DEATH [illegible] ISLAND

LYNNE MARIE TAYLOR

BLOODHOUND
BOOKS

First published in 2026 by Bloodhound Books.

www.bloodhoundbooks.com

Print ISBN: 9781917705622

MALTESE PRONUNCIATION GUIDE

There are some different pronunciations of letters and extra consonants in the Maltese alphabet, for example:

Ċ = ch, like church
Ġ = j, like jump
J = y, like yes
Għ = silent
H = silent
Ħ = h, like hat
Ż = z, like zebra
Z = ts, like pizza

Characters' names:
Bonnici = Bon-ee-chee
Borg = Borj
Sciberras = Shi-berr-ahs
Zija = Tseeyah
Rożi = Roh-zee
Grech = Grek
Galea = Gah-lyah

Other vocabulary:
Għonnella – Awn-nel-lah
Dgħajsa – Dye-sah
Karrozzin = kar-ro-tseen
Fejn = feyn
Pulizija = poo-lee-tsi-yah
Ajma = ahy-mah
Ħanini = hah-nee-nee

VALLETTA
Sliema
Sliema Creek
Gżira
Manoel Island
Hospital
Fort
The Lazzaretto
Lazzaretto Creek
Quarantine Harbour
Fort St Elmo
Valletta
Fort Ricasoli
Grand Harbour
Fort St Angelo
Bighi
Floriana
Senglea
Vittoriosa
Cospicua

For Daniel, Tasia and Penny

CHAPTER ONE

Valletta, Malta. Sunday, 17 October 1880

Detective Inspector Sam McQueen was roused from a less than refreshing sleep by a steady thumping on his bedroom door.

'Inspector! You're needed. Now,' came the voice of Sergeant Galea of the Maltese Police. His eager voice betrayed his excitement – something important was happening.

'Hang on there, son. Give me a moment,' McQueen called out. Getting up, he shook his head slightly to test the damage – a dull pain, but not too bad. His mouth felt dry and tacky, and he reached for a swig of water before pulling on his trousers. He vaguely remembered staggering back in the early hours, after a night of whist in the Mess Room of the Royal Engineers. Worse off by at least ten shillings. The dual sins of gambling and intemperance; his minister father would have instantly disowned him – if he had not already done so fifteen years previously.

He opened the door to reveal the smartly dressed young officer, who saluted him.

'They've found a body, sir,' Galea said.

'What?'

'A body in Lazzaretto Creek – drowned.'

'Is Superintendent Ellis there?'

'Yes, sir, and Doctor Bonnici.'

'What's the time now?'

'Around six – marine police pulled the body out about an hour ago.'

McQueen splashed some water on his face and finished pulling on his clothes, making sure to stuff his notebook into his jacket pocket.

'Well, who are we to hold them up, Sergeant? Let's get moving,' he said. 'A body, eh? That'll liven things up.'

Drafted over from Edinburgh, Inspector Sam McQueen had been living in Malta since the summer, working with the Maltese police. To some extent he had acclimatised to the heat, but now they were in October he found it hard to accept it still reached eighty degrees in the daytime. Stepping out of his lodgings he appreciated the cool, early-morning breeze as he followed Sergeant Galea down the few short streets to the landing place at the foot of Marsamuscetto Steps.

They stepped down into a water-taxi, known as a *dgħajsa tal-pass,* which took them across the harbour from Valletta to Gżira. The boat was able to get close to where the body had been pulled out of the water, crunching to a stop in the gravel that passed for a beach. Climbing out, they approached the huddle of men surrounding the corpse. Doctor Bonnici – Police Physician – was searching for something in his medical bag. He looked up and greeted McQueen with a nod and a half-smile. Police Superintendent Ellis was issuing orders to the local officers, insisting they move back the ragged line of onlookers beginning to form on the shore. Spotting McQueen he stepped forward, shaking his hand with a forceful grip.

'Good to see you, Inspector. Shouldn't have to trouble you too much. A drowning. Drunk and lost his footing, I expect. Soon have this cleared up, I'm sure.' He gestured to a young officer in dark blue uniform, standing next to him. 'This is Inspector Azzopardi, from the Marine Police. He oversaw the retrieval of the body from the creek.'

Colonel Hugh Ellis had been in post for less than a month. The governor had insisted on appointing an Englishman, after former Police Superintendent Riccardo Borg had been forced to step down, facing charges of corruption. A typical colonial approach, to bring in one of their own, someone with military experience. It had not gone down well with the Maltese.

McQueen had taken an instant dislike to Ellis. Every time he saw the man's spare, slightly stooped frame, that hawkish profile, he felt the same rush of irritation. Thirty years in the British Army, serving in the West Indies and India, Ellis thought he knew everything about leadership and getting the job done. But he had not the first idea about policing. Brought in three months ago to solve the murder of a high-profile British admiral, McQueen had been asked to stay in Malta to set up a detective department. Although the work was going well, the arrival of Ellis had started him thinking perhaps his time on the island was coming to an end. Another few weeks and he would head back to Edinburgh.

'Any idea who it is?' he asked, approaching the body.

'Yes, we found a calling card – name of Buchanan, Captain. Must be ex-army, British. A magistrate from Bombay.'

McQueen walked around the corpse slowly, noting the

well-cut clothing that marked out a gentleman. Tall and well-built – stocky even. He was surprised the man had not been dragged down by the weight of his clothes and boots. A healthy man in his prime, who should not have met this fate. He crouched down to look at the face. A high forehead, the more exposed as the longish hair was plastered down with water. Grey eyes, open and glassy. A long nose and thin lips. Handsome enough, McQueen thought. A look of the military about him.

He patted down the sides of the body, pulling open the jacket and feeling inside the pockets. Water pooled out, smelling of the oil and coal that characterised the harbour.

'Inspector Azzopardi has already done all that,' Ellis said sharply. 'Found these.'

A leather pouch containing smoking paraphernalia, and a money clip — holding several disintegrating pound notes — lay dripping to one side.

Ignoring him, McQueen continued to check the clothing. The waistcoat pockets yielded nothing. However, feeling down the sides, he detected a split in the material. Quickly he undid the buttons and pulled back the waistcoat, revealing the shirt underneath. He looked up.

'Look at this, Doctor,' he said to Bonnici. Even in the murky light of the dawn, a dark patch could be seen, staining the shirt material. 'Could be blood.'

Bonnici knelt next to him and carefully peeled back the shirt to reveal a small wound in the side of the body, halfway down the ribcage.

'A puncture wound,' he murmured. 'Looks to be deep.'

'Was it the cause of death?' McQueen asked.

'I don't know,' Bonnici replied. 'Could be, if he didn't drown. We'll find out in the post-mortem examination.'

'Whichever way, it must have been foul play. Don't you agree, Colonel?'

Ellis pursed his lips, his eyes narrowing. For a moment he looked as though he was going to snap back, but then he recalculated, looking steadily at McQueen as he responded.

'Absolutely. No doubt about it. Right, Sergeant, get the body taken away. McQueen, you're in charge. I'll get back to the office, inform the magistrate and order the post-mortem. Azzopardi, come with me.'

Ellis walked away, Inspector Azzopardi behind him. McQueen did not know Azzopardi well; he had not had to deal much with the marine police. His impression was that the inspector was efficient, probably ambitious. Young and good-looking, but distinctly cool and unfriendly. He nodded at McQueen on his way past, but without any emotion registering on his face.

McQueen called Galea over.

'Find out if anyone knows more about who our dead fellow is, where he has come from.'

'Yes, sir.'

He turned to Bonnici who was still examining the body. Even at this time in the morning, the doctor was impeccably turned out. *How did he do it?* Smart black jacket, hair neatly combed, clean-shaven, he looked ready to attend an important function rather than a murder scene. The closest McQueen had to a friend on the island, he knew he could rely on Bonnici's expertise and support.

'Anything else you can tell me about him?' he asked. 'Any idea how long he's been in the water?'

'Not long. A few hours perhaps. He was face down when he was found. The skin is puckered but not yet bloated. No other injuries I can see, apart from this wound. The animals of the sea can get to work very quickly you know, so I don't think he's been there for much time.'

Sergeant Galea approached with a short, stocky ferryman. The sailor was wearing a stripy shirt, grey waistcoat and trousers, a squashy red cap on his head. A long-stemmed pipe was clenched between his teeth.

'Inspector, there's someone here who thinks he might know something. Can he see the body?' Galea asked.

'Certainly, bring him over.'

The ferryman took the pipe out of his mouth as he leant down to look at the dead man's face. As he stood, he gesticulated toward the body with the bowl of the pipe, explaining something to Galea in a cascade of Maltese. McQueen was impatient, unable to understand a single word. He had expected the Maltese language to be similar to Italian; thought perhaps he might be able to pick up a word or two. However, he had soon discovered that Maltese was more akin to an Arabic dialect. Despite his efforts, he struggled to make any sense of the language.

'What's he saying?'

'He thinks it might be one of the English people from Manoel Island. He took several groups over there from the steamship *Poonah* earlier this week. They are in quarantine at the Lazzaretto.'

'I know about that,' Bonnici said. 'Cholera on board. The first-class passengers are in quarantine for ten days.'

McQueen was aware of the Lazzaretto, an old quarantine hospital on Manoel Island, linked to Gżira by a narrow bridge. Any ship carrying people showing symptoms of cholera, yellow fever or other deadly disease was obliged to wait in Quarantine Harbour, marked by a yellow flag, until it was declared 'in pratique'. Affected passengers and goods had to be taken to the Lazzaretto, goods fumigated, and passengers kept in isolation.

'How sure is he that this man is from the *Poonah*?'

'He's quite sure. He recognises his ring.'

McQueen had also noticed a gold signet ring on the man's left hand, with a heraldic crest depicting a shield above the family name.

'Right,' McQueen said. 'Bonnici, you stay here with the body until the wagon arrives to take it away. Sergeant Galea, come with me to Manoel Island. We need to find out if they are missing a certain Captain Buchanan.'

McQueen was fond of Galea. He had taken the young sergeant under his wing and was training him in the art of detection. As they headed to Manoel Island on the *dgħajsa*, he asked him what he knew about the Lazzaretto.

'Oh, it's a terrible place, my mother says. One of her cousins used to be a health guard there. They supervise the people, make sure they are keeping to the laws of quarantine. This cousin says they built the Lazzaretto over the plague pits from hundreds of years ago. He says that at night-time you can hear the groans from the bones of all the plague victims. It keeps him awake. But he likes to tell these stories, my mother says. I don't think it's as bad as all that!'

McQueen laughed. 'Who's in charge of the place?'

'The Keeper of the Lazzaretto? It is Angelo Sciberras. He has been there for some years. They say he is very efficient. Keeps things running smoothly.'

'I still don't see why we have to go by boat.'

'It's the rules. You can't walk up to the Lazzaretto unless you have written permission.'

The ferryman rowed the *dgħajsa* alongside Manoel Island. The Lazzaretto loomed above them. A huge, elegantly-proportioned stone structure with a series of fine arches just above the waterline. The *dgħajsa* stayed bobbing in the water as the ferryman shouted across to the open window of a room at sea level. A face appeared at the window. A voluble exchange then took place.

'He's going to get Sciberras,' Galea explained.

McQueen felt ridiculous, trying to keep his dignity whilst rocking from side to side. Why on earth they could not just walk across the bridge from the mainland, he could not understand.

Eventually the keeper of the Lazzaretto appeared at the window. A craggy-faced man in his late forties, he seemed displeased at their early-morning arrival.

'What's going on?' he shouted. 'I hear you are police and you need to see me?'

'Detective Inspector McQueen,' he shouted back. 'We've found a body in Gżira, washed up from the creek. An Englishman – we think his name is Buchanan. He may have been staying at the Lazzaretto. Do you know him?'

'Yes, but that can't be right. There is a man here with that name, but he is in his apartment. He's travelling with the Indian gentleman.'

'Can you check? We're sure of the name.'

'All right. I'll send a guard to find out. Wait there.'

Galea chatted with the ferryman, while McQueen sat back down. The sky was overcast and although the air was warm, a strong breeze blew across the water, making the boat roll from side to side. He took out his notebook and sketched the Lazzaretto, admiring the clean lines of its functional design, broken up by the elegant arches. It was a wide structure, stretching some two hundred and fifty yards, built right on the edge of the island, flat honey-coloured limestone with small windows to keep out the intense heat of the summer.

After a few minutes Sciberras reappeared at the window.

'Buchanan has disappeared,' he shouted. 'I don't know how it happened. Nobody has seen anything. Even the Indian gentleman who he shares the room with.'

'I need to come in, to ask some questions,' McQueen shouted back.

'Impossible. This is quarantined.'

'I'll get a warrant!'

'Warrant or no warrant, no one can change the rules of quarantine.'

'Just you wait! I'll be back soon. You'll have to let me in.'

'Not a chance. We can talk at the parlatorio, but you can't come any further inside.'

Sciberras moved away from the window. Interview over.

McQueen felt a rush of frustration. He had to get into the Lazzaretto and find out what had happened to Buchanan, how he had ended up in the creek.

'What is this parlatorio?' he asked Galea.

'It's a room in the Lazzaretto where you can meet people, but at a distance.'

'This is ridiculous. We'll have to go back to Valletta, sort out a warrant, just to get inside and ask questions.' He sat back as the ferryman started to row back to shore.

This was going to be a long-winded investigation. McQueen could feel it in his bones.

CHAPTER TWO

Gżira, Malta. Sunday, 17 October 1880

Having been left with the dead body, Bonnici was beginning to feel uneasy. If this man Buchanan had arrived on the *Poonah,* he may have been in contact with cholera. One man had already died from cholera on the ship and the whole point of quarantine was to prevent the disease from spreading. Now here was a body, that he had already examined, lying out in the open. Unlikely to be contagious, but you never knew.

He placed his cane down carefully and knelt next to the corpse to take another close look. It was difficult to tell, as the body had been floating in water for several hours, but the man's skin appeared plump, not shrivelled. He pinched the flesh on the corpse's arm. It felt firm. One of the main characteristics of cholera was that the body was literally purged of liquid, in no time becoming almost desiccated, the skin taking on a blue colour. It was even known as the blue death. People suffered terribly with diarrhoea, vomiting and stomach cramps. Death could be swift, within hours. Bonnici felt sure this man was not a cholera victim himself, but he could still be carrying it in its early stages.

The worst cholera epidemic in Malta had been in 1837, two years after Bonnici was born. It was still strong in people's memories, as the outbreak had cost the lives of nearly half the Maltese population. A terrible time. He recalled the sorrow with which his mother talked of family members lost to the disease. A further breakout had happened in 1850 and then in 1867, when he was already practising as a doctor. In 1867 there had been over one thousand cases with around four hundred fatalities – the death rate being much higher in the poorer Maltese communities. Bonnici vividly remembered the weeks of treating patients at the cholera hospital, the fatigue, the few cases where patients recovered, the awful regularity with which they were lost, and the fear that he himself would develop symptoms. He could hardly bear the thought of another epidemic on the island.

He called over a police sergeant, ordering him to make sure no one came within one hundred feet of the body. He also sent a message to Colonel Ellis instructing him to ensure that the men coming to take the body away were properly protected and that they knew not to touch the skin of the victim. He washed his hands with alcohol. He was waiting for McQueen to return, knowing that if Buchanan was indeed from the Lazzaretto, there was a difficult decision to be made. According to the strict rules of quarantine, he and McQueen would have to join the residents on Manoel Island for at least ten days.

Watching McQueen stepping out of the ferry boat and

stomping up the beach, Bonnici could tell the inspector was frustrated.

'You'll not believe this,' McQueen yelled as he approached, running his fingers through his hair. 'Our friend Buchanan here *has* come from the Lazzaretti or whatever you call it, but we can't get on the island to investigate.'

'Did you speak to Sciberras?'

'Aye, but only for a few seconds. Wouldn't let us on the island without a warrant. Even then he said we have to meet at some place called the parlatorio.'

'I think you should prepare yourself for some bad news. I believe you *will* be able to get on the island, in fact you won't be able to leave it.'

'What do you mean?'

'Think about it, McQueen. You and I have both examined the body of this man Buchanan, who is in quarantine. Not just his clothing, his skin. Without gloves. I have absolutely no doubt that Sciberras will tell you we'll need to join the other *Poonah* passengers in the Lazzaretto. And stay there for at least ten days.'

McQueen stepped back, his boots crunching on the gravel, his face a picture of confusion and disbelief.

'You what? I can't do that!'

'It's cholera, McQueen, it has to be contained. If there's even the smallest possibility that we could have picked up the infection, we have to keep away from other people. Besides, it's the only way you're going to be able to ask questions of the passengers travelling with Buchanan.'

Bonnici could see the inspector working through the logic of the situation.

'It's your fault,' McQueen said, glaring at him. 'You could've warned me!'

'Well, we had no idea where he was from at that stage,' he replied mildly.

'What about Azzopardi? He touched him as well.'

'He was wearing gloves.' *If only they had taken the same precaution.*

At that point the wagon arrived to take the body away. Bonnici supervised the men, making sure they were wearing gloves and instructing them to wrap scarves around their faces. They had to work in twos, using long stretches of canvas passed underneath the corpse so they could carry it at some distance from themselves.

'Take the body to the isolation hospital,' he said. 'I'll do the post-mortem there, myself, later today. We can keep him there until we decide where he's to be buried.'

McQueen stood watching, frowning.

'I don't know how you can be so calm,' he said. 'My head is reeling. I won't be able to do that. I can't be cooped up in one building for that long. I'll go insane.'

'You can, if it needs to be done. I've seen cholera many times, McQueen. I'll do whatever it takes to keep it away from the people on my island.'

'There must be another way. I'll find another way, I'll not go.'

'By all means, speak to Sciberras and to Colonel Ellis. But I wager two guineas we'll both be in quarantine by the end of the day.'

'Over my dead body.'

Five o'clock that afternoon, McQueen was unpacking his bag in a small apartment in the Lazzaretto, throwing his clothes roughly into a chest of drawers. About eleven feet by fourteen, his room contained a bed and a washstand, a table and two armchairs, next to the fireplace. On the opposite side there was a desk, and another table with a pitcher of water and a carafe of wine. He looked out of the window – a drop of about ten feet to the water and a view out across the creek.

He was seething. Meeting him at the parlatorio — through an iron mesh partition separating the two different parts of the room — Sciberras had the self-satisfied look of someone who enjoyed his power rather too much. Despite being of medium height and build, he gave off a heaviness, a sense of the weightiness of his position. His face was dark, with a black beard and brows. He looked incapable of breaking into a smile. Defensive from the outset, Sciberras declared he could not understand how Buchanan had been found off the island. No one under his watch had ever broken quarantine.

McQueen asked him about Buchanan's character:

'Captain Buchanan was difficult from the start, insisting on this and that. The Indian man he was travelling with, also. Demands for special food, special linen even. This is not a hotel, this is quarantine.'

'Who is this Indian man, why are they travelling together?'

'He is some kind of prince. His name is Singh, the son of an exiled Indian ruler. He was being guarded by Captain Buchanan, to make sure he got back to England. I don't know what the story is, but he is not allowed to go to India. He tried to land at Bombay, but he was arrested and was being brought back.'

When McQueen had stressed once more that he needed to go into the Lazzaretto, to interview Singh, and all the passengers travelling with Buchanan, Sciberras had repeated that he would have to go into quarantine. For one thing he had been in direct contact with Buchanan, and for another it was the only way he could conduct an investigation inside the quarantine walls.

After the interview, McQueen spoke with Colonel Ellis, reluctantly agreeing this was the only course of action open to him. He would operate from inside the Lazzaretto, with Sergeant Galea as his go-between with Ellis, via the parlatorio. He sent a message to his landlady, *Sinjura* Caruso, asking her to pack his clothes and take his bag down to the harbour.

So, here he was, stuck on the island for over a week. Either he could find out that one of Buchanan's fellow passengers was guilty of his murder, or he was being forcibly prevented from following lines of inquiry that would take him back to Valletta. It was not a comfortable position to be in. At least he had Doctor Bonnici with him, who would be a more than useful ally. Also, he would have full access to all the suspects. Because they, like him, were unable to go anywhere else.

Bonnici was also unpacking his bag, in the next apartment, neatly arranging his soap, shaving cream, brush and razor on the washstand. He hated staying away from his home in Valletta; he could never settle in a strange environment. The room was pleasant enough, but it was not as clean as he would have liked. Little balls of dust were hiding in the corners, and the washbowl needed a good scrub. He would have to go back to the entrance where servants congregated alongside the tradesmen, making themselves available for hire. A mature woman who took pride in cleaning would be the perfect choice. There seemed to be any number of candidates. It was quite something to be prepared to work in the Lazzaretto, where you could contract a deadly disease from someone in quarantine, but the wages were good and there were plenty who were prepared to do it.

He thought about Carmela Caruso, McQueen's landlady.

He had been 'walking out' with her for the past two months. It had been difficult telling her that he had to stay at the Lazzaretto for ten days. They had been growing ever closer; it felt as if their relationship could develop into something serious. This was a novel feeling for him, after fifteen years a widower. It was good to have some joy in his life again. He hoped the time apart would not cause any problems.

A bang on the door and McQueen walked in.

'Well, Doctor, here we are! Let the adventures begin.' He dropped his heavy frame into an armchair. 'At least I have you here with me. You can help me form a plan.'

'Absolutely.'

He folded away his washbag and sat opposite McQueen by the fireplace.

'Tell me, how did you get on with the post-mortem examination?' McQueen asked.

'It was interesting.' He cast his mind back to the room at the back of the isolation hospital, the familiar smell of formaldehyde. 'I have sent the notes to the magistrate. Buchanan was a healthy man, around thirty-five years of age. Time of death around five hours after the last meal, so if we can establish what time he ate, we can estimate that quite well. Cause of death was not drowning. There was no water in the lungs. It was without doubt the knife wound, which went straight through the ribs, piercing the heart. Death was virtually instantaneous. And I would say that whoever wielded the knife knew exactly what he was doing. One swift strike. Accurate and deadly.'

'Would that be a long blade then?'

'Around five inches. Very sharp. And I think a slight curve to it. The shape of the wound is quite distinct.'

'We should concentrate on finding the murder weapon. It

may well have been thrown in the creek, but we should have a thorough search of this building anyway.'

'I am just the police physician, remember.'

'You're also the only man I've got in here. Sorry, Doctor, but I am co-opting you onto my team for the duration of our stay.'

Bonnici felt a tiny thrill at those words. He did not like to admit it to himself, but he had enjoyed the challenge of working with McQueen on their last murder investigation. It had taken him into a life-threatening situation, and he felt he had risen to the challenge well, staying calm and using good judgement.

'I dare say I can cope with that,' he said to McQueen, with a small smile. 'What should we do first?'

McQueen jumped to his feet and started pacing up and down.

'We need a list of all the passengers and a plan of the Lazzaretto showing where everyone is staying. We'll have to divide up and interview them, find out what they know about the deceased and where they were at the time when he died.'

'All right. Also, we should establish when Buchanan took supper and what he ate. If it was at seven o'clock we'll know he was killed around midnight.'

'Good point, Doctor. You go and get that information, while I find out all I can from Sciberras. Let's meet up later to plan the interviews and how we're going to get the building searched. I'll start with Buchanan's apartment. Time is fast running out today. We must find out as much as we can. The first hours after a murder are the most important in the whole investigation. We've lost time already.'

CHAPTER THREE

Manoel Island, Malta. Sunday, 17 October 1880

The Lazzaretto was made up of six different buildings, all connected to one another. The main section contained all the apartments; at least twenty rooms, with numbers of occupants depending on the class of persons. McQueen's apartment was on the first floor of the so-called New Palace. Here the rooms were reasonably comfortable, but he had heard that in times past, hundreds of lower-class passengers in quarantine used to be crammed into long, narrow dormitories. Sciberras's office was in the oldest part of the Lazzaretto, originally built in the seventeenth century. McQueen climbed the stone steps up to the first floor and knocked on the two-hundred-year-old door, where a brass sign declared *Quarantine Office* in flowing letters. Invited in, he was struck by the impressive view from the window of the office, which looked out over Lazzaretto Creek.

Each time he had met Sciberras, McQueen could view him a little more closely. First time seen in the distance from the ferryboat, second time at the parlatorio, eight feet apart and through an iron mesh. Now they were closer, he could see that the man's dark face was badly pockmarked. Cruelly ironic for the keeper of the quarantine hospital.

'I hope you find your apartment acceptable?' he asked, his voice deep and monotone.

'Passable,' McQueen said. 'It'll do, while I'm here.'

'If you need anything, let me know. We can get most things here on Manoel Island. Of course, it takes a great deal of time, making sure everybody abides by the rules. I'll expect you to comply, as well. Bear in mind that communication between parties should be held only at a distance, and without contact of hand or breath. No goods must pass hands. My team of guards are very thorough.'

McQueen gritted his teeth. *This was going to be a trial.*

'How many people are staying here?' he asked. 'Are they all from the *Poonah*?'

'Yes, just twenty-four passengers. They're all from first class. They're the people who had contact with the steward — the one who went down with cholera. I have a list of them, with the rooms they are staying in.' He handed over a ledger, open on a page showing a column of names, each with a corresponding number. 'Our records are accurate. I run a tight ship, you know.'

McQueen was already finding Sciberras tiresome. How he would be able to stand ten days cooped up with him, he didn't know.

'Perhaps not so tight,' he said drily. 'Laurence Buchanan walked out of the Lazzaretto sometime last night or early morning — as far as we know without being seen — and ended up floating in the creek.'

He scanned the list of names. Captain Buchanan had been in Apartment Four with Prince Sundar Singh. Apartment Three appeared to have two lady occupants, Miss Louisa

Copeland and Miss Eleanor Templeman, Apartment Five a French family called Trévissier – father, mother and two children. Another six apartments grouped together along one corridor. So many people to interview. He would start with Apartment Four and work his way outwards from there.

'Can you show me where Buchanan was staying?'

'Let me get the guard who was assigned to the captain. He can take you.'

Sciberras got up, crossed the room and opened the door. 'Fetch Grech,' he said to the servant waiting outside.

'Grech's a good man,' he said as he sat back at his desk. 'He's usually very reliable. But let me tell you, if I find out he broke the rules, there'll be hell to pay.'

The man clearly took every opportunity to reinforce his authority.

Grech, when he turned up, was short and scrawny, with evasive dark eyes. He hovered in the doorway, seemingly unwilling to enter the room.

McQueen could not tell if he was afraid of Sciberras, perhaps because he had not fulfilled all his duties, or if he was holding back information about Buchanan's disappearance. But it looked as if something was troubling him.

'Ah, Grech,' Sciberras said. 'This is Inspector McQueen. He is investigating the death of Captain Buchanan. Take him to Apartment Four, will you, and answer any questions. Truthfully, now. I expect nothing but honesty and integrity from my staff.'

He picked up his fountain pen and began to write. Clearly, he had no more time to give them.

McQueen followed Grech down the corridor, emerging into a courtyard. The sun was low, making it cool and shady. Bright pink bougainvillea plants, growing up the side of a staircase, were just coming into bloom. Three walls of the courtyard featured arched entrances leading into separate corridors. The guard walked with a slight limp, but it did not seem to slow him down. He led McQueen up the staircase, then veered off into a corridor on the right. McQueen had to stride quickly to keep up with him. The passageway was dark, seeming to go on indefinitely. Just as his eyes adjusted, Grech stopped outside the door of Apartment Four.

'Here is Four,' he said, edging away as if hoping he could escape any questions.

'Hold on a minute,' McQueen said. 'Before I go in, I'd like you to tell me about Buchanan. What was he like?'

Grech screwed up his face as he thought about what to say.

'He was officer. Did not like quarantine. Shouted.'

'What about?'

'Things. He wanted some things. Wanted to send messages.'

'What sort of things?'

Grech shrugged. 'Paper, ink, envelopes. I fetch.'

'When did you last see him?'

'Last night. Late. I checked him and the prince ten o'clock. He write at desk with lamp. I go back six o'clock this morning. I bring water for washing. He not there.'

McQueen watched the guard's face, saw him struggling to keep a guileless expression. He felt sure there was more to find out.

'Did he give you letters to send?'

'No.'

'Did you find any on the desk?'

'No.'

'So, you have nothing else to tell me?'

Grech shook his head vehemently. 'I go now,' he said. 'I have duties.'

'All right,' McQueen said. 'Off you go then, but I'll need to speak to you again.'

He watched the rapidly-retreating figure go back down to the courtyard. He wondered what had been going on between Buchanan and the guard. There was definitely something to follow up on. He turned to knock loudly on the apartment door.

McQueen studied the young man sitting opposite him. Prince Sundar Singh was elegantly dressed in an oxblood velvet jacket, dark trousers and brown Oxford shoes. A cream-coloured silk scarf, tied at his neck, was matched by a silk turban. He was small and slight, with a dark, youthful beard. He ran his slim fingers through the ends of the scarf as he spoke. McQueen noted the ring on his right little finger, a large ruby set in heavy gold. It must be worth a fortune.

'I have nothing to tell you,' Singh said. 'I was asleep the whole night. The guard woke me in the morning and asked where Buchanan was. I had no idea. I only found out later he had drowned.'

His accent was cultured, English. With heavy-lidded eyes and a full mouth, he gave the impression of being at once sulky and bored by the questioning. He would not look McQueen in the eye.

'What was your relationship with Captain Buchanan?'

The prince sighed. 'I'm sure you'll have heard, Inspector. Captain Buchanan was accompanying me back to England, after my thwarted attempt to find my roots in Mother India. The man took great pleasure in never leaving my side.'

'And how did you feel about him?'

Singh lifted his eyes and looked directly at McQueen for the first time. A slight smile played on his lips. 'My dear Inspector,' he said, 'I hated him.'

'Are you sure it's wise to tell me that?' McQueen asked. 'Given the situation you're in?'

The prince shifted up in his armchair. 'It's well-known,' he said. 'Everybody will tell you the same thing. Put yourself in my place, Inspector. I am a Sikh. My father is Sir Anokh Singh, the rightful ruler of the Sikh Empire. He was Maharaja of the Punjab, Kashmir and Jammu, until the British took his kingdom from him, when he was young. Now he lives in exile in Paris – not even allowed back in Britain. The son of a Maharaja, I attempt to travel to India to meet my people, to learn what it is to be a Sikh warrior, and I'm stopped, prevented, brought back like a naughty schoolboy. How do you think I feel? Buchanan treated me like I'm ten years old, and I won't have it!' He slapped the arm of the chair, his dark eyes flashing with anger.

McQueen suppressed a smile. The young prince was full of swagger, but he looked far more like a petulant child than a warrior.

'So, you're glad he is dead?' he asked.

The prince folded his arms, thinking before he spoke next. 'No,' he said eventually. 'I don't know what has happened here, but it's nothing to do with me. Buchanan was a boor. I disliked him intensely. But I wouldn't wish him dead.'

McQueen believed him. The lad looked to him like an open book. For all his bravado, he looked a little lost now he no longer had his companion – however much he hated him.

He stood up. 'I need to go through Buchanan's belongings.'

The prince waved toward the far corner of the room. 'His stuff is all over there. I doubt you'll find much. He was very proud of travelling light, said it was the mark of a true soldier. Made fun of me, my five trunks of luggage, but, you know, I have to remember who I am. I must make the right impression. These things are important.' He put his fingertips together and looked at McQueen over the top of them as if daring him to say something.

'Thank you, that's it for now. Don't go anywhere, will you?'

'Ha!' said the prince. 'As if I could.'

He picked up a book and started to read.

McQueen began to sort through Buchanan's belongings. His bed was made, pyjamas neatly folded under the pillow. McQueen shook them out, raising an eyebrow at the silk. He could not imagine wearing such fancy, slippery material. What was wrong with a flannel nightshirt? He stripped the bed of its blanket and sheets, checked underneath the mattress. Nothing there. Next to the bed there was a small table. A pair of wire spectacles were balanced on a book – *Michael Strogoff* by Jules Verne. He turned it over, leafed through the pages, read a few paragraphs. It looked interesting, about a Russian agent sent to Irkutsk on a mission. He put it down again and picked up a framed photo. It showed a slightly younger Buchanan in an officer's uniform, with proud parents alongside him, a fine-looking manor house in the background. The man clearly lived a privileged life. He peered at Buchanan's image more closely, detecting in the tilt of his chin and the slight downward turn of his mouth a kind of disdainful pride that was far too common amongst the English upper classes. He could see in the father what Buchanan would have become, the stockiness turned to portliness, the facial expression signalling satisfaction with his lot. Well, his world was soon going to be turned upside down when he found out about his son's death. McQueen put the photo down, glad he would not be the person delivering the news.

He checked the washstand, nothing remarkable there. Buchanan did not appear to set great store by men's toiletries. Just the plainest of soaps and shaving creams. McQueen moved on to the trunk at the foot of Buchanan's bed, pulling out the clothes neatly piled up inside. All quite plain but good quality. About halfway down, he found a bundle of papers, tied together with a ribbon. He sat down on the bed, placing the bundle next to him, and untied the bow. A big bunch of correspondence spilt out, letters and telegrams. McQueen riffled through them: short letters from Buchanan's mother and father, who appeared to live somewhere called Great Fallow Court in Wiltshire, longer letters from a Letitia professing to be his fiancée in Gravesend, Kent, and some official telegrams from a Sir Arthur Gambol in Whitehall. These looked like instructions on how to deal with the prince. Putting them to one side to read more thoroughly later, he finished searching through the trunk, throwing everything back in again after finding nothing out of the ordinary.

He pulled out his pocket watch. It was close to seven. No wonder he felt hungry.

'What time is dinner?' he asked.

Prince Sundar looked up from his book. 'Mine is brought here at seven thirty,' he said. 'I suggest if you want to eat you make your way now. The restaurant serves dinner between seven and eight thirty. If you wait too long all the decent food will be gone. I recommend the beef ragout. It's just about edible.'

McQueen met Bonnici on his way to the restaurant. A handsome room with limestone walls and a high vaulted ceiling. They made their way in and sat at a table. There were around a dozen tables, but only five were occupied by diners. The sounds of cutlery on plates and subdued conversations echoed strangely around the half-empty room. A few servants bustled around serving plates of food. McQueen called a young man over to their table. 'What can we get to drink around here?' he asked.

'Wine. Is good, Maltese.'

He pulled a face. He had not yet got used to the rustic nature of the local wine. 'I suppose it'll have to do,' he said. 'A bottle of red to start, if you please.'

'So, what did you find out?' he asked the doctor.

'Not much,' Bonnici said. 'Apparently Buchanan ate with Prince Sundar at half past seven yesterday, soup and fish. That fits with the timings I estimated. What about you?'

'Well, no love lost between the captain and the prince, for one thing. But apart from that not a great deal. No one seems to have heard Buchanan leave the apartment. Although I suspect the guard knows more than he is letting on. I've got Buchanan's papers. Nothing much there.'

The waiter brought bowls of soup to the table. McQueen tucked in hungrily, dipping in hunks of bread. The wine had also arrived. He poured them each a glass then drained his in one, before filling it up again.

'God knows how we're going to survive in this place,' he said, coughing. 'If this is all the drink we can get.'

'You can order in other supplies in the morning. There are traders who wait by the gate for orders. It'll be expensive though.'

'Colonel Ellis will have to foot the bill. I can't stay here without a decent drink. I'll see him tomorrow, let him know what we need.'

The soup bowls were cleared and the main courses arrived. Beef ragout with vegetables. As he ate, McQueen set out his plan to question all the passengers, starting with those nearest to Buchanan's apartment, and to search for a murder weapon. 'We're going to need more men, at least two to search all the buildings.'

As they finished eating, the level of noise suddenly rose in the room. McQueen looked over to the door, where a woman appeared, looking wildly around. She spoke to one of the servants who pointed to their table, then she ran over, hair dishevelled, tears running down her face.

'Are you a doctor?' she cried, looking at Bonnici. 'It's my husband. He's sick. Please come and help. I think it's the cholera!'

CHAPTER FOUR

Manoel Island, Malta. Sunday, 17 October 1880

Bonnici pushed down a momentary feeling of panic as he got to his feet. He knew that direct handling of a cholera patient would put him at risk. But as a doctor his first duty was to treat the sick. If this was cholera then he had to act quickly and decisively, showing no fear.

'Madame, don't worry, we'll come straight away. McQueen, can you get my medical bag and meet us there? Which room is it?'

'Apartment Five – please come quickly, Doctor, he's not breathing well.'

Bonnici called over a servant. 'Run to Sciberras,' he said. 'Tell him we have a suspected case of cholera. He needs to notify the quarantine doctor at once.'

Using his cane to walk as quickly as he could, he followed the stricken woman out of the restaurant through a mêlée of people, who had heard the word 'cholera' and were pushing their way back to their rooms.

Entering the apartment, he could see two small children huddled together on an armchair, tearfully reaching out for their mother, who went to comfort them. The patient was on a bed at the far side of the room. There was just one oil lamp, making it difficult to see.

'More light please,' he said. 'Bring the lamp closer. What is your husband's name?'

'It's Pierre – Pierre Trévissier – we are from France.'

He spoke gently to the patient. 'Monsieur Trévissier? Do not worry, I'm a doctor. I'm just going to examine you.'

Trévissier looked at him with an expression of pure terror. His eyes were sunk into his head, his lips black. He tried to speak but his voice was just a whisper. It sounded like '*Aidez-moi*.' Then he slipped into unconsciousness.

Bonnici felt for his pulse. It was weak and intermittent. His body temperature was low, with a clammy skin, despite the warmth of the room.

'How long has he been ill?' he asked.

'Just a few hours.' Madame Trévissier was trying to hold back the tears. 'I was sick yesterday. I thought perhaps it was the food. When Pierre was also ill, after luncheon, I was sure it would be the same for him. But he's been so bad, Doctor, vomiting and purging, then complaining of cramping pains. He was angry, Doctor, he wouldn't let me fetch any help. I was busy clearing up after him, trying to persuade him to drink water, time has passed so quickly. Then he sank into this weakness.'

'We need to warm him up. Find servants to help, we need warm water and flannels, hot stones to place around him.'

Madame Trévissier ran to get more help, almost bumping into McQueen who had just arrived with Bonnici's medical bag. 'How is he, Doctor?' he asked, his face full of concern.

'It's bad.' Bonnici pulled down the sheet and unbuttoned the patient's shirt. The man was thin, his abdomen severely retracted. His skin was a bluish colour, with patches that were almost black. His fingertips and toes were wizened, his nails a blue-white. 'There's little we can do now, I'm afraid. His body is shutting down. We can only ease the pain. I need to keep my hands clean. Pour me some water, please.'

McQueen poured water into the washbowl. Bonnici washed his hands before opening his medical bag.

'It's important to avoid touching the patient and anything he's touched.'

He prepared a hypodermic syringe with morphine and administered it to the patient, watching him closely as his breathing, which had been shallow and rapid, settled to a gentler rhythm.

Although trying to remain detached, he felt an intense sympathy for the wife who was about to lose her husband. He could remember the pain of watching his own lovely Liena pass away, her body consumed by tuberculosis, and the helplessness of not being able to cure her. Being able to ease the suffering of others had given him some sense of purpose but it did not help with the grief and anger, the feeling that this should not be happening to the person you love. Lost in his thoughts for a moment, he closed his eyes and silently mouthed a prayer, finishing with 'Holy Mary, Mother of God, pray for us sinners now, and at the hour of our death. Amen.' Then he shook his head and stood up briskly, shutting his medical bag as Madame Trévissier came running back, followed by two women carrying towels and hot stones.

Before they could start to place them around the patient, though, a booming voice came from the doorway. Sciberras.

'Stop, at once!' he said. 'If this is cholera, everyone must step away from the victim. Doctor, can you confirm that this man has cholera?'

'Yes,' Bonnici replied.

'Right, then. He must be taken immediately to the isolation hospital. Guards, now.'

Sciberras stepped back to allow two burly guards to enter the room, faces covered with scarves, carrying a stretcher. Madame Trévissier gave out a moan.

'He's too ill to be moved,' Bonnici said. 'I'll treat him here. He can be taken to the hospital later.'

'No,' Sciberras said. 'No one is to touch him. Only these two men, who will be thoroughly cleansed and their clothes fumigated afterwards.'

'That's inhumane,' Bonnici said. 'The man needs care and attention. He should be treated with dignity.'

'Doctor, you know as well as I that cholera should be prevented from spreading at all costs. Take him away, now.'

The two guards wrapped the sheet around Trévissier and lifted him from the bed on to the stretcher.

'No, please,' Madame Trévissier cried. 'Let me go with my husband.'

One of the guards pushed her away, which made McQueen step forward. 'Leave her!' he said. She collapsed against him, overcome with grief.

'I'll go with your husband, Madame,' Bonnici said. 'I'll take good care of him, trust me.' He picked up his cane and walked behind the guards past Sciberras, who had backed away across the corridor.

'I'll come and find you later,' he said to Sciberras. 'We need to talk. You may be Keeper of the Lazzaretto, but I am a police physician.'

The isolation hospital was a small building some four hundred yards from the Lazzaretto on the west side of Manoel Island.

There were two wards containing ten beds, one on each side of a courtyard. The guards took Trévissier to a side room, dropping him unceremoniously onto a bed, then left the building. Bonnici lit an oil lamp on the bedside table, turning the wick down low for a comfortable light. He checked the patient, counting the heartbeats per minute. Trévissier opened his eyes momentarily, looking wildly around and attempting to lift his head, before collapsing back against the pillow. He murmured some words which Bonnici could not make out, then sank back into unconsciousness.

Bonnici sat in vigil, dozing off every now and then. Beyond the soft light from the lamp, the darkness had taken on a reddish-brown unreal quality. He had the impression that shadows were shifting around, as though kindly spirits were hovering at the edges, ready to welcome a stranger at the moment of passing. He rubbed his eyes, shaking his head to rid himself of such fanciful thoughts. He wished McQueen was there, who would change the atmosphere with a dram of whisky and a joke.

The door opened, making him jump, and a young man appeared. Small and slight, with a serious expression, wire spectacles framing his dark eyes. 'Good evening, *Dottore*,' he said in a whisper. 'Lorenzo Cassar. Quarantine doctor. Sorry I am late. I'm new here, just taken over from the previous doctor. How is the patient?'

'I don't think it will be long,' Bonnici replied. 'His breaths are getting more drawn out now. Perhaps it's time to call for a priest.'

The young doctor had a closer look at Trévissier.

'Is there nothing more we can do?' he asked.

'I'm afraid not. I had to give him morphine a couple of hours ago. By the time he had been moved to the hospital, it was too late to try any treatment. Is there a priest here?'

'*Dun* Niccolò. I'll go and see.' Cassar left the room quickly, as if glad to get away.

Several minutes later, he returned with an elderly priest, with swept-back white hair and a white beard. The priest walked stiffly across the room, nodding at Bonnici as he approached the patient. In the lamplight, Bonnici could see the deep wrinkles in his forehead and the sides of his face.

'Blue cholera. Excuse me if I don't get too close,' he muttered.

He sat down heavily in a chair, about four feet from Trévissier. He was carrying the sacrament kit in a battered leather case, which he placed next to him on the floor. He pulled out his stole, draped it over his shoulders, and began to recite the familiar prayers and blessings. Bonnici joined in with the responses, wishing that Trévissier's wife could be there. It was one of the cruelties of a disease such as cholera, that relatives could not witness the last sacrament, or pray for their loved ones as they passed from one life to the next.

He watched the priest anointing the dying man with holy oil, using a cotton swab so as not to touch the skin and jerking his hand away as soon as he could. In a low, quavering voice, the priest rattled through the Lord's Prayer, then commended Trévissier's soul to God's care. It felt as though he could not get through the sacraments quickly enough, to get away from the pestilent air. Giving all the responses, Bonnici found himself praying this would not be an epidemic. McQueen had asked him to be part of the team, to help find the murderer who had killed Captain Buchanan. How would they be able to conduct a proper investigation if cholera was claiming victims all around them, cloistered up as they were in the confines of the Lazzaretto?

He heard the last words '*Pax Domini sit semper vobiscum,*' and responded automatically '*Et cum spiritu tuo.*'

The priest stood up, nodded at the two doctors, gathered up his sacrament kit and left the room as fast as his arthritic knees would take him.

Doctor Cassar got up and checked the patient's breathing. 'I think he's gone, *Dottore*. That was good timing, calling for the priest.'

Bonnici sighed. 'I suppose it was,' he said. He stood up abruptly, brushing away the melancholy that threatened to overwhelm him. There was work to be done.

'Can you speak to the sisters? Make arrangements for the body to be prepared for burial? I'll go to Madame Trévissier and pass on the sad news.'

'Thank you, *Dottore*, yes I will.'

Bonnici glanced back at Cassar as he left the room. He looked so young, so unsure of himself. If they continued to have cases of cholera, if it spread through the Lazzaretto, it would be a severe test of his skills and his character.

McQueen had gone back to his apartment. He was concerned for Bonnici. Why had he taken it on himself to tend to that poor man, knowing he was dying of cholera? He knew the answer already – Bonnici was dedicated to his profession. But for how long would he be gone? Now there was no one to work with or talk to.

What did he have to go on, so far? He sat down heavily at his desk, wishing he had a glass or two of whisky at hand. He started to leaf through the correspondence from Buchanan. He pulled out the notes and telegrams from Sir Arthur Gambol and arranged them in date order. They were addressed to *Captain Buchanan – Magistrate, Bombay*. Over a period of six months, he could trace Buchanan's orders. It appeared that Sundar

Singh, who had graduated from Trinity College, Cambridge, in July, was in frequent correspondence with his father's cousin, Tejbir Singh, a prominent Sikh leader living in Amritsar. Their letters were being copied and passed on to the India Office, who appeared to be paranoid about a possible uprising by the Sikhs. McQueen guessed that memories of the Indian Rebellion of 1857 were still fresh.

The orders had come directly from the Viceroy of India himself. Sundar Singh was to be stopped from returning to India. Tejbir Singh was plotting with the prince, encouraging him to embrace his Sikh faith and to return to the Punjab to reclaim his empire. Gambol wrote that the prince's father, Sir Anokh Singh, had a hugely symbolic significance as he was son of the famous 'Lion of the Punjab'. But he was suffering ill-health, living with delusions of grandeur in Paris. Instead, Sikh leaders were turning to Sundar, the young heir to the kingdom. The Indian Rebellion had been suppressed but it would not take much encouragement for the people of India to rebel again – especially those princes who had lost their power and riches.

Buchanan's orders were to stop Prince Sundar Singh on his arrival in Bombay, to deny him the right to continue his journey in India, and to return with him on the next steamship back to Southampton.

McQueen was intrigued by what he was reading. It appeared that the powers-that-be in the India Office had spies watching for signs of rebellion everywhere, that even a young Sikh brought up in England had to be stopped from returning to his native land in case he stirred up trouble. He had heard of the prince's father, Sir Anokh Singh, who had lived in Scotland for many years. Now he needed to find out more about the Sikh Empire and how it had been absorbed into the British Raj. He put the correspondence to one side, to report to Colonel Ellis in the morning.

It was late. He stepped outside his apartment for a smoke. A long terrace ran along the whole building, with views out across the creek. It was peaceful. All he could hear was the lapping of water against the rocks, ten feet below him. He wondered what had happened to Buchanan. What had taken him out of his apartment at night? Who had lured him away, and why? And where had he been killed? It seemed a callous act; a knife through the ribs, the body dropped into the water. Ruthless, probably silent and swift, like an assassination. Nobody had reported hearing anything, which was strange in this eerie, quiet space.

McQueen dropped his cigarette and ground it out on the limestone floor. He could hear a faint noise, farther along the terrace. Quietly, he moved toward it. He stopped when he realised it was coming from Apartment Five. The sound of muffled sobbing. Madame Trévissier. He hesitated outside the door, feeling it was not his place to offer comfort, but hating to hear her distress. After a few moments he made his way back to his room to attempt to get some sleep. The whole place felt oppressive to him; fear and sorrow permeated the fabric of the building. He was not sure how he would be able to stand it for ten days.

CHAPTER FIVE

Manoel Island, Malta. Monday, 18 October 1880

After a restless sleep, much interrupted by the persistent buzz of mosquitoes, McQueen breakfasted at the restaurant then headed out to the Lazzaretto entrance. A handful of hawkers were milling around, selling different wares. He called one over and asked him to get a couple of bottles of Scotch, wincing at the price but reckoning it was a necessity. The hawker, short and solid, said he would have them there later that day.

The weather was fair and fresh, the water brushing against the sides of the pier. McQueen stood for a moment, enjoying the sea breeze. It was busy, with about a dozen *dgħajjes* lined up, some just waiting to be booked, others with passengers stepping off onto dry land. One such passenger looked familiar, and he was pleased to recognise the good-natured features of Sergeant Galea. He waved at him, then pointed out where the parlatorio was, before turning to make his way there.

He had to go down a short corridor to the left of the main

entrance to reach the room via an internal door. The other way in was from the outside of the building. The parlatorio was made of plain concrete, separated into two halves by a thin partition wall, a wire mesh in the middle. He waited for a couple of minutes before Galea entered the room from the other side. They were told they had to stay eight feet apart, a beefy guard glowering at them to make sure.

The young sergeant was smartly turned out, as ever, his uniform pressed, his moustache neatly curled at the ends. McQueen felt the strangeness of the situation, not being able to shake his colleague's hand, or clap him on the back. He was fond of Galea, who although still inexperienced, had proved himself to be a dependable, willing officer during their last case.

'Good morning, sir,' Galea said, from the other side of the partition. 'How is it at the Lazzaretto?'

'It's a bloody nightmare,' he said. 'It stinks, there are a million mosquitoes and now there's a case of cholera. Dr Bonnici treated the patient, a Frenchman, who died last night.'

Galea's eyes widened. He pulled back slightly to make even more distance between them.

'Don't worry,' McQueen said, amused. 'You won't catch it just from talking to me.'

'Sorry, sir.'

'Right, to business.' He pulled out the papers he had taken from Buchanan's trunk. 'You can take these to Colonel Ellis. I found Buchanan's orders from the India Office. He was a magistrate in the Civil Service in Bombay, charged with escorting Sundar Singh back to England. There's a link straight to the Viceroy.'

As he went to hand over the papers, the guard shouted from the other end of the room. 'No goods!'

'You can't pass anything over,' Galea explained. 'You have to leave it in the room, then it gets fumigated before anyone can touch it.'

'Oh, for goodness' sake!' McQueen put the papers away, frustrated. 'Get your notebook out then, you'll just have to take this down. Buchanan's orders came from Sir Arthur Gambol, India Office. Tell Ellis to get hold of him, to report the death and find out all he can about Buchanan.'

Galea wrote quickly, frowning in concentration. 'Gambol?' he asked.

'Yes, G-A-M-B-O-L. And tell Ellis I need two officers. We have to search the whole of the Lazzaretto. Today. Too much time has passed already. I'll expect them early afternoon to give us enough time before dark. They'll have to be paid extra, I imagine, to get them to come over, but it has to be done.'

'But what about the cholera?' Galea asked. 'What if everybody gets ill?'

'It's a risk we must take, Sergeant. We have a murder to solve. The killer is likely to be one of the passengers on this island. We must find out who.'

The two Maltese police officers who arrived at the Lazzaretto that afternoon looked distinctly wary. Both on the short and stocky side, with tunics tight around their middles, caps squashed down on their heads.

'Ah, Tweedledum and Tweedledee! Thank you for joining us in the land of quarantine,' McQueen said, enjoying the blank looks on their faces.

'Genovese and Battista,' one of them muttered, indicating himself and his colleague. 'Reporting for duty.'

'Excellent. Right, what I want you to do is to go through all the rooms. A thorough search. Under mattresses, through drawers and cupboards. Empty out the passengers' luggage. Look for anything out of the ordinary. Anything that people seem to have hidden away. And of course, the murder weapon, a dagger. We have twenty-six rooms and three hours before it gets dark. Three of us, so roughly twenty minutes per room. All clear?'

The constables nodded in unison.

'Let's get going then. You two go to the New Palace – through there. Genovese, take rooms one to ten on the left side of the courtyard, Battista, take those on the right. I'll go through the apartments in the Old Palace. Come and get me if you find anything.'

'Yes, sir!'

'And make sure you wear gloves at all times. Keep your distance from the passengers, otherwise you'll be kept here for ten days.'

The two officers visibly blanched. They set off, pulling on their gloves, looking as if they wanted to get the job done as quickly as possible and get away from this plague island.

McQueen knocked at the door of Apartment Three. His notes from Sciberras told him that this room was given to two single ladies, travelling back to England from India: Miss Louisa Copeland and Miss Eleanor Templeman. The door was opened by a tall, slender woman, who looked at him blankly. She looked typically English: blue eyes, pale skin, light blonde hair. An aloof air about her.

'Yes?' she asked. 'What do you want?'

'Detective Inspector McQueen, police. It's about the murder of Laurence Buchanan. I need to search your apartment.'

'Who is it?' a concerned voice came from farther inside the room.

Eleanor turned her head. 'It's the police. About that man who died.'

'Oh, goodness!'

The speaker, who was sitting by the fireplace, got up and joined her companion. Quite the opposite in looks, she was small, compact, with plain dark hair, and sincere brown eyes. A few years younger than her companion, he thought; barely over twenty years old.

'I am Miss Copeland,' she said, 'and this is Miss Templeman.'

The blonde woman nodded her head slightly.

'I'm sorry to break in on you like this, ladies, but we're searching the whole building.'

'Of course,' Louisa said. 'Please, come in. We did hear about Captain Buchanan. It's so terrible.'

'Did you know him?'

'No, not really – just talked to him on board a few times. He was with that mysterious Indian prince. What happened to him? Are you allowed to tell us?'

'Louisa, please,' Eleanor murmured. 'Let the officer go about his task.' She turned to McQueen. 'Do you have the necessary permission to do this? It seems rather a liberty to turn up unannounced and go through our belongings.'

'Aye, I do,' said McQueen. 'I'll be as quick as I can.'

The two ladies went back to their armchairs, but he felt aware of their eyes on him as he searched through their belongings, the dark eyes of Miss Copeland watching with interest, the light blue of her companion coldly surveying him. He could feel his face burning as he sorted through silks and cotton petticoats. On one bedside table he found a book of poems by Elizabeth Barrett Browning.

'Who's the scholar?' he asked, holding it up with a smile.

'Oh, that's Miss Templeman. I'm far more of a practical mind,' Louisa said. She jumped up and crossed the room to pick up a copy of *Mrs Beeton's Book of Household Management* from the other bedside, holding it up so he could see the title. 'I'm to be married soon. I can't wait. I'll have two houses to manage – one in London and one in Hertfordshire. So much to think about!'

She took the book back to her armchair and began to leaf through it.

McQueen completed the search, finding nothing of interest. Correspondence, a few books. A letter opener on the desk, shaped like a dagger but with blunt edges and a rounded tip. Impossible to inflict any damage with that.

He pulled out his notebook.

'Thank you, ladies. Now can I ask a few questions?'

'Certainly,' Louisa said. 'But I assure you we don't know anything.'

'That's fine. I have to ask everyone the same. How long had you known Captain Buchanan?'

'Just a few weeks, during the voyage. Although didn't you meet him in Bombay, Eleanor?'

'Once or twice. At the Governor's Ball and some music evening. Total bore. Arrogant too – typical Old Etonian,' Eleanor said, looking as if she had smelt a foul odour.

'He wouldn't say exactly why he was escorting that young Indian back to England. Something political, I suppose. Rather thrilling,' Louisa said.

'What did you know about him?'

'Ah, well, he said he was from Wiltshire originally. Ex-army, hence the "Captain", then Indian Civil Service. Doing well, I believe. Did he say he was getting married, Eleanor? I think he did.'

'Yes, I believe so. A Miss Letitia Fox.' A flicker of amusement crossed Eleanor's face. 'Came out with the Fishing Fleet.'

'The what?' McQueen asked.

'Women who travel to India to catch themselves husbands,' Louisa explained. 'All rather desperate, I would say. Anyway, he seemed very happy about it, kept saying how life would be much better with someone to look after him. I got the impression he had perhaps grown weary of the bachelor life.'

'How did he spend his time on board the ship and here in quarantine?'

'For the most part he was cooped up with the Indian. When we did see him in the saloon or on deck, he was rather rude about the prince. Said he was tedious company and deluded – ideas above his station.'

McQueen frowned. He was not forming a pleasant impression of this Buchanan.

'What about the night of the murder? Two nights ago?' he asked. 'Did you see or hear anything from their apartment? It's only two doors away.'

'D'you know, Inspector, we've asked ourselves that, and we really don't think we heard a thing,' Louisa said. 'We got back from dinner at around eight o'clock and spent the evening reading and talking. It's so dull here. We can't wait to be released.'

'It was mid-morning before we heard what had happened,' Eleanor said. 'One of the health guards came and told us. It was a shock.'

Realising he had spent sufficient time there and that he needed to move on, McQueen snapped his notebook shut.

'Thank you, ladies. I'll take my leave for now. You've been very helpful.'

'Do come back with any more questions, Inspector,' Louisa said. 'Let us know if there's anything we can do to help.'

McQueen stood outside the next-door apartment for some time, periodically bashing it with his fist, before it was eventually opened by a dishevelled young man. Jacketless and with shirt unbuttoned, he had a sickly air about him. He looked as if he had not shaved for two or three days and his sandy-coloured hair was unbrushed, sticking up at all kinds of angles.

'Gilbert Browne?' McQueen asked, having read his name on Sciberras's list.

'Yes,' Browne said. 'Who're you?'

He was standing in the doorway, blocking McQueen from seeing inside.

McQueen pushed open the door and stepped past him. 'Police. Detective Inspector McQueen. Investigating the murder of Laurence Buchanan. Here to search your room.'

The apartment smelt unaired, musty. The shutters were partially closed, keeping out the light. McQueen strode over to open them, then turned to face Browne, who stood bewildered in the middle of the room. The bed was unmade, with sheets twisted and crumpled. From his state of undress and the languor of his movements, the young man looked to have been pulled out of a drug-induced stupor.

'Wha... wha's happening?' he asked, backing away.

McQueen took him by the shoulders and pushed him firmly back onto the bed. 'You, sit there,' he said. 'I need to look through your belongings – I'm checking through all the apartments.'

Browne made a feeble attempt at protesting, then sank back against the pillows, eyes closed. McQueen wondered what he had taken, where he had got it from, and why he was in this state of stupefaction in the middle of the afternoon. Was it to counter the sheer boredom of quarantine, or were there other reasons? He glanced around, looking for evidence. On the floor, by the side of the bed, he found a small yellow tin, black tacky syrup melded around the lid. Prising it open, he saw it was stuffed with a dark brown sticky substance. He smelt it – a cloying, sugary odour with flowery overtones. Raw opium, no doubt about it.

'Where d'you get this?' he asked.

Browne opened his eyes and gradually focused them on the tin.

'India,' he said faintly. 'For headaches. Terrible headaches. Migraine.'

'How often do you take it? How much?'

'No' much. No' often. Just today. Bad head.'

McQueen was concerned. He wanted Bonnici to see Browne. The young man's breathing was slow and shallow, his pupils like tiny dots. He told Browne not to move, that he would be back soon with a doctor. As he left, he took a cursory look around the room, forming the impression of a gentleman of some means, with fine clothes, quality belongings. A few ornaments collected from North Africa and India. A young man who liked to travel. He would have to question him later, no point when he was in this state.

McQueen crossed through the Old Palace to see if he could find someone to send for Dr Bonnici. He took the steps two at a time to get from the top level, where the apartments were situated, down into the courtyard. He called over one of the servants, bustling through with an ewer of water. At that moment,

Genovese appeared on the other side of the courtyard, Battista right behind him. 'Inspector, sir,' Genovese shouted. 'Come, quick, we find something!'

'What is it?'

'Come, see.'

McQueen followed the constables through corridor after corridor, feeling like the place was a rabbit warren.

'I start here,' Genovese explained, shouting over his shoulder. 'Where you said. New Palace. Then maid scream and I run to see – here, in laundry.'

They entered a large, airy room with open windows. A tiled floor, with wooden tables against every wall. A big stove stood on the right-hand wall, opposite the windows, and a huge mechanical mangle was in the middle of the room. Wooden airers were suspended from the ceiling, with sheets draped over them.

'Here, here,' the constable said, running over to the corner opposite the door. McQueen could see a stack of giant canvas bags, full of bedding ready to be washed. 'Laundry maid find this.'

He explained that the maid had pulled out a couple of sheets, then had seen a muslin cloth, stained a dark, rusty red. She had opened out the cloth, revealing this item, which had made her scream – very loudly. So loudly he thought someone was being murdered.

The muslin had fallen back down over the object. Carefully, McQueen reached over and pulled it back. Underneath, surrounded by material soaked in blood, was a dagger with a silver handle, beautifully embellished with an intricate design of leopards and leaping antelopes. The blade, around five inches long, was curved, with sharp, serrated edges.

'Well done, Constable,' he said, looking up at Genovese. 'I believe you've found the murder weapon.'

CHAPTER SIX

Manoel Island, Malta. Monday, 18 October 1880

Word had got back to Sciberras. He appeared in the laundry room, flanked by three of the health guards. McQueen inwardly groaned. The keeper of the Lazzaretto would no doubt want to assert his authority.

'What's this? I hear you've found a dagger! Is it the murder weapon?' Sciberras demanded.

'It's possible,' McQueen said. With relief, he saw Bonnici arriving through the doorway, medical bag in hand.

'Take a look, Doctor,' he said. 'Could this be the blade used on Buchanan, d'you think?'

He held up the muslin package with the knife. As Bonnici came close to view it, he thought his friend looked weary, dark shadows under his eyes and lines etched around the corners of his mouth.

Bonnici studied the dagger for a moment, then looked up.

'I think it likely,' he said. 'Not only is it the right length, but also it has a curvature which fits with the wound on the body.'

'Thank you, Doctor.' McQueen patted him on the shoulder. 'You all right?' he asked quietly.

Bonnici smiled slightly and nodded. 'Of course,' he said.

'Let me see,' Sciberras commanded, almost pushing Bonnici away. He took a quick look before announcing: 'I knew it! It belongs to the Indian. Buchanan handed it in when the passengers arrived. It was locked in the storeroom. The Indian must have got hold of the key, found his dagger, and used it to kill his captor.'

He glared at the health guards. 'One of you must have helped him! He couldn't have done this on his own.'

'Let's not jump to conclusions,' McQueen broke in. 'Where's this storeroom? We need to see if the dagger has been taken.'

Together, the whole company marched back through the endless corridors of the Old Palace and the New, until they reached the administrative offices at the front of the Lazzaretto. Sciberras stopped outside a heavy metal door and tried the handle. It was locked. He pulled out a heavy ring packed with keys, selected one and used it to open the door. The room was dark and cool, with one tiny, barred window at the back. It was lined on three sides with shelves, filled with small suitcases, jewellery boxes, metal safe boxes and other miscellaneous items. Sciberras clearly knew exactly where the dagger had been stored. He strode over to the far right of the storeroom, where an ornate wooden casket sat on the middle shelf. McQueen kept close to him, watching his every move.

'Look!' Sciberras said. 'There, see – the lock is open.'

He lifted the lid of the casket. 'This is where the dagger was.'

McQueen peered over his shoulder as Sciberras put his hand inside the box and pulled out a beautiful, curved silver scabbard, embossed with the same design as the handle of the dagger. 'This is it. It belongs to the Indian prince. You should arrest him immediately!' Sciberras said triumphantly.

'Thank you,' McQueen said. 'I'll take it from here.'

He took the scabbard from Sciberras. 'We'll go and talk to Singh. But, if it *is* his dagger, it's not evidence that he himself is involved.'

'Oh, come on, Inspector! The man's clearly dangerous. Who else would want to kill Buchanan? It's *his* weapon. You must lock him up in solitary confinement, now. I'll send word to Colonel Ellis.'

'No, I'll decide what information is to be shared with Ellis,' McQueen said. 'That'll be all. Dr Bonnici, Genovese, you come with me; Battista, you go with Sciberras. Interview the health guards. Find out if any of them know anything about the key to the storeroom.'

Walking back to the prince's apartment, McQueen let Bonnici in on his thoughts. 'We need to find out about this dagger, what it's for and why Singh has one. Did he know where it was being stored? If he did have a plan to murder Buchanan, why choose his own weapon?'

'Indeed. It's led us straight to him, which doesn't make much sense,' Bonnici said. 'There's also the question of where the murder took place.'

'Exactly. There are no signs of disturbance in the apartment. And the prince hasn't been able to leave it. How would he have been able to get hold of his dagger, then lure Buchanan out of the compound, before killing him and dropping his body in the harbour?'

'And yet he's an obvious suspect.'

'Agreed. We're going to have to lock him away. I can't see how we can avoid it.'

When they got to the apartment, Sundar Singh let them in warily, eyes glancing from one to the other, trying to read what level of trouble he was in. He was wearing a fine blue tunic, with a white silk turban. He looked calm and composed.

McQueen indicated that Genovese should stand at the doorway, then pulled up two chairs opposite the prince's armchair so that he and Bonnici were facing him.

'There's been a serious development,' he said, watching Singh's expression carefully. 'Doctor, the dagger, please.'

Bonnici unwrapped the muslin, revealing the knife. McQueen placed the scabbard next to it. Singh's eyes flashed with recognition, but he remained still.

'Can you confirm that this is your dagger?'

He nodded. 'Yes, it is my *kirpan*.' He raised his chin proudly, then went to unbutton the top of his tunic.

'Hold it,' McQueen said sharply. 'Stand up.' He patted Singh's jacket to check for weapons. There was a shoulder strap but nothing within it, and nothing in any of the pockets.

'All right, you may show us,' he said.

Singh undid the tunic to reveal an ornate blue shoulder strap, with loops to hold the knife. He took it off and handed it to McQueen.

'This is where my *kirpan* should be. By my religion it should be worn at all times. When I was handed into the care of Captain Buchanan, I was forced to give it up,' he said, doing the buttons back up again, 'which shows your British lack of respect for my culture. I've not seen it since.'

'Did you know where it was stored here at the Lazzaretto?'

'No. No idea.'

The prince's eyes kept flicking to the knife in the muslin.

'Yes,' Bonnici said. 'If you're wondering if that's blood, it is.

We believe that this is the weapon used to kill Captain Buchanan.'

Singh swallowed.

'So, you can see that it looks extremely bad for you,' McQueen said. 'Your knife was used, and you have a strong motive for wanting Buchanan dead.'

Singh closed his eyes for a moment, then opened them with a sigh.

'But that's crazy,' he said. 'For so many reasons. Firstly, the *kirpan*. It is a symbol. It represents the honour of compassion, kindness and mercy. We're taught that it should be used as a last resort, only in defence, and never in anger. I would not have used it against Buchanan. And if I had, why would I have stayed here? Surely, the whole point would have been for me to escape? Please credit me with some intelligence.'

'But perhaps it was so important to you that you bribed one of the guards to find your *kirpan* for you. Did you and Buchanan argue? Did it turn into a physical attack, forcing you to pull out your dagger?'

'No!' Singh replied forcibly. 'We never argued. I couldn't stand the man. We were forced together, but we simply ignored each other. He had his job to do, and I had to put up with him. There was no way I could escape. Even if I could, where would I go? This is a tiny island. I don't exactly fit in.' He gestured at his turban. 'How could I get to India, when everyone here would be on the lookout for me?'

'So, you have been thinking about escaping,' McQueen said. 'Look, there is strong evidence here – so much so that I am going to have to move you to a locked room where we can safely hold you. We'll question you again tomorrow.'

Singh dropped his head into his hands for a moment, his body tense. When he raised his head again his eyes were wide and pleading. 'I haven't done anything,' he said. 'Can't you see?

Someone has used the *kirpan* to make it look like me, but I didn't do it.'

McQueen believed him, for all the reasons the young man had given him. He stood up and put his hand on Singh's shoulder.

'It's difficult, I know,' he said. 'I'm not charging you – yet. We're continuing the investigation. We'll find out the truth of what's happened. But you have to be kept under lock and key. Genovese, take him to Sciberras and find out where the room is. Look after him, make sure he has blankets, food, all the essentials.'

He waited until the young Sikh had been taken out of the apartment. 'I can't see it,' he said. 'He's so young. I don't think he has it in him. Not to kill a former soldier like Buchanan.'

'He's also small and slight,' Bonnici said. 'You saw the size of Buchanan, he was tall, bulky. To be able to close in on him, use the dagger with such precision and force.' He shook his head. 'It is difficult to imagine.'

'We need to find where the murder took place,' McQueen said. 'There may be evidence there that will help tell the story of what happened. It's all conjecture at the moment. Conjecture and a bloody knife!'

With Singh safely held in a locked room, McQueen took Genovese and Battista out to search the shoreline of Manoel Island. He was annoyed with himself. He should have organised this sooner. They only had around an hour before dark. They took sticks with them, and a lantern. One of the health guards came to show the way, a lively little man who said he knew the island and the waters better than anyone. Given where Buchanan's body washed up, he said, it was likely he was dropped into Lazzaretto Creek from the east shore.

The guard led them out of the back of the New Palace through an iron gate. The ground was dry and hard, with scrubby bushes on either side of a rough path. Ahead of them they could see the high walls of Fort Manoel, about five hundred yards away. The sun was low, hovering above the Valletta skyline, wreathing the clouds in orange and yellow. The air grew cooler as they drew closer to the water. McQueen took in a deep breath. It was hard to believe that these tranquil surroundings could have been the scene of a violent crime.

They headed down a path to the right, leading toward the harbour. 'Spread out,' McQueen said. 'Look for signs that someone's been here. Any trampled undergrowth, any marks in the ground. Anything that would indicate a struggle.'

They moved along slowly in a triangle, the guard ahead on the path, Battista some way behind him. McQueen was walking to the left of the path, in the scrubland, Genovese to the right. As he swept through the low bushes with his stick, McQueen wondered whether Buchanan had been enticed out of the Lazzaretto. If so, did he know that he was in danger? Was he perhaps armed, himself? Or was he heading toward some kind of rendezvous, unaware that someone was intent on murder?

They made slow progress, with the sun rapidly disappearing. The path had taken them along the shoreline, as far as Fort Manoel, its bastions looming above them on the left. McQueen's frustration grew with every step. After around twenty minutes, he was about to call off the search when Genovese gave a shout. 'There's something here!'

McQueen strode rapidly across to see Genovese pointing at a dark stain on the ground. It was getting too dark to distinguish colours. 'Quick, light the lantern,' he ordered. As Battista struck a match and the flame began to take hold, it revealed a deep brown stain on the surface of the sandy soil. McQueen knelt to look at it closely. It looked like dried blood. There were no footprints or tracks coming away from the spot, but the ground and the path bore the faint marks of having been brushed, perhaps by some twigs.

'Over here,' called the guard.

'Battista, the lantern,' McQueen called as they moved over to see what had been found. The path came to an abrupt end at a slipway leading down into the now inky black waters. Halfway down, there were smudges of blood.

'Well,' McQueen said. 'I think we have our answer. This is where Buchanan met his fate and ended up in the water.'

'Detective Inspector McQueen. This way!'

As they got back into the Old Palace, Sciberras appeared suddenly from his office doorway. *What is it now?* McQueen was weary. It had been a long day.

'Colonel Ellis is here. He's waiting for you in the parlatorio,' Sciberras said with great relish.

He must have sent a message to the superintendent, telling him about the kirpan.

'Fine,' McQueen said, through gritted teeth. 'I'll be on my way then. No rest for the wicked.'

He told Genovese and Battista they could head back to Valletta, thanking them for their sterling work.

It was dark when he got to the parlatorio. A guard stood just inside the door, a disconcertingly solid presence. Two lamps had been lit and placed on tables, one either side of the wire mesh partition. Ellis stood restlessly on the far side.

'Ah, McQueen, at last!' he said sharply. His gaunt face looked eerie in the warm yellow lamplight, the shadows around his eyes a strange grey-green colour. 'Where have you been?'

'We went to identify where Buchanan's body was pushed into the water. Looks like it was the place where he was murdered, over by Fort Manoel.'

'Ah. Look here, McQueen, why did I have to hear about the murder weapon from Sciberras? You should have informed me immediately.'

'A few things I wanted to check first. We had to get outside before we lost the light.'

'The thing is, this makes it crystal clear. It was Prince Sundar Singh's dagger that killed Captain Buchanan. It's obvious that he is the murderer. I can't believe I've had to come all the way over here to tell you to place him under arrest.'

'With respect, Superintendent, I don't think we have enough evidence. The prince has been placed in a secure room, to keep him safe, while we put the case together. It's not crystal clear, in fact there are some serious issues, such as how he could have obtained the dagger when he was under virtually constant observation from Buchanan.'

'He could easily have found a means. Who else would have wanted Buchanan dead? McQueen, you have no idea how much pressure we're under to get this young Indian troublemaker severely dealt with. At least you've put him under lock and key. I'll go back now to see the magistrate and get a warrant for his arrest.'

'I just need a bit more time, a day or two, to gather more evidence.'

'Your request is denied. I'll confirm the arrest warrant tomorrow. In the meantime, I will *not* grant you any more time, or support from police officers, to pursue further inquiries.'

'I think you're being short-sighted,' McQueen said. 'There's more to this story than meets the eye.'

'I don't care what you believe, McQueen. The prince is guilty. He is to be watched at all times until quarantine is over, when he can be moved to the police cells in Valletta.'

Ellis turned and stalked out of the parlatorio into the darkness of Manoel Island, slamming the door behind him.

'That's all very well,' McQueen said to the guard standing in the shadows. 'But why doesn't he tell us what he really thinks?'

He set off back to his apartment, wending his way through the dark corridors of the Lazzaretto, feeling oppressed by the weight of prejudice and suspicion.

CHAPTER SEVEN

Valletta, Malta. Monday, 18 October 1880

'You can go, Papà,' Maria Tanti said. 'I'll lock up later, when I've finished.'

'I don't like to leave you here on your own.'

'I won't stay long. I'm waiting for more information about the body found near the Lazzaretto. I went to the police office earlier, spoke to Sergeant Galea. He said he'd send me a message when he heard more.'

Maria's father, Michele Tanti, was the editor of the *Malta Post*. A leading member of the Malta Chamber of Commerce and Enterprise, he was running late for their monthly meeting.

'I told you, a simple statement reporting the death of an Englishman is enough. I don't want you writing anything speculative, stirring things up.'

Maria had only recently started working with her father on the newspaper, after begging him for a chance to prove herself. She counted herself lucky, being able to work in a job that she loved. Women were expected to marry young and remain at home, taking care of all the household duties. But thanks to her beloved Papà, she had been given a good education and now worked alongside him as a writer and deputy editor.

'But, Papà, it's an important story. We can find out from Inspector McQueen exactly what is happening. He's there, on Manoel Island. We can steal a march on *The Standard*, get first-hand information about the investigation.'

There were only two English language newspapers published in Malta, theirs which came out weekly and *The Standard* – with an English editor – which was published every other week. Maria knew her father would love to get ahead of his rivals.

'All right, all right. But I will have the final word on the report – yes? I have to go now. Lock everything up carefully. I'll see you for dinner. Remember *Zija* Paolina has invited *Dun* Filippo. Don't be late.'

She smiled after him as he bustled out of the office, typically late and carrying a bulging briefcase of papers. She knew the meeting would not start until he had arrived. He was an unapologetic Anglophile, which put him at odds with many of the local businessmen, who looked to Italy for culture and commerce. But his easy charm and practical nature made him a popular member of the board.

She liked the office in the evening. The compositors only worked in the mornings, so it was quiet, giving her space to think. The printing press, in a large room at the back of the building, came to life on a Friday night. Once cranked up, it rolled all night to produce the nine hundred newspapers ready for distribution on Saturday morning. Even when dormant, the smell of oil and ink permeated the building, which for Maria was the smell of home. The printers' office, which she shared with her father, was a wonderful jumble of papers, reference books and filing cabinets. They had a desk each. Unlike her father, she liked to keep hers ordered, with a good supply of sharpened pencils and paper at hand.

Maria settled down to writing her piece on the death of Captain Buchanan. A high-ranking English civil servant, drowned in Lazzaretto Creek. Who was he? One of the passengers from the *Poonah*, currently being held in quarantine, but what was his story? How had he ended up dead? She wondered how Inspector McQueen was getting on. She had found out from Sergeant Galea that he was staying at the Lazzaretto. Having joined forces with him on his previous case in Malta, she knew he was a man of action. Being cooped up with strangers, without access to a bar, would be his idea of hell. He would need to solve the case quickly just to stay sane.

She heard the bell at the front of the office and went to the door. Her heart lifted as she saw the message boy standing outside. It was Antonio, smiling, his untidy black hair sticking up awkwardly on one side. He waved at her, holding a folded piece of paper in his hand. Just ten years old, he earned pocket money by running errands for the police.

She opened the door and gave him a quick hug. She was fond of the boy, known as Ninu, having got to know him well over the past few months. The son of *Sinjura* Caruso, McQueen's landlady, he was devoted to the Scottish detective, following him around and 'helping' him with his investigations.

'Ninu, come in. Have you got a message for me?'

'It's from Sergeant Galea. Here, read.'

She opened the note:

Sinjorina Tanti,

There is cholera and Inspector McQueen is in quarantine. You must go to meet him at the parlatorio, at the Lazzaretto, tomorrow morning at 10am. I will come with you. You must not publish anything in the newspaper.

Prince Sundar Singh is going to be arrested for the murder of Buchanan. This is confidential. McQueen does not think he is guilty. He hopes you can help.
Giuseppe Galea (Sergeant)

'Goodness,' she said. *So, it was murder*. She folded the letter back up. 'This is quite the tale.'

'What is it?' Antonio asked, hopping from foot to foot.

She was thinking quickly, wondering how she could find out more. She had a vague memory of seeing something about an Indian prince, being returned to England. The newspaper received weekly information from the P&O office about the travellers on each passenger ship that arrived in Valletta. She would have to go through the telegrams.

'Nothing for you to worry about,' she said, ruffling Ninu's hair. 'Stay there while I get you a penny. I'll write you a reply and you can take it to the sergeant.'

She went to her father's desk to rifle through the petty cash box. Then she penned a quick note to Galea.

I'll be there, 10am tomorrow. Tell McQueen to stay clear of the cholera. Will do what I can to help, Maria.

'Here you go,' she said, handing the note to him. 'Now get yourself back home. Aren't you at school now?'

'Yes. I go every day except Sunday. Finish at three.'

'Do you like it?'

He scowled. 'No. I wanted to go, but I hate it. The teachers are always angry.'

She thought perhaps he just needed to adapt to the discipline. He had been used to his freedom. School was a new thing. His mother had not been able to pay before but now she was being helped by Dr Bonnici.

'Now, Ninu,' she said, 'you know you have to work at school. You'll be fine. You just have to catch up with the other boys.'

'Yes,' he said, looking at the floor. 'But it's hard.'

She gave him the penny. 'You're a brave and very helpful boy. Be good now, and I'll see you soon.'

She watched him leaving the office and running up the road, cheerful again with his money in his hand. Perhaps she had not said the right thing. She did not seem to have that knack with children that people like McQueen had. She shrugged. Just as well, she was not likely to be having a family herself. Now she was 'damaged goods'. Damned by association with the disturbed individual who had been her fiancé. No man in Malta would ever be interested.

She sighed and went to look through the recent P&O announcements.

The next morning, Maria met Sergeant Galea at the entrance to the Lazzaretto. She had travelled from Valletta in a *dgħajsa tal-pass*, with her maid as her companion. Rożi, who hated anything to do with water, complained all the way.

'Why are you making me do this? You know I feel sick, every movement. Now I know you don't like me.'

Maria had known Rożi all her life. Her mother had died when she was very young and Rożi had always looked after her. *Zija* Paolina, her father's sister, had also been there, but theirs was a different relationship, one that was much more focused on trying to get Maria to behave in a more becoming way.

Galea greeted them with a salute. 'Good morning, ma'am, *Sinjorina* Tanti.'

He was so serious nowadays, now he was training to be a

detective. She smiled at his formality. 'Sergeant. How are you? Is Inspector McQueen ready to see us?'

He nodded. 'Yes, it's this way.'

He led the way to the parlatorio, talking over his shoulder as they went in: 'We have to stay on separate sides of the room and talk through a partition, from a distance. To stop the cholera from spreading. There are other people there, too, having meetings. I expect it will be noisy.'

He was not wrong. About fifteen people were packed into the parlatorio, which echoed with loud conversations. She spotted McQueen on the far side of the room and made her way over toward the iron mesh that separated those in quarantine from their visitors. As usual, he was a good head taller than the people around him, looking bulky in his woollen suit. He was frowning, looking on edge, she thought, until he caught sight of her and broke into a rueful smile.

'Here's a turn-up,' he said. 'Good to see you, lassie.'

'How are you?' she said. 'What's happening?'

'You got my message, about Prince Sundar Singh?'

She nodded.

'Colonel Ellis has gone to see the magistrate. The prince is going to be arrested but he'll be kept here in the Lazzaretto until quarantine is over. I'm stuck inside and so is Doctor Bonnici. It's no fun, I can tell you.'

McQueen ran his hand through his hair. He looked almost comic in his despair.

'How's Dr Bonnici?' she asked.

'He's been treating a cholera patient. I hope to God he doesn't go down with it. He insisted on staying with him in hospital.'

'*Sinjura* Caruso is so worried!'

'I can imagine.'

'What can I do for you, Inspector?'

'I need more information about Buchanan. I don't believe the prince is guilty. In which case, we have to find out more about Buchanan and work out who else might have wished him dead. Ellis won't hear of any police officers taking time to work on this. Can you find out what you can?'

She felt a surge of excitement. There was nothing she would like to do more than help McQueen with the investigation. It appealed to her sense of adventure and her love of digging out a story.

'What kind of information do you need?'

'Anything you can find out about the first-class passengers from the *Poonah.* They are all here at the Lazzaretto. I need to know if anyone had any reason to want to get rid of Buchanan.'

She took out her notebook and quickly wrote a couple of notes.

'Then there's his romantic entanglement. I found a letter from a Letitia Fox who purports to be his fiancée. What can you find out about her? Were there any other women in his life, previous to her?'

'I'll see what I can do.'

'And finally, what about his army career? He was a captain. Which regiment was he in? Had he been to war? Are there any stories linked to his record?'

She looked up from her notebook. 'Goodness, that's a lot to find out.' Her mind was already racing, thinking of people she could ask, favours she could call in.

McQueen shrugged. 'Hate to ask,' he said. 'But I'm stuck. Can't do anything myself. If you send anything you find to Sergeant Galea here, he'll get it over to me. Right, Sergeant?'

'Yes, sir!'

'I'll send something to you in a couple of days,' Maria said. 'In the meantime, what can we report in the *Post*?'

'Ellis would have to tell you that,' McQueen said with an

edge in his voice. 'Why don't you go to the police office with Sergeant Galea, and find out what you can and can't say? As far as I can make out, the superintendent is completely blinkered. Only interested in pursuing one suspect. If he and the governor want to publish details of the arrest, then so be it. But I'd be careful. Keep an open mind.'

'I will,' she said.

She hated the thought of McQueen being cooped up like this on Manoel Island. The guard shouted that the parlatorio session was over. She watched McQueen as he turned to leave with all the other quarantined. He looked back and raised his hand, looking rather like an ox being led away to market. So far, he was going along with it, but she wondered how long it would be before he kicked out against the system.

CHAPTER EIGHT

Manoel Island, Malta. Tuesday, 19 October 1880

On his way back into the main buildings of the Lazzaretto, McQueen could hear raised voices from the crowd that hung around the main gate. Local traders and servants, hustling for money from passengers quarantined within the building. As he walked toward the noise, he could see a tall woman, standing head and shoulders above the Maltese, addressing them with considerable energy.

'It's not as if I'm asking for much,' she was saying. 'I just want a newspaper that's got today's date on it, not one from five days ago!'

She had a strong voice with an American accent, and he got the immediate impression she was used to getting her way. A clamour of Maltese voices tried to explain how this was impossible. He could see how she was getting more and more infuriated as he walked up.

'Can I help?' he asked.

She turned to look at him. She had a direct gaze, appraising him with a haughty air. He was struck by the intensity of her green eyes, and the confident set of her mouth.

'Who the hell are you?' she asked.

He laughed at her directness and tipped his hat.

'Inspector Sam McQueen, Edinburgh Police. Trapped in quarantine like you.'

'Police? Is this to do with the murder? Tell me, what's going on? I've been trying to find out and I can't even get a current newspaper. It's driving me crazy.'

'You are?'

'Nellie Byrne.'

McQueen cast his mind back to the list of passengers, recalling that Nellie Byrne was an independent traveller on her way back from India.

'Let's go inside to your room,' he said. 'I need to talk to you anyway. I'm interviewing everyone who was staying near the victim's apartment.'

'I'm not having you come to my apartment,' she said. 'We can walk to the terrace.'

She led the way. Having been in Malta for a few months, McQueen had got used to being a good deal taller than everyone around him. This woman, striding ahead, was at least five feet ten, just a couple of inches shorter than him. She radiated an unusual strength and confidence, and he wondered about her background. What had led her to a life of adventure, travelling alone?

After leading the way through the corridors, Nellie stopped at the terrace running along the front of the Lazzaretto, where the arches offered a view out across the creek.

She pulled out a tin of Egyptian cigarettes from a pocket in the skirts of her dress, a navy-blue serge, the bodice plain and close fitting. She offered him one, which he took, masking his surprise at a woman smoking a cigarette. He lit a match for her, watching her closely as she drew in the smoke and let it out slowly from her mouth.

'So, Inspector. How come you're from Scotland?'

'It's a long story. I'm here to help the Maltese police for a wee while. What about you? What journey have you been on?'

'I'm on my way to England, after a trip to India. I'm a woman of means, Inspector, I go wherever I fancy. I get bored if I stay still for too long. That's why I can't stand it now, stuck here in quarantine.'

'I'm the same,' McQueen admitted. 'But with cholera here, we have no choice.'

Nellie took another deep drag of her cigarette, staring out over the water.

'What about Captain Buchanan, being found dead? What's the story?' she asked. 'All I know is that he was found in the harbour.'

'Yes, the body was found by a fisherman. Did you speak with Buchanan on the voyage?'

'Only a couple of times. Fancied himself as a ladykiller. I know the type. He drank too much one evening, approached me in the clumsiest way. I told him what I thought of him. He avoided me from then on. No doubt he spread gossip about me to anyone who would listen. Some men just can't stand being turned down. Can't believe any woman can resist.'

'I thought he was engaged to be married?'

'Oh, he told me all about that. The lovely Letitia, and how "what she didn't know wouldn't hurt her". Did he not see how insulting that is to her – and to me? Such a pig.'

'No love lost between you, then.'

'No, but I wouldn't wish him dead, Inspector, if that's what you're implying.' She dropped her cigarette and ground it beneath the toe of a fine-looking silk shoe, watching him steadily.

'Did you talk to Prince Sundar Singh at all?' McQueen asked.

'Well, as it happens, yes, I did. I am acquainted with the prince's father, the Maharaja. I met him in Paris. I've been kind of looking out for the prince, I feel sorry for him. All he wanted to do was to follow his roots, find out about the Sikh religion, and his heritage. Instead, he was forced to turn back to England, with Buchanan as his guard.'

Interesting. She must know more about the prince's background.

'You say you know his father. What's he like?'

'Not in good health, Inspector. Apoplexy has left him somewhat depleted. He's been exiled from India most of his life, but now he's exiled from England as well. He's a bitter man. A bit weak, I would say, certainly one for the high life when he had the money. Not much left now. I think he sees young Prince Sundar as his last chance to reinstate his former glory.'

'The young heir, eh? Tell me, Miss Byrne, the prince's apartment was a few doors away from yours. Did you hear anything at all, the night that Buchanan died? Saturday, three nights ago?'

'Not a thing. I was reading a book and writing my journal. First I heard was at breakfast on Sunday morning.'

'What do you think happened to him?'

'I have no idea. Somebody said today that the prince has been arrested. Is that right? Do you think he did it?'

'It's possible.'

Nellie glanced at him quickly.

'I think it unlikely, Inspector, don't you? He seems to me to be such a young man. In so many ways.'

'What do you mean?'

'Oh, come on,' she replied. 'Surely you've met him? The boy

has no more grit than a mouse. There must be other people with more reasons to want Buchanan dead.'

'Like who?'

'Oh, I don't know! That's your job, not mine.' She yawned. 'If we're done, Inspector, I'd like to retreat to my room. Scintillating though your company is, I've got some letters to write. Bound to see you again soon in this godforsaken place.'

McQueen watched as Nellie Byrne strode back toward the apartments. The atmosphere had lightened up a little since meeting her. He took out his pocketbook and made a few notes.

McQueen met Bonnici in the restaurant at lunchtime. The doctor looked freshly shaved, his hair neat with pomade and his clothes smartly pressed. Feeling large and shabby, McQueen ran his fingers through his hair before sitting down at the table.

'Good day, Doctor,' he said. 'You look as if you've managed to get some rest.'

Bonnici smiled. 'I have. And you? What have you found out?'

'I met with Sergeant Galea and Maria Tanti at the parlatorio. Miss Tanti is going to do some digging, find out more about Buchanan, the other passengers. And I've just met with Nellie Byrne. Interesting woman, American. Claims to know nothing about the murder, but I'm not sure. I'll need to talk to her again.'

Bonnici raised an eyebrow. 'I've heard about her – an American heiress with a generous allowance. Her father has made a fortune in steel production. A formidable young lady, I believe.'

'She certainly is. And she did not like Buchanan at all.'

One of the waiting staff brought soup, bread and cheese to

the table. McQueen immediately started spearing food onto his plate, his mouth watering.

'There's someone else I want you to see, Doctor,' he said as he tore up a piece of bread. 'It's Gilbert Browne. Young lad. Titled gentry. On his way back from India. I interviewed him on Monday. He was lethargic, in a stupor, induced by opium-eating. I assume he's all right now, but I think you should take a look at him.'

He stuffed the bread with a big piece of cheese into his mouth. He was used to Maltese cheese now, often made from ewe's or goat's milk, strong-flavoured and salty.

Bonnici rather more delicately took a corner of bread and buttered it.

'Of course. What else do we need to do?'

'We should go back to Sciberras. There's something about the disappearance of the dagger – how he seemed so certain of what had happened. He's up to something, I'm sure. And we should check on the prince, see how he's being treated and ask him some more questions about Buchanan.'

Intent on his plate of food, McQueen did not see Eleanor Templeman approaching their table. The blonde Englishwoman from Apartment Three seemed to suddenly appear next to them, pale and colourless, like a ghostly apparition.

'Do you mind if I sit with you?' she asked. 'I have no companion. Miss Copeland is indisposed.'

'Of course,' Bonnici said. 'I hope it is nothing serious.'

'No, no, she says she'll be fine, just a stomach ache. A lie-down will do her the world of good.'

A slight look of concern crossed the doctor's face. 'I'll come by and look at her later,' he said.

A bowl of soup was placed before Eleanor and she began to eat it almost mechanically, her mind clearly elsewhere.

McQueen found her difficult to read. She was distant, withdrawn.

'We're about to visit Gilbert Browne,' he said. 'What do you know of him?'

Browne's name seemed to focus her. She looked at McQueen coldly. 'That fool! He's the worst of the aristocracy – lazy, immoral and profligate.'

McQueen and Bonnici exchanged glances. Having made this declaration, Eleanor carried on eating the soup, which was full of beans, cabbage and other vegetables.

'Do you know of his family? Anything about him?' McQueen ventured.

'Not a thing,' she replied. 'I've simply heard him holding forth in the first-class lounge, telling the most appalling tales of his journeys in India and the Far East. Not at all suitable for the company of ladies. He thinks everyone should listen to him and applaud his stories of drunkenness and debauchery. Well, I for one will *not*.'

With that emphatic despatch, she finished her soup, touched the edges of her mouth with a napkin, and took a drink of water.

She stayed for a little while longer, engaging in a bit of small talk, then took herself off back to her apartment.

'Well, she's not one to hold back, is she?' McQueen said. She amused him, but at the same time there was too much that reminded him of the extreme respectability of the world in which he grew up. The strict rules of the Scottish Presbyterian Church which he had left behind a long time ago, but which had stultified him with boredom. Everything was frowned upon – drinking, dancing, playing games. Sundays spent sitting still, listening to sermons, reading and praying. Even the thought of it had him itching to punch something and run straight to the bar for a drink.

The Gilbert Browne who opened the door to them a little later was very different to the drugged young man McQueen had met the day before. Bright-eyed and cheerful, he welcomed them into his room. It was a fine afternoon, and the sunlight was slanting through the windows, bouncing off the limestone walls to bathe the room in a warm glow. Browne was exceptionally good-looking, with bright blue eyes, dark-blond curls and a winning smile – the type of looks that as a child and a young man could charm anyone, but that so easily turns to baldness and corpulence in middle age.

'Do come in,' Browne said. 'It's Inspector McQueen, isn't it?'

'Aye, and this is Doctor Bonnici. After our last meeting, I wanted him to see you. You were not in a good way.'

'Well, as you can see, I'm fine. You caught me at a bad time – I took a little too much medication – I get these headaches, you see. But all good now.'

Bonnici stepped forward. 'Do you mind?' he asked.

'Of course, be my guest.'

The doctor put his hands on either side of Browne's face and tilted it toward the light. 'Watch my finger,' he said, moving his index finger in front of Browne's right eye and then his left.

'Good, good,' he muttered. Then he took Browne's wrist and held it for thirty seconds or so, while looking at his watch.

'You're fine,' he said, after a moment. 'But you must be careful. Treat opium with respect. Too much can kill you.'

'Oh, I know, Doctor, I know. You don't need to worry about me. I've got it all under control. It was just being cooped up here, the murder, my headache. It was all a bit much... you know.'

He was trying hard to keep his tone light, but McQueen

detected an undercurrent of unease and decided to push him for more information.

'What do you know about Laurence Buchanan? Did you speak with him on the voyage?'

'Yes, a little. I don't think he liked me. Kept telling me to hold back on the booze, which was a bit rich coming from him. He lives in Bombay, works for the Indian Civil Service. Thought he was some kind of government agent because he was tasked with escorting the Indian prince, but it all seemed a bit lame to me. I believe I've seen more of life than he has.'

Browne broke off at this point, seeming to remember that he was talking about a murder victim. He had the good grace to look a bit embarrassed, muttering, 'Not to speak ill of the dead, naturally.'

McQueen gestured at the ornaments displayed on the table. 'I can see you're well-travelled. Where have you been?'

'Oh, South Africa, China, India, Egypt.'

'Where did you pick up the opium habit?'

Browne smiled slightly. 'China – it's everywhere. And India. The opium dens, those are the places to go. Nothing like it.'

'What else did you get up to?'

Browne licked his lips. 'Just travelling around, you know. Meeting people, seeing the sights.'

'On your own?'

'Yes.'

'How long have you been travelling for? Must have cost a lot, this trip of yours.'

'Six months.' Browne looked at McQueen with narrowed eyes. 'I don't know what you're fishing for. I have plenty of money – I have a trust fund. Got a bit of business going too. Not short of cash.'

'Business, eh? Care to tell me what that's about?'

'Not really, Inspector. Don't see why I should.'

McQueen made a mental note to look into Gilbert Browne's circumstances. This evasion certainly must mean something.

At that moment, there was a thump at the door. Browne opened the door to reveal one of the health guards. 'Doctor Bonnici, you're needed, quick!'

Bonnici picked up his medical bag at once. 'What is it?'

'It's cholera – English lady, Miss Copeland.'

McQueen felt sick as Bonnici rushed out with the guard. *The poor lassie.* This whole situation was terrible. Stuck in quarantine, with two killers on the loose – one a human, the other a deadly disease.

CHAPTER NINE

Manoel Island, Malta. Tuesday, 19 October 1880

As Bonnici arrived at Apartment Three, a maidservant was bustling out, carrying a chamber pot covered with a cloth. The smell was enough to tell him this was a case of diarrhoea. 'Stop, let me see,' he ordered. Gingerly he lifted the cloth; the substance beneath was like rice water. This was a bad sign.

'Be careful,' he said to the servant, who looked at him, wide-eyed. 'Do not allow any of this effluence to touch you. And put a mask around your face so you're not breathing in tainted air.' She left quickly, looking terrified.

Entering the chamber, he found it dark and foul-smelling. The shutters were closed, and a lamp lit, giving the room a murky brown colour. Louisa Copeland was lying on her bed, stripped down to a long chemise. She was rolling from side to side, crying out with pain. Eleanor was sitting by her side, holding a damp cloth, murmuring words of comfort to her friend. She stood up as Bonnici approached, her face taut and white.

'Thank you for coming, Doctor. I'm sorry to send for you, but Louisa is so much worse. Is there something you can give her?'

'Of course,' he said. 'Has she been vomiting?'

'Yes, it came on suddenly, with the cramps, about thirty minutes ago.'

Bonnici took the patient's pulse, which was extremely weak. She looked awful. Her eyes were sunken and dark with terror. She felt cold to the touch, and her skin had taken on a bluish colour. She clutched at him, only able to speak in a hoarse whisper.

'Help me, Doctor,' she said. 'It hurts. I feel so bad.'

He tried his best to sound reassuring, despite knowing that this was the gravest of situations. 'Don't be fearful,' he said gently. 'We're here to take care of you. We'll stay with you until you're well again.'

Bonnici turned to Eleanor, speaking softly so that Louisa could not hear. 'You did well to call me,' he said. 'It *is* cholera, still at the first stage. She's fit and strong, we can but hope that she'll pull through. I'll do everything I can. Will you assist?'

Eleanor replied without hesitation. 'Yes, Doctor. I have nursed before. Just tell me what to do.'

'First, we need to inform Sciberras that we have another case of cholera. She's to be moved into isolation at the hospital. Once there, we need to get her warm. Find servants who can bring hot water bottles. Also, we need ice – plenty of ice and water – and some cognac. If you want to help, you'll have to come to the isolation hospital as well, and you know what that means. It puts you at greater risk. It'll be a long night. Are you prepared to do that?'

Eleanor nodded, her expression set and determined. 'Of course, Doctor. Whatever it takes, I'll do it.'

Sciberras despatched Grech with the key to the room where Prince Sundar Singh was being held. McQueen waited while Grech unlocked the door and let him in, then heard the key turn in the lock behind him, leaving him alone with the prince.

Prince Sundar was lying propped up on a pillow on a single bed. It was a plain, black, cast-iron bed, the mattress covered with rough cotton sheets and a grey blanket. His hands were clasped behind his head. He was wearing the same cream silk turban that McQueen had seen before, but his jacket and trousers were plainer and there was no silk scarf.

'Inspector, how good of you to call by,' he said. 'Here I am, at home, just waiting for my busy social life to take off. I'm expecting a steady stream of visitors, you know.'

'Afraid it's just me,' McQueen said, drawing up a chair and sitting down. 'How are they treating you?'

'Well, apart from the fact that I'm a prisoner here, and have no books, paper, pens or anything to keep me occupied, I suppose I'm tolerably well looked after. The same food is brought to me as before. They allow me visits to the water closet and bring me water for my ablutions.'

'Good. I'll see what I can do about getting you some books from your apartment.'

Singh dropped his nonchalant pose and leant forward. 'If you could, Inspector, I would be genuinely grateful. I must admit, I feel like I'm slowly going out of my mind.'

'I can understand that. Look, I have to be honest with you. It's not looking good. You are to be brought before the court on a charge of murder as soon as your quarantine is over. In the meantime, is there anything more you can tell me that could possibly help? Cast your mind back to the days before

Buchanan disappeared. Tell me what was going on, your relationship with him.'

Singh rested his head in his hands, thinking, before eventually lifting his gaze and staring above McQueen's head.

'We arrived here on the twelfth of October. I remember being so angry. Bad enough that I'm being taken back to England like a bloody naughty schoolboy, now I'm being delayed – for over a week – in quarantine. Buchanan was also unhappy. He was going to meet his fiancée's family, I think, in Berkshire. He'd been so pleased with himself. Boasting to me that she's from money, that he'd done well. I told him he couldn't impress me. My grandfather was one of the richest men in India, I couldn't care less about Buchanan's so-called fortune. We got to the point where we didn't speak to each other at all. Couldn't bear to be in the same room, but there we were, cooped up.'

As if feeding off the remembered tension, Singh stood up and started pacing around the room.

'We had a routine going. He would go out and get the post, while I washed and dressed. Of course, he locked the door when he left. We'd both read, write letters in the morning, then after luncheon he would escort me out for a walk around the grounds. It was so dull.'

Singh wheeled around, gesturing at the walls.

'Little did I know I would end up in here, so much worse.'

'Did nothing happen that struck you as strange or unusual in this time? Who did he get letters from?'

'There were daily telegrams from his employer at the Bombay office. Things he had to reply to. He was muttering about one of them. Something about diamonds from South Africa? I'm not sure. It seemed to put him in a bad mood.'

McQueen pulled out his pocketbook and noted this down.

'Oh, and he had a letter from Letitia, his fiancée. Made me sick, reading bits out to me. She sounded so annoying. But I don't know – I think maybe something was worrying him. Not sure what it was. Truthfully, I was not listening.'

Singh leant back against the windowsill. 'There is one thing, now I remember. I think one of the health guards gave him a note. There was a knock at the door and a bit of a conversation. I think Buchanan was given an envelope, but he only glanced at it and put it in his pocket.'

'When was that? This could be important.'

'Oh, I don't know. Every day seemed the same.'

'How close was it to the night he was killed?'

'Not sure, perhaps the day before? It was the evening, after dinner.'

'Which one of the guards was it?'

'No idea. Some chap with a limp. He has a whiny voice.'

McQueen made a note. *Could it be Grech?* Something to check up on.

'And you have no idea what time he went out?'

'No, and that's strange, Inspector. I normally sleep very lightly, and the night Buchanan disappeared I was out like a light and slept right through to morning. I've even wondered if he slipped something into my drink?'

'I'll try and find out,' McQueen said. 'One other thing. Your dagger – *kirpan* was it? – when did you last see it?'

Singh gave a big sigh. 'They took it off me in Bombay. I haven't seen it since. I think they put it in a safe on the *Poonah*, then transferred it to the storeroom when we were moved here. Believe me, Inspector, I have no idea where it has been. I wish I did. Whoever took it, whoever used it, they clearly wanted to frame me for the murder.'

McQueen put his hand on Singh's shoulder and assured

him he would do what he could. He then rapped on the door to be let out. Looking back as he left, McQueen saw the prince had thrown himself back on the bed, looking crushed. It seemed that reality had caught up with him. He would be spending days in custody, then facing a murder charge. If found guilty, there was only one way it would end.

In the isolation hospital, approaching midnight, Doctor Bonnici and Eleanor Templeman were taking care of Louisa Copeland. It was the same room where Bonnici had spent the night just forty-eight hours ago. He was deeply concerned but determined to treat Louisa with everything he could think of. She was showing every sign of going the same way as the previous patient. He had given her a preparation to relieve the vomiting, which had had some effect. But her body continued to be racked by diarrhoea. Her skin was growing darker and darker, her hands and feet desiccated like a mummy. Her arms and legs were icy cold. She had completely lost her voice and could only communicate through her eyes, which reflected anxiety bordering on terror.

Bonnici gave her an injection of sulphuric ether to help with the pain and to encourage sleep. Earthenware bottles filled with hot water had been placed around her, and Eleanor had been continuously rubbing her hands and feet with a strong-smelling oil, a mixture of camphor, ammonia and cumin seed.

'You're doing well,' he said to Eleanor. 'Keep going, the cramps seem to be abating a little.'

After the injection, Louisa seemed quieter. She became very still, her pulse almost undetectable. Bonnici was not sure if this was a good sign or not. They were at a critical point where she could easily slip away.

He became aware of the silence, watching and waiting for every tiny shallow breath.

'I don't know how you can do this,' Eleanor said suddenly from the shadows, her voice making him jump.

'I do it precisely because I can,' he replied. 'I have my medicines, my tools, my preparations. I know what *will* work, what *might* work, what could be worth trying. That's all doctors can do — continue to learn and try our best to save lives.'

'But over and over,' she said. 'When you inevitably have to watch people die.'

'Can I ask you a personal question?'

'Yes, of course.'

'Have *you* watched someone you love take their last breath?'

She was quiet for a moment. 'Yes, I have.'

'Even though you can't save them, it's important that you are there. Important to them, and important to you. It's hard, I know, but I always think it's the right thing to do. I do my utmost to save someone, but if it is God's decision that it is their time, I'll be there for their passing.'

'Well,' she said slowly, 'I suppose I do think someone should be present, to witness the moment.'

They sat in silence.

It was not long before Louisa woke up again, her arms and legs jerking. She tried to cry out but could only make hoarse whimpering sounds. Her tongue protruded from her mouth, pale and cold. She was clearly desperately thirsty.

'Try giving her some ice,' Bonnici suggested. 'It may provide some relief.'

Eleanor held a cube of ice in the patient's mouth, as she was too weak to take it herself. Meanwhile, Bonnici had prepared a poultice of cumin seeds, camomile and mustard meal, and applied it to her chest and abdomen.

Throughout the night, they continued with the same

treatment – keeping Louisa warm, applying friction to her hands and feet, and every hour trying to get her to take a preparation of cognac, ether, camphor and camomile. They worked together as a team, taking it in turns to sleep for an hour, the other keeping watch. Around four in the morning, they were both awake. It was the time of night when the fatigue was so extreme, it hardly seemed possible to keep going. Eleanor, her face pale and shadowy in the lamplight, suddenly spoke. 'It is Louisa's tender heart that has led to this, you know.'

'In what way?' Bonnici was surprised by the slight edge in her voice.

'She looked after Madame Trévissier's children, when their father was taken ill. She went into their apartment, played with them. I told her she shouldn't go, but she insisted. God, this place. I hate it.'

'It's possible she was already infected,' Bonnici said gently. 'Do not blame her.'

'Oh, I don't – not really. But we should keep ourselves to ourselves, try and keep safe. Not just from the cholera. There are bad things going on in this place, I'm sure of it.'

'What do you mean?'

'Strange noises at night, people creeping around, up to no good. That Gilbert Browne, he takes drugs, I am sure of it. I've seen him looking so strange, it made me fearful. And that American woman, Miss Byrne. I had to fetch some water from the kitchens late one night. I saw her out on the terrace with Captain Buchanan, in the shadows, close as you like, virtually embracing. It was unseemly, immoral. Then, of course, he was murdered...' She tailed off.

'When was that? Do you remember?' Bonnici wondered if McQueen knew about this meeting.

'Not sure. Perhaps two days earlier?'

He would have to pass on this information when he saw McQueen next. It sounded important.

Louisa stirred and whimpered slightly. She opened her eyes, looking blankly at him. He reassured her that she was doing well, gesturing to Eleanor to pass him a warm cloth. They went back to their routine, the night's shadows continuing to close around them. It would be at least two hours before the dawn.

CHAPTER TEN

Valletta, Malta. Tuesday, 19 October 1880

Walking briskly, Maria Tanti crossed Piazza San Giorgio – St George's Square. At four in the afternoon it was busy. British soldiers were stationed in front of the Main Guard, opposite the Governor's Palace. Beggars were lazing around by the benches on all sides of the square. She noticed a group of barefoot boys playing by the fountain. She looked hard but Antonio was not among them. *Good, he's supposed to be in school.* Two women were chatting under the canopy of a pharmacy, both wearing the traditional *għonnella*, a long black cloak with a starched hood. Maria had one at home, but she only wore it when trying to walk around the city incognito. Today, she was wearing a navy-blue jacket and matching dress. Smart and practical.

The Governor's Palace was built between the sixteenth and eighteenth centuries, when Malta was ruled by the Knights of St John. Formerly called the Grand Master's Palace, it was designed to impress, its elegant frontage stretching across the whole length of the square. Maria approached one of the two arched entrances – the one on the right, used by the governor's office. It led into Prince Alfred's Courtyard, with its elegant orange and palm trees, bird fountain and Moorish clock. She always felt a bit of a thrill walking into the palace, thinking of its history, of the Grand Masters who had made it their headquarters. It was a very different place now; the British having been in charge since 1800. Only soldiers and administrators marched about the place, looking officious and important.

Maria presented her papers to the guard in the reception area and was taken by a smart young officer to the office of Lieutenant Carstairs, aide-de-camp to the governor. They took an informal route across the Prince of Wales Courtyard and up a winding staircase to the offices on the first floor. Carstairs's room was next door to the governor's office, so he could constantly be at His Excellency's beck and call. It was large and elegant, with green wallpaper and panelling. She was especially taken by the fresco at the top of the walls, depicting the history of the Order of St John.

Maria had not seen Carstairs for a few weeks. Deeply involved in the case that had brought McQueen to Malta, he had been a good support to her afterwards, as she tried to come to terms with what had happened. She was fond of him, finding his English awkwardness endearing.

As she walked into his office, Carstairs jumped up from his desk, where he appeared to be writing a letter, and came round to greet her.

'How nice to see you, Miss Tanti,' he said. 'I trust you're well?'

He looked as smart as ever, his short hair parted on the side, clean-shaven apart from his neat moustache, the exact width of his top lip. She thought he looked tense. He gave her a fleeting smile, but his eyes were focused elsewhere.

'I am fine. Thank you for agreeing to see me,' she said. 'I'm sure you must be so busy.'

'Have to say I'm a little distracted,' he replied. 'But happy to help, as always, if I can. Please, sit.'

Maria sat on a green armchair in front of the desk. Carstairs sat down opposite her, pulling out his pocket-watch and frowning momentarily.

'Is something the matter?' she asked.

'Oh sorry, don't mean to be rude. I'm waiting to hear from the governor about the cholera outbreak at the Lazzaretto. He is at the Board of Health meeting right now. We can't afford to have another epidemic – the last one was devastating. And now there's been this murder. All a bit much, really!'

He took a breath and smiled, revealing his slightly protruding front teeth. 'Now, what can I do for you?'

'It's about the murder. I assume you've heard that Inspector McQueen is stuck with the passengers on the Lazzaretto? He's asked me to do a bit of detective work for him.'

'Ah, I see.'

Maria got out her notebook and pencil.

'The man who died, Laurence Buchanan, he worked for the Indian Civil Service. Apparently, he was very good at his job, quite high up, a magistrate. Before that, he was a captain in the army, 8th Punjab Infantry. Inspector McQueen asked me to find out where he'd been stationed, any battles he might have fought in, that kind of thing. I thought perhaps you could help. You're still in the army, aren't you?'

'Indeed, I am. Royal Engineers, seconded. I've not heard of a Captain Buchanan. Do you by any chance know when he was discharged?'

Maria looked down at her notes. She had sent a telegram to

the India Office who had responded with a few details. 'Well, I know he started his job with the Indian Civil Service in late 1878, so it could be earlier that year?'

'You should be able to find his discharge papers. They'll be stored with his regiment, at their headquarters. Any idea when he joined the army?'

She checked her notebook. 'October '65.'

'8th Punjab Infantry. Let me think. Tell you what. Why don't you contact this chap?' Carstairs pulled out a sheet of paper and wrote down a name. 'Peter Fellowes. Works for the Commander. If anyone can, I bet he can track down the records. From memory, I believe they might have been deployed in Afghanistan, but I wouldn't swear to it.'

'Thank you.'

'But I thought they had already arrested someone – that Indian prince? Colonel Ellis has been keeping the governor up-to-date.'

'Yes, but Inspector McQueen doesn't think it's him. He's doing his best to investigate, but he can't do much, stuck on Manoel Island. I hope they'll soon be out of quarantine. Thank you, anyway. I'll contact this Fellowes and see if I can obtain any military records.'

Maria got up to take her leave, picking up the piece of paper and tucking it into her reticule with her notebook and pencil. As Carstairs stood up, there was a loud knock at the door and a messenger appeared. He handed over an envelope, which Carstairs immediately tore into.

He read it quickly, then shook his head. 'Oh, no!'

'What is it?' Maria asked.

He looked up, his eyes full of concern. 'There's another case of cholera, a young Englishwoman. It seems to be spreading.'

With Carstairs disappearing quickly to meet the governor, Maria felt strangely deflated. Everything was happening on Manoel Island, while she was stuck here in Valletta. But then she realised what an awful thought that was. Cholera was deadly, horrendous.

She decided to head back to the *Malta Times* office to write about this latest development. The news that a young woman had contracted cholera, following on so swiftly from the reported death of Monsieur Trévissier, was extremely concerning. How many of the twenty-four passengers might get infected? Would it prove impossible to keep the disease contained within the Lazzaretto? The fear of cholera amongst the Maltese people was very real.

It was just a five-minute walk to Strada San Giovanni. It was one of the steepest streets leading down from the city centre toward Victoria Gate. She tried not to rush too fast, knowing she could easily slip on the stone steps as she made her way down. Concentrating hard on watching her feet, she didn't see a man lurking in the shadows until he stepped out in front of her, right by the printing office. She jumped. A small, scruffy individual dressed in a dark-brown cotton suit. All she immediately took in was his fierce black eyes and long hair. Pushed back from his gaunt face, it hung jaw-length over his ears.

'*Sinjorina* Tanti,' he said, his voice low but insistent. 'I've been waiting for you.'

Maria brought her left hand up to her heart. '*Ajma!*' she said. 'You gave me such a start.'

Giuseppe Trapani was a young firebrand, a pro-Italian and passionate supporter of the new Anti-Reform party speaking up for Maltese rights, in opposition to recent edicts being pushed through by the British government. She had interviewed him for the *Malta Post*, her father's newspaper. She respected some of his views, but was wary of him, knowing that his politics were so radical he would not be afraid of using violence. Months earlier, she had exposed a failed plot to cause an explosion that could have killed the Queen's son, Prince Alfred, on a visit to Malta. However, there was not enough evidence for him to be charged, and he had been let off with a caution.

'Can I come in?' he said. 'I need to talk to you about something.'

She thought quickly. Her father was due to arrive at the office shortly, so it was probably safe enough, but she wished she had a chaperone with her. She looked around, but she could not see anyone in the street who would notice.

'All right,' she said. She got out the key and let him into the building.

Once inside, she led Trapani into the printers' office. She left the door open and leant against a table, piled high with ledgers and books. She knew he would not sit down. Trapani had a restless energy that meant he was perpetually on the move.

'What is it you want to discuss?' she asked.

'Do you know what's going on at the Lazzaretto?' He paced up and down the office as he spoke, picking up random books every now and then, glancing at them and placing them back down. 'An Englishman has been drowned, and an Indian man has been wrongfully arrested for killing him.'

'How do you know this?'

'From *l-Avukat* Marsat.'

'What is this to do with me?'

'I hear you met with Inspector McQueen. I want to know what he said. What's going to happen to the Indian?'

'Why?'

'Because we believe he is being victimised by the British. They don't have enough evidence, yet they are charging him with murder.'

'How is this your business?'

He whipped around, fiercely. 'We can't get let them away with this. If he's found guilty, he will be executed, yet he is an innocent man. We stand shoulder to shoulder with those who are oppressed, as we are, by the British. We aim to make a stink about this, make sure everybody knows.'

'When you say "we", who do you mean?' Maria asked.

'The *Gruppo Militante Pro Italiano.*'

The breakaway group from the Anti-Reform party. She thought they had dispersed, but apparently not.

'We knew that Superintendent Borg was corrupt, but he is Maltese. This new English Superintendent – Ellis – he is blinkered and biased. Marsat has said there is no real evidence against the prince, and yet he is assumed guilty and thrown into a cell, purely because is Indian.'

'Why are you telling me this, exactly?'

'Two reasons. Firstly, we want you to tell us what is happening with the investigation. If any new evidence comes to light, we want to be kept informed.' He picked up an old copy of the *Malta Post* from her father's desk and held it up. 'Secondly, we want you to report it in your newspaper. Your father is pro-British, everybody knows that. We want him and your readers to see what the British are really like, how they treat people in the colonies. We have to take a stance.'

Maria took exception to the implication that the *Malta Post* was partisan.

'You can't tell us what to write. My father might be pro-British, but we're always fair and honest in our reporting. What about that piece I wrote on the Anti-Reform Party? Did you not agree that it was impartial and clearly stated your case?'

'Yes, but your father's editorial in the next edition showed that he disagreed with us. It's the Language Question. He is in favour of this new reform which says that children should be taught English rather than Italian. But we're against it. The British had always promised us that we can maintain our way of life, allowing us our traditions. We speak Maltese at home, and Italian for all official business. This is our identity. They have no right to go back on their promise and impose English on us.'

'My father does agree with the reform, but he is allowed to do so. He trusts that the colonial government has our best interests at heart. You have to admit that Malta has prospered under British rule.'

'The foreigners and the rich people have prospered. The majority of Maltese are exploited and remain poor.'

'Look, I promise we'll report everything about the murder in a fair and just way, no matter what the outcome. But as for reporting to you about what Inspector McQueen is up to, I see no reason why I should do that.'

'I appeal to you to support us. We only want to help this prince. There is no one else who will fight for him. Think about it. You'll get a good story for the paper. People will be able to see the British version of justice, which places their needs above all others.'

Maria trusted McQueen to judge the Indian prince fairly, but she remembered what he had said about Colonel Ellis; how he was blinkered, preventing the inspector from carrying out a full investigation.

'All right,' she said. 'I'll let you know when I have any news.'

'Good,' Trapani said. 'You can send a message to me here.' As he was handing over a paper with an address scrawled on it, she heard the front door opening. Her father's cheerful voice rang out, 'Are you here, *ħanini*?'

Quickly, Maria put the paper on the desk behind her. Holding her in his intense gaze, Trapani put his finger to his lips.

'I've had the most interesting meeting at the Chamber of

Commerce,' her father was saying loudly as he approached the office door. 'The railway plans are progressing at quite a pace. Work is about to start at Victoria Gate.'

He stopped abruptly when he saw Trapani standing inside.

'What's happening here?' he asked.

'Nothing,' Maria said. '*Sur* Trapani is just leaving.'

CHAPTER ELEVEN

Manoel Island, Malta. Tuesday, 19 October 1880

Sciberras, the Keeper of the Lazzaretto, was making McQueen feel as welcome as a dog with fleas.

'I have too many worries,' he said, gesturing at the pile of paperwork on his desk. 'We have the killer, and we have the weapon. Why do you need to ask more questions? I have the health board demanding what is happening to halt the spread of cholera. Have you any idea what will happen if the disease reaches Valletta? Let me get on with my job.'

Light slanting in from the window accentuated the dark circles under his eyes. Clearly, he was a man under pressure.

'I understand, but I also have to do my job. I need more evidence,' McQueen said. 'This is not enough to convict. How could the prince have got hold of the dagger?'

'Don't bother me with such things. He must have bribed one of the guards.'

'Constable Battista reported they all denied they had

anything to do with it. However, from what you have just said, I see you don't trust them. Who do you believe could be bribed?'

'I don't know, Inspector. Surely anyone can be bribed if enough money is involved? Can't you leave it now?'

McQueen checked his notebook. 'What about Grech, the guard with the limp? Can you fetch him here so I can talk to him?'

Sciberras slammed his hand down on the desk. 'No, Inspector,' he said loudly. 'Grech is busy. Let me tell you again, we're dealing with cholera. Just get out!'

Walking back to his apartment, through the courtyard where the staircase was flanked by brightly coloured bougainvillea, McQueen caught sight of a small shadowy figure scurrying away down a corridor.

'Hey – you – Grech – come here!' he called out.

Reluctantly, the shadow stopped, turned around and walked back toward him, head looking down at the ground.

Scarcely taller than five feet, Grech had the perpetual look of someone who wanted to be elsewhere. His limp seemed to be caused by his right foot, which turned inwards slightly, but he moved quickly and there seemed to be strength in his wiry frame. He stopped in front of McQueen, looking up at him with his head tilted to one side.

'Yes, sir?'

'Listen,' McQueen said. 'I know you gave Captain Buchanan a message the day before he died. Who was it from?'

Grech cast his eyes upwards, pursing his lips.

'I not know.'

'What do you mean, you don't know? Of course you know! Who gave you the envelope?'

Grech shook his head emphatically. 'I not know. Is woman. She stop me. I not see her – it is dark and she wear cloak.'

McQueen did not believe him for one second. *Damn the regulations.* He wanted to pick the man up and shake him, to rattle the teeth in his head.

'Were there other times?' he asked. 'Was the woman-in-darkness in the habit of giving you messages for Buchanan?'

Grech looked away again, as if trying to remember. His acting skills were pitiful. Finally, he came up with an answer.

'No. No more times.'

McQueen tried another tack. 'What about the dagger, the *kirpan*? Do you know anything about where it was kept and who could have taken it?'

Grech looked at him as if he had spoken in double Dutch.

'Who took the dagger, the murder weapon from the storeroom?' he repeated.

'I not know.'

'Did anyone pay you for the key?'

He shook his head hard enough to scramble his brains.

'No. Not me,' he said, his eyes darting about, desperate for escape.

He was saved by the voice of Sciberras from the other side of the courtyard.

'Grech! Where are you?'

Finding him with McQueen, Sciberras's fury was written all over his dark features. He strode across.

'I told you Grech was too busy to talk.'

McQueen shrugged. 'We met,' he said. 'So, I asked a question or two.'

'Go, take this message to the quarantine doctor. Now!' Sciberras ordered Grech. 'And as for you...'

'Yes?'

'Nothing. Just stay out of my sight.'

'Feeling's mutual.'

When he got back to his apartment, McQueen opened the door to see an envelope lying on the floor, his name written on the front. The handwriting was distinctive, orderly and neat, with a peculiar way of writing a Q and an R that he had not seen before.

Intrigued, he opened it and took out a sheet of white notepaper.

It was an invitation from Nellie Byrne, asking him to meet her on the terrace later that evening, to share a drink. She had, she said, something to discuss with him.

Well, he thought. *Why ever not?*

By ten o'clock at night the Lazzaretto was deadly quiet. Practically all the quarantine inmates were shut in their rooms, either sleeping or quietly passing the time, hoping they would be spared from the contagion.

A bottle of good whisky stashed under his arm, McQueen left his apartment for the terrace. He found Nellie Byrne leaning on the balustrade, looking out across Lazzaretto Creek. The air was distinctly cool, a fresh breeze coming from the dark waters. A steady clanking was coming from ropes hitting against wooden masts, as small boats rocked gently to and fro. From across the harbour, the occasional roar of noise from a rowdy group of sailors, too far away to be distinct.

'It's so weird being locked away from real life,' Nellie said, so quietly that he almost missed what she was saying. 'I'd give anything to get away from here.'

'Strangest place I've ever stayed,' he replied. 'And I'm not getting much help here, on the case.'

He stood next to her, facing the other way, leaning back on the balustrade, so he could roll a couple of cigarettes. Good quality black tobacco from Turkey. He took out generous pinches from his tobacco-pouch and rolled them, using scraps of paper, a habit he had learnt from police colleagues returning from the Crimea. He struck a match against a stone wall, lit a cigarette to pass to Nellie, then lit his own, turning round to join her looking out to sea.

They stood in silence for a while. He could not remember meeting anyone with the same air of confidence and self-assurance as this American. She seemed to have no need to make conversation just for the sake of it. He felt deeply conscious of how close they were standing to each other. There was no denying her good looks. She was dressed in a long jacket, in the same dark-green wool check as her dress, her hair pinned up at the back but curled softly around her face. He could tell from the amused set of her mouth that she was aware of his glances.

'So, Inspector. I've never met a police detective before. Plenty of army types on my travels, and even the occasional police officer, but never a detective inspector. How d'you like your job? Would you say you enjoy it?'

He laughed. 'No, I would not. There was a time, perhaps, when I was younger. Now, though...' He dropped his cigarette end over the balustrade. 'I've been around too long. Seen too much. Annoyed too many people.'

'Still, it brought you to Malta. That can't be bad, surely?'

'Oh aye, it's all right here. Well, it was, until I had to stay in this bloody place.'

'I haven't even seen the main island yet. I've just been stuck in quarantine. They say that Valletta is lovely. It certainly looks good from a distance.'

Nellie had brought out two small glasses and a bottle of French brandy. She poured a couple of drinks and passed one over. He tasted it. It was good, but not as good as his whisky.

'What took you to India?' he asked. 'Very brave, to travel there on your own.'

She rolled her eyes. 'God, Inspector, you're as bad as all the rest of them. I go wherever I want to go. So many people have said I can't travel alone as a woman, but I've proved them wrong. Here I am now, safe and well, after travelling half the way around the world. I like India. It's interesting.'

He held his hands up. 'All right,' he said. 'You've made your point.'

He drained the brandy, then showed her the bottle of whisky.

'Here, try this – it's an Ardbeg, from Islay.'

'Islay?'

'An island in the Inner Hebrides. Considered small in Scotland, but almost twice the size of Malta. Home to the best whiskies in the world.'

He felt homesick just talking about it. He poured a couple of drams into the glasses.

'Here,' he said, holding his glass up. 'You have to say *Slàinte Mhath*. It means Good Health.

'Oh, I know that,' Nellie said. 'My father's from Ireland, Irish through and through. It's pretty much the same – *Slàinte Mhaith.*'

They clinked glasses.

'So, what was it you wanted to tell me?' McQueen asked.

'Ah, yes. It's about Buchanan. I wasn't sure if I should tell you this, but I think maybe it could be important.' She hesitated for a moment.

'Go on.'

'It's just that quite soon after we got here, to the Lazzaretto,

I overheard an argument between Buchanan and that blond kid, Browne. They came out to the terrace one night, like this, when I was smoking a cigarette. I was kind of round the corner, so I don't think they knew I was here.'

She took a sip from her glass.

'Did they seem to know each other?'

'Yes. They were talking real quietly but I heard Buchanan say something like, "I'll have to report it, you know that." Browne was agitated. He said, "Look, give me a chance. It will destroy our family, you know that. Think of Alexander, what it will do to his career." Then Buchanan said, "You should have thought of that yourself. Leave it with me. I don't know what I'll do yet. You've put me in an impossible situation."'

McQueen was intrigued. 'Have you any idea what they were talking about?'

'No, but sounds like Browne was up to something he shouldn't have been.'

'Did you hear any more?'

'No, Buchanan left after that. Browne stood there for a while, then he swore under his breath and left as well.'

'What night was that?'

'I think it was the day after we arrived here. So, like the thirteenth? I figured you might want to know.'

'Why didn't you say anything before?'

'It was when I found out that Prince Sundar was going to be arrested for Buchanan's murder. I know it wouldn't be him, so I was wondering who else might have a reason. Then I remembered that conversation.'

They stood in silence, McQueen thinking of the timeline. If Nellie's account was right, Buchanan clearly had a hold over Browne. It was something to go back to the young man with, press him for the truth.

He swallowed his whisky, poured another. He proffered the

bottle to Nellie. 'Go on then,' she said. 'I'm not sure how much I like this whisky of yours, but it sure is different.'

They clinked glasses again. McQueen caught himself admiring her green eyes, which glinted with amusement. Was there more to this than just passing on some information?

The moment was broken by the arrival of the health guard, Grech, who stopped abruptly when he saw the couple together. He walked over, holding out an envelope.

'Sciberras sent me to find you, Inspector,' he said, looking from one to the other. 'Message from Colonel Ellis.'

As he took the envelope, Grech smirked. 'I have to report you,' he said. 'Terrace is for walking, not for meeting.'

McQueen had had enough. He was back in the most intensely frustrating situation he could ever remember.

'Get out of here!' he said, lunging forward and raising his fist. 'Before I do you some serious harm.'

He towered over Grech, who backed away, hands held up in front of him. 'All right, all right,' he said, maintaining his silly grin.

'I'd give you a kicking,' McQueen called after him, 'if it weren't for the bloody regulations.'

McQueen opened the message from Ellis. He had obtained a warrant for the Indian prince's arrest. Ellis declared there could be no other explanation than that Prince Sundar Singh was guilty. *The insidious violence of the act, the finding of the weapon which has sacred meaning for the Sikhs, the fact that they are notorious warriors. This would be enough for any magistrate to agree to charge him,* he wrote.

McQueen tossed the sheet of paper to the ground. 'I don't like this,' he said. 'Ellis is completely blinkered. He's only interested in wrapping the case up neatly. He wants the prince taken to the police office as soon as he's out of quarantine.'

'What are you going to do?' Nellie asked.

'Nothing for now. It's late, I'll leave Ellis to his beauty sleep, go and talk to Browne first thing in the morning.'

'Well then, Detective,' Nellie said, 'let's go somewhere a little more comfortable. Try some more of this whisky. You never know, I might get to like it.'

CHAPTER TWELVE

Manoel Island, Malta. Wednesday, 20 October 1880

At around 5am Bonnici woke Louisa to give her some water and brandy. As he lifted her head and shoulders from the pillow, she opened her eyes. She clutched weakly at his arm. Her breathing was laboured. She was struggling to get enough oxygen. She tried to speak but could only produce a faint, hoarse whisper. He thought he could hear her saying 'the noise, my ears.' She looked distressed and highly confused, her eyes unfocused.

'Bring the lamp closer,' he said over his shoulder.

Eleanor lifted the lamp, flinching slightly at the sight of her friend, whose face was by now virtually black in colour.

He waved his hand in front of Louisa's face. As he suspected, there was no response. Blindness had set in. He lifted her wrist, his fingers pressing down as hard as he dared, barely able to find any pulse. Quietly, he laid her back down.

'I think you should go to Sciberras. I suspect it won't be long. It is time for a priest.'

Eleanor bit her lip, her eyes dark in the shadowy light.

'Are you sure?'

'Her heartbeat is very slow,' he said as gently as he could. 'We must prepare.'

Eleanor stood for a moment, her face set, almost like a mask, before nodding and leaving the ward. He was impressed by her composure. *Quite remarkable. A natural nurse, knowing when emotions need to be firmly in check.*

With Eleanor away, Bonnici sat watching the patient. Unexpectedly, Louisa woke again, groaning. The symptoms had returned, the cramps in her stomach, the flux. *Is this the last attack?* She could not survive much longer. It was hard to witness her agony. *Is it time to give her one large, final dose of morphine?*

He went to his medical bag, started sorting through the bottles, looking for the morphine preparation. Eleanor slipped quietly back into the room. She gave a small cry as she saw her friend in pain again, but quickly got back to work, cleaning up the clothing and the bed. Bonnici's hand hovered over the morphine bottle, but he hesitated. What if he could take some of the pain away, but at the same time stimulate the system? There was one other treatment that might work. He searched until he found a bottle of ether, then prepared a hypodermic syringe.

'Turn her on her side,' he said. 'I'm going to try this. It should make her more comfortable.'

He gave Louisa two injections in the spinal column, one at the top and one at the lower part. Gradually, she quietened down again, lying completely still as if in a coma. This was likely to be the end. She had no strength left to fight the disease.

'Now we leave her,' he said. 'No more medicines, no water, no stimulation. Did you manage to find out about a priest?'

'There's no one available. Not until the morning.'

They sat in silence, listening for every breath, waiting for the dawn.

McQueen stayed in Nellie Byrne's apartment longer than he intended to. They had taken care not to be seen, but he knew how bad it would look if he were to be found spending time alone with a single woman, especially during an investigation. She was not exactly a suspect, but no one could be ruled out.

'Don't worry about my reputation, Inspector,' Nellie had said with a smile. 'That went out the window years ago.'

She asked him about how he came to be a policeman. He told her about his father, the minister, so popular in his parish that contributions from the congregation had enabled the building of a brand-new church, large enough for a thousand people to listen to his sermons. How he and his brother, when old enough, had been taken out to the poorest parts of Fountainbridge, frequently witnessing drunkenness and violence.

'My father is a big man, strong, you know. There's a weight about him. He would step in, break up fights. But his answer to problems was always to lecture folk. He would tell them to renounce the devil drink, to turn to prayer and faith. Well, let's just say I couldn't see it the same way. To me, that was a waste of time. They'd always go straight back to their old ways. I had some kind of idea I could make more of a difference in the police, putting my faith in justice instead.'

'Your father sounds like quite a character. I guess he's well-known in Edinburgh.'

'Aye, he is. But we went our separate ways, a long time ago. It's black or white with him. I turned my back on his way of life, and he turned his back on me.'

He raised his glass of whisky. 'Just as well. I could never give this up: *uisge beatha* – the water of life.'

They clinked glasses.

'What about your father?' he asked. 'A rich man, by all accounts.'

'Oh, God. Talk about a big personality. Left Ireland in '47 because of the Great Hunger. Went to Pittsburgh, started working in an iron foundry. Worked his way up, and in the late '60s set up a steel mill with a friend of his. Long story short, made his fortune in steel. A real big fortune.'

'Are you close?'

Nellie sighed. 'It's complicated. We clash, we're too much alike – stubborn. I guess that's one of the reasons I'm always travelling. I'm away for weeks, I miss him, I go back, then we have another bust-up. There's not a lot we agree on. My mom died, five years ago, and I kind of blame him for not taking better care of her.'

'That's difficult.'

'Yep!' Nellie seemed to want to change the subject. 'So, tell me, going back to the case, what do you think happened to Buchanan? I think we both know Prince Sundar Singh did not kill him.'

McQueen had had a few whiskies. *It can't hurt, surely, to share a few details?*

'It could be anyone,' he said. 'We don't have many leads. We know someone managed to get the key to the storeroom and fetch Singh's dagger. Probably by bribing one of the guards. We think he was killed outside, near Fort Manoel, a single knife wound. Then his body was rolled into the water. Who else would have wanted him dead, we've no idea. No one seems to have a good word to say about him, and you've reported that he argued with Browne. That's it.'

'I guess he had some skeletons in his closet, huh?'

'Could be. Trust me, I'll find out what happened.'

'Let's drink to that, Detective.'

They stayed up drinking and talking until the early hours, before McQueen staggered back to his apartment and dropped heavily into his bed.

Bonnici woke at seven. Daylight was slanting into the room through the unshuttered windows, uncomfortable on his eyes. He rubbed them, then stretched his arms out, yawning. He was so stiff. Two nights of catnapping in a chair had not done him any good. He stood up carefully, straightening his back. His left leg was aching. He reached for his cane, unable to move without its support.

Across the bed, Eleanor Templeman was sleeping, her head lolling forward. He could hear her gentle breathing and stayed as quiet as he could. She should sleep as long as possible. He leant over the patient, who lay as still as she had in the middle of the night. Was she still alive? Placing his hand in front of Louisa's face, he thought he could feel a very slight movement of air. He reached for her wrist and pressed firmly. There was a pulse, weak, but regular. More importantly, her arm felt warmer to the touch. He felt the skin higher up on her arm, then her legs and her feet. All had lost their icy coldness. His heart leapt.

'Doctor, how is she?'

Eleanor's voice was urgent. She must have woken and watched him checking for signs of life.

He tried not to sound too hopeful. It was important to keep a sense of perspective. The patient's condition could change at any moment. But he felt sure that a corner had been turned.

'She's still with us,' he said. 'She's had a couple of hours of sleep.'

'Thank God,' Eleanor murmured. She leant forward and brushed a lock of hair away from her friend's face.

'Thank God, indeed.' He felt some energy returning. 'I'll go and order some good warm broth. Hopefully she'll take some nourishment.'

As Bonnici got to the hospital entrance, he was dismayed to see two patients being brought in on stretchers, carried by health guards wearing masks and gloves. Doctor Cassar brought up the rear, directing the bearers to the hospital ward. His face lit up when he saw Bonnici.

'*Dottore!* I am so pleased to see you. I didn't know if you would still be here. We have more cases – two from the same family. Please, can you help? I have not much experience of cholera.'

Bonnici felt acutely aware of his exhaustion, and for one split-second was overwhelmed at the thought of treating new patients. Then he looked at them, at their suffering, and his professionalism took over.

'Of course, *Dottore*, follow me.' He went back into the hospital. 'We need nurses, clean bedding, hot stones. Above all, everything they have touched or worn must be disinfected.'

It was going to be another long day.

CHAPTER THIRTEEN

Valletta, Malta. Wednesday, 20 October 1880

Maria walked up the steep stairs of Strada San Giovanni and made her way to the P&O offices in Strada Mercanti. Always a busy place, it was noisy and stuffy inside, with three long queues in front of the counter. Harassed clerks were attempting to deal with all the bookings and inquiries. She waved to get the attention of one of the men, Enrico Vassalli, who was a family friend. He waved back, smiling, then excused himself from the customer he was dealing with, an Englishwoman, who looked around crossly to see who had interrupted her transaction.

'Just a moment,' Enrico said. 'I'll be back soon.'

'Well, really!' the customer said.

Enrico lifted up the countertop, to the right of where he was standing, and beckoned Maria to come through. She felt the customer's judgemental eyes boring through her as she passed.

She hid a smile as she followed Enrico into an office to the left, behind the counter. 'I hope I'm not going to get you into too much trouble,' she said.

'No, it's fine. The lady can wait a minute or two.'

She liked Enrico. A similar age to her, he had chubby features, combed-back black hair, and an easy-going manner. She did sense, however, that he had a new awkwardness around her. Perhaps she was overly sensitive, but she felt like friends and family were not quite sure how to act around her. Just a few months ago, she had been engaged to be married to a handsome young lawyer, which had turned out to be a big mistake. Would anyone be interested in her now? But she would just have to ignore people's reactions and keep moving on with her life, she thought.

Enrico showed her to a table. 'Right, I have found the passenger list for you. Hope that gives you what you need.'

'Thank you.'

He disappeared back to his disgruntled customer.

Maria pulled out her notebook in readiness, then began to read all the entries under First Class Passengers sailing on the SS *Poonah* from Bombay to Southampton. For each name, there were details of age, date of birth, occupation, and a destination address. She checked this against the list of people Inspector McQueen had given her, noting down all their details. Of all the passengers forced to stay at the Lazzaretto, only one was intending to disembark in Malta – Gilbert Browne. All the others were staying on board until they reached England.

The Hon. Gilbert Browne was listed as being twenty-six years old, born in April 1854. He had given his occupation as Gentleman. The destination address was c/o Mr and Mrs R Pelham, Strada Zaccaria, Valletta, only two streets away. Maria decided to pay the Pelhams a visit, to find out what she could about Browne. McQueen had said he was returning from a year spent travelling abroad. What an enviable way of life. It was all she had ever wanted to do, to see the world beyond the shores of her island home. *One day*, she thought. *One day*.

Maria gathered up her things and left the P&O office, waving her thanks to Enrico on the way out. Ten o'clock in the morning was a decent time to call on the Pelhams, she reasoned. She found the address; a handsome townhouse with an enclosed wooden balcony, freshly painted in the rich green colour much favoured in Valletta. The door knocker was a highly polished lion's head, with a ring through its mouth. She knocked and handed over her card to a housemaid, explaining that she would like to ask Mrs Pelham a few questions about Mr Browne, due to stay with her soon.

After a few minutes, she was welcomed into the hallway and shown into a sitting room on the right. Mrs Pelham soon appeared. Maria thought she recognised her, perhaps from one of the talks that she had attended at the Governor's Palace. Medium height, with blonde hair, a round face and lively eyes.

'Miss Tanti, from the *Malta Post*? This is intriguing!' she said, holding up the calling card. 'Do sit down. How may I help you?'

'Thank you for agreeing to see me. Sorry to call on you out of the blue. It's about Mr Browne. I believe he's going to be staying here, when he gets out of quarantine?'

'Yes, he's my cousin. Haven't seen him for a few years. It's one of those things, isn't it? He's travelled halfway around the world without encountering any difficulties, and now he's stuck in quarantine. Frankly, it sounds terrifying. I heard that someone had died in mysterious circumstances – one of the passengers. Is that right?'

Maria wondered how best to get information from Mrs Pelham without giving away that her cousin could be a suspect.

'Yes, it is. I'm trying to write a piece about the situation there, but it's almost impossible because of the quarantine regulations. I wondered if you've heard from him?'

'Well, yes. He sent a note asking for some money. Apparently, it costs a great deal to stay at the Lazzaretto.'

'Oh,' Maria said lightly. 'Does he not have enough funds?'

Mrs Pelham sighed. 'He never has enough money. He said he'd spent it all on his trip. Look, I shouldn't be telling you this. I sent him ten shillings. My husband doesn't know.'

'Would your husband not approve?'

'It's just that Gilbert always seems to be in some kind of trouble, it gets rather tiresome. He gambles, I think. But he promised he can pay me back when he gets to England. Says he'll have plenty of money soon. Some art investment that he said was going to make him a fortune.'

'Does his note say anything else about what's happening in the Lazzaretto?'

'No, he says he's just bored. I hope he gets out soon. I'm worried about him. Do you think he's safe there?'

'The police are on the island. Hopefully the case will be solved soon. You seem fond of your cousin?'

'Yes and no. Gilbert is very charming. He has a way of winning everyone over. Getting his own way. Always has. But he's not someone you can rely on, not by any stretch of the word. Anyway, listen to me, rattling on. Tell me, do you write for the *Malta Post* regularly, Miss Tanti?'

'Yes, my father is the editor of the newspaper. I'm deputy editor. Always working on a story.'

'How thrilling! Sorry I could not be more useful. Perhaps we can meet up again once this awful business is over.'

After exchanging more pleasantries, Maria left, feeling she had got some useful information to pass on. Browne was a gambler, he needed money, and he clearly had plans that would net him some profit soon.

From Strada Zaccaria, Maria went on to the telegraph office on Strada Reale, to check if she had a reply from Fellowes, Carstairs' colleague in India. A telegram was indeed waiting for her. She glanced at it quickly, then tucked it inside her notebook, thinking she would read it more thoroughly later.

It was close to midday when Maria got back to the *Malta Post*. She was pleased to find her father in his office. Busy talking to the compositors, he did not break off but looked up over his spectacles and smiled. The paper was usually printed overnight Friday ready for Saturday morning. Galley proofs were done, but there was a lot to do that afternoon. No rest for the workers, even though it was a hot day. Maria put her notebook on her desk and settled down to write up her findings.

Eventually her father finished talking through the tasks for the compositors. 'I want the galley proofs corrected by five o'clock,' he said, ushering the two men out of the office and into the workshop. 'Then Maria and I can check them before the formes are made ready tomorrow.'

He shut the door behind them and turned to face her.

'*Allura, ħanini,* how quickly the week goes. I can't believe it is Wednesday again. I think I am beginning to get too old for this. Every week the rush to get the paper finished, printed and out of the door!'

'Ah, Papà, you can't say that. You're not even fifty! Besides, I don't believe you. You love the rush. Where would you be, without your newspaper to air your views?'

'That's true enough. I think I'm just too hot today. It's too much. Why is it eighty degrees in October?'

'I don't know. Hopefully we'll get some rain soon.'

'Not soon enough! And what have you been up to this morning, *ħanini*?'

'I'm finding out about some of the people in the Lazzaretto. Went to see a nice English lady in Strada Zaccaria, who knows one of the passengers. Oh, and I have the service record for Captain Buchanan, the man who was killed.'

Her father's eyes lit up. 'Oh, anything of interest we can use for the paper?'

'Papà! You know we can't report it – I'm just helping out for Inspector McQueen.'

'Still, let me know. What does it say?'

She read out the telegram. '"Captain Buchanan commissioned Second Lieutenant 8th Punjab Infantry 1865, promoted Lieutenant 1868, Captain 1871, left army 1878. Mainly stationed Malerkotla, Punjab. Hope useful. R. Fellowes."'

'So, after the army, he joined the Indian Civil Service, is that right?'

'Yes, he stayed in the Punjab at first. Got a job as a magistrate. Then he moved to Bombay, a promotion. He was there to meet Prince Sundar Singh when he arrived. Got him arrested, then insisted that he himself should escort the prince back to England.'

'Ha! The prince has got the British worried. They'll do anything to stop him getting back to the Punjab.'

Her father sat on the edge of his desk, re-energised by this information.

'Pass me that telegram, will you, Maria. There's something I want to check.'

She gave him the piece of paper and watched his face as he read it. His eyes crinkled at the corners, and he pursed his lips, deep in thought.

'There's something rattling around in the back of my head,' he said. '*Malerkotla*. I'm sure it's something about that place. Let me think. Hang on...'

Suddenly he left the office, leaving her wondering what on earth he was up to. He came back in a couple of minutes later, holding a large, heavy cuttings book.

'It's in here somewhere. It's something to do with a rebellion in the Punjab. Some years ago.'

He put the book on his desk and started flipping the pages over from the back. '1875,' he muttered. '1873... Ah, here it is. 1872.'

He put his finger firmly on the left-hand side of a double-page spread. He looked up at her, his eyes deeply troubled.

'This is beyond belief. This is one of the worst atrocities ever perpetrated by the British in India. I remember it. It was talked about for many months, if not years afterwards.'

Maria came round behind her father to read the newspaper article, dated January 1872:

> At the Malerkotla Parade Ground, the Lieutenant Governor of Punjab ordered the execution of 66 Namdhari Sikhs, accused of fomenting rebellion against British colonial rule. The Sikhs were executed by a means called 'blown by cannon': strapped to the front of cannons, which were then fired.

Maria's knees shook. She collapsed onto a chair, gazing in horror at her father. She felt sick. Tears sprung to her eyes.

'Oh my God,' she whispered. 'Oh, my good God. I have never heard of such a terrible act. How could they? How could they do that?'

'I know,' her father said. 'I can't help thinking: if Captain Buchanan had anything to do with this barbarism, it may have a bearing on the case.'

CHAPTER FOURTEEN

Manoel Island, Malta. Wednesday, 20 October 1880

McQueen made it to the restaurant just in time before they stopped serving breakfast. He saw Bonnici sitting at their table, eating bread and cheese. The doctor looked haggard, staring straight in front of him as he chewed, as if his thoughts were miles away. McQueen felt guilty, knowing his friend had been treating patients through the night, while he had drunk whisky and spent time talking with Nellie Byrne.

'Is there any change,' he asked, 'with Miss Copeland?'

Bonnici nodded, with a slight smile. 'Yes, thank God. A small improvement. Miss Templeman is giving her some warm broth, which hopefully she will take down. It was touch and go. A long night.'

'Miss Templeman stayed the whole time?'

'Yes, she's a true friend, don't you think? A good nurse too.'

'Indeed.'

McQueen asked a passing servant for some breakfast. 'Bring me bread, cheese, eggs, anything you have. I'm hungry.'

'She did tell me something I think you should know,' Bonnici said, before taking a delicate sip of coffee. 'You know the American, Miss Byrne?'

McQueen nodded, thinking this might not be the best time to say any more.

'Miss Templeman saw her on the terrace with Captain Buchanan at night, two days before the murder.'

'What?'

'Yes. Apparently, they were in close conversation. Quite intimate.'

What did this mean? She had not said anything about that, quite the contrary. She had said she had little to do with him. He felt a flicker of disappointment, and something that felt suspiciously like jealousy.

'That *is* something. I'll have to follow up on that. Thank you.'

'Any other leads? Sorry I've not been around to help.'

'I'm still trying to track down who could have got into the storeroom – I think Grech is involved. I'm going to try and rattle his cage.'

'Good luck. Well, I have to go. There is bad news. Two more cholera cases have just been admitted to the hospital. The quarantine doctor needs help – he's willing but sadly lacks experience.'

Bonnici stood up, leaning heavily on his cane.

'You need to rest as well, Doctor,' McQueen said, concerned for his health.

'Don't worry, I will when I can.'

McQueen watched his friend walk away, his limp more pronounced than usual. This was a testing time. He could see the pressure was taking its toll, but he knew Bonnici would keep going for as long as he was able.

McQueen dashed off a note to Galea and took it to a messenger outside the Lazzaretto entrance. He asked the sergeant to find out what he could about Grech, the health guard. Where did he live, when he was not on Manoel Island? What were his circumstances? Did he have any criminal connections? Galea had taken well to the role of police detective. He should be able to find out that kind of information without any difficulty.

McQueen then went back into the building. He felt he needed a different space for interviews; a room that was neutral, less comfortable than an apartment. He was concerned he might have stepped over the line with Nellie Byrne. It was not a good idea to drink with potential suspects, still less to spend time with them in their sleeping quarters. What did he really know about her? The news that she had spent time with Buchanan was unsettling. He decided to speak to her again, to ask her more questions in a formal setting. It would be uncomfortable, but it would be better to remind her where they both stood.

He demanded an office from Sciberras, who reluctantly agreed. It was a small, bare room at the end of a corridor, dark and stuffy. He managed to get hold of a desk, a few hardback chairs and a kerosene lamp. It would have to do. He sent one of the guards with a message for Nellie Byrne to meet him there, then sat back in one of the chairs, feet on the desk, waiting for her to arrive.

'Why, what's this, Detective Inspector?' she said, the moment she appeared in the doorway. 'You're trying to tell me something, aren't you? Nice office. Now, what's this all about?'

He brought his feet down with a clatter, almost stood up, then sat back down again clumsily.

'Please sit down. Thank you for coming,' he said. He gestured at one of the chairs on the other side of the desk.

Nellie sat down elegantly, carefully arranging her skirts so they draped neatly over the top of her feet. She sat very upright, her hands clasped loosely on her lap.

'So, what can I do for you, Inspector?' she said, with deliberate politeness, a smile playing at the corners of her mouth.

McQueen felt awkward, as though he was getting everything wrong. 'Sorry about this,' he said gruffly. 'I have to ask you some difficult questions. I thought this might be better... a bit more formal, you know.'

'Oh, I *do* know, Detective, I most certainly do. All right, I'm here, fire away.'

'It's about Captain Buchanan. I have been passed information that you were seen with the captain, at night, on the terrace, shortly after you all arrived here at the Lazzaretto. Two nights before he died – that would be the fourteenth. Can you tell me what you were talking about, what the nature of your relationship was?'

He watched her carefully, saw her jaw clench and her eyes narrow. When she spoke, her voice was cold.

'I told you there was no relationship,' she said. 'Your source is wrong. I did not meet Captain Buchanan on the night of the fourteenth. As I said to you, I couldn't stand the man.'

He sat back, folding his arms. Did he believe her? A voice in his head said, *Well, she would say that, wouldn't she?*

'Is it possible you had a rendezvous? Perhaps some business together? Did it slip your memory?' he asked.

'Oh, for goodness' sakes, no! Quit asking me stupid questions. I've given you my answer.'

'All right. But I am wondering, why were you so keen to tell me about Buchanan meeting with Browne? Why is it important to you that we look to someone else, other than Prince Sundar Singh?'

Nellie leant forward, hands on her knees.

'Because, Detective Inspector, I believe in doing the right thing – and I thought you did too. That young man is innocent. He's done nothing wrong. The odds are stacked against him, and I want to stop a terrible miscarriage of justice.'

She stood up, towering over him across the desk, her eyes flashing with anger.

'Do your damn job, McQueen. Find who did this. And get this into your head. It's nothing to do with me.'

He watched as she left the room, taking her anger with her. What kind of game was she playing? Was she as straight as she presented herself, standing up for the wrongly accused, or was she a superb actress, trying to deflect him from an awful truth?

Later that day, McQueen received a short note from Sergeant Galea.

> *Grech lives in Senglea. Married with four children. Found out from Grech's neighbours he has been spending money recently. His wife has new clothes, and he has a new boat – worth 150 scudi.*

Interesting. Now he had some ammunition to go back to Grech, shake him up and get some more answers. He summoned the guard to his new office, not bothering to let Sciberras know. If the Keeper of the Lazzaretto was not going to be helpful, he would just work around him.

Grech arrived promptly and McQueen pulled him into the room. Initially the man looked defiant, hands in his pockets, chin pointing upward. But as McQueen pushed him down into a desk chair and drew another chair uncomfortably close, he seemed to shrink backward.

'Right, you,' McQueen said. 'It's about time you gave me some proper answers. Your master isn't here to protect you. It's just you and me. And if I don't get the truth this time, there will be hell to pay. You'll not just lose your job, you'll lose your liberty, as you'll spend at least two years in prison. Let's see how your wife does then, in her fine clothes, with no husband to support her.'

Grech squirmed away from him in the chair.

McQueen got even closer. 'I know you've been accepting money,' he said. 'Someone paid you to get them the key to the storeroom. Fact! Come on, admit it. It will go easier for you if you do.'

The guard thought for a moment, then nodded slightly, swallowing.

'If you tell me who it was, you'll be helping the investigation,' McQueen continued. 'I can tell the magistrate that you've been useful, and he may view your case more leniently.'

Eventually, Grech shifted in his seat. 'All right,' he said. 'I tell you.' His voice had a sulky tone. 'Is not to do with murder. Is Mister Browne. He want key, to see statues. He give me plenty money.'

'Gilbert Browne?'

'Yes. He has statues from India, in storeroom. He go check they still there.'

What on earth?

'When was this?'

'I give him key Friday morning. He give it back later, same day.'

McQueen thought quickly. Was this what Browne and Buchanan had been talking about? Some Indian statues? Or had

Browne known about the *kirpan* and gone to the storeroom to find it?

'Take me to those statues now,' he demanded.

They marched back through the corridors to the storeroom, near the front entrance of the Lazzaretto, McQueen thinking about why Browne would want to 'check on' his souvenir statues. They must have significant value.

Grech unlocked the door. 'Here statues.' He indicated three substantial wooden crates, stacked on top of each other to the right of the door. A label on the lid of the top crate identified it as belonging to the Hon. Gilbert Browne, address Tilehurst House nr Reading, Berkshire, England. It was nailed shut.

'Get a crowbar,' McQueen said. 'Now.'

Grech scurried off.

McQueen cast his eyes around the room. Prince Sundar Singh's travelling luggage was directly opposite, underneath the shelves where they had found the box containing the *kirpan. Could Browne have taken the dagger, to use it on Buchanan and throw the blame on the prince?* The *kirpan* and scabbard were now being held elsewhere, in a locked storage case, ready to be taken to the police office as evidence.

Grech returned, wielding a small iron crowbar. McQueen took it from him, slid the flat end under the lid of Browne's top crate and eased it up. He moved along the lid, gradually increasing the gap until he was ready to put some strength into it, pushing down on the handle and making the lid fly up with a crack.

'Got you!' he said, under his breath.

Inside, the crate was full of a coarse straw. He fished around until his hand touched a smooth wooden surface. He pulled it up gently, brushing away the straw, to reveal a wooden statue of an Indian elephant pulling a large log with a rope. It was around ten inches in length, eight inches in height. It looked to be carved out of a single piece of wood, including a heavy base. Putting it to one side, he felt around in the crate, finding and pulling out five more elephants until he had a full set of six.

They were standard tourist souvenirs, of good quality but not great value. There had to be more to it. Was there a way in which these were being used to hide other objects? He examined the first elephant more closely, turning it over in his hands, and shaking it rapidly. Could he hear a faint rattling? There was just one place where he could possibly detect a crack in the wood. At the front of the log. He ran his finger over the surface of the wood. Yes, there was a small round section that could have been removed and plugged back in again. He pulled out his penknife. 'I've never been much good at whittling,' he said. 'But needs must.'

It took a good few minutes of carving before he finally managed to remove all the pieces of what turned out to be a wooden plug, a half-inch in diameter, which revealed a hollow chamber inside the log. Tipping the elephant forward, he watched seven small crystals toppling out. He picked them up, put them in the palm of his hand, then held one up to the light. It was dull, a light-grey colour, looking like a piece of sugar, ready to drop into a cup of coffee.

'Well, I think I know what these are,' he said. 'A clear case of diamonds in the rough. What *have* you been up to, you high-born scoundrel?'

McQueen sent a message to Gilbert Browne, summoning him to his office. He had placed one of the elephant statues on his desk. The young man arrived promptly and stood in the doorway looking wary. His eyes took in the statue. He blinked heavily, showing no expression on his face.

'Come in, come in,' McQueen said. 'Take a seat.'

Browne walked in slowly, choosing the chair furthest away from the desk before sitting down.

'How are you?' McQueen asked. 'Are you well?'

'Not really,' he muttered. 'My head...'

Of course, those famous headaches.

'Do you recognise this wooden statue?' McQueen asked.

'No.'

The charm he had displayed last time they had spoken was well and truly gone. He looked like a sulky child.

'I'm sure you do. It's one of yours. There are half a dozen of them packed in a crate, with your name and address on it, currently in the Lazzaretto storeroom.'

'I've never seen it before,' Browne said, stonily.

McQueen was getting tired of being lied to.

'You mean to tell me you have a whole crate of merchandise, in your possession, and you've no idea what the items are?'

'That's right,' Browne said. 'A friend of mine gave them to me, told me to take them back to England for him.'

'And let me guess, you did not know that the statues also contained a selection of uncut diamonds?'

His eyes widened in fake innocence. 'No. Really?'

'Who did you say gave them to you?'

'Look, he's a friend. I can't give you his name. He said he'd collect them after I got back to London.'

'For God's sake, do you think I am stupid? We can find out who it is, you know. You might as well tell me.'

Browne shrugged, looking down at the floor.

'Right, well let me tell you what's going to happen,' McQueen said. 'You're in a hell of a lot of trouble. Two things. One: you have been caught with smuggled goods in your possession, worth hundreds of pounds. This carries a hefty sentence. Two: you were seen arguing with Buchanan three days before he was killed. He was onto you, wasn't he? He knew you were smuggling diamonds for a criminal organisation. He was threatening to turn you in. That gives you a motive for silencing him. What do you say to that?'

Browne had gone incredibly pale. He looked as if he was going to slip down the chair and onto the floor at any second.

'I didn't... he didn't... it's not true,' he stuttered.

McQueen had had enough. 'I'm going to walk you back to your apartment now. Then I'm going to send a request to the magistrate to get a warrant for your arrest. You're not to move from your room. I want you to think about the story you're going to tell. If you're innocent of Buchanan's murder, you'd better tell me all about what happened between you. And the more truthful you are about the smuggling, the better it will be for you, when you come before the judge. Do you understand?'

Browne nodded miserably.

McQueen marched him back to his apartment via Sciberras's office, where he explained what was happening and collected the key. He deposited the young man in his room, locking the door from the outside and taking the key back to the office. Then he sent a long message to Police Superintendent Ellis explaining the situation and requesting an arrest warrant from the magistrate. Now Ellis would see that there *were* other possibilities, that it was not a cut and dried case.

CHAPTER FIFTEEN

Manoel Island, Malta. Thursday, 21 October 1880

The next day, McQueen had in his hand a warrant for Gilbert Browne's arrest. Taking Sciberras with him as a witness, he went straight to Browne's apartment and knocked. No answer. He put his ear to the door. Silence from within. He banged on the door, calling out a warning, 'Browne, it's Inspector McQueen. I'm coming in.'

No response. He unlocked the door and entered the room, Sciberras close behind him. The scene inside was almost the same as the first time he saw Browne. The room was in semi-darkness, the shutters half closed. He strode over to open them. The light streamed in, revealing Browne on his bed, fully clothed, on top of the sheet. He looked to be deeply asleep, lying on his side, arm across his body.

Irritated, McQueen went to shake him awake. Browne was unresponsive. His face was white-pale, his skin clammy and cold to the touch. McQueen rolled him over onto his back. He felt on his neck for a pulse, expecting to get a weak, slow beat.

Nothing. He put his hand to Browne's mouth – no breath. *Damn it – the man has gone too far, taken too much.* He was beyond saving.

'Get Doctor Bonnici – now!' he ordered.

Cursing under his breath, Sciberras left the room.

McQueen looked around. Browne's luggage trunk was open; his clothes scattered around the floor. It looked as if he had been scrabbling around to get to the bottom of the trunk. Sure enough, the same yellow tin containing dark-brown opium resin was on the bedside table. The lid had been left open. McQueen checked Browne's right hand. His index finger had a smudge of a tar-like substance on the tip and under the nail. No doubt, then, that he had taken another dose of raw opium. And this time, more than his body could cope with. McQueen shook his head. *What a waste.* Browne was young; he had his whole life ahead of him. More than that, he had been given every advantage.

McQueen stepped back and took out his notebook to sketch the scene. He had just finished, when Bonnici arrived.

'What do we have, Inspector?'

'Overdose of opium, I suspect. You'll need to confirm the cause and estimate the time of death.'

'Foolish young man. I warned him to take care, do you remember?'

'Aye. There's something more. I've just found a stash of rough diamonds, hidden in a batch of souvenirs, in his luggage. He was attempting to smuggle them to England from India.'

Bonnici was busy checking Browne's eyes and mouth. He looked up, eyebrows raised. 'You surprise me,' he said. 'That's risky, no?'

'Extremely. I have got a warrant here for his arrest. Perhaps he was looking for an easy way out. Couldn't face the music. What time do you think he died?'

Bonnici pulled back Browne's clothing to examine the state of his body.

'There is not much stiffness yet. Rigor mortis usually sets in after two to six hours, so that's some indication.'

He pointed to the left side of the chest and the hip area. 'Can you see the discolouration here?' McQueen nodded. 'That's where the blood is beginning to settle. Half an hour up to three hours after death.'

Eventually Bonnici finished the examination. He pulled out his watch. 'The time is now 10am. I think the deceased must have died sometime between four o'clock and eight o'clock this morning.'

McQueen shook his head. Such a stupid, pointless death. 'We must get a message through to Colonel Ellis as soon as possible. He'll let the magistrate know and arrange for the body to be removed. They can decide if a post-mortem examination is needed. It's one bloody thing after another.'

Around two o'clock, one of the guards brought McQueen a message. He glanced at the note. Maria Tanti was at the Lazzaretto. She wanted to speak to him.

He made his way to the parlatorio where Maria was waiting, her maid Rożi by her side. He lifted his hand as he went in. She looked well, her eyes bright with excitement. It was good to see a friendly face.

'What's happening?' she asked as he got close. 'I saw the police constables setting off shortly before me. Police milling around on the quay.'

'Another person has died. Accidental,' he said.

'What? Who?'

'Gilbert Browne.'

Maria clapped her hand to her mouth. 'No! What happened? That's the person I came to tell you about.'

'Looks like he took an overdose,' he replied. 'We don't know yet.'

'I can't believe it.' She shook her head. 'My God, this place. Another death! This is too strange.'

'I know.'

'I can't take it in,' Maria said. 'I was just talking to Gilbert Browne's cousin yesterday. She was looking forward to seeing him. Is it really true? That he's dead?'

'Afraid so. I found him this morning. What was the information you wanted to give me?'

'It's not that much, but perhaps it might be useful.' She gazed into space for a moment, lost in thought.

'Go on,' he prompted.

She shook her head slightly. 'I don't know. I got the impression he was a bit of a black sheep. I tracked down his cousin from the P&O records, went to see her. She said he needed to borrow money, to pay for food, essentials, while staying here. Apparently, it was normal for him to need funds. She said he had a gambling problem.'

'Ah.' That could explain his money-making scheme.

'Yes, but she also said he'd hinted he would soon have plenty of money and would be able to pay her back.'

'Interesting. We certainly have evidence that he was up to no good. And it's not been ruled out that he could have been involved in Buchanan's murder in some way.'

'Really? It shows you never can truly know what people are capable of. His cousin said he could be annoying, but she seemed fond of him. Said he could charm his way out of any situation.'

'Unfortunately, he was also an opium-eater. And this time, he took too much.'

'I don't think his cousin knew anything about drug-taking. It's going to come as such a shock.'

'It's good you found relatives. The police can inform them of the death if you pass on the details.'

'Of course,' Maria said.

'Have you managed to find any more information? Anything on Buchanan?' McQueen asked.

'Oh yes! That really is something.' She pulled out a piece of paper. 'I managed to get Buchanan's service record. His army career was spent entirely in the Punjab. He was definitely there throughout most of the '70s. I don't know if this is true or not, but it's possible he took part in the execution of sixty-six Sikhs at Malerkotla, in 1872. My father kept a cutting.' She showed him the news item, through the partition. 'It caused a terrible commotion in the press. It was horrendous, evil. Not even a trial. The deputy commissioner said they were guilty of insurrection and ordered them to be killed. Blown by cannon.'

McQueen read through the copy, feeling a surge of anger against the cruelty, the inhumanity of this act of British oppression. He wondered if Colonel Ellis knew anything about it. This definitely needed to be followed up.

'Thank you for doing this,' he said. 'This is significant. You have been a great help, especially as I'm stuck here for now.'

'How much longer?'

'Just five or six more days. Bonnici will have to stay longer, as he's been in contact with cholera patients.'

'How is Miss Copeland?'

'I believe she's slightly better. The doctor's hopeful she may survive.'

'Well,' Maria said, 'that's about the only bit of good news today. What about the Indian prince, how's he getting on?'

'He should be out of quarantine in a couple of days. Then he'll be taken into custody at the police office in Valletta to be charged. That doesn't give me much time to get to the bottom of this mess.'

Maria stood up, linking her arm in Rożi's. 'We'll leave you to it, Inspector. Hope to see you soon, back in Valletta.'

'You've no idea how happy I'll be to be off this island,' he said.

He watched her walking away, wishing he had her freedom.

Later that day, McQueen received a visit from Police Superintendent Ellis, accompanied by Inspector Azzopardi from the Marine Police. They met at the parlatorio.

'I have co-opted Azzopardi to the Interior Police,' Ellis said. 'He has been invaluable to the case. I've assigned him to work alongside you, Inspector. You'll find him to be an excellent officer.'

McQueen looked hard at Azzopardi, who returned his stare, a slight smile playing about his lips. It would not pay to be too antagonistic, but he wondered why Ellis had made this move. Did Ellis just need a hanger-on, someone sure to do things his way?

'We'll see about that,' he said.

'Plenty to fill you in on,' Ellis said. 'I've spoken to the magistrate. This latest death, Gilbert Browne. Doctor Bonnici can carry out a post-mortem examination at the isolation hospital, as soon as possible. Then we can get him buried here on the island. Looks to be cut and dried. An overdose, yes?'

'I think so.'

'Then we need to announce it as a natural death. Deal with it as quickly as possible. People need to know it's not another case of cholera. We can say it's heart failure, or something equivalent. Let's see what Bonnici says.'

'What about the diamonds?' McQueen asked.

'I've contacted the Indian Imperial Police. We can send the diamonds and the statues back to Bombay. They will investigate, find out where they've come from. Then they will talk to the India Office, perhaps even Scotland Yard, to work out if Browne was part of a criminal ring.'

'I have good intelligence that Captain Buchanan may have found out what Browne was up to. Browne could have had access to Singh's dagger. He could have wanted to silence Buchanan before he reported him and had him arrested.'

'What are your sources?'

McQueen explained about the overheard conversation on the terrace, and Maria's information from Browne's cousin.

Ellis shook his head. 'This is all hearsay,' he said. 'I specifically told you to focus on the prince. He is the dangerous party here. He is the one with the strongest motive to kill Buchanan.'

'Yes, but from what I've found out, he couldn't have had access to the *kirpan*. Browne could. He was in the storeroom, the night before the murder.'

Azzopardi chipped in. 'Perhaps Singh told him, or paid him, to get the *kirpan* for him. He is the one who would want his precious weapon back.'

McQueen could feel his blood beginning to boil.

'There's sufficient doubt for us to keep digging before Singh is brought before the magistrate. There isn't evidence enough to make his charge stick. On the contrary, the more I find out, the *less* likely it seems to me that he is the culprit.'

'You're not listening, Inspector. You do not seem to grasp the political significance of this situation. We're talking about the defence of the Empire. A Sikh plot to start a large-scale rebellion and overthrow British rule in India. Have you any idea how much our country stands to lose, if this were to take place? The prince is guilty, and he'll pay the price.'

'What happened to "beyond reasonable doubt"? You're not giving us the chance to prepare the evidence, which means the prince won't be given a fair trial.'

'Don't worry, the matter will be dealt with swiftly and fairly. I have all the evidence I need that Singh was planning what would no doubt be a wholesale massacre of innocent people. He would stop at nothing to make this happen, including the murder of Captain Buchanan.'

McQueen could not understand why Ellis was being so dogged. Was it something to do with his time in India as an army officer?

'You were in the Punjab, weren't you, Colonel?' he asked.

'Yes, I was. Brigade Commander. What has that to do with anything?'

'Any involvement in the Malerkotla executions?'

Ellis stared at him with eyes of flint. 'None of your business. What if I was?'

'Did you know Captain Buchanan? I have evidence that he was at Malerkotla. Is there a link between this and your fears of a Sikh uprising?'

'Absolutely not. I did not know Captain Buchanan. Thought I might have recognised the name, but no, I did not know he was at Malerkotla. This has nothing to do with Singh. I am quite clear that he is guilty.' Ellis turned to Azzopardi. 'Singh is clear of quarantine in two days, yes?'

'Yes. He has been in isolation for eight days.'

'In which case, I want him transferred to the police cells at the Auberge d'Auvergne on Saturday morning. He'll be brought to trial as swiftly as possible.'

If found guilty, the sentence would, of course, be death by hanging. A problem averted, and a clear message sent out, just as it had been in Malerkotla. McQueen felt deeply disturbed by the form of British justice he could see acting out in front of him.

'Not yet, I need more time. A few other lines of inquiry to follow up.'

'Absolutely not. I will send Sergeant Galea here first light on Saturday to take the prisoner to Valletta. You are to remain here until your quarantine is over. That's an order.'

McQueen retreated to his apartment with only a bottle of whisky for company. With Dr Bonnici at the hospital, he had no one to talk to about the case. Not only that, but he was living amongst the very suspects he was investigating. Now there was another death, another twist in the story. Gilbert Browne had taken the dagger from the storeroom, he felt sure, but had he used it to kill Buchanan? Why would he do that, and why would he want to throw suspicion on Prince Sundar?

The situation with Ellis was uncomfortable. Both he and the police superintendent reported directly to the governor. But as head of the police, Ellis had a direct line to the magistrate. He was using this to his advantage. McQueen was frustrated by the lack of agency he had on Manoel Island, his inability to stop Ellis from his near-sighted pursuit of the prince.

Truth be told, he was beginning to resent his position in Malta, feeling he was being made complicit in British treatment of the colonies. Malta was of vital strategic importance to the British Empire. It was treated as a kind of fortress, with all government decisions made in the name of Her Majesty Queen Victoria – not just Queen of the United Kingdom of Great Britain and Ireland, but also Empress of India. In Edinburgh, he felt somewhat shielded from this empirical view, comfortable that as a Scot he was in some ways at an ideological remove. But here in Malta, he was witnessing first-hand colonial attitudes and prejudices he found unacceptable.

He began to think about returning to his life back home. He did not have to stay much longer in Malta. Yes, he had a battle on his hands to complete this murder investigation, but once the case was solved, he could get back to familiar surroundings and people. Not that there were many people waiting for him there. Of his family, he only spoke to his brother, who had followed his father into the Kirk. And the woman he had loved – or so he thought – had told him she did not want to see him anymore.

He poured himself a large dram of whisky, took a swig and sat staring into the amber liquid in the glass. A melancholy settled on him as he thought about Jeannie. He had brought her to live with him in his apartment, having taken her away from the bordello where she had been living under the thumb of her ponce, Quinn. She was a poor wee creature, reliant upon laudanum, given to her by that bastard to keep her compliant. He had felt compelled to take her away, to protect her. Gentle-natured and trusting, she did not deserve the life she had been driven to lead.

At first, they had been happy together, but over time things had changed. How could he have thought it was enough, just to provide a roof over her head? He remembered the arguments, her accusations that he was never there, that he paid her no attention. She must have been feeling so neglected. He was out every day, working long hours. He should have thought much more about what she needed to make her happy. She would be better off now, he thought, living with her brother in Leith. He had heard she was doing well, that she had found work with a milliner.

He swirled the whisky around the glass. Before they separated, she had told him he was drinking too much. He did not agree. It was not too much. Just the occasional night in the Fountain Inn, after a long day dealing with ne'er-do-wells. But he had promised her, told her time and time again he would not drink; that he would never turn on her, as her alcoholic father had turned on her mother. Then one night, they had an argument, after he returned late from the bar. He pushed her, caused her to be hurt. It had been an accident, but it had changed their relationship forever. Thinking about it made him feel guilty. He threw the whisky down his throat. Perhaps she was right. He should cut down.

A tap at the door brought him out of his reverie. He opened it to find a guard outside. 'You're to come to the mortuary,' the guard said. 'Doctor Bonnici wants to see you.'

He grabbed his jacket and followed the guard to the isolation hospital. The mortuary was in an annexe to the hospital, a small room with a high ceiling. When he arrived, McQueen was relieved to see the post-mortem was finished. He was not a keen observer of the process. Gilbert Browne's body lay on the examination table, covered with a white cloth. Bonnici was wearing a white apron and rubber gloves. He was working with a hospital orderly, busy washing and tidying the scalpels and other instruments that had been used. There was a strong smell of formaldehyde, but none of that cloying smell of decay that McQueen found hard to take, presumably because the body was so fresh.

Bonnici looked up from his cleaning.

'Aha! Good to see you, Inspector. As you can see, we're nearly done.'

'Pleased to hear it. I'm not sure my stomach would cope with watching you at work. What have you found out?'

'Well, the external examination showed bluish skin around the lips, fingertips, and toes which suggests poor oxygenation. Also, the pupils of the eyes are still constricted. These are signs of opium poisoning. In addition, I found the lungs were heavily congested, filled with fluid. A sign of respiratory failure, associated with the effects of the drug. These findings are strongly suggestive of an opium overdose. However, the stomach contents contained only a small amount of raw opium. Unlikely to be enough to kill. And here, this is the interesting thing.'

Bonnici moved over to the table and pulled up the white cloth to reveal the top of the left arm.

'I missed this when we initially found the body.' He pointed to a small red dot. 'Subcutaneous injection.'

McQueen leant over for a closer look. 'Yes, I see.'

'We know that Browne liked to take opium by mouth. But this strongly suggests he had been given an injection. A lethal dose of morphine.'

CHAPTER SIXTEEN

Manoel Island, Malta. Thursday, 21 October 1880

Bonnici finished clearing up. He looked around the mortuary, assuring himself that everything was back in its place, then used the pull-chain to close the valve on the gas lamp, plunging the space into darkness. Gilbert Browne's body had been moved to a cool room, ready for burial the next day. He could not help thinking of how difficult this would be for Browne's family in England. Their loved one buried so far away, unable to be brought back to them because of the fear of contagion.

Bonnici made his way back to the ward to check on his patient. He found Eleanor still sitting by Louisa's bedside.

'How is she doing?' he asked.

'Not too bad,' Eleanor replied. 'She vomited around seven o'clock, but she said she felt a little bit better afterwards. She's had broth every two hours, just a few sips, and a little bit of wine.'

Bonnici tilted his head to one side, looking closely at Louisa's face. Her colour was better; the black hue was retreating. She opened her eyes, as if conscious that someone was looking at her. She gave a tiny half-smile in recognition.

'Good evening, Miss Copeland,' he said. 'I am just going to check your temperature. You're doing so well.'

He felt her hands and her feet, reassured to find them slightly warm to the touch. 'Let's leave her to sleep for a few hours,' he said to Eleanor. 'One of the sisters will stay with her. I'll go and speak to the quarantine doctor.'

He left Eleanor by her friend's bed and went to find Doctor Cassar, who was treating cholera patients in one of the main wards. The doctor had managed to draft in five sisters and the same number of hospital orderlies. Bonnici had spent time advising him. Between them they had set up a nursing and cleaning regime that hopefully would help the patients and stop the spread of the disease.

'How are they doing, *Dottore*?' he asked, referring to the two new patients brought in the previous night.

Cassar was standing at the bedside of a woman in her forties, preparing to give her an injection. She was propped up by pillows, her face gaunt and lined, her eyes rolled up, revealing the whites. A few beds away, a man of about the same age was being looked after by two nurses, who were rubbing his arms and legs to encourage circulation and keep him warm. Cassar concentrated on the injection then looked up. 'Just making this brave lady more comfortable,' he said, then moved away from the bedside, taking Bonnici with him.

'It's not looking good,' he said quietly, when they were out of earshot. 'They had both been hiding their symptoms for several hours, not wanting to be kept in quarantine any longer. The cholera has taken a strong hold. We're doing what we can. This lady is Mrs Fairfax, that's her husband over there. I think he is a bit stronger than her, perhaps he has more of a chance.'

'Keep up with the treatment,' Bonnici advised. 'Is he managing to take in any fluids?'

'Just about. But not his wife. She can't tolerate anything, not even a sip of brandy. I just gave her some morphine, to keep her sedated.'

'Is it just them in their apartment?'

'Yes. The orderlies have taken away all linen for boiling and have disinfected the room. The water closets have been treated with carbolic acid and vitriol.'

'Make sure everyone is vigilant with their own protective clothes and regularly washing their hands with disinfectant. We have to stop this spreading to more people.'

Cassar nodded, his eyes bright behind his round spectacles. Bonnici knew what he was going through, recognising the young man's fear, but also his determination to do the right thing.

'You're doing well, *Dottore*,' he said. 'We have a good system and good staff. We'll get through this.' He patted Cassar on the shoulder. 'Can you arrange for a sister to sit with Miss Copeland for a few hours? She's resting quietly. She can have some beef tea when she wakes. Miss Templeman needs to get some rest.'

'Of course.'

'I will be back in the morning. But come and get me if you need any help in the night.'

He left the ward to get some much-needed rest.

The following morning, despite a deep, dreamless sleep, Bonnici woke up feeling exhausted and headachy. His body was unwilling to move, but still he managed to dress carefully and shave, before dragging himself back to the hospital to check on the patients. Sadly, Mrs Fairfax had just passed away. Doctor Cassar was grey with fatigue, overseeing her removal to the mortuary, and the disinfection of her clothing and bedding. Bonnici assured the young doctor he had done all he could and said he would come back and relieve him from his duties shortly, once he had caught up on news from McQueen.

He made his way to McQueen's apartment. The big man, looking as dishevelled as ever, was sitting at the table, writing in his notebook. He had clearly been running his fingers through his hair, as it stood up from his head in comical tufts.

'I think you're in danger of doing too much thinking,' Bonnici said. 'Your hair is protesting.'

McQueen flattened his hair down with a smile and pushed his chair away from the table.

'How's it going, Doctor? Any news?'

'Miss Copeland is doing well, sitting up, drinking beef tea. She's weak, unable to move her arms, but she's making progress. Unfortunately, not the same for the other patients. One has died in the night, a Mrs Fairfax. The other, her husband, is also unlikely to pull through.' He sighed. 'I'll go back soon, after breakfast. The quarantine doctor's good, but in danger of being overwhelmed. He needs a few hours to catch up on some sleep.'

'God, we're easy prey, here in quarantine, cooped up in small spaces.'

'We have to be vigilant. Clean water, disinfection. We're doing everything we can.'

He pulled up a chair opposite McQueen and sat down.

'What's happening with the investigation?' he asked. 'Did you let Superintendent Ellis know about the hypodermic mark?'

'Aye, I did. Sent a message – not heard anything back yet.' McQueen pulled over a sheet of paper. 'I was trying to get my thoughts in order. I want to list out all the leads we've had and then work out what we need to do, to move things on. Three things happened in the run-up to Buchanan's death. I'm going to give them arbitrary dates. Here's when the ship anchors in Quarantine Harbour.'

He wrote down *12th October*, then underneath that *Poonah arrives in Malta. Steward dies.*

'Then we have Buchanan seen arguing with Browne the night after they went into quarantine. Let's put that here.'

He added another heading: *13th October – Buchanan + Browne.*

'The following night, Buchanan was seen talking to Nellie Byrne. So that's the fourteenth.'

He added: *14th October – Buchanan + Byrne.*

'Then, the night before he was murdered, he receives a note from a mysterious woman.'

He wrote: *15th October – note delivered to Buchanan.*

'So, he could either have been deliberately lured out by a woman who wanted to harm him – although why, we have no idea – or it was by chance that Browne found him out on the night of the sixteenth and killed him.'

'Agreed,' Bonnici said, pleased to see some kind of order being made of a jumble of information. 'How likely do you think it is that Buchanan was killed by Browne?'

'He had a strong motive. If he could stop Buchanan reporting him to the authorities, he could still hope to smuggle the diamonds into England and eventually receive his payment. It feels like he was getting desperate, his debts catching up with him.'

'But if that's the case, who then murdered *him*? And why?'

'Exactly. I need to do more digging. There have to be more links we don't know about yet.'

'What about Nellie Byrne? What have you found out about her?'

McQueen coloured slightly.

'Well, as it happens, I did spend a fair bit of time with her the other night,' he said, with a note of feigned detachment.

Bonnici immediately suspected his friend of being quite taken with the American heiress.

'Oh, yes?'

'It is interesting. She says she knows Prince Sundar's father, the Maharaja, having met him in Paris, where he lives in exile. She's been asking me questions, trying to find out about the investigation, claiming that she knows the prince is innocent and wanting to help him.'

Bonnici thought for a moment. 'Is there a way to verify that story? A letter from Paris she could show us, perhaps? Also, could she be the mysterious woman?'

'I don't know. That stupid guard, Grech. Seriously, I could throttle him. Our only witness and he's incapable of giving a coherent description. Look, I'll talk to her again, see what else I can find out. I get the feeling she's genuine, but you never know.'

'I hope you're treating her exactly the same as you would any suspect.' Bonnici could not imagine McQueen's judgement being swayed by an attractive woman, but it was always possible.

'Don't worry about that,' McQueen said. 'I'm not in her good books at the moment anyway.'

'So, how long do we have before Prince Sundar is moved to the police cells?'

'Just one day. Ellis says he'll be transferred first thing tomorrow morning.'

'Well, you know where I'll be, if you need anything.'

When Bonnici got back to the hospital, Cassar was nowhere to be seen. He went over to Eleanor, who was patiently giving Louisa some warm broth.

'Have you seen Doctor Cassar?'

'He was here up until a few minutes ago. One of the nurses came to tell him something, and he disappeared with her. He looked concerned.'

Eleanor looked cool and calm as she gently wiped her friend's mouth with a muslin cloth. A little bit of rest had done her good, he could see, helped no doubt by seeing Louisa begin to recover.

Bonnici murmured a few words of encouragement and said he would be back soon. He left, thinking he might find Cassar in the doctor's office, opposite the ward. No one was in there. The place was in disarray, paperwork spread all over the desk. He heard voices farther away down the corridor and followed the sound to find Cassar standing outside the door to the storeroom, berating one of the nurses. She was looking down at the ground, a red flush creeping up her neck to her cheeks. Bonnici could see she was trying to hold back tears.

'What's going on?' he asked.

Cassar turned to him, his eyes looking hunted behind his spectacles.

'We're running out of laudanum,' he said. 'I have to have some, now. We've just checked the stores. We're low on medication, cleaning products, everything.' Panic and desperation had clearly set in.

'Well, it won't be the sister's fault, will it? You may go, Nurse. Please don't worry, we'll take care of the situation.'

The nurse nodded and scurried away.

Cassar took his spectacles off and rubbed his eyes. The dark stubble around his jawline, after two days of not sleeping or managing to shave, made him look older, unkempt.

'I'm sorry,' he said. 'But I couldn't believe what I was seeing. I don't know what's gone wrong, or where the fault lies, but there are serious shortages. God knows how many more patients we're going to be receiving. We have to be ready.'

'There will be a solution. Don't worry. We'll start by making an inventory of what we need.'

It took them around an hour to work through the list, starting with four dozen bottles of Condy's Fluid, and supplies of carbolic soap, laudanum, ether, camphor and morphine. The absolute essentials for tackling cholera.

'I don't understand,' Cassar kept saying. 'I'm sure I ordered more stock a week ago, but I can't find the paperwork.'

Bonnici felt sure that Sciberras would be the one at fault. As Keeper of the Lazzaretto, hospital supplies were part of his remit. He was either incompetent, or he was corrupt. Either way he was putting lives at risk. He had held the post for at least ten years. He had got used to running things his way, with no one checking up on him. No doubt he had deliberately kept stocks low, leaving them ill-prepared for a serious outbreak of disease.

'I'll take this list to Sciberras and watch over him while he places the order,' he said. 'In the meantime, I'll send a message to the Civil Hospital where I work. They can get the essential medicines over here within a couple of hours.'

There was a great deal to be done. The Lazzaretto was being badly run. Standards of hygiene were not being met. Despite his fatigue, he felt determined to turn things around. If they were going to get on top of this cholera outbreak, he would have to be prepared to speak up, tackle ineptitude and work harder than he ever had.

By the time he had emerged from a long and fractious

meeting with Sciberras, it had grown dark. He made his way as best he could back to the hospital, the muscles on the right side of his body aching with every step, only to find that there was to be no respite that night. Three more patients had been admitted with cholera. One of those was a small child.

CHAPTER SEVENTEEN

Paola, Malta. Friday, 22 October 1880

Maria and Rożi walked slowly along the paths of the Cimitero di Santa Maria Addolorata. Situated three miles from Valletta, on a hill in Paola, it was a grand, new cemetery, boasting a fine chapel, several hundred graves and a growing number of family vaults. The temperature had dropped; dark clouds scudded across the sky. Maria was wearing her *għonnella*, holding it tight across her as the wind whipped up the dark silk. She hated wearing the traditional cloak, but it was useful for concealing her identity.

'Tell me again why we're meeting *Sur* Trapani here, *Sa* Maria? It's too cold!' Rożi complained.

'It's a place where we could be seen talking and have good reason to be here. We could easily both have family graves that we're visiting.'

'You know I don't like *Sur* Trapani. He is trouble, I'm sure of it.'

'I know, but it's all right, he just wants to ask me some questions. We'll be out of here in a few minutes.'

At that point, Trapani appeared, walking briskly toward them.

'Follow me,' he said, leading them away to a path on the right. He stopped in front of a gravestone. Maria read the inscription:

SALVATORE TRAPANI 1835 – 1874
LA MORTE NON È LA FINE, MA L'INIZIO DI UNA NUOVA VITA.

'My father,' Trapani said. 'He came here from Sicily after the *Risorgimento*. He was a true republican, a follower of Garibaldi. There was a group of them here in Malta.'

'I'm sorry that he has now passed away,' Maria said.

'So am I, I miss him. And my mother does too. She has to work now. Housekeeper for a rich English family.'

He turned away and walked to a wrought-iron bench, where he sat down, head in his hands. Maria sat next to him, with Rożi standing a short distance away, watching with evident disapproval.

Eventually, Trapani looked up, his eyes dark and intense.

'So, do you have news from the police?' he asked.

'Yes,' Maria said. 'There's been another death. An Englishman called Gilbert Browne. Took an overdose of opium. McQueen said he might have been involved in Buchanan's murder.'

'Oh, yes? How?'

'I don't know. He was up to something, apparently, but I've no idea what.'

'When did he die?'

'Yesterday.'

'Anything else? Do you know what's happening to the Indian prince?'

She thought for a moment. 'I think McQueen said he was going to be moved to the police cells once his quarantine was over. In a day or so.'

'All right.' He stared into space as though making plans in his head. His expression hardened, and Maria felt apprehensive.

'Listen,' she said. 'I haven't told you anything definite, just a few things I've heard. I don't want any part in any trouble you might be brewing.'

'If there's any trouble, believe me, it will be for a reason. We must take a stand, fight for what's right.'

'Is this the *Gruppo Militante Pro Italiano*? How many of you are there?' she asked. Was it growing in popularity? How much of a threat did the group pose?

'About fifteen. All hate British rule. Malta should be part of Italy, and Italy should be a republic, not a kingdom.'

With her father editing an English-language newspaper, growing up amongst so many British people, Maria had never questioned whether it was a good thing to be a part of the British Empire. It was just how it was. Now her eyes were beginning to be opened, she was starting to see how others could have a different outlook.

'Where and when do you meet?' she asked.

He barked out a short laugh. 'I can't tell you that,' he said. 'It is good of you to help with information, but I am not a fool. You could give us up to the police, I know.'

She had to play a game here, keep the dialogue going. This was a good story in the making. One that she wanted to cover in the paper.

'You know I don't share all your views, but I think you're right about the way the prince is being treated. It is troubling.

I'll let you know if I find out any more about what's happening.'

'All right. We can always meet here again if we need to.' Trapani stood up and pulled a shabby blue cap over his unruly hair. '*Saħħa.*'

'*Saħħa.* Goodbye.'

He marched away, head down, a man on a mission.

Rożi came close to Maria. 'He worries me,' she said. 'He is too angry. He only sees things one way. His way.'

Maria sighed. 'I know. But he is right about some things. Perhaps we need people like him, not afraid to stand up for what they believe?'

Rożi snorted. 'I don't trust him one bit,' she said.

Back at the printers, Maria found her father poring over the galley proofs of the *Malta Post*. He had all twelve pages on the large desk in front of him, and was leaning over page three, pen in hand. He looked up and greeted her distractedly, a smudge of ink on his right cheek.

Maria stood next to him, looking down at the proof pages. 'How are you doing, Papà?' She picked up the front page. As well as the election results, it featured her piece about the death of Captain Buchanan.

Her father looked at her over his spectacles. 'Well, I would have been much further on if I'd had help from my deputy editor. Honestly, young people are so unreliable.'

'Sorry, Papà. I was following up on a story.'

'I hope it was worth it, leaving your poor father slaving over the galleys.'

'Of course! Anyway, I'm here now. I'll start at the beginning.'

Maria usually did the second proofread after her father, then he did one final check of the form proof before printing. She took the front page over to her desk and sat down to read it, starting with the first column.

She was pleased to see that the compositor had managed to set her late-night addition announcing the death of Gilbert Browne. Of course, there was little detail to report, but it would certainly capture their readers' interest. She had written about the sense of menace that hung over the Lazzaretto: a murder, the overriding fear of cholera, and now a sudden death. *The Standard* had already printed their next edition, so this would be the first report that people would see.

'It's a shame we can't write anything about Buchanan yet, his possible links to the Malerkotla Massacre,' she commented. 'Hopefully Inspector McQueen will be able to find out more about that and we can follow up next week.'

'We need to tread carefully,' her father said. 'The establishment will not want us to stir anything up unnecessarily. I have more news on that. Colonel Ellis may also have been involved. He was Brigade Commander, in charge of forces in the Malerkotla–Ludhiana region of the Punjab. They are not going to want us to divulge that information.'

Maria wondered if she might have a battle on her hands if her father was reluctant to run with a story that was deeply critical of the British. She knew she would not be able to back down if she felt the truth needed to be told.

The second and third columns, written by her father, were about the threat of cholera. She read his report on Wednesday's meeting of the Central Committee, appointed by the governor to prevent the spread of the disease. The hospital had been reorganised to enable it to meet the needs of the new situation with greater efficiency. The medical staff was being increased, and the supplies of disinfectant. The Admiralty was to lend casks for carrying water to the hospital from the mainland and lanterns and candles to light the hospital at night. It was known that a foul water supply could be a carrier of the disease and that good water was the best medicine. They were trying to prepare for the worst.

Her father was watching her read the columns.

'I am worried,' he said. 'They go so far, but not far enough. We know from the last epidemic that the places where the greatest number of deaths occurred were in crowded areas where the water supply has been contaminated. They talk about how it is vital there is pure water to drink. But what have they done to improve conditions in poorer quarters like the Manderaggio?

'I saw the chief police physician and he said there had been no funding to improve the sanitary conditions. There are families of ten, fifteen people living in cramped rooms with no water supply. Easy prey. I am so concerned, Maria. I can't face the idea of living through an epidemic again.'

Something in her father's tone of voice made Maria look up. He seemed a little unsteady on his feet, and she could see a film of sweat across his brow even though the room was not particularly warm.

'Papà?' she said. 'Are you all right?'

'I don't know, *ħanini*, I'm not sure. Something here.' He pressed his hand to his chest. 'A little pain.'

She hurried over to him. He looked disorientated, a little perplexed as well as pained. He smiled wanly. 'I think, just a touch of dyspepsia.'

'Come and sit down.'

She gently sat him in his chair, loosened his collar. He leant forward, his breathing shallow and rapid. 'I'll – be – all right – in – a moment,' he said between breaths.

'Try to relax, Papà. I'll get you some water. We must send for the doctor.'

She tried not to show how she was feeling, but she was terrified. As far back as she could remember, her father had never shown any signs of illness. The occasional chill or headache, nothing more. Now here he was, struggling to catch his breath. She ran next door to get a glass of water and called for one of the pressmen to run for Doctor Mifsud. Then she ran back to him. He was still leaning forward, his breathing laboured.

She took his hand. It felt clammy. He gripped her hand tightly for a moment.

'Don't worry,' she said. 'Help is on its way. Honestly, what can we do with you? You're making yourself ill, with worrying about others.'

After a few minutes, with Maria murmuring foolish things to try and make light of the situation, her father sat back, his hand flat on his chest. 'Thank God,' he said, weakly. 'A bit better now.'

She stroked the side of his face. 'Good,' she said. 'Don't scare me like that.'

Gradually, the colour returned to his cheeks and his breathing became easier. By the time the doctor arrived, he seemed a great deal better. After examining him, the doctor advised that he should get home as soon as possible and rest in bed.

'Don't worry about anything,' Maria said. 'I'll finish the proofreading. We'll get the paper out. You must not think about it at all.'

By the time Maria arrived back at her family home on Strada Mezzodi it was close to two o'clock in the morning. Proofreading done, final formes checked, she had left the pressmen in charge of running the printing press overnight. The urgency of the task had given her all the energy she needed to keep going, but as she let herself into the house, she felt exhaustion sweep over her. She was standing in the hallway, taking off her bonnet and cloak, when her aunt appeared, wringing her hands.

'*Zija* Paolina! Why are you still up and about?'

'Oh, Maria – I couldn't sleep. How could you think it? I've been waiting for you to get home, worrying about you. Walking home at this time of night, it could be dangerous. And your father being taken ill like that. I am terrified!'

'How is Papà?'

'He is sleeping now. The doctor has given him a draught. He was much better by the time the doctor left.'

'Thank goodness for that.'

She loved *Zija* Paolina, her father's sister, dearly. She had moved in with the family while Maria was still a baby, to help care for her and run the household. In some ways it was reassuring to have her constant presence, but she fretted and worried so much it could be wearing.

'The doctor has given me all the instructions. Your father is to have drops in brandy and water every three hours during the daytime. It is his heart. He needs to rest – lots of rest. Of course, I won't be able to stop him from getting up from his bed. You know what your father is like. Can you imagine trying to keep him from his blessed newspaper?'

'Don't worry, *Zija*. I can look after things for a while.'

'The doctor has written you a note. Come to the kitchen. I'll make you a warm drink. I put the envelope on the table.'

Maria followed her aunt into the kitchen, a cascade of words washing over her. Finding the envelope, she opened it and pulled out the doctor's note.

> *Dear Sinjorina Tanti,*
>
> *Your father has the symptoms of angina pectoris. This can be brought on by overexertion, and by nervous strain. He has been lucky, the episode was short-lived, but he must rest and recuperate. I have left a phial of amyl nitrite. Two drops are to be placed under the tongue if your father has another similar episode. For now, I prescribe a mild sedative. But I must stress that this is a long-term condition. He could have another attack at any time. He will need to moderate his diet and have minimal stimulation. I will call back in the morning.*
>
> *Doctor Giuseppe Mifsud*

Maria stood holding the note, feeling a cold fear run down her body. Her beloved Papà. She could not bear the thought of losing him. Her mind flashed to a place where he was no longer around, then she shook her head to rid herself of that image. It was not going to happen! If things had to change, to make sure he stayed with them, she would do whatever it took. She would step forward, run the newspaper for him. He would be able to see how capable she was and take life a little easier.

She accepted a milky drink from *Zija* Paolina, who smiled at her tiredly. 'Here, drink this, *ħanini*. You look as though you need it.'

'Thank you,' she said. 'Now we must go to bed and get some sleep. There will be a great deal to do in the morning.'

CHAPTER EIGHTEEN

Manoel Island, Malta. Saturday 23 October 1880

McQueen woke early. There was a slight chill in the air and for once he was glad of his woollen suit. He went out of the front entrance to find Galea waiting. The young sergeant was smartly turned out, as always, looking keen as mustard.

'Good morning, Sergeant. Early enough for you? Ready to spring into action? I'll help you fetch the prince.'

'Yes, sir. We have a boat waiting near Fort Manoel,' Galea said. 'We have instructions to move the prince as quickly as possible before it gets light, and to draw no attention to ourselves. No one is to see the prisoner in transit.'

'Of course,' McQueen said. 'Heaven forbid.'

They stopped at the keeper's office to collect the key to the room where Singh was being held. Sciberras handed it over with a triumphant smirk. McQueen would have dearly loved to wipe off the smile, a careless elbow, perhaps?

On the way through the corridors, he asked Galea if Ellis

had received his message about the result of Browne's post-mortem.

'Yes, he did.'

'Clearly it didn't change his mind about the prince.'

'No, sir. He said he didn't have time to look into it now. We're to proceed as planned.'

'That's hardly unexpected. He's not one to be swayed.'

They stopped outside the door. 'Do you have handcuffs?'

'I do.' Galea pulled out a pair of heavy screw-key handcuffs, his face set with determination. McQueen smiled inwardly, sure that the young prince would not give them any trouble.

'Right, let's go in and pick him up,' he said.

McQueen banged on the door and motioned Galea to unlock it.

They went in to find Prince Sundar sitting on the edge of his bed, bag packed at his feet. His turban had been taken away from him, and his thick, long hair had been pulled into a topknot. He looked younger, more vulnerable, his eyes radiating hostility but also a flicker of fear as Galea ordered him to put his arms out in front of him. The sergeant fixed the handcuffs to Singh's wrists, keeping a tight grip on his left arm.

'No progress, then, Inspector?' Singh asked. 'On finding out the truth? You know I didn't kill anyone.'

What could he say? He had so many doubts but had to follow orders.

'I'm doing what I can, but for the moment, you're being moved.'

'I'm not sure I want to be moved. I hope the accommodation will not be worse than this pathetic excuse of a room.'

'Don't hold your breath. A police cell is not the most hospitable of places.'

'It's not fair. I've done nothing, broken no laws. I don't deserve to be placed in a police cell.'

'Well, it is as it is just now. Let's go,' McQueen said shortly. 'We need to get you over there by dawn.'

Galea pushed Singh out of the door and walked with him through the corridors to the back entrance.

They took the path, the same way that McQueen had gone to find where the murder took place. The prince stumbled a few times, complaining loudly about being forced to walk in handcuffs. They arrived at the same slipway, by Fort Manoel, as the first haze of light began to appear on the horizon. A rowboat, slightly larger than the traditional *dgħajsa* was tied up to a wooden post, two boatmen on board. One taller and thinner, with a black moustache, the other shorter, balding, with a grey beard. They wore traditional clothing: breeches, a sash tied around their waists, caps on their heads. Sergeant Galea called out to them in Maltese. The taller man shouted out a response and indicated they should climb into the boat.

McQueen's senses were tingling. This boat, and these boatmen, were different to the normal ones used in the harbours. The men looked tense, edgy. There was something about them that made him feel uneasy. He pulled Galea back by the shoulder.

'Are you sure about this?' he asked. 'Is this really your transport? Do you know these men, this boat? I don't like the look of them.'

Galea looked surprised. 'Yes, I am sure,' he said. 'Inspector Azzopardi gave me instructions. This is just as he said. A boat, two men, to take us to the landing place in Marsamuscetto, where police officers are waiting.'

The shorter boatman called out in Maltese, his voice gravelly. He sounded irritated.

'We have to go now,' Galea translated. 'It's beginning to get light.'

McQueen had already decided he was going to leave the island. Now he decided he could not leave Galea alone with these boatmen. He was going to go too. He would deal with the consequences later.

Galea pushed Prince Sundar toward the boat and stepped on board with him, helped by the shorter man. The taller man was working on unknotting the rope linking the boat to the wooden post. McQueen was at the water's edge and tried to join Galea on board. Instead of waiting for him, the bearded man started to propel the boat forward. The other man pulled in the rope and set to rowing with his oar. 'Hey!' McQueen shouted, splashing into the water up to his knees. He grabbed the side of the boat, but the boatman pushed him forcibly away. He lurched forward, trying to get to the boat again, but he was off balance, and ended up with his face in the water. He lost his footing and floundered, his suit and heavy boots pulling him down.

'Sergeant, watch out!' he called. He could see the taller boatman raising his oar behind Galea's head. *Too late*. The boatman hit Galea, and as he crumpled, pushed him into the water. Then the two men set to, rowing efficiently and swiftly, pulling away into the harbour.

McQueen splashed through the water as best he could, keeping his eyes on the point where Galea had gone down. He could see nothing. The young man seemed to have disappeared. But as he got closer, he could just about make out a dark shape coming up to the surface. He grabbed for it, his hand closing around the collar of a police tunic. He hauled it upward with all his strength. Galea's head came out of the water, spluttering. *Thank God for that, he's alive.*

'C'mon!' McQueen yelled. 'Let's get out of here.'

He pulled Galea back toward the slipway, splashing backward with an attempt at a swimming stroke. It was cold and the water was unpleasant; salty and filthy. He had to get them out of there as quickly as possible. He kept trying to find solid ground under his feet, eventually feeling some rocks. They were slippery, but he got just enough traction to be able to stumble forward. He threw Galea onto the slipway, then pulled himself out, working hard to get his breath.

'Made it,' he said.

Galea rolled over and sat up, rubbing the back of his head and coughing up water. McQueen sat down heavily next to him, pulse racing. Together they looked out at the rowing boat which, instead of crossing the harbour toward Valletta, was passing in front of Fort Manoel, heading toward the other side of the island.

'Not our greatest hour,' McQueen said. 'Who the hell were they?'

'I don't know, but they've got the prince.'

'Told you I didn't like the look of 'em.'

Galea was a picture of misery, sitting on the ground, seawater pooling around him. His face was pale in the faint light, his teeth chattering. Drops of water ran down his face from his sodden hair. 'What's going to happen?' he asked. 'I failed in my duty. What's Colonel Ellis going to say?'

'Don't you worry about him!' McQueen pulled Galea up to his feet. 'You did nothing wrong.'

He clapped the young man on the back. 'Go and get changed into warm clothes. The important thing is that you're alive and on dry land. Just you leave Superintendent Ellis to me.'

A couple of hours later, a genuine *dgħajsa* delivered McQueen and Galea to the quay at Marsamuscetto. McQueen counted fifteen police officers milling around, talking in groups. Police Superintendent Ellis stood in their midst, Inspector Azzopardi by his side.

'What the hell happened, McQueen?' Ellis said sharply.

'You tell me!' McQueen looked pointedly at Azzopardi. 'You set it up, Inspector. Sergeant Galea was quite clear about where the boat would land. Do you have any idea who those men were?'

Azzopardi shook his head. 'The boatmen who were supposed to take you were overpowered early this morning. They were left tied up in a boat store. Those two men took the boat, they must have found out about the plan.'

'They knew what they were doing, I'll give them that,' McQueen said. 'The boat disappeared off at a good speed.'

'It's been found, in Sliema,' Azzopardi said. 'They tied it up and left with the prince on foot. Nobody has seen them since; we have no idea where they've taken him.'

'For God's sake, McQueen!' Ellis said. 'This is a real crisis. The prince is dangerous. He's now at large, a murderer. Heaven knows what he's capable of. You need to find him, fast. I assume you're out of quarantine?'

McQueen nodded, patting his jacket pocket. 'I have a letter from the quarantine doctor.' He felt guilty, having practically forced the young doctor to give him written permission to leave the Lazzaretto, without Bonnici's knowledge. But this was more important. There was no way he had picked up the disease; he had been careful while inside.

Finding the prince would surely not take long. He thought about the network of contacts he had been building up with Galea over the past few months. It was a good time to draw on informants. Someone must know something.

'It's a small island, an even smaller city,' he said. 'He can't go far, or stay hidden for long without us finding him.'

'Marine police will search every boat, every ship leaving port,' Azzopardi said. 'He won't be able to get away by sea.'

'You'd better be right,' Ellis said. 'I'm going to see the governor now. He is not going to be happy, not at all. Inspector McQueen, come with me, now. Sergeant Galea, get back to work.'

Galea looked back at McQueen as he walked away, in the manner of a lamb being led away to slaughter.

Standing in the governor's plush office, McQueen was glad to be out and about again after being cooped up on Manoel Island but irritated beyond belief that he'd been made to look a fool by the men who had taken Prince Sundar.

The governor, sitting behind his oversized mahogany desk, was furious. He glowered at McQueen and Ellis from underneath his bushy white eyebrows.

'This is appalling,' he said. 'The Secretary of State for the Colonies is going to have to be informed. We must assume that having arranged this escape, the prince will go back to his plan to sail to Bombay and travel on to the Punjab.'

'I'm not so sure,' McQueen said. 'To me, it looked as if the prince was as surprised as we were when the boatmen took him. I don't think he had any idea of the plan.'

'Of course he did!' Ellis said. 'Who else would have wanted to make it happen? He must have found a way; bribed the guards.'

'I don't agree. I think this was organised by outsiders, but I don't know why.'

'Well, due to your negligence or incompetence, Inspector,

our prime suspect for the murder of Captain Buchanan is now on the loose. Further to that, he is a dangerous insurgent who poses a threat to the security of our empire,' the governor said.

'I'd argue that the Marine Police who organised the boat are equally to blame, would you not agree? How were we to know the boat we'd been directed to had been stolen?'

'Don't try and dodge the blame, Inspector. Listen here, I shall send my aide-de-camp Lieutenant Carstairs to work with you. We must work quickly, leave no stone unturned, find this Sikh nuisance as soon as we can. I will not be made a laughing stock. Get the so-called prince back and behind bars as soon as possible.'

CHAPTER NINETEEN

Valletta, Malta. Saturday, 23 October 1880

Under cover of darkness, it appeared no one had seen the two mystery boatmen and the prince once they had landed at Sliema. McQueen had called a team together at the police office. He had a room assigned to him, optimistically called the 'detective department'. It was on the ground floor, boasting three desks, various chairs, a filing cabinet, and a blackboard on a wooden stand. A big improvement on the cupboard he was given when he first arrived in Malta.

The team comprised Lieutenant Carstairs, Inspector Azzopardi, Sergeant Galea, two other sergeants and a police constable. When all the general chat had died down, McQueen stood by the blackboard, stick of chalk in hand.

'The big questions are: who knew the prince was being moved, and who stood to gain from kidnapping him before he got to the police cell? Any ideas as to who might be behind this?'

Azzopardi spoke first. 'I arranged the boat with my contact Schembri. I know him well. He told me he did not inform anyone of the plans. I believe him. The real boatmen agreed to meet at Barriera Wharf. The men that attacked them had scarves around their faces, so they could not be identified. Also, it was dark. They dragged them into a boat storeroom, by Nix Mangiari Steps.'

McQueen sketched a plan showing Manoel Island, Sliema, Marsamuscetto Harbour and Valletta. He drew a tiny boat at the Marsamuscetto landing place, with arrows showing the route to Fort Manoel and then round to Sliema.

'We know the boatmen were Maltese, but that's all. I've been wondering if there are any people from India living in Malta, who might be involved? Could there be any Sikhs? I'm looking to you, Carstairs. Any military?'

Carstairs shook his head. 'Not really. From time to time, we have Indian troops here, but none at the moment. Perhaps worth checking out the areas near the harbour?'

'I'll take some constables to the docks and the Three Cities,' Azzopardi said. 'We'll sweep through the area, asking at the boarding houses if anyone has heard or seen anything suspicious.'

'Good idea, take plenty of men. Make your presence felt.'

McQueen added the Three Cities to his plan. These were dockyard areas across the harbour, where many working families lived, packed into old townhouses.

'What else can we do? Any ideas?' he asked.

'We could go back to Manoel Island,' Galea suggested. 'Talk to Sciberras and the guards again. See if anyone can tell us anything new?'

'Good idea, Sergeant. You and I will do that. Carstairs, can you go to the telegraph office and get someone to check all the telegrams going out from Valletta since yesterday morning. Anything that could be a coded message, that could give the game away?'

'Certainly. My pleasure.'

McQueen turned to the rest of the officers. 'I'd like you men to go to Sliema. Start knocking on doors, check if anyone saw three men on the move. Somebody must have seen something.'

A couple of hours later, McQueen was back at the Lazzaretto packing up his belongings as quickly as he could, keen to get away. He heard a knock at the door and looked up.

'It's open,' he said.

Nellie Byrne appeared in the doorway and stood watching him.

'Inspector, I've been waiting to see you.' She nodded toward his bag. 'Are you leaving us?'

'Yes, allowed out, thank God.'

'I'm hoping I can go soon as well, maybe tomorrow, if I get permission from the quarantine doctor. I'm going to stay in Valletta for a week or two.'

'Right, well, I've got to go now.'

He finished stuffing his Gladstone bag, fastened the clasp and went to walk past her.

'Wait. I wanted to ask you about Prince Sundar. Someone told me he'd escaped. Is that right?'

Is nothing secret around here?

'What have you heard?'

'That he got taken away by boat.'

'Aye, that's right enough.'

'I need to know what's happening, Inspector. Do you know anything about who has taken him?'

She was talking in a low, earnest tone, without her usual detached, somewhat amused manner.

'You know I can't discuss that with you,' he said. 'It's a police matter.'

'Sam, *please.* I promised the prince's father that I'd look out for him. I'm worried for him. He could be in danger. I want to know if he's in safe hands or not.'

She pressed a folded piece of paper into his hand.

'I'm going to be staying here when I get away from this prison.'

He opened it up to read *Hotel Britannia, Strada Reale.*

'Please, let me know if you find him.'

He tried to read her expression. She was deadly serious. *Why is it so important to her?*

'I cannot stress too much how crucial this is, Sam,' she said. 'I need to know at once, before anyone else.'

He folded up the piece of paper again. 'I'll see what I can do,' he said. 'Got to find the little beggar first.'

As he walked past her, she put her hand on his arm.

'You have to trust me, Sam. Can you do that?'

He looked into her clear, green eyes, seeing intelligence and a steely determination. She knew more than she was letting on, he was sure. He nodded slightly. 'Aye, maybe,' he said, pulling away.

'I'll see you again when I'm off the island,' Nellie called after him as he walked down the corridor. He put his hand up in acknowledgement, without looking back.

McQueen headed back to the Lazzaretto quay, where Galea was waiting for him. He had suggested the sergeant should talk to the servants and merchants who congregated there from early morning. The interview with Sciberras had been a total waste of time. It was nothing to do with him, or his staff, he had said. The prince had been well looked after while in his charge, safely kept under lock and key. He seemed to take great pleasure in rubbing in that it was under police custody that Singh had been taken. McQueen, who had had enough of the Lazzaretto and its keeper, did not bother to stay for long.

As he got to the quay, McQueen saw Galea deep in conversation with one of the boatmen. He noticed the sergeant slipping the man a few coins, thanking him profusely, before turning away.

'Got any good information?' he asked.

'Very good information,' Galea said, looking pleased with himself. 'But not about the prince. It's about Sciberras.' He nodded toward the boatman, who had walked back to his water taxi. 'That man says we should do some checking about the quarantine grain stores. He says it is well-known that grain keeps disappearing – into thin air. He thinks perhaps it is being smuggled into the port in Valletta, sold on the black market.'

'Any proof of this?'

'No, just stories. But we should find out, yes?'

'Perhaps, but not just now.' He would love to see Sciberras unveiled as the scoundrel he had always suspected he was, but finding the prince had to be the priority.

'Let's get back to the mainland, away from this godforsaken place,' he said.

As they climbed down into the waiting *dgħajsa*, McQueen remembered he had not gone to the hospital to see Bonnici, to let him know what was happening. He felt a pang of guilt. Here he was, relishing the chance to quit Manoel Island, getting out of quarantine a few days early, and leaving the doctor behind without even saying farewell.

CHAPTER TWENTY

Valletta, Malta. Saturday, 23 October 1880

McQueen was never happier to be back at his lodgings in Strada Ponente. A typical townhouse, tall and narrow, it was run with efficiency by his landlady, *Sinjura* Caruso. She greeted him at the door in her usual cool manner. He never could tell what she thought of him. She disapproved of the work he did, believing he was a bad influence on her ten-year-old son Antonio, but she did not appear to dislike him. The fact he got on so well with Bonnici was in his favour, given that she and the doctor were now courting.

'Oh, so you're back,' she said, letting him in. 'Well, your room is not ready. You should have let me know.'

'Pleasure to see you too, Mrs Caruso. How's that little scamp of yours?'

As he stepped into the entrance hall, McQueen heard the scrape of a chair, then footsteps as Antonio came running up, a big grin on his face.

'Mister McQueen – you are here. I miss you!'

McQueen ruffled the boy's already untidy hair. 'I hope you've been keeping out of trouble, eh?'

He was fond of the lad, who had worked for him as a message boy for a few weeks in the summer, until he started school. This arrangement had led Antonio into great danger, the main reason why his landlady was wary of him.

'Did you see any ghosts?' Antonio asked. 'My friends say people hear screams at night at the Lazzaretto. I wish I stay there!'

'No ghosts, but I'm glad to be away from the island, I can tell you. Any chance of a beer?'

He went into the kitchen and sat at the old scrubbed-pine table, making himself at home as *Sinjura* Caruso poured him a beer. Antonio was chatting away nineteen to the dozen, telling him all about school and his new friends.

'Hush, Ninu,' *Sinjura* Caruso said. 'You make too much noise.' She placed the beer glass in front of McQueen.

'Please, tell me, how is Doctor Bonnici? I am so worried about him. There is the cholera, yes?'

There was no way of hiding the truth from her. 'Yes, I'm afraid so. At the moment he is treating an Englishwoman, Miss Copeland. He is hopeful she will recover. But there are other patients who are not doing so well.'

'He risks his life. I don't like it. What happens if he gets the cholera?

'He is careful, I can tell you that,' McQueen said. 'He knows what he's doing, and he is taking every precaution.'

'But he's not strong. I wish he would leave it to the doctors at the Lazzaretto and come back here.' *Sinjura* Caruso turned away and started scrubbing the kitchen work surfaces with vigour.

'He'll be back soon, I'm sure.' He wished he felt as certain as he sounded. He knew the doctor would always put duty above his own health issues.

However, there was no time to dwell on such concerns. He had a job to do. He stood up purposefully.

'Time and tide wait for no man. I'll be heading back to the police office.'

'It is your favourite rabbit stew for dinner, Inspector. Don't be late.'

He pulled a face behind her back. He was served rabbit stew at least twice a week and the novelty was beginning to wear thin.

'I cannot wait, Mrs Caruso. I cannot wait.'

McQueen arrived back at the detective department to find a note folded up on his desk. He recognised the careful handwriting of Sergeant Galea.

'I have information about the grain store,' he read. 'Meet at Attard Brothers warehouse by the waterfront in Senglea at three o'clock.'

Instantly annoyed, he scrunched up the note and threw it into the wastepaper basket across the room. It would take close to an hour to get there, walking to Grand Harbour and taking a water taxi. He wanted to get on with the search for the prince, not waste time on this trifling matter. He had not given Galea permission to run his own investigation. The sergeant was too keen by half. A few weeks of detective training and he thought he was Scotland Yard.

He sighed but decided he had better set off. It might provide a chance to meet up with Azzopardi as well, who was in Senglea knocking on doors. Striding through the streets of Valletta, he was glad of his linen suit. When would the weather finally cool down? Here it was, the third week in October and it felt about eighty degrees. By the time he got to Lascaris Wharf, he could feel sweat beginning to drip down his face. He took off his hat to mop his forehead and his damp hairline. There was barely anyone around. After several attempts, he managed to get the attention of a boatman, napping under the canopy of his *dgħajsa,* who reluctantly agreed to row him across the harbour. The man did not speak any English, but spent the whole twenty-minute journey delivering a monologue that McQueen imagined to be along the lines of 'don't you know it's siesta time, when decent folk should be resting in the shade?'

Reaching the dockyard, McQueen alighted, giving the ferryman a generous tip, to make up for disturbing his slumber. He set off in search of the warehouse, stopping a passerby to check the address. The warehouse stretched along the southeast of the main waterfront, a flat-fronted limestone building with ten offices, each with a doorway featuring an arched window above it, and two small windows on each side. Attard Brothers was the third office from the right, indicated by a placard on the left-hand door. It declared the brothers' business to be 'Import and General Export Provision'.

The painted wooden doors were closed, with an iron bar through the handles and a padlock. The padlock had been opened. McQueen bashed on the door, with no response. He looked around. It was quiet everywhere, no one in sight. His senses were tingling. Something did not feel right. Where was Sergeant Galea? He pulled out his pocket watch. It was just before three o'clock. He banged on the door again, but there was no sound from inside. He felt he should go in to see if Galea was there already. Taking the padlock off, he slid the iron bar out from the handles and opened the door.

It was dark inside, barely any light getting through the grimy windows at the front. A little sunlight slanted through two small windows at the back. The space was largely empty, just a few crates on the left-hand side. The floor was dusty. He called out: 'Is there anyone here?' There was a rustle at the back of the room. He jumped, but it was just a cat emerging from behind a crate. It bolted past him out of the front door, which he had left slightly ajar. Still, he sensed he should not be there. He had been set up. Galea was not going to arrive.

McQueen looked around for possible weapons. He thought he could make out a broken crate. Perhaps a piece of wood. He walked toward it, but before he got there, he heard a crash as the front door slammed shut behind him. He spun round and saw three figures coming toward him. The two on the outside were heavy-set muscle men. In between them a small, shabby creature who looked familiar – something about the way he moved. As he got close, he could see the man's face, grinning at him with a gappy smile he instantly recognised.

'Inspector McQueen. I have message for you.'

'Camilleri.' This was the informant who used to work for disgraced former police superintendent Captain Borg. 'What do you want?'

'Message is – stay out of our business. Boys, hold him.'

The two bruisers moved forward. McQueen stepped back but was not quick enough. One grabbed him by the left arm, the other by the right. However much he fought against them, they held him firm.

Camilleri brought his face unpleasantly close. 'You ask too many questions. This is warning. It is worse next time.'

McQueen saw Camilleri's arm move back, a leather cosh in his hand. He tried to pull back but heard a loud crack as the cosh hit him on the right side of his forehead. The henchmen dropped his arms. He fell straight to his knees, watching the hard floor come up to meet him. Then everything went black.

McQueen came back to consciousness, feeling intensely nauseous. Sergeant Galea was crouching next to him looking deeply concerned.

'Are you all right, sir?'

He went to sit up. 'Give me a moment,' he said groggily. 'Got to check the damage.'

He put his hand up to his forehead – no blood, but an egg-shaped lump above his right eye. His ribs hurt too. He hauled himself off the ground.

'What happened?' Galea asked. 'When I got to the door, I saw two big men standing to the side and that pest Camilleri kicking you. They saw me and pushed past. I tried to catch them, but they got away.'

'That little bastard Camilleri coshed me. Said he had a message – for us to stay away.'

'I'm sorry, sir, I was late. I got held up. There was this accident with a cart, down the road.'

'No doubt planned. You know what?'

'What?'

'This has all the hallmarks of your uncle's work. Wanting to get at me, but to keep you out of it.'

Captain Borg had been stripped of his post as police superintendent for obstructing McQueen's previous investigation. He was awaiting trial but somehow seemed to keep avoiding it. Every time the date approached there was another complication and a postponement. He was also known to have dubious business connections with his brother, Gabriel, but there was never enough evidence to convict. Galea was trying his best to distance himself from this branch of his family.

'Sorry, sir. I hope it is not him.'

'Let's get out of here.'

They came out of the warehouse, the bright light making McQueen wince.

'Could you turn the sun down a bit, Sergeant?' he asked.

He could just about make out a silhouetted group of men running toward them. Inspector Azzopardi, along with two police constables.

'What's happened?' Azzopardi asked. 'We heard the whistle.'

'It's nothing,' McQueen said. 'Sergeant Galea set up a meeting with a person of dubious character. We'll be sorting it out later, won't we, Sergeant?'

Galea was a picture of unhappiness. McQueen almost felt sorry for him, but he did not like being shown up in front of Azzopardi. Also, the way that Galea had been set up was distinctly annoying. Following up on the grain-smuggling was not a priority and now McQueen felt he was at a disadvantage.

Azzopardi peered at him. 'That's a serious black eye you're getting there, Inspector,' he said.

'Och, it'll be fine.' He was not looking forward to what he would see in the mirror. His thumping head was suggesting perhaps it would not be great. 'Have you heard anything that can lead us to the prince?'

'A lot of what we heard is not repeatable. How many Maltese swear words do you know, Inspector? When people did answer their doors, and mostly they didn't, there were crazy rumours. That a madman from India was on the loose who would murder everyone in their beds. That he was armed with a giant sword. Oh, and that the cholera is rampant, two hundred people already dead and soon to be spread over the whole of Malta. I don't know how these stories spread so quickly.'

So much for his first day out of quarantine. A wild goose chase followed by a head injury. Things were going to have to start getting better.

'Let's get a beer,' he suggested to Galea. 'Then think of another plan.'

CHAPTER TWENTY-ONE

Valletta, Malta. Sunday, 24 October 1880

The next morning, McQueen walked to the Auberge d'Auvergne, his head thumping with every step. He was trying to work out his next move. Who had taken the prince? Who would want to save him from custody and a trial? Sikh followers, clearly. But Carstairs had said there were very few Indians living in Malta and Azzopardi had not found any staying near the docks. So, who could have organised the escape? They would have to have known when the prince was going to be moved.

McQueen thought about who was privy to that information. Colonel Ellis, Azzopardi, and Galea, obviously – all very committed to bringing the prisoner safely across to the police cells. Was there anyone else he had discussed the case with? He cast his mind back to the Lazzaretto. He had spoken to Nellie, of course. She had been so keen to pump him for information about the abduction. But that was afterwards. He would swear she had no idea it was going to happen.

He also remembered telling Bonnici that the prince was about to be moved. Yet he knew the doctor would have spoken to no one. He was fully taken up with caring for cholera patients, from that time right up until Singh disappeared. *Was there anyone else?* An image of Maria Tanti, walking away from the parlatorio after their last meeting suddenly came to him. She had asked about the prince, and he had told her about the plans to move him. Why had he done that? He should not have trusted anybody. Had she passed this information on to someone, either deliberately, or without realising? He quickened his pace. The *Malta Post* was at the foot of Strada San Giovanni, only a few minutes away. He needed to speak to Maria, as soon as he could.

When McQueen was shown into the editor's office, he found Maria on her own. A pile of newspapers was on the desk. She was poring over some sheets, pencil in hand. She jumped up immediately, looking at him in shock.

'Inspector McQueen! What are you doing here? And what in God's name have you done to yourself?' she asked.

He had forgotten about the large lump on his forehead and the deep burgundy swelling around his right eye.

'It's nothing,' he said. 'Looks worse than it is.'

'Did someone hit you? Who was it? What's been going on? And why are you out of quarantine?'

He explained that he had been given permission to leave the Lazzaretto, to track down the prince after his escape. That the black eye was nothing to do with it – something he had to sort out later.

'Oh, my goodness,' Maria said. 'Prince Sundar has escaped?

I had no idea all this was going on! I've been head down, getting the newspaper printed and out of the door.'

'Where's your father?'

'Taken ill, resting at home. He's all right, but he had an attack of angina. The doctor says he has to rest.'

McQueen frowned. That was bad news. He liked Tanti a great deal. 'Let him know I asked after him,' he said. 'Wish him a speedy recovery.'

'I will.'

'Listen, this is important. I'm following up on everyone who knew that Prince Sundar was going to be moved to the police cells in Valletta. When you came to the Lazzaretto, with the information about Browne, I'm fairly sure I said something to you. Does that ring a bell?'

'Oh, um...' Maria looked away for a moment.

'I see I've hit a nerve,' he said. 'Come on, you have to tell me.'

'All right,' she said eventually. 'I *might* have said something about the prince being moved, but I didn't know exactly when it was going to happen. I didn't realise it was told in confidence, sorry.'

'Who?' he asked. 'Who did you talk to?'

'Giuseppe Trapani. He came to me, said he wanted the *Malta Post* to tell the story about Sundar Singh's arrest. He was angry, said the prince was being scapegoated. But I didn't know he was planning anything.'

Trapani – that young firebrand. What the hell is he up to?

'Where is he? Do you know where to find him?'

Maria nodded, jumping up from her chair. 'I think so.' She ran over to her reticule, which was hanging from a hook on the back of the door. 'He gave me this address. Said I could contact him there.'

She pulled out a piece of paper and handed it over.

'I'm sorry, I just wanted to see if there was a story that we could cover in the paper. I didn't know the prince had disappeared. If I had, I promise I would have let you know.'

McQueen looked at the paper: *45 Strada Santa Lucia*.

'Where's this then?'

'It's right by the entrance to the Manderaggio. I wouldn't go there myself. It's too dangerous.'

Finally, thank God, he had something to go on. That stupid young man, Trapani. McQueen had little time for him. Trapani saw himself as a patriot and an agitator, with grand ideas of leading a movement to throw off British colonial rule. In reality, he was little more than a troublemaker with ill-thought-through plans. What was he trying to achieve, if he did take the prince?

'Right,' he said. 'Time for me to pay *Sinjur* Trapani a bit of a visit.'

'Be careful, he has associates that are known to be violent – you remember the Gruppo Militante Pro Italiano?'

'I'll take Sergeant Galea with me. That'll put the fear of God in 'em.'

Maria smiled, then shook her head.

'Don't underestimate them,' she said. 'Let me know what happens. And please, don't let Trapani know I helped you. I want him to keep talking to me, so I can follow up on the story.'

The girl was incorrigible.

McQueen went back to the police office to pick up Galea. Over the past couple of months, they had ventured into the area known as the Manderaggio several times.

An overcrowded district known for its poverty and lawlessness, it had been the home of criminals and outcasts for hundreds of years. He had explained to Galea that they needed to have a reach into the parts of the city seen as off-limits. People they could pay, if necessary, for information on the criminals operating there, and the crimes being committed. The young sergeant had an air of innocence about him. He needed to get a bit rougher around the edges. To give him his due, though, he was making an effort.

They found the building on Strada Santa Lucia. It was old, made of a soft limestone, four storeys high. Steps led up to the building entrance, where a thin young man was leaning against the doorway, smoking a pipe. He stared down at them with open hostility. As they got closer, he looked to be no older than fifteen, wearing a grimy white shirt, coarse cotton waistcoat, and brown trousers rolled up at the hem. His feet were bare. He had a black cap on his head, covering up unruly curls. He was no doubt very proud of the downy dark hair on his top lip that passed for a moustache.

'I'm looking for Giuseppe Trapani?' McQueen asked. The lad looked at him blankly.

'Giuseppe Trapani?' he said again.

'Stay here,' the young man muttered. He disappeared inside the building. Eventually they heard footsteps, then Trapani appeared. He stopped and looked at them for a moment, then shrugged.

'Come in,' he said. His voice was strongly accented. McQueen knew his English was a little limited.

He led them into a room on the left of the hallway. It looked like an office, with a large rickety desk and about ten chairs scattered around. He leant back against the desk, glaring at them, arms crossed in front of him. His long hair hung around his face, making him look unkempt and a little wild.

'What you do here?' he growled. 'How you know this address?'

'It wasn't hard,' McQueen said. 'Perhaps you think you've done a good job hiding yourselves, but it didn't take long.'

'What you want?'

'Where's Prince Sundar Singh? We know you have him.'

'No idea what you talk about.' Trapani's bravado was impressive. His eyes gave nothing away as he continued to glare at them.

'Come on, man,' McQueen said. 'The two boatmen who abducted the prince. We know they are part of your militant group.' *Not strictly true, but an easy deduction.*

Trapani launched into a tirade in Maltese, walking around the room, waving his arms. McQueen sighed. 'What is he saying?' he asked Galea.

'Oh, he says we're always blaming him and his group, that they have done nothing wrong. We are the problem, working for the British, and I am a traitor to my people.' Galea looked a little indignant at these last words.

'Don't worry about it, Sergeant. You'll get that a lot in your job. Tell him to speak English, or I'll arrest him for obstructing the police. I don't have time for this.'

Galea spoke to Trapani in Maltese, who went back to leaning on the desk, facing them.

'Let's just drop the pretence, Trapani,' McQueen said. 'You're in trouble, and you know it. You've taken him, haven't you? You know how important Prince Sundar Singh is to the British, how they need him to be in custody. Did you think you could use him to lever some of your political demands from the governor? Is that why you've kidnapped him?'

Trapani rolled his eyes, saying nothing.

'The problem is, we know you've got him. You won't get away with it. You've hidden him here, in the Manderaggio. I'll go and get a search party, and we'll find him in no time. Isn't that right, Sergeant?'

'Yes, sir!' Galea said smartly.

'The penalty for aiding and abetting a prisoner to escape from custody would be imprisonment. I think even you can admit there's not a lot of insurrection you can organise from a prison cell. If you take us to him instead, that will save a lot of time and a lot of man hours. I think the magistrates will be less inclined to go for the full penalty. Your role could be minimised, likely leading to just a fine and a slap on the wrist.'

McQueen watched Trapani carefully. He gave nothing away with his eyes, but there was a slight shift in his shoulders. He was thinking about it.

Suddenly, it came to McQueen in a moment of clarity. 'In fact,' he said, 'now you've met the prince, I'll wager you've not found him to be the character you thought he would be. He'll have been complaining about his quarters, saying he didn't ask to be saved. I know, I've met him. Is he worth it, Trapani? I think you're concerned the governor won't want to negotiate for his release. Why don't you lead us to him now, and we'll take him off your hands.'

He waited, while Trapani thought it through. Finally, the young man spoke. 'I say nothing,' he said. 'Perhaps we have a plan, perhaps not. But what if my friend takes you to a place, where you find the Indian? Is still the case he is innocent of the crime, no? If you take him to police cells, I do not believe he will get a fair trial.'

'I understand your concern. But you have my word I'll do everything in my power to make sure he is treated fairly. It'll be better for everyone if he is taken back into safekeeping, I guarantee.'

McQueen felt this was as much as he could promise. He could sense Trapani relenting. The young man raked his long hair back with his fingers, then straightened his shoulders. 'Wait there,' he said.

He left the room. McQueen looked at Galea and nodded as they heard low voices murmuring in the hallway outside.

'I think we've got him,' he said. 'He'll do it.'

Trapani came back in, bringing the young lad with him, along with an older, tough-looking character, arms covered in tattoos. 'This is Luigi,' he said. 'He will take you.'

'Did you know this is called the *tomba tal-Mandraġġ?*' Galea said as they followed Luigi down the steep steps into the depths of the Manderaggio. 'That means the tomb, or the grave.'

'Very reassuring,' McQueen said. 'You wouldn't want people thinking they were going anywhere cheery.'

A narrow street lay in front of them, getting increasingly narrower as they made their way farther into the district. Unlike the straight, ordered streets of Valletta, the Manderaggio was a labyrinth of alleys and irregular buildings. It was dark and filthy. No sunlight could get through. McQueen could feel the humidity pressing down on him. *Imagine what this would be like in the hottest part of summer.* They passed by noisy, barefoot children playing in the dirt, a young woman washing her feet at the water pump, groups of women gossiping at street corners and hard-faced men watching suspiciously from doorways.

Eventually, Luigi led them up crumbling steps and through a heavy door into a dirty old building. They carried on up a narrow staircase for two more floors, before entering a dark corridor. Luigi stomped up to the last room on the right and bashed hard on the door, calling out in Maltese. No sound from inside. Luigi stood waiting impatiently, muttering to himself as he shifted his weight from one side to the other. Finally, he reached in his pocket for a key and unlocked the door.

McQueen could hear him calling out as he entered the room, but there was no response. Galea followed Luigi in, McQueen close behind. All he could make out inside was a vague outline of a bed in the corner, with an inert body slumped on top. Luigi ran over to the body, shaking it while rattling off a volley of words in Maltese.

McQueen strode over to see who it was. A stocky square-jawed man with short, dark hair, evidently an associate of Luigi's. He was beginning to come to, eyes slightly open, trying to speak but slurring his words.

'For God's sake, what's the man saying?' McQueen asked. 'What's going on?'

'Someone forced his way into the room. He had a knife. He threatened this man, knocked him out,' Galea translated.

'Where is the prince? Ask him, where is he?'

The man shook his head, mumbling something almost inaudible.

'He's gone. He's been taken.'

'God damn it! Who was it? Who was it that took him? Does he know?'

Galea asked in Maltese.

Even McQueen understood the answer. *Borg's man again.*

'Camilleri. It was Camilleri.'

CHAPTER TWENTY-TWO

Valletta, Malta. Sunday, 24 October 1880

A few hours later, McQueen was back in the police office, feet up on the desk, hands behind his head. He was simmering with frustration. The second time Camilleri had crossed his path in as many days. The man was everywhere. What was Borg up to? How many pies did he have his fingers in?

He and Galea had given up after a wild goose chase around the Manderaggio, asking if anyone had seen Camilleri, with or without a turbaned young man. Nobody would talk to them. Why would they? Especially him, standing out as a foreigner as well as a police officer. Since then, he had sent Galea home for his traditional Sunday meal with his parents. McQueen was thinking he should go back to his lodgings as well, but in his current mood that was probably not the best idea. He was not sure he could be civil to anyone, even Antonio. He would not want to scare the boy by saying or doing the wrong thing.

Inspector Azzopardi had made an appearance at the office a

short while ago. He was also leaving at the end of the day. He and his officers had made extensive inquiries, looking for information about Indian visitors to Valletta, but they had drawn a blank. Azzopardi had also set up a watch at the two main harbours in the city, looking out for suspicious people or activity. He made it clear he was having to do a lot of extra hours, which he was perfectly happy to do, of course, as a result of McQueen's shortcomings.

A knock at the door interrupted McQueen's brooding.

A young police officer appeared and handed over an envelope, saluting before disappearing again. At least someone was still showing him some respect.

He recognised the distinctive handwriting on the front at once. It was from Nellie Byrne. He tore it open and pulled out a sheet of paper:

> *Inspector McQueen*
>
> *I have something important to discuss with you. Please come to my rooms at the Britannia Hotel at 8pm. It's essential that you come alone.*
>
> *Nellie Byrne*

He raised his eyebrows. *What is this going to be about?* He pulled out his pocket watch. A couple of hours to go. He dashed off a note to *Sinjura* Caruso, telling her not to expect him for dinner. He would get something to eat, with a beer, before heading to the hotel.

Nellie opened the door to her suite almost as soon as McQueen knocked. Behind the door was a small hallway.

'Hi, come in.' She smiled briefly, then led him into a private sitting room. The room was well-lit, with a ceiling-mounted gaslight and four pairs of wall lights. It was comfortably furnished with soft armchairs and a writing desk. A small table was laid out with a tray of glasses and a whisky decanter. He could see floor-to-ceiling windows at the end of the room, with doors leading on to a balcony, but it was dark, and the windows were closed.

'What did you want to see me for?' he asked. He didn't feel the need for social niceties. She had asked him there for a reason.

'Drink?' she asked. 'I ordered some whisky.'

'I'll not say no.'

She poured him a glass of whisky, then handed it over, a slight smile hovering at her lips.

He took it and sat down in one of the armchairs, stretching his legs out, knowing he was acting unmannerly, but not caring.

'You look rough,' Nellie said. 'What's with the black eye?'

'All in a day's work,' he said. 'A lot's been going on.'

He took a sip of the whisky, watching her carefully. She sat opposite him and smoothed down her skirt. She looked composed but a little tense, the corners of her mouth twitching every few moments as she looked down into her drink. He wished she would get to the point. He was tired, irritable. He took another sip.

'Go on,' he said. 'What is it?'

'It's Prince Sundar,' she said. 'If I tell you something, you have to promise to follow my wishes.'

'I'll do no such thing.' He was not in the mood to play games. 'Just tell me, then I'll decide.'

She stared at him for a moment, before making up her mind and nodding. 'All right then. I'll tell you. He's here. I've got him.' She took a big swig of her whisky, looking at him expectantly over the top of the glass.

McQueen sat upright. 'You what? How?'

'I want your help to get him away from here.'

'I can't do that. He's to be locked up, charged.'

'You know as well as I do that he's innocent.'

'How did you find him?'

'That doesn't matter now. Let's just say it's all about knowing the right people.'

McQueen thought of the link between Sciberras and Borg. Clearly, they were working together. It was Borg's man who took the prince.

'Sciberras,' he said. 'You've been talking to him all along, haven't you? How much have you paid him?'

'Enough,' she said. 'Apparently, it's easy to find someone in the Manderaggio, if you know who to ask. The Gruppo Militante weren't exactly quiet about it, and the prince is pretty noticeable, you know.'

'Where is he?' McQueen felt anger bubbling up inside him. He could not believe she had done this, snatching the prince just as he was about to re-arrest him.

'He's safe, that's all you need to know.'

'But why? Why would you do this?'

'That's easy. I'm being paid. I told you I know Sir Anokh Singh, the prince's father. It's more than that. I'm working for him. My orders are to keep him safe and to get him back to Bombay, where his cousin is waiting for him.'

'That's not going to happen.'

'It is, Sam. And I want your help. Look, I know you don't believe the prince is guilty. If we leave it up to Colonel Ellis, he'll be tried and executed within weeks. If I didn't involve you, I reckon you'd find out what's going on and stop me. I'd rather you were on side, that you know what the plan is. You can turn a blind eye, then everyone gets what they want.'

'You're taking a big risk.'

'I know what I'm doing.'

McQueen threw the remainder of the whisky down his throat.

He leant forward. 'So, let me get this right. You expect me to aid and abet the prince's escape because you don't think he'll get a fair trial. But you know full well I'm a police officer and that I have to follow orders and procedure.'

Nellie laughed. 'Oh, come on, Inspector, I've seen the look on your face when you talk about Ellis! You can't stand the man. You'll enjoy stealing a march on him. I'm not asking you to do anything. You just need to look the other way.'

She got up and moved across to the table to get the decanter. Then she leant across to pour him another drink. He watched the whisky spilling into the glass, to try and distract himself from how close she was to him. But he could not help catching her eye as she straightened up. She smiled at him, tilting her head to one side, an expectant glint in her eye.

The air seemed to change between them. He had struck up a good understanding with Nellie, the time they had spent together in quarantine. Now it seemed he was being pulled in deeper. He was attracted by the merriment in her eyes, her quick wit and intelligence. It was unexpected, that he should be drawn to her so strongly. But this was a murder investigation. She was somehow at the centre of it, attempting to pull the strings. It was a bad idea, he knew it.

He cleared his throat, sensing his feelings were being betrayed by the colour rushing to his face. He shifted in his seat, feeling bulky and awkward. Did she see something in him, or was it all just a game? She went back to her seat, picked up her drink and watched him as she took a sip. It was up to him to make the next move.

'So, where are we then?' he asked gruffly. 'What's your plan?'

'I've booked a first-class ticket to Bombay on the SS *Arcadia*. The prince will accompany me as a manservant, along with my lady's maid. They are booked in the servants' quarters. The ship leaves around dawn on Tuesday, so we just have one day to lie low and stay undiscovered.'

'You think you'll get away with that?'

'I do. It's pretty common for someone like me to take an Indian servant on a trip like mine. Helping to smooth the way, carry the bags, that kind of thing.'

'Not sure he'll be too happy with that.'

Nellie shrugged. 'He doesn't have much choice.'

'I still don't see why you're doing this. You say you're being paid, but I thought you had plenty of money.'

'I do, but a girl can always use more. Have you any idea how expensive it is to travel? Besides, I'm easily bored. I like a challenge. Throw in a bit of danger and I'm there.'

Nellie leant forward, tucking a stray strand of hair behind her ear.

'So come on, Inspector. What do you say? Will you keep your distance and allow us to get away? Do we have a deal?'

'I don't know,' he said slowly, swirling the whisky around in his glass. 'I have to think about it.'

A sudden loud knock broke through the quietness of the room. Nellie sprang to her feet. She put her finger to her lips, signalling to McQueen to get up.

'Who is it?' she called out.

'Captain Borg,' came the muffled response through the door. 'I need to see you.'

'Just a minute!'

McQueen's instinct was to confront Borg and send him packing. How dare he call on a woman on her own in her hotel suite? But then he remembered his own situation. He should not be found here, himself.

Nellie pushed him into her bedroom and went to shut the door.

'Stay in there,' she said in a low voice. 'I'll get rid of him as quickly as I can.'

'Be careful,' he said. 'Don't trust him. He's a nasty piece of work.'

McQueen put his ear to the door, listening as Nellie let the captain into the sitting room. *Will he notice the two glasses, the whisky decanter?* He heard the rumble of Borg's deep voice, Nellie's firm responses. He could not hear the words, but the exchange seemed to be getting increasingly fractious. It went on for some time, Nellie's voice getting more and more strident. Finally, he heard her call out, 'How dare you? Get out!' He had his hand on the door handle, ready to burst through and confront Borg, but the voices died down. Instead, he heard retreating footsteps and a door banging shut.

As he opened the door, Nellie came back from the hallway, cheeks glowing. 'Did you hear that villain?' She laughed. 'I sent him packing. He was trying to get more money out of me.'

'I've had dealings with him before. Police are keeping an eye on him. He'll not get away with it.'

'That's what I like about you, Sam. You go after your man.'

She drew close and straightened his collar. 'You *are* going to wait until we've gone, though, aren't you?' she said softly.

He took her hand and moved it away, looking into her eyes. He was attracted to her, but still unsure of what game she was playing.

'Promise me you'll do the right thing and let the prince go?' she pleaded. 'He's just a boy, he doesn't deserve to be treated this way. He needs protecting.'

McQueen pulled her close for a second. She rested her head on his shoulder. He could feel her heartbeat.

'I'll see what I can do,' he said.

He was drawn to her, her compassion, her lively spirit and her wit. She felt warm and strong in his arms. But it was late, he needed to get back to his lodgings. People would be wondering where he was. He remembered Bonnici, tending the cholera patients in hospital. He owed it to everyone not to get involved.

'I have to go,' he said, pulling away. Could he trust her? Or was she just trying to use her charms to get her way?

As he left, picking up his hat from the table in the hall and placing it firmly on his head, he knew he was not going to do as she asked. It was not in his nature to look the other way when a crime was being committed.

CHAPTER TWENTY-THREE

Valletta, Malta. Monday, 25 October 1880

Maria felt she had been left high and dry. Inspector McQueen had not sent any messages since he disappeared into the Manderaggio. She did not dare follow up with Trapani until she knew what had transpired. Yet she wanted to keep working on the story of Buchanan's murder, and what had happened in the Lazzaretto. She had been thinking of different angles, wondering if she could get more information from the people who were now coming out of quarantine. She had heard that Nellie Byrne, the well-known American heiress and traveller, had left Manoel Island and was staying in the Britannia Hotel. So, dressed in her smartest day clothes, with her notebook and pen in her reticule, she set off to try and get an interview.

The man at the reception desk was exceptionally well turned-out. She suspected he was the manager. Perhaps in his early forties, sporting a shiny waxed moustache, the same black colour as his combed-back hair, he looked down his nose at Maria when she presented her card.

'Miss Byrne gave strict instructions she's not to be disturbed,' he said in a haughty voice.

'I'm from the *Malta Post*. Please send a messenger with a note from me. I want to write about Miss Byrne's amazing adventures. I am sure the readers will want to hear that such a famous traveller is currently staying at this esteemed establishment. Surely you know we have the widest distribution to English speakers in Malta.'

He thought for a moment, his moustache twitching from side to side.

'Very well,' he said. 'You may send a message – but of course she'll most likely refuse to see you.'

'Thank you.'

Maria scribbled a note and sent it with her card.

I am working with Inspector McQueen on the investigation of Captain Buchanan's death. Please will you allow me to come and talk to you about your experience at the Lazzaretto? Every detail is important as we piece together the story of what happened. I would so value your time.

Yours Faithfully, Maria Tanti.

She stood impatiently by a stand covered in tourist brochures as the note was taken away by a message boy. Her eyes roamed over offers of boat trips to see the Blue Grotto, ferries to Gozo, day trips to Città Vecchia or the temples at Ħaġar Qim. Eventually the boy came back and handed her a note.

Certainly, come on up! Nellie Byrne.

'She says yes,' Maria told the hotel manager, trying not to sound too triumphant.

'Very well. It's the Majestic Suite, third floor.'

As she walked up the three flights of stairs, Maria could not help feeling a little nervous. It was her dream to travel the world – anywhere away from Malta. To have so much money, the freedom to go wherever she wanted. That, to her, would be heaven. And to have the confidence to travel alone. Nellie Byrne must be a formidable woman. Would she really be prepared to talk to the deputy editor of a small Maltese newspaper?

When Nellie Byrne opened the door and invited her in, Maria's worst fears were realised. She felt small and insignificant, her clothes dowdy and plain, as she followed Nellie into a sitting room. The room was so grand, and Nellie herself so tall and confident, Maria immediately wished she had not come. The American was younger than she had expected, stylish but in an understated way, and with an aura about her that was completely intimidating.

'Come in, sit down, what can I do for you?' Nellie asked. Her voice was warm, with a slight accent. Maria took a deep breath. She needed to sound confident herself, even if she was not feeling it.

'Thank you for seeing me. I appreciate it,' she started.

'I felt I had to,' Nellie said. 'I was intrigued by you saying you were working with Inspector McQueen. Did he send you?'

Maria wished she had not used his name so blithely. What if word got back to him and he disapproved?

There was a pause as Nellie looked at her expectantly, her direct gaze making Maria even more uncomfortable.

'Ah, not exactly,' she said. Then before she could stop herself, a whole load of words came tumbling out. 'The thing is, I'm writing a piece for the newspaper. I want to know the whole story about what happened – on the island – what happened to Captain Buchanan? Was it the prince? If it wasn't, who else could it be? You were there, I wondered if you'd seen or heard anything...' She tailed off, feeling about two inches tall.

Nellie looked puzzled. 'Wait a second. You mean you've made your way into my apartment, and you have no authority at all? You've used McQueen's name, but he doesn't know you're even here?'

'Well, no.'

'Are you working with him, or are you not?'

'I am. I know he went to look for the prince yesterday. He came to see me first. I had an idea where he could start looking. But I haven't heard from him since.'

'I see. But I don't get why he would work with you?' Nellie looked at Maria's calling card. 'It seems to me you're just a journalist, looking for stories.'

Maria felt colour rush to her cheeks.

'I'm not just a journalist. My father owns the newspaper. I'm a writer and an editor. Inspector McQueen asked me to find out information for him when he was stuck on the island. And I helped him on his last case.'

'All right, all right. I get it.' Nellie got up and walked over to the windows, which led onto the balcony. 'Only he was here last night, and I thought he must have told you...'

'Told me what?'

'Never mind.'

Maria felt the opportunity slipping away from her. She had to find some way to get Nellie to at least give her some background, or further information. She thought quickly. If McQueen had been there and had information from Nellie, it could only mean one thing: the American must know something about where the prince had gone.

'Please help me. Don't you see how important this story is?

An innocent Indian prince, accused of murder? The whole history of his family, how they've been stripped of their land, their wealth, everything? People here need to know the truth. I want to be able to tell them. Do you know where he is?'

Nellie laughed. 'Of course not.'

'I don't believe you. You said McQueen was here. Why? You must know something. If you know where the prince is, let me speak to him. I want to hear his story.'

Had she done enough? Her words fell into an awkward silence. Nellie stood staring at her, clearly mulling something over in her mind.

'All right,' she said eventually. 'I can see why McQueen trusts you. You have something about you. Quite the firecracker, aren't you? Look, if I let you in on something, you're going to have to keep this to yourself for a time. There's someone I can let you meet. But you *cannot* – and I mean *cannot* – use this story until well after this someone is far away and completely safe. What do you say?'

Maria nodded mutely, feeling excitement bubble up inside her. This sounded like an opportunity that could not possibly be turned down.

Nellie led Maria out of the hotel suite, along to the end of the corridor where a heavy door opened onto a discreet staircase. They went up a narrow flight of stairs to the top floor, where they were faced with a long line of plain doors.

'Servants' quarters,' Nellie said, stopping before a door with a metal number 59 nailed on the front. She knocked lightly on the door, then took out a key and unlocked it.

'It's for his own protection,' she explained. 'My maid is next door. She also has a key.'

Not sure if she was going to meet the prince himself, Maria's stomach was churning with excitement. As they went into the room, which was reasonably well lit by a window and an oil lamp, she could see a young Indian gentleman, sitting in an armchair. He looked up as they came in and carefully placed down the book he was reading. He squinted at Maria.

'Who is this?' he asked.

He was young, with a soft, black beard. A light cream-coloured turban was wrapped from the centre of his forehead over his ears. His good looks were striking, but to Maria's eyes, slightly marred by the petulant set of his mouth. She had to admit she was a little disappointed that the prince was not more – well, prince-like.

'This is Miss Maria Tanti, Your Highness,' Nellie explained. 'She wants to write your story in her newspaper, the *Malta Times*. I've said she can interview you, as long as nothing is printed until you're safely away from Malta.'

The prince raised his shapely eyebrows. 'Well, that will at least help pass the time,' he said, in his cultured English accent. 'I've been dying a slow death through boredom, up here in this garret prison.'

Maria sat in an armchair opposite him and took out her notebook and pencil. Nellie stood on the other side of the room, gazing out of the window.

'Thank you,' Maria said. 'Our readers will be thrilled to find out about your life, I am sure.'

The prince smiled slightly and waved his right hand graciously. 'Go on then, fire away. Ask me all your questions.'

Maria asked him about his childhood and was amazed to hear about castles in Scotland, shooting parties, and his father mixing with the Prince of Wales. School was boarding at Eton, university was Trinity College, Cambridge. She commented that this was the classic upbringing of someone born into the British aristocracy.

'Yes, but always this sense that we didn't belong. We were exotic, different. When he was young, my father was a great favourite of the queen. She made such a fuss of him, he thought he could have anything he wanted. But as he got older, he found he was in turn fawned over and then berated. He had to ask for every penny from the India Office. He had to have permission for everything he bought, everything he did. It made him so angry. He hates the British government now.'

'The Maharaja lives in exile,' Nellie said from across the room. 'He is bankrupt. The India Office stopped supporting him. It's taken its toll on his health.'

'It's so unfair,' the prince said bitterly. 'They made him what he is. They took away his land, his rights, his riches. Made him leave India, when he was just a boy. Our family used to own fabulous jewels, diamonds even, but they've all been stripped away. My father is a broken man.'

Maria found it hard to believe that the British government had simply taken possession of the Punjab, but it seemed this was completely true.

'What were you hoping to achieve by travelling to Bombay?' she asked.

'I went to meet my father's cousin, Tejbir Singh. He'd been writing to me. He wanted me to know more about my heritage. My father was brought up a Christian, as we were too. I wanted to find out what it means to be a Sikh. Tejbir Singh said I should take my rightful place as Maharaja of the Punjab, ruler of the Sikh Empire.'

'Can I ask what happened, when you met your cousin?'

The prince sighed. 'It was the best thing that's ever happened to me,' he said. 'He organised for me to take part in the *Amrit Sanchar* ceremony. It's how I was initiated into the

Sikh faith. That's when I was given my *kirpan,* you have to wear it. My father had taught me the meaning of the whole ritual. I was so proud to take part. To become a true Sikh prince.'

'Does it take long?' Maria asked, intrigued.

'About two hours. Lots of prayers, drinking *amrit* – a sugar drink like nectar – making pledges, more prayers, then a meal with all the community.'

'What happened afterwards?'

'My cousin told me we were going to travel up to the Punjab. He had a party of men with him. They all took part in the *Amrit Sanchar*. He'd ordered *tangas* to take us to the station. Apparently, it takes about five days to get to Amritsar by rail. We were all ready to go, with luggage loaded. Then we were surrounded by British military and the Indian Police Force. We'd done nothing. I don't know what happened to Tejbir Singh, or the others, but I saw them being beaten by *lathis*. They tried to fight back, but from what I saw they were outnumbered and easily subdued.'

Prince Sundar was lost in thought for a moment, gazing down at the ground. Then he looked up again, his eyes darkened with hatred.

'I was taken to the Bombay police office, thrown into a cell. Then they put me on the *Poonah* the next day, with that wretch Buchanan to accompany me.'

'And if you go back to Bombay now, would you do the same thing again? Try and get back to the Punjab?'

'Of course!' he said, glancing quickly at Nellie.

Maria sensed that behind the bravado there was a great deal of fear. The prospect of leading from the front, in what was to him an alien country, must be a daunting one. He seemed to shrink back in his seat thinking about it.

There was one other question she was dying to ask him.

'Prince Sundar, are you aware of the execution of Sikhs by the British, at the Malerkotla Parade Ground, eight years ago?'

'Yes. My father told me about it. Another example of British brutality.'

'What if I told you that Colonel Ellis, who was so keen for you to be arrested, gave the order for the prisoners to be executed? And that Captain Buchanan was one of the officers present in Malerkotla? That he may have ordered the cannons to fire?'

The prince narrowed his eyes. 'Then,' he said bitterly, 'I would say that Buchanan deserved to die. And if it *had* been me, I would have twisted that knife so hard I would have pulled out all his entrails.'

CHAPTER TWENTY-FOUR

Valletta, Malta. Tuesday, 26 October 1880

'Let's face it, Sergeant, they are not coming.'

It was eight o'clock in the morning. McQueen and Galea had been watching and waiting for over two hours. The SS *Arcadia* was preparing to depart from Grand Harbour. Berthed at Pinto Wharf, the steamship had been a bustling centre of activity since before dawn. Stevedores had carried on fresh provisions, the passengers' luggage had been loaded, and finally the passengers themselves were arriving. McQueen had checked that Nellie Byrne was registered on the ship, with her two servants. She was preparing to leave Malta that morning, but so far she had not appeared at the harbour. He cursed under his breath.

'Shall I go and ask the ship's captain when they are leaving – check he hasn't seen them?' Galea asked.

'Aye, if you would.' He felt too frustrated to go and ask himself.

He stayed in the entrance to Pinto Stores, surveying the busy harbour scene, as Galea approached the *Arcadia*. There were a dozen ships in harbour, most at anchor a little way out. The noise was overwhelming, the sound of coal being tipped by the ton into a ship's bunker, the shouts of the harbour supervisors, the stevedores, and the many boatmen, as they steered their *dgħajjses* from ship to shore. Galea boarded the ship and talked to the captain. Now he walked down the gangplank and came back, shaking his head. 'Nothing,' he said, shrugging. 'No luggage. No sign of her, or the servants. The ship is going to sail in half an hour.'

The SS *Arcadia* was the only ship going to Bombay that week, they *had* to be on it. Or did they? A persistent doubt had been nagging at his thoughts, ever since their meeting. Nellie had fed him all the information, begged him not to pass it on. Yet she must have known that his sense of duty as a police officer would mean he could not turn a blind eye. Was she deliberately telling him they were leaving for Bombay to put the police off the scent?

He cast his mind back to the exact words Nellie had used. She had said that the prince was just a boy, that he needed protecting. *Of course!* She was never going to put him on a boat back to India. It was too dangerous. She had always intended to keep him safe. She would be taking him back to England instead.

He turned to Galea. 'You know all the ship's sailing schedules, don't you?'

It was basic intelligence-gathering they had set up over the past few weeks.

The young sergeant nodded. 'Yes, I think so.'

'Is there a P&O steamer leaving today for England?'

'Well, yes. There should be. The *Cathay*. Sailing this morning.'

'Right, come with me,' McQueen shouted, sprinting away as fast as he could. 'We have to get to Marsamuscetto, now.'

They ran from Grand Harbour up the steep steps to Victoria Gate, and through the crowded streets of Valletta, pushing aside early-morning shoppers. Their boots pounded on the stone. They arrived at the top of Marsamuscetto Steps, panting. McQueen could feel sweat dripping down his face. They looked down onto the harbour. A large white ship had pulled up its anchors and was beginning to move slowly away.

'Quick!' he shouted.

They ran down the steps as fast as they could, but by the time they had reached the wharf, the *Cathay* had pulled out to the centre of the harbour, moving at a majestic but unstoppable speed. McQueen stood watching, hands on his knees, trying to catch his breath. He looked across at the ship. He thought he could see the silhouette of a tall, elegant woman watching from the deck. He could imagine the smile playing on her lips.

Nellie Byrne. That scheming, American, hustler of a woman. He had to hand it to her. She knew what she was doing.

'She's on there,' he said. 'She's got away.'

As ever, Galea's emotions were writ clear on his face. He looked crestfallen.

McQueen put his hand on the youngster's shoulder. 'Ach, well, Sergeant. Happens to the best of us. She had us all for fools.'

McQueen and Galea walked to the P&O office and asked the booking clerk, a young Englishman with dark-rimmed spectacles, about passengers on the SS *Cathay*. Yes, Miss Nellie Byrne had booked a first-class passage to England, together with two personal servants.

'When does it get to Southampton?'

'In ten days, on November 5th.'

'Any stops on the way?'

'No, none.' The booking clerk peered at him across the counter. 'Are you by any chance Inspector McQueen?' he asked.

'Aye, I am.'

'Only Miss Byrne left an envelope for you.' He handed it over.

McQueen tore it open and glanced at the paper inside. It was a long note, written in Nellie's distinctive hand. He got the gist, that she was sorry to have misled him, but that she hoped he would understand. It was all for the right cause. He folded it back up roughly and stuffed it into his jacket pocket. No time to read it now. He looked at Galea.

'As far as you know, Sergeant, this note doesn't exist. You never saw it, understood?'

Galea nodded.

'Right then, we'll have to get back to the police office. We're going to have to face the music. Ellis is not going to be happy to hear about this.'

At least it was not Bombay. Ellis would have his guts for garters if the prince had escaped back to India.

They found Police Superintendent Ellis in the main hall of the Auberge d'Auvergne, talking to Inspector Azzopardi. McQueen marched over. *Might as well come straight out with it.*

'Prince Sundar got away,' he said. 'On the P&O steamer to Southampton.'

'What? You said you'd find him and bring him in today. I

was counting on getting him back into custody. This is not good enough, Inspector.'

Ellis's eyes were blazing with contempt. Had he been in the army, McQueen felt sure he would have instantly faced a court martial. But he did not have to answer to Ellis and he was damned if he was going to apologise.

'It's not the end of the world,' he said. 'There are no stops en route. The prince can be arrested when he gets to England.'

'You're damn right. We'll have that ship surrounded before it gets into port. It'll be searched from top to bottom. There's no chance this murderer will escape from us again.'

Ellis turned to Azzopardi. 'You, Inspector, set that in motion. Send a telegram to the port authorities. I'll inform Scotland Yard, and the Colonial Office.'

'Yes, sir,' Azzopardi said, glancing at McQueen with a hint of triumph before smartly turning on his heel and setting off for the telegraph office.

'And as for you, Inspector McQueen, I'm removing you from the investigation. You've lost our prime suspect twice and made us look like a laughing stock. You can go back to whatever it was you were doing before this whole sorry episode started.'

Conscious that he probably weighed half as much again as Ellis, McQueen was entertaining himself with images of turning the man upside down and shaking him until all the contents of his pockets fell out. It was either that or punching him.

'With all due respect, sir, I report to the governor, not you. There is still work to be done. We don't have sufficient evidence to support Singh being charged with murder. There are other strands to follow up. For a start, there's Gilbert Browne. I need to find out what happened to him. It wasn't an accidental death. Someone injected him with morphine. He was involved in the case, I'm sure. He's the most likely person to have taken the dagger from the storeroom.'

Ellis looked every bit as if he was going to strike him. 'You're like a bloody dog with a bone,' he said through gritted teeth. 'You just won't leave it, will you? Fine, I'll speak to the governor. I'm sure he'll be every bit as displeased as I am. I think you've done enough damage for now. Get out of my sight.'

'With pleasure.'

McQueen tipped his hat and left, taking Sergeant Galea with him. 'Let's go for a beer,' he said, 'do some thinking. We've got ten days until the *Cathay* arrives in Southampton. Ten days to find out who really did murder Laurence Buchanan – and Gilbert Browne.'

CHAPTER TWENTY-FIVE

Manoel Island, Malta. Tuesday, 26 October 1880

'How many is it now, *Dottore*?'

'Nine.'

Dr Vittorio Bonnici was feeling bone-tired. He and the quarantine doctor, Lorenzo Cassar, had been working round the clock for seven days. They had just admitted another two cholera patients. The ward was full. Luckily, they had eight Sisters of Mercy working with them. The doctors had set up a clear regime. Patients were constantly tended. They were kept warm, clothing and bedding clean, with frequent medication given in brandy and water. But despite their efforts, four patients had died. Of the current sufferers, most were responding well to treatment. The ones who appeared to be deteriorating were older people, and those with weaker constitutions. There was little to be done for them, except to try and keep them comfortable.

'I am going to step outside for an hour, *Dottore*,' Bonnici said. 'When I return, you can take a little time away.' He wanted to look in on Louisa Copeland who, one week from the onset of the disease, was now much better. She was out of bed and had been transferred to her apartment to continue her convalescence.

On the way to the Lazzaretto, Bonnici thought about McQueen. He had heard about the inspector leaving the island after Prince Sundar had been abducted. He felt deeply disappointed that McQueen had walked out of quarantine before the ten days were up. It was desperately important that the cholera stayed on Manoel Island. So far, there had been no cases reported in Valletta. What if McQueen was carrying the infection, unbeknownst to him, and passed it on to those he came in contact with? To his mind, there were no mitigating circumstances that could justify McQueen's decision to leave.

It was good to be outside, breathing in the fresh air. The short walk from the hospital did him good. The temperature had dropped a little over the past few days. Was it finally autumn? He stopped for a moment, leaning on his cane, to look across the creek, gaining some strength back before entering the Lazzaretto.

He found the two English ladies in good spirits. Louisa was pale, but looking much healthier, sitting up in an armchair, firmly wrapped in a shawl, a blanket over her knees.

Eleanor had lit a fire and was tending to it. They had a servant girl with them in the apartment and when Bonnici arrived, Eleanor sent her off to fetch a large pot of tea.

'It's so good to be out of hospital, Doctor,' Louisa said. 'I feared I would never leave the place.'

'You've done well, Miss Copeland. It's good to see you finally out of bed again. May I?'

He checked her pulse. Although not particularly strong, it

was good and regular. He felt an almost overwhelming sense of relief. He had helped at least one person to recover, one who was young, with her whole adult life ahead of her. He smiled. 'Now, you still need to rest,' he said. 'Take it easy, until you're feeling strong again. No dancing yet.'

'Oh, I don't think there's much chance of that,' Louisa said. 'Not around here anyway.'

'Doctor, you're looking fatigued,' Eleanor said. 'Please, sit down.'

He sat in the armchair by the fire, enjoying the warmth and the chance to rest his aching leg.

'What has been happening while I was in hospital?' Louisa asked.

'I can answer that,' Eleanor said with obvious relish. 'So much has been going on. Prince Sundar Singh was arrested for the murder of Captain Buchanan, but he's escaped. Isn't that right, Doctor? Oh, and that idiot Gilbert Browne has killed himself with an opium overdose.'

Bonnici kept quiet about the autopsy findings. It was not for him to say if there were developments in the case.

'Oh, my goodness!' Louisa said. 'Mr Browne is dead? That's awful. And where has the prince got to? What's going to happen?' She looked genuinely upset, her eyes darting from Eleanor to him and back again, as if checking that all this news was true.

'Please, do not get agitated,' Bonnici said. 'It's all under control. Inspector McQueen has left Manoel Island. I'm sure he'll soon find where the prince is hiding and bring him back into custody.'

'I'll tell you who else has left the island,' Eleanor said. 'That Nellie Byrne. Left early on Monday. There's something strange about her, don't you think? I told you, Doctor, didn't I, that I saw her talking to Buchanan a couple of nights before he died? I've also seen her talking with Inspector McQueen. Alone. What business does she have with these men? She's certainly of dubious moral character. I think she's involved in something underhand. Although what, I have no idea.'

'Oh, Eleanor, you always think the worst of people. It is none of our business whom she chooses to spend time with.'

Eleanor sniffed disapprovingly.

'Ah, here's the tea,' Louisa said.

As Eleanor busied herself with sorting the tea tray, pouring the tea into cups, Bonnici found his thoughts drifting away. Before he knew it, his eyes started to close. He fought against it, trying to keep them open, but he was pulled by an invisible force into slumber.

Eventually, Bonnici returned to consciousness, feeling himself emerging from a deep, dark place of rest. He kept his eyes closed. He was embarrassed he had fallen asleep in company. The two women were talking in low voices. He let their words wash over him, unwilling to face reality, at least for a little while longer.

'We'll have to stay in Malta until you're ready to travel,' Eleanor was saying. 'I'll book a hotel in Valletta. The sooner we get off this poisonous island the better. I have to get back to England. I need to start my new position. They won't wait for me forever.'

Louisa murmured something about it being a while before they would be out of quarantine.

'Well, that hasn't stopped the detective inspector, has it? He and that American woman, both gone. A good riddance to them.

They're as bad as each other. He's hardly the gentleman, and she's certainly no lady. That health guard, Grech, he told me he saw the inspector leaving her room early one morning. At the end of that first night, when you were taken into hospital. I call that downright immoral.'

That must have been the night McQueen had told him about. He had said they had spent time together, but nothing about spending the whole night. This did not sit well with Bonnici, but he knew he was old-fashioned. It struck him that she was quite the fount of information, this Miss Templeman. He was surprised at the side of her character that was being revealed. Clearly, she had a watchful eye, and an ear out for gossip. Perhaps she did not have enough of interest in her own life and revelled in hearing the details of other people's.

'I hope they find the prince. It's concerning that he's escaped,' Louisa said.

'Yes, he needs to be found. But I'm not holding my breath. The police are useless, if you ask me.'

Perhaps it was time to make his exit. Cautiously, Bonnici opened his eyes and made a pretence at yawning.

'I'm so sorry, I must have dropped off. So rude. I really need to go, get back to the ward.'

He made his goodbyes, glad to see Louisa's progress, and intrigued at the prickly nature Eleanor Templeman had just revealed, very different to the caring nurse he had spent time with at the bedside of her friend.

Bonnici made his way back, feeling slightly rejuvenated by the unplanned nap. Arriving on the ward, he was pleased to see one of the orderlies, a vigorous woman in her sixties, mopping the floor. An important part of the regime was floor-washing every two hours during the daytime. But something caught his eye as he walked past, and he stopped short.

'What's this?' he asked. 'The water is so pale, barely pink. Have you used the right amount of Condy's?'

As a solution of potassium permanganate, Condy's Fluid should be dark purple in colour. When diluted, it should be a pale purple. This had hardly any colour at all.

'Yes, *Dottore*. One wine glass full for each pail of water.'

'Then why is it so light in colour? Show me.'

The woman took him into the sluice room. She indicated the sink, where a bottle of Condy's Fluid stood on the worktop.

'I used that one,' she said.

Just by eye, he could see that it was not the colour he would have expected.

'Where did you get it from?' he asked.

'Over here.' She showed him where a stock of around twenty bottles of Condy's stood on shelving on one side of the room. He pulled out a few at random, checking the colour of the fluid inside the glass.

'Can you ask Doctor Cassar to come in here, please?' he asked. The orderly disappeared at once.

Cassar arrived almost immediately, his brow furrowed with concern. 'What is it, *Dottore*?'

'This disinfectant. Is this the new batch you ordered?'

'Yes, four-dozen bottles. Some here, some in the main storeroom. Why, what's the problem?'

'It's the colour. Look! This is not Condy's. Or if it is, it's been watered down. Did you not notice?'

Cassar gulped. 'I wondered. I wasn't sure. But there's so much to do, I pushed it to the back of my mind.'

Bonnici felt his legs go weak beneath him. He looked around for a stool and sat down, gathering himself. After a couple of moments, he addressed the young doctor in as low and measured a tone as he could manage. He did not want to lose his composure.

'Surely you realise the significance of this? How can we contain this disease if the disinfectant we're using is not effective? This is important. Did you check with Sciberras that he got exactly what we ordered?'

The young doctor stuttered. 'I… I… No. I'm still new here. I didn't think it was my place.' He looked like a drowning puppy, searching around for someone to save him.

Bonnici was reminded of what he had been like at Cassar's age. Desperate to prove himself, to get everything right. But also hopelessly naïve, thinking everyone working in medicine could be trusted.

'All right,' he said gently. 'I do understand. But if there's one thing I've learnt, *Dottore*, it's that you should always trust your instincts. And if something is wrong, you should immediately tackle it. Especially when, as now, the risks are so high. Let's go through the orders now.'

Together, they went through the copies of all the orders, comparing against the items received. Then, armed with two bottles of disinfectant and a long list of questions, Bonnici set off to confront Sciberras. He had never felt more fuelled by anger.

The shadows were beginning to lengthen by the time Bonnici reached the keeper's office in the Lazzaretto. He went in without knocking and placed a bottle of Condy's Fluid on Sciberras's desk.

Sciberras looked up and scowled.

'What do you want? Can't you see I'm busy?'

'I want an explanation. Why is this bottle of disinfectant watered down?'

Sciberras pushed his chair back, glaring at him. 'I have no idea what you're talking about. It's Condy's Fluid. You can see it on the label.'

Bonnici pulled the second bottle from his jacket pocket. 'No, *this* is a bottle of Condy's. See the colour difference?'

There was a marked contrast between the two shades, one bottle looking about half as dark as the other.

'This is genuine Condy's Fluid. We found an old bottle in stock. See how dark the colour is. Compare it to this bottle, taken from the recent delivery. Whoever you bought this product from, it has been doctored. Diluted in water. It is no longer effective.'

'You're talking nonsense. It's fine,' Sciberras blustered.

'Listen to me, *Sinjur*. Doctor Cassar and I have spent two hours this afternoon going through the stock, comparing the items we ordered with the items you provided. Two hours when we're needed to tend to our dying and seriously ill patients. How dare you sit there and question what I am telling you?'

Sciberras looked out of the window.

Bonnici continued. 'You're a thief, Sciberras. A scoundrel and a thief. Your greed may have cost lives. It's not just the disinfectant. There are products missing, and items which are cut-price alternatives to those we'd ordered. You can't do that with medical supplies. If we're not able to contain this cholera outbreak, I'll hold you responsible.'

'What are you going to do?' Sciberras asked.

'I'm going to report you to the police, as soon as I get an opportunity,' he said. 'But for now, I'm going to concentrate on looking after my patients. And you're going to reorder the correct products and have them delivered here tomorrow, however much it costs. Do I have your assurance you'll do that?'

Sciberras nodded, his eyes narrowed.

Bonnici left Sciberras sitting at his desk in the semi-darkness, his silhouette resembling the hulking vulture that he was.

He made his way slowly back to the isolation hospital, leaning heavily on his cane. He had truly had enough. Conspiracy and unpleasantness lay all around him. And the spectre of cholera still had its icy fingers over Manoel Island.

CHAPTER TWENTY-SIX

Valletta, Malta. Tuesday, 26 October 1880

By the time McQueen got back to his lodgings, he had sketched out a plan with Galea, starting the following day. They needed to go back to the Lazzaretto and ask more questions about people's whereabouts on the night Browne was murdered. *Who could have slipped into his room and injected him? Who would have a reason to do so?* There had to be a clue somewhere. McQueen did not want to go back to Manoel Island, but that was where the answers lay. The thought of it had put him in a foul temper.

Sinjura Caruso had saved him some dinner. He sat on his own in the sombre dining room, surrounded by religious paintings and small statues. The sideboard opposite him featured a large photograph of his landlady with her husband, holding baby Antonio. *Il Kapitan* Caruso, a ship's captain, had died at sea, six years ago. *Sinjura* Caruso liked to light candles around the photograph. The flickering flames seemed to change the expressions on the serious faces of the young couple the more he looked at it. She had been broken by her husband's death, he knew, and worried about the future for her son. But thanks to Dr Bonnici, her step was now a little lighter. She smiled at McQueen as she brought him some pasta and a glass of beer.

He pulled out the letter from Nellie and placed it on the table to read while he ate his meal. Something had caught his eye when he first glanced at it. Nellie admitted that she had not been truthful with him. As well as working for Prince Sundar's father, she said, she was under instruction from 'powers that be' to ensure the prince was returned to England. Was she some kind of spy? Who was this woman? She had told him of her time in Paris, where she said she was mixing with Irish revolutionaries and Russian diplomats, as well as Sir Anokh Singh. And yet here she was saying she was working for 'powers that be', with the implication that this was the British government. How did this American woman, on her own, find herself playing such an extraordinary role?

She was highly intelligent, that much was obvious. He thought of her clear green eyes and how she had looked at him with amusement. There was a challenge there, which he had enjoyed. She had got the better of him on this occasion, but if he ever saw her again, he would know not to trust her. It would be fun to pit his wits against hers, even if she got the upper hand again. She wrote:

> *I know you'll be angry with me, but I want you to know that I genuinely did enjoy spending time with you. You're a good man, Sam McQueen, and in any other circumstances, I would have wanted to get to know you better. I admire the way you look for the truth and don't give up until you find it. I have every confidence you'll uncover what happened to Buchanan, and to Browne. Believe me, I had nothing to do*

with either case. I was happily fulfilling my mission of getting the prince back, this has all been a crazy interruption. Good luck, Inspector. You never know, I may see you again one day.

Yours, Nellie.

Truth to tell, Nellie Byrne's departure had left him feeling empty. He had felt a spark with her he had not experienced before. Part of him wanted to book a ticket immediately and follow her to England. He would not, of course. He had responsibilities, a case to solve, and besides, what encouragement had she given? He sighed, picked up the glass and drank down the beer.

There was another letter, up in his bedroom. It was from Jeannie, the woman he had left behind in Edinburgh. He had received it when he got back to his lodgings. A crofter's daughter from the Isle of Skye, Jeannie had not had much education. Her handwriting was childish, and she had struggled with some words. It would have cost her a huge amount of time and effort to write it. He wished she had not bothered. She was telling him clearly that their relationship was over. She cared for him and would be forever grateful for his help and support. But she had been seeing someone else. A temperate man, a man from the Kirk. She said she was happy and that she wished him well.

A temperate man. Thinking about her words, he felt a bitterness well up inside him. He could understand to some extent. Her father was a drunkard who had beaten her and her mother. But why hold up this 'ideal' of temperance? Was there no such thing as acceptance and moderation? It brought up all his anger against his father, the non-stop sermonising, the suffocating way of life dictated by the Church. A life to be spent in duty and piety, where anything and everything was frowned upon, if it so much as hinted at enjoyment or fun. He pushed his chair back and stood up. He was going out for another drink.

McQueen's drinking den of choice was a tiny bar at the end of Strada Stretta. Barely enough room to swing a cat in, but a good range of whiskies. No single malts – that would be too much to ask – but good blended whiskies such as Walkers Old Highland. The barman was deftly efficient and not prone to chatting, which suited McQueen's mood well. He ordered a double, downed it in one, then ordered another. He felt the warmth of the whisky coursing through his body, its relaxing effect just what he was after. He took his drink and sat in his favourite corner. There were sketches on the wall, street scenes from Valletta including one depicting Carnival. The strangeness of the costumes, with people dressed as harlequins, fools, clowns and satyrs reminded him of how far away he was from his normal life. The idea of Carnival was bizarre: an annual, boisterous street party before the onset of Lent. In his father's church, you could never cast off your cares. It was all one monotonous existence of abstinence and repression.

To some extent, he had enjoyed his stay in Malta. The architecture in Valletta appealed to him and the blue skies and sea breezes lifted his spirits. He felt useful, passing on his experience to the police force. He thought he would be able to leave at least Sergeant Galea with a solid grounding in detective work. But now it had all started to unravel. He had trusted Nellie Byrne, which had proved to be a big mistake. It had left him exposed to ridicule, not helped by the crimson swelling around his eye. The whisky was numbing, but not enough yet. He drained the glass, went back to the bar and paid for the remainder of the bottle. Sitting back on the bar stool in his corner, he got out his notebook and amused himself by sketching caricatures of Ellis, with his lean figure and hawk-like profile.

Several whiskies in, McQueen was in a fog of concentration when he felt a tap on his shoulder.

'I say, Inspector, found you at last. Been everywhere looking for you.' It was Lieutenant Carstairs, aide-de-camp to the governor. 'Mrs Caruso said you'd gone out, and here you are.'

McQueen looked up at him blearily. 'Join me?' he said.

Carstairs, smart as ever in his dark uniform, hesitated, but pulled up another stool and sat opposite him. 'All right. But just the one.'

McQueen called over to the barman, 'Another glass, for my friend here!'

He poured Carstairs a generous measure from the bottle and refilled his own. 'Good to see you,' he said. 'You'll have heard what happened to the prince. I'm drinking to his health, him and the lovely Nellie Byrne.' He held up his glass. 'Bon voyage to the both of them.'

Carstairs clinked glasses with him, his eyes blinking nervously from behind his spectacles. He took a quick sip, then rested his glass on the table. 'Um, with respect, Inspector, I think you should perhaps call it a day. I came to find you because the governor wants to talk to you tomorrow morning. He's at his residence in the country. San Anton Palace. I can take you there, pick you up first thing.'

McQueen sighed. 'What does the old goat want with me now? It's that Ellis, isn't it? He wants me off the investigation.' He showed Carstairs the sketches he had made. 'What d'you think? Caught the likeness?'

Carstairs attempted a laugh, whilst taking another sip of whisky. It came out more like a hiccup which turned into a cough. 'Look, I don't know exactly what he wants. He's got some information from Whitehall. It's important.'

'Oh, aye? Well, must not let the great man down.' McQueen felt a surge of annoyance. 'Can't even leave me in peace for a moment.'

He stood up and picked up the whisky bottle. 'I'll away to my bed then.'

'Good idea, Inspector,' Carstairs said, his attempt at a soothing tone irritating McQueen still further. 'I'll walk you back to your lodgings.'

Not trusting himself to speak without cursing, McQueen raised his hand in acquiescence. He headed out of the bar with Carstairs in tow.

Strada Stretta – or Narrow Street – was called that for a reason. At only nine feet across, and the focus of most of the bars and houses of ill-repute in Valletta, it was crowded with groups of raucous soldiers and sailors. McQueen scanned the lane ahead of him, an ingrained habit, looking out for possible trouble. He saw the usual mêlée, all seemingly good-natured. Then a blue cap caught his attention, about four yards ahead of them. The man wearing the cap dodged away into a doorway, but not before McQueen recognised him. Camilleri, again – on his own this time. He was sick of being watched and followed by that worthless coward. His blood boiled. Pushing his way through the hordes, he strode after Camilleri, finding him backed into the entrance of a brothel.

Camilleri put his hands up defensively. Without thinking, McQueen reached out and pulled him up by his greasy lapels, holding him against the wall. The little man, cursing in Maltese, tried to wriggle out of his grasp, kicking out wildly. One of his feet caught McQueen in the kneecap, which hurt like hell. He buckled for a moment, then straightened up. He leaned in harder, his arm across Camilleri's throat, so close he could smell the smoke and garlic on the man's breath. 'Will – you – leave – me – alone?' he snarled. He watched Camilleri's face turning red, his eyes beginning to bulge as he struggled to breathe. Yet still he carried on pressing against his throat, Camilleri turning weaker under his grasp. He only stopped when he heard a peremptory voice behind him.

'McQueen, stop! Drop him, now.'

He let go of Camilleri, turning round to see if it was Carstairs.

Police Superintendent Ellis was standing behind him, in full uniform. Inspector Azzopardi was also there, truncheon out ready to strike. Carstairs stood to one side, hopping from one foot to the other, anxiously looking on.

'He's a suspect,' McQueen explained thickly. 'He's the one that took the prince.'

He realised he was still holding the whisky bottle and went to put it down on the ground, next to Camilleri who lay curled up, groaning.

'McQueen, you're drunk,' Ellis said. 'We'll deal with this.'

'He's working with Borg. They helped Nellie Byrne get the prince away.'

He felt shattered now, the rush of anger beginning to subside.

'That's as maybe,' Ellis said. 'You've caused enough trouble. You need to leave. Inspector Azzopardi here will escort you back to your lodgings. Sleep it off.'

'I'm going to take him to see the governor tomorrow morning,' Carstairs said, his earnest face bobbing into view. 'I'll pick you up at eight o'clock, Inspector, if that's all right?'

McQueen nodded wearily. There was nothing for it, he had to comply. As he walked back through the streets of Valletta, Azzopardi by his side, he was reminded of the first time he went to an inn, aged sixteen. His brother Andrew had been sent by his father to pull him out of the bar, to be marched home in disgrace. There he was subjected to a long haranguing and the seething disapproval of his father, who could not abide to see any man or boy drunk. It was his own anger toward his father that had led him to the inn. He had wanted to defy his father's authority and try for himself what was forbidden. It had not felt much like a triumph. Now, here he was, still trying to shake off this perpetual feeling of not living up to expectations. He had to get a grip on himself. He could not let the police chief have the upper hand.

He stopped outside the door of his lodgings in Strada Ponente. Azzopardi stood watching him, his blank features giving nothing away as McQueen focused hard on fitting the key into the lock.

'I'll wish you a good night then, Inspector,' McQueen said. 'So good to run into you. Although, I've been in better company. Why don't you try and lighten up a bit, toss your cares to the wind? It'll do wonders for you.'

As Azzopardi muttered a good night and turned away, McQueen thought about the whisky bottle he had left in the street. Should he go back and retrieve it? *Perhaps not such a good idea. Unlikely to be there anyway.* He pushed the door open and made his way upstairs. He dropped onto the bed fully clothed, falling into a dreamless sleep.

CHAPTER TWENTY-SEVEN

Valletta, Malta. Wednesday, 27 October 1880

An hour and a half in a swaying carriage, on bumpy roads was not the ideal way to start the day. There had already been two stops for McQueen to complete the job of voiding his stomach contents.

'Excuse me for saying it, Inspector, but you really do not look well,' Carstairs commented.

'I'm all right,' he said, lying through his teeth. Today was going to be one of those days he would just have to get through. One saving grace – the sun was hidden behind scudding clouds. The temperature had dropped a few degrees, and a fresh wind was blowing. McQueen sipped water from a flask, watching the countryside go past, vowing never to drink whisky again.

'What happened to Camilleri?' he asked after a while. 'Is he in custody?'

'Good grief, no. The Police Superintendent let him go. He ran off like a scalded cat.'

McQueen had to admit it was a good thing Ellis had appeared when he did. He knew he had lost control. It happened very seldom, but it was concerning when it did. However, part of him was not sorry for at least making a point. Perhaps Camilleri would think again before crossing his path.

He noticed dully that they had turned off the road, through ornate white iron gates, and were now travelling along an avenue of cypress trees. A grand two-storey limestone building came into view. McQueen's head hurt so badly, he could scarcely take in the elegance of the house and surrounding gardens. It was as much as he could do to climb down from the carriage without throwing up again, as they came to a stop at the steps leading up to the palace.

'Just give me a moment,' he said, steadying himself and taking a few deep breaths.

They were greeted by a footman and led inside, through a marble-floored hall, and along echoing corridors before reaching a small state room with white-panelled walls and ceiling, gold paint outlining the panel edges. Four chairs were arranged around a table. A giant portrait of a grand figure sporting an eighteenth-century wig and ermine-edged robes dominated one wall, a religious painting of Christ with the Apostles on the other side. Sir Thomas Grant, Governor of Malta, was writing at the table. He stood up as they entered and gestured for them to sit down. His bushy white eyebrows rose up as he greeted them.

'Sorry to drag you all the way over here, McQueen. But we have an important reception being held here in a day or two, and I have to oversee the preparations.'

'No trouble at all, Your Excellency,' McQueen said, thinking the exact opposite.

'Hope you like the palace. It's far and away my favourite place on the island,' Sir Thomas said. 'Beautiful gardens, and all that. Did you know Princess Victoria Melita was born here a few years ago? The Duke of Edinburgh's second daughter.'

McQueen had been introduced to Prince Alfred, Duke of Edinburgh, when the prince had visited Malta the previous month. He had not formed a favourable impression of the Royal family.

'Anyway, the reason I've called you here is that I've received a missive from the India Office. It's about Miss Byrne. It's strictly confidential, but I thought you ought to know.' He held up a sheet of paper that had been lying on the desk.

McQueen sat forward in his chair. 'What is it?'

'It appears she's well-known in top circles and is in close contact with key personnel at the Home Office. Keeps them informed of matters pertinent to British security. I can't stress enough how important it is that this goes no further. Miss Byrne has been passing on correspondence to do with Prince Sundar Singh's intentions in India. The prince's cousin is waiting for him in Bombay, to lead a Sikh rebellion. As grandson to the Lion of the Punjab, and son of the Maharaja, Prince Sundar could be a powerful figurehead. Because of that, Miss Byrne was given explicit instructions to return him to England. It's imperative that he's taken back home, where it's hoped interest in him will die down.

'Now, Miss Byrne has also informed the India Office she's confident Prince Sundar wasn't involved in the murder of Laurence Buchanan, and that you'll be able to uncover the culprit.'

'That *is* my intention.'

'So, it appears Miss Byrne has done you a favour and that Ellis may have been jumping the gun after all.'

'You don't say.'

'I want this wrapped up quickly, McQueen. Find the killer,

get him locked up. I've enough to worry about, with the threat of a cholera epidemic. There's panic out there and we need to quash it.'

'I'm still on the case then?'

'Absolutely, I'll let Police Superintendent Ellis know. Carstairs here will offer any extra support you need. Won't you, Carstairs?'

'Yes, sir.' Carstairs stood to attention and saluted.

McQueen went to get up.

'And, McQueen?'

'Yes, sir?'

'Get yourself tidied up, man. You look like you've been through the wars.'

McQueen picked up Sergeant Galea on his return, and they took a *dgħajsa* back to Manoel Island. While in Valletta, he made sure to go back to his lodgings to wash, shave and change his collar, before a hearty lunch at his favourite café. He felt more human. Energised by the job that had to be done.

'Sergeant, I want you to get all Browne's belongings packed up and sent over to the police office. Then come over to the parlatorio. I'm going to talk to Sciberras.'

'Yes, sir.' Galea marched off to talk to one of the health guards near the entrance to the Lazzaretto.

McQueen sent a message to the keeper's office, then went to wait at the parlatorio. The shoe was on the other foot now. He was the visitor who could leave at the end of the meeting. He stood impatiently waiting. Eventually, Sciberras appeared, scowling in the doorway.

'You back again?'

'Aye, I am. And this time you're to provide me with all the help I need. Governor's orders.'

'What do you want?'

'I need statements from all the guards and residents who were here the night before Gilbert Browne died. My sergeant will organise a schedule. They'll each have to be brought here for questioning, at the times we've set them. Is that clear?'

'Inspector, you're aware we have cholera to deal with. I have no time.'

'Aye, but this is also important. The sooner you sort this out, the sooner we'll be out of your hair. Get me a list of the guards.'

'Very well.' Sciberras turned to go.

'How is Dr Bonnici?' McQueen asked before he walked away.

'The doctors are very busy.'

'Tell him I'm here, if you would.'

Sciberras grunted as he left the room.

Sergeant Galea reappeared. They wrote down the names of passengers who were still in quarantine. Grech turned up with a list of guards, handing them over sullenly without meeting McQueen's eyes. Galea drew up a timetable and gave it to Grech to take to Sciberras.

The next four hours were spent meticulously mapping out where everybody was between the hours of 9pm on the 20th October and 9am on the 21st. During that time, Gilbert Browne was locked in his apartment, and yet someone had managed to get to him and inject him with an overdose of morphine. Most likely in the early hours of the morning, sometime between 4am and 8am. Nearly everyone questioned said that they were still asleep at that time. Only two of the guards were on duty that night, but they both claimed not to have seen or heard anything. When pressed, it appeared they had been dozing in different parts of the building. There was just one useful piece of information. One of the guards was waiting in the small reception area next to the keeper's office. He had the set of keys with him, which included the key to Browne's room. He had left them on the wall hook while he rested. He could not swear that they had not been taken and returned while his eyes were closed.

The last passenger to arrive was Eleanor Templeman. She was as calm and poised as ever. McQueen asked after Miss Copeland and was told that she was well on the mend.

'We hope to be out of quarantine within a few days,' she said. 'It's been a long, terrible time. I am so thankful for the care and treatment Louisa had from Dr Bonnici. He saved her life, I am sure of it.'

She was very pale, her features looking pinched. McQueen could see the ordeal had taken its toll on her.

'I'm sorry to pull you in for these questions,' he said. 'But it is important. I need you to tell me where you were on the night of 20th to 21st October.'

'That's easy, Inspector. I was by Louisa's bedside. Dr Bonnici will vouch for me. I stayed with her from the night of the 19th, when Louisa was taken to the hospital, right through until the 22nd, when she was well enough to be left for a few hours. She was finally allowed to get out of bed a couple of days ago.'

'Are you sure? You did not leave that morning at any time?'

'Quite sure, Inspector. Ask the doctor. What is this about anyway?'

McQueen thought quickly. She must know that Gilbert Browne had died. It would not do any harm to let her know he had been murdered.

'You'll have heard that Gilbert Browne died on the 21st?'

'Yes, an overdose. I'm not surprised. I told you before that I thought he was taking drugs. Opium, was it?'

'No. We believe he was injected with morphine.'

Eleanor raised her eyebrows slightly. 'Oh, really?' she said. 'I find that hard to believe. Perhaps he is one of those who injects himself? It has been known.'

'If he did, there was no evidence of it. No hypodermic syringe, no morphine preparation.'

'That's just ridiculous. I'm sure there must be some explanation.' She made to stand up. 'Well, if you've nothing else to ask me, I should get back. Louisa may need a drink, or some food.'

McQueen sensed a discomfort with the subject, that she was keen to get away. He leant forward.

'Are you not more interested in this?' he asked. 'Don't you feel alarmed at the idea that Mr Browne was likely murdered? In his own room?'

Eleanor looked him squarely in the eye. 'No, Inspector, I'm not. Mr Browne was a stupid, privileged young man and quite frankly I couldn't care less that he died. Whoever did it, I imagine he brought it on himself.'

She had a point. It was likely that his death was somehow linked to the diamond smuggling he was involved in. However, her indifference bothered him. He decided to ask a few more questions.

'Miss Templeman, I understand you've been a tireless companion and nurse to your friend Miss Copeland. It is admirable, how you've stayed by her and helped the good doctor. You must've been wondering about the investigation, following the death of Captain Buchanan. What've you heard?'

'Not a lot. I was focused on looking after my friend. Dr Bonnici did tell me that the prince escaped from custody.' She brushed imaginary crumbs from her skirt. 'That seemed to me to show gross incompetence on the part of the police. He was clearly guilty of the crime.'

Sergeant Galea coughed suddenly, as if to mask an expression of annoyance. She gave him a cold look.

'What if I told you,' McQueen said, 'that the prince has been exonerated of the murder? That he's not guilty? What would you think then?'

'Then, Inspector, I would think that you need to get on with your job of finding out who *did* do it. I have no opinion on the matter.'

She stood up. 'I'm not staying any longer,' she said. 'I need to get back to Louisa. She's still not strong. She needs constant care.'

As she left the room, McQueen jotted down a few notes.

'She's a strange one, isn't she?' he remarked to Galea. 'I'm going to write a message to Dr Bonnici. We could do with seeing him and finding out if she really was as zealous in her bedside vigil as she says she was.'

'Are many Englishwomen so rude?' Galea asked. 'She should try standing on a rocking boat and being hit on the head by a big wooden oar. I nearly drowned!'

McQueen laughed, patting him on the back. 'Your bravery is duly noted, Sergeant. I'll make sure she finds out what really happened.'

He dashed off a message to Bonnici, asking him to come to the parlatorio as soon as he could, to help with the investigation.

Looking forward to seeing you, my friend, he wrote.

A half-hour later, as he and Galea were finishing off their notes from the interviews, he was taken aback by the response to his note, brought to him by one of the health guards.

It was curt and to the point.

I regret that I can't meet with you at the moment. The urgent situation at the hospital makes it impossible for me to leave the patients. Bonnici.

This did not sound like the considerate, obliging man that he knew. Something was amiss.

CHAPTER TWENTY-EIGHT

Valletta, Malta. Thursday, 28 October 1880

'Right, Sergeant, what do we have?'

McQueen, Carstairs and Galea were at the police office going through everything they had on the case.

'Who is not accounted for, on the night Browne died?'

Galea consulted his notes. 'Most residents were in their rooms, sleeping, and have people who can confirm that. There are the two guards who say they were napping. No one saw them, so we only have their word for it. Also, Sciberras. He's not able to prove where he was. He has his own rooms, and says he was there, but we don't know for sure.'

'Sciberras, eh? One thing I was wondering was whether he found out about the diamond smuggling. I wager he would have gone to Browne, asked for a cut. What if Browne refused? Perhaps that's a reason to dispose of him.'

'There's still the missing grain to find out about. I've got the ledger where Sciberras keeps the record of goods taken into quarantine at the Lazzaretto. I took it from his office.'

'Excellent, Sergeant. Carstairs, can you find out from Customs if the records match with theirs?'

'Absolutely!' Carstairs said enthusiastically.

'I suspect we'll find that the quantities listed at the Lazzaretto are significantly smaller than the amount that left the ships. Also, we need to know if anyone has seen suspicious activity between Manoel Island and the Cospicua docks – particularly at night-time. If we can get enough evidence to charge Sciberras, and link him to Borg, we should be able to get him talking.'

'I can ask Inspector Azzopardi. He knows nearly everybody working in the harbours,' Galea said.

'All right. Might as well give him something to do. Put it on your list.'

'Yes, sir.'

'Now then, I've been going through Browne's belongings. In his correspondence, there was a letter from his brother Alexander. Browne must've told him that he'd met Buchanan in Bombay and that he was going to be travelling with him on the *Poonah*. This letter, which reached Gilbert in Malta, tells him to pass on his congratulations to Buchanan, on his engagement. It seems they were friends, at school together. So, that corroborates the account I had from Miss Byrne that Gilbert Browne and Laurence Buchanan knew each other, and that Buchanan had a hold over Browne.'

'Is that his stuff here?' Carstairs asked, glancing at the trunk of clothes.

'Aye, it is.'

'Only, this is an old Etonian tie.' He pulled out a black-and-light-blue-striped tie from the top of the trunk. 'That'll be where Browne went to school – same as his brother, of course.'

'If you say so. The point is, I'm sure this connection

between them is in some way linked to the case. It's too much of a coincidence not to be significant.'

McQueen stood and picked up his hat.

'Right then, you two have things to do. I'm going to make one more trip to Manoel Island. I need to speak to Dr Bonnici. He said he was too busy yesterday, but today's another day and I'm going to insist.'

Out on the water in a *dgħajsa*, McQueen determined once again this would be his last visit to the Lazzaretto. He had had enough of the place and these journeys across the harbour. He was no seaman. His weight meant that any movement in the boat made it rock alarmingly. He had already had one experience floundering about in the water in a heavy suit and he did not want to repeat it.

It was a fresh, blowy day, with a few dark clouds in the sky. They had not had rain in Malta since the summer storm in August. The farmers relied on the autumn rainfall. They would be happy if it was on its way. McQueen welcomed the temperature drop but had to admit he had got used to the intense blue skies that characterised the Maltese climate.

Landing at the Lazzaretto, McQueen sent a message to Sciberras advising him he was there, together with a note for Bonnici, asking him to meet him at the parlatorio. Knowing it would take the doctor a while to extricate himself from his work, he started to walk toward the isolation hospital, thinking he might catch Bonnici on his way. Approaching the hospital, his attention was caught by a cemetery to the right of the path, and he decided to go in. As he wandered through, he read the inscriptions on the headstones. Names from many different nations, a wide range of ages, people who had succumbed to the plague, to cholera, to yellow fever, dying alone on a tiny island.

Musing about the blows dealt by fate, he caught sight of Bonnici, dressed in his usual top hat and smart coat, walking at some speed, aided by his cane. 'Doctor!' he called out, lifting his hand in greeting, 'over here.'

Bonnici stopped and looked over, an expression of extreme annoyance on his face. McQueen had seen that look just once before, when they had first met. They had not got off to a good start, when he had deliberately needled him, not knowing Bonnici would be his best ally in Malta. The doctor hesitated for a moment, then slowly approached him in the cemetery. McQueen moved forward, holding out his hand, but Bonnici stopped him.

'No,' he said sharply. 'Keep your distance. If we're to meet here, you need to keep well away from me. It might have escaped your notice but I've just come from the bedside of a patient who's dying of cholera.'

So, this is what it's about.

'Yes, of course,' he said, hastily pulling his hand back. 'You're still in quarantine.'

'As you should have been when you left the island.'

'I'm aware of that, but in the circumstances...'

'Have you any idea how serious this situation is? We've lost four patients. We may still lose more. Cholera's a terrible disease. We can save some people, perhaps more than half, if we treat them early and they're strong. But the weak succumb in no time, McQueen, quite literally in hours. In '37, nearly half the population of Malta died. And fifteen years ago, we lost near to four hundred people. I know all about it. I was there. We can't allow the disease to get onto the islands. And yet you willingly took that risk.'

McQueen was taken aback by Bonnici's tone. He noted how drawn his colleague's face had become, the dark circles under his eyes. It had been eleven days, he calculated, since Bonnici had willingly gone into quarantine. Ever since then he had been tending to the sick and watching people die. No wonder he was angry.

He held his hands up. 'I'm sorry. It was a risk, but not without some thought. I was close to the end of quarantine. I hadn't been in direct contact with the disease. It was necessary. The prince had escaped. I was needed on the main island. I had to get on with finding him.'

Bonnici looked down at the end of his cane. 'Not good enough. You went behind my back, getting Doctor Cassar to give you permission to leave, knowing he would be biddable. I'm disappointed in you, McQueen. I can't believe you would leave like that. It's been hell here, and you just walked away.'

There was an uneasy silence. McQueen thought about the best approach to take. He had to win back his colleague's trust.

'Let's take a walk,' he said eventually. 'Keeping our distance, of course. I'm sure you could do with some fresh air, a break. Perhaps I shouldn't have left, but at the same time, I felt I had to go. It was my fault Prince Sundar escaped, right from under my feet. I had to be the one to find him again, to put it right.'

Bonnici sighed. 'All right, I'll walk with you. You can tell me about the investigation. But understand that I will never condone what you did.'

'Aye, well, the situation is what it is. We'll have to live with it.'

They left the cemetery and followed the path through the scrubland, where there was room for them to walk side by side. McQueen explained all that had happened – Nellie Byrne's involvement, the prince's journey to England, the suspicions about Sciberras working with Borg, and his attempts to work out who could have given Browne the lethal injection.

'I imagine you're smarting from the way that American woman used you?' Bonnici said.

'Oh, aye. Not sure I want to talk about that.'

'Hard to believe she's effectively a spy. For the British.'

'Hard to believe, but it's a good guise, isn't it? An heiress, with money, travelling around the world.'

'I think you became close to her, didn't you?'

'There was a certain appeal.'

He was not going to be drawn to say more.

'So, at this stage do you know that Buchanan's killer was definitely not the prince, and that Miss Byrne had nothing to do with it?' Bonnici asked.

'Aye. For sure.'

'Sciberras is a shady character, I'm certain of that. I have evidence that he's been cutting corners with supplies, pocketing large sums of money by substituting low-quality products. Perhaps Buchanan caught on to what he was up to.'

'That's interesting. We know that Sciberras has been siphoning off supplies of goods and selling them on. Could Buchanan have found out about all these schemes? Was he threatening to report him? Also, Sciberras could have wanted a share of Browne's smuggling operation. If Browne refused, perhaps he had to be eliminated.'

'Hmm. But how would he have administered the injection?'

'I wondered about the quarantine doctor. We don't know for certain that he was accounted for at the time when Browne died. Perhaps he's in the pay of the keeper?'

Bonnici shook his head. 'I can't see it. I don't think he is capable of anything like that. He's without guile, I'm sure of it. What are the exact hours we're looking at? Seems like a long time since I did the post-mortem.'

'Between four and eight o'clock in the morning. The twenty-first – a week ago.'

Bonnici stopped and leant on his cane as he thought. 'It's hard to remember when things happened. But I think that was the night when we had to admit two more cholera cases... Yes, I'm sure of it. I was with Doctor Cassar all that night. We set up an intensive regime for the patients. There was no time to get away, or to do anything else.'

'What about the nurses?'

'It's possible. I don't know them so well. There are eight sisters at the hospital. they come and go round the clock. But they don't give hypodermic injections.'

'They might've observed how to do it though.'

They had started walking again. A fine drizzle had settled on the island, which reminded McQueen of Edinburgh weather, without the chill of the northeast wind.

'What about Miss Templeman? She was with you in the hospital at that time. Can you vouch for her? She says she was at Miss Copeland's bedside.'

'Well, yes, she was. So attentive to her friend. Quite remarkable.'

They walked in silence for a while, McQueen thinking about Eleanor Templeman. There was something bothering him.

'You know, when I asked Nellie Byrne what she was discussing with Captain Buchanan on the night of the 14th, she flatly denied she'd met him. I now know that it *couldn't* have been true that they were on the terrace, as Miss Templeman described. There was no connection between them. Why do you think Miss Templeman came up with that story?'

They had walked the length of the island and had come to a stop at the landing place, where Laurence Buchanan's body had been rolled into the sea. They stood, looking across the harbour at the fortified walls of Valletta. The city looked unchanging, permanent, a silent witness to the tumult that had been happening on Manoel Island.

'I can't guess. Perhaps she was mistaken,' Bonnici said slowly. 'You know, she's a complex character. A harsh outlook on life and the people around her, which seems at odds with her devotion to Miss Copeland. I didn't warm to her, despite my admiration of her nursing skills.'

'Is it possible she was away from the bedside that morning?'

'I suppose it is. She could've slipped away, to freshen up, or to take breakfast. I wouldn't necessarily have noticed.'

McQueen started thinking about all their encounters with the pale, aloof Englishwoman. What did they know about her? What was her history? Was there a connection with Buchanan they did not know about? He needed to get back and look through his notes.

'Something else,' Bonnici added. 'I overheard Miss Templeman say that she's starting a new position, as a lady's companion. I did wonder what reason she had for leaving her previous employment. Do you know?'

'I don't, but I can find out. Thank you, Doctor, you've been a great help.'

They turned back toward the hospital, the doctor walking with more difficulty than McQueen remembered. He worried that Bonnici had worn himself out with the long hours and constant stress of tending the sick.

'Are you winning the battle?' he asked. 'Against the cholera outbreak?'

Bonnici sighed. 'I hope so. I can't say for sure, but if, after the next day or so, there are no new cases, it's possible. I daren't say any more than that.'

McQueen would have loved to clap an arm over the doctor's

shoulders, to reassure him that all would soon be well. But of course, he could not.

'Well, Doctor, you have my utmost regard. Have in mind that one day soon you'll be back in Valletta. We can break open a bottle of the fine stuff together. If you can bring yourself to be in my company?'

The beginnings of a smile crossed Bonnici's face. 'Perhaps,' he said. 'But I make no promises.'

CHAPTER TWENTY-NINE

Valletta, Malta. Thursday, 28 October 1880

'Papà, you know you should be at home resting.'

Maria was trying not to show her irritation, but her father was pushing her patience to the limit. They were in the office, looking at galleys.

'The next edition is nearly ready to print. Look, here's the editorial you wrote on Monday.' She showed him the front-page proof, which had his piece about the first meeting of the new council following the elections.

'Hmm, all right,' he said, skim-reading. 'Not too bad. Bit short, perhaps. I'd like to add a bit more. What else have you got to do?'

Maria wanted to cover the latest in the murder investigation, but her hands were tied. She had written all she could about Prince Sundar. The official line was that he was in police custody, even though she knew about his departure for England. She would have to wait for permission before she could run her article describing his life, his recent adventures and how he had been treated by the India Office and the police. At this stage, she could not tell her father what she knew.

She had also not got any more background on the story about the cholera outbreak. This is what she wanted to add, on the second page of the paper.

'I've got the chance to interview and write about the two English ladies travelling together,' she said. 'Miss Copeland was lucky enough to survive cholera. Dr Bonnici was in charge of her treatment, and her companion, Miss Templeman, helped nurse her back to health. They've been allowed out of quarantine. I'm going to go and see them at their hotel. I want to show how Dr Bonnici has been dealing with the disease, a success story to make people feel less frightened that the cholera will get out of control.'

'But, Maria, you're leaving it too late. You'll have to have the story written and typeset by tomorrow afternoon.'

'It's fine, I have it all under control. Please, I want you to go back home and rest. You can see we're nearly there. There's just this perfect space, here, for the cholera story. I'll go and get some good content about life in quarantine, especially what it was like being in the isolation hospital. People will want to read this. I know they will.'

'Very well, but I also want to add some more to my editorial piece. I'm going to stay here until it's done.'

A peevish note had crept into his voice, which Maria had not heard before. It was difficult, juggling the demands from all sides as the newspaper production was nearing completion. The last thing she needed was him putting his oar in at this stage. But she respected him as well as wanting to protect him. She thought quickly. Perhaps she could leave him in the office for a couple of hours. She could interview the Englishwomen, then get back and make sure he went home.

'All right, but please, just do the bare minimum. Remember you're not to stress yourself with work!'

'Fine, fine, you go.' He had taken off his spectacles and was peering at the print. She felt a surge of affection, remembering how hard it was for him not to be in total control of his baby, the newspaper. She kissed him lightly on the cheek as she went out.

'I'll talk to Pietro,' she said over her shoulder. 'Make sure he keeps an eye on you.'

'Go, go,' he said, waving his spectacles as he spoke. 'I'm perfectly well.'

Maria had arranged to meet the two English ladies at the drawing room of the Grand Hotel in Strada Reale. She left her jacket, bonnet and gloves at the cloakroom and smoothed down her hair before going in. It was an elegant, airy room, with a high ceiling and large arched windows letting in plenty of light. She always enjoyed pretending she fitted in with this refined setting, even if she could not keep up the façade for long. It was a constant battle for her, not to do or say anything ever-so-slightly outrageous, just to shake things up a bit and see the expressions on people's faces.

The hotel attendant took her to a group of three armchairs, facing each other around a small mahogany table. Maria was pleased to see that morning coffee was laid out, with cups and saucers, plates, and a stand of dainty pastries and cakes. The two ladies rose to greet her as she approached. The smaller woman, with rich dark hair and lively eyes, spoke first.

'Miss Tanti? How do you do? I am Miss Copeland, and this is my friend Miss Templeman.'

Maria nodded at both ladies in turn. Eleanor Templeman seemed reserved. She was tall, pale, with a long aquiline nose.

She looked exhausted. Maria would have believed *she* had been ill rather than Louisa Copeland, who seemed charming.

'How do you do?' she answered. 'Pleased to make your acquaintance.' She felt faintly ridiculous spouting such English expressions. Louisa caught her eye, and they laughed at the same time. She felt she was meeting a kindred spirit.

'Sit down, do. Let me pour you some tea. I'm so happy to be better again, to be back in the land of the living. I can't tell you what a nightmare it's been,' Louisa said.

'I can imagine,' Maria said. 'Thank you so much for agreeing to talk to me, so soon after your illness.'

'Oh, don't mention it! You're so young though! I can't believe you work for the newspaper as a writer, and an editor. I am so impressed. You are truly of the modern age. Don't you agree, Eleanor?'

Eleanor smiled slightly and inclined her head, but Maria did not get the impression she entirely approved.

'I was brought up to believe I could contribute much the same as a man,' Maria explained. 'My father made sure I had the same education a boy would. The *Malta Post* is his newspaper. He set it up.'

'Oh, I'd like to meet him.'

'I'm sure you will. How long are you staying in Malta?'

'Just a week or so. We haven't booked our journey home yet.'

'Miss Copeland needs to be back to full strength before we travel,' Eleanor said. She looked at Maria coldly.

Discomfited by this, Maria pulled her notebook out of her reticule. 'Miss Copeland, do you mind if I ask some questions straight away?'

'Not at all, please do.'

'Can I start by asking about you two, travelling together. How well do you know each other? Did you meet in Bombay?'

Louisa looked at her friend quickly before answering. 'Yes,

we did. What was it, about a year ago?' Eleanor gave a slight nod, her face impassive. Louisa continued. 'I went there to see my parents. They've lived in Bombay for years. I love to spend time with them when I can. I've been living in London with my aunt.'

'So, you hadn't seen them for a while?' Maria asked.

'No. I'd been away for a year at finishing school. Then I stayed with my aunt during the London winter season. She took me to all the events and evening gatherings. That's when I met Mr Fenton and we got engaged. I'm getting married next year.'

'But he wasn't with you in India?'

'Oh no, he's a lawyer with his father's practice. He's always there, in Hertfordshire, working. But I admire him for that. It's a highly respected firm and he's doing well.'

Louisa put her hand on Eleanor's arm. 'That's how we met, isn't it?' she said. 'Two singletons on our own, at the Bombay social events. Naturally we started talking. We soon became fast friends.'

Eleanor looked away, unwilling to be drawn into the conversation. Maria wondered how it was they had formed such a friendship, when their characters were so very different.

'Anyway, thank goodness we had each other on the voyage and in quarantine. I couldn't have stood it on my own.'

'What was the reason for returning to England?'

'I'm going back to stay with my aunt for a few months. My parents will return for the wedding, but it's not until next spring.'

Maria moved on to ask Louisa about the experience of falling ill, how she felt about being taken to the isolation hospital. Louisa spoke freely of her appalling feeling of terror when she realised she had cholera. Once the disease had taken hold, however, she had hardly been aware of what was happening.

'It was like a bad dream that went on and on. Darkness, shadows, voices coming from a long way away. The thirst was terrible. I felt I would die for want of a drink. But then I remember cool hands, holding ice cubes for me. And Dr Bonnici telling me I was going to be fine. He was so utterly reassuring, it helped me get through it.'

'He's a good doctor,' Eleanor confirmed. 'He saved your life.'

'And you, of course. You were a constant. I can never thank you enough.'

Eleanor patted her on the hand with a slight smile.

'How was the experience for you?' Maria asked Eleanor. 'Over in the hospital?'

'Unlike Miss Copeland, I've no desire to talk about what's happened. I'm simply relieved that it's over, and that we're now off the island. A horrible place.'

'Yes, it's not just the cholera,' her friend chipped in. 'It's bad enough that while you're in quarantine, you're defenceless against it. The conditions in there are not good, you know, it's not clean. But it's also the atmosphere. You can feel a kind of horror lurking in the walls. I think it's the sheer number of people who've died there. There are ghosts, I'm sure of it.'

'You're being fanciful,' Eleanor said. She poured another coffee into her cup and added cream and sugar.

'But what about the murder?' Maria asked. 'Didn't that affect your feelings about the place? After all, there could've been a killer amongst you in the Lazzaretto?'

Eleanor narrowed her eyes. 'Well, I certainly didn't think *we* were in danger,' she said, taking a sip from her cup then placing it carefully back down. 'Why would we be? It's obvious it was that Indian prince who killed Buchanan. It was his dagger that was used, wasn't it? Besides, I'm positive Captain Buchanan was involved in some shady dealings. I saw him talking to more than one person late at night, receiving and sending messages. A person like that is looking for trouble, if you ask me.'

'Yes, but perhaps the place does have something to do with it,' Louisa said. 'Could it be that the sense of foreboding, the tainted air, the dark history of the place, makes it more likely that evil thoughts can take hold of a person? When I first went in there, I thought it was fun, like being in my own Gothic tale. But when I was ill, it really got to me. There's something awful about the whole island.' She shivered. 'I heard that there used to be a gibbet standing between the Lazzaretto and Fort Manoel, set there to deter those thinking of breaking quarantine. I can't think of a more suitable symbol. Anyone looking across the harbour at the island would be warned about what awaits them there.'

'Don't be ridiculous!' Eleanor said. 'The gibbet is long gone, the cholera outbreak is under control, and you, I'm pleased to say, are recovered.'

She turned to Maria. 'Have you all your answers, Miss Tanti? Miss Copeland is clearly fatigued, and in need of rest.'

'No, no, I'm fine,' Louisa said. 'Take no notice of my strange fancies. Tell me, Miss Tanti, what should we do while we're here in Malta? Have you any suggestions?'

Maria noted the deliberate change of subject.

'It depends on your interests. There's a great deal to see here in Valletta, particularly churches and palaces, a reminder of our history under the Knights of St John. Our countryside offers picturesque walks, including the spectacular cliffs at Dingli. And if you're interested in ancient history, there are archaeological sites around the islands, dating back thousands of years.'

'Now that sounds fascinating,' Louisa said. 'I love anything to do with ancient ruins.'

'If you like, there's a talk at the Ladies' Guild on Saturday afternoon,' Maria said. 'Professor Attard from the University of Malta is giving a lecture about the ancient temples at Ħaġar Qim. I'd be happy to take you there.'

'Let's wait and see,' Eleanor said. 'Only if Miss Copeland is well enough.'

'Oh, I will be, don't you worry about that.' Louisa held out her hand. 'It's been a pleasure meeting you, Miss Tanti, and we'd love to see you again.'

'Thank you so much for your time. It's been so helpful.'

Maria shook hands with both English ladies and made arrangements to meet up with them again at the weekend. She left with a stack of notes, knowing she had good material with which to describe the experience of one who suffered from and survived cholera. But she also felt uneasy. These two women had safely escaped from Manoel Island, but the killer had not yet been found. Was the murderer still on the island, or had he also left? Was he now abroad in Malta, or even on the streets of Valletta? After she had written her piece, she would try and speak to Inspector McQueen. She needed to know where he had got to with the investigation.

CHAPTER THIRTY

Valletta, Malta. Friday, 29 October 1880

The Customs House was a handsome neoclassical building on the waterfront, looking across Grand Harbour. Carstairs had sent a note asking McQueen and Galea to meet him there at eight o'clock in the morning. On arrival, they found Police Superintendent Ellis and Inspector Azzopardi talking with Carstairs in the entrance hall. It was the first time McQueen had seen Ellis since the governor had given him carte blanche to continue the murder investigation. He greeted him warily, wondering what his intentions were. Was he there to hinder or to help? Ellis returned his greeting with a brusque nod.

Carstairs took the lead, taking them into the Records Office at the back of the entrance hall. A series of ledgers lay open on a long table in the centre of the room.

'We've trawled through the records from the past year,' he said. 'Of the nine thousand ships that came into harbour, eight hundred had to go into quarantine. Of those, roughly a third were carrying cargo. We've started the process of comparing the weight of goods recorded against the quarantine records held at the Lazzaretto. And you'll not believe this...' He looked around the group, his enthusiastic smile revealing his protruding front teeth. 'Sciberras has been siphoning off over sixty per cent of quarantine goods, particularly the grain.'

'I knew it!' Sergeant Galea piped up. 'I'm not surprised about the grain – it's so expensive.'

'Well, we have a long way to go, and we'd need more manpower to get all the evidence we need, but it's clear as daylight that he's been profiting from stolen goods.'

'Good work,' Ellis said. 'I can certainly assign more men to assist you – those who are reasonably literate. In the meantime, we should ask Sciberras to explain himself, under caution.'

'Did you find out any more about where the goods have been sold?' McQueen asked.

Inspector Azzopardi pulled out his notebook. 'You were right about those warehouses in Cospicua. We have an informant who told us consignments of goods are being unloaded under cover of darkness, at least once a week. They're dealing with a great deal of produce coming in and out, some of it legitimate, but clearly not all. I've traced the ownership of the company that runs the business – import and export. Ultimately, it leads back to Riccardo and Gabriel Borg. I think we have grounds for a search warrant, to go through all the company records.'

'Indeed, we do,' Ellis said. 'I'll go to the magistrate immediately.' He turned to McQueen. 'Is this linked to Buchanan's murder, d'you think? Is it possible he found out what was going on and threatened to expose Sciberras? Was he killed to silence him?'

'It's possible.' McQueen thought of the beating he had

received from Borg's men. 'They'll go to any lengths to cover their tracks.'

'Let's move as fast as we can then. The whole police force can be pulled in. Inspector Azzopardi can take charge of raiding the warehouse. We'll take as many men into custody as possible. We're looking to gather enough evidence to be able to charge both Sciberras and the Borg brothers. This is good news, well done. Now, everyone, get to work.'

As they made to leave, Ellis took McQueen to one side.

'Finally, some progress. There've been too many blunders, too much time wasted. I expect this investigation to be wrapped up within a week. It's gone on far too long.'

Thinking of all the time wasted while Ellis blindly pursued Prince Sundar Singh, McQueen resisted the temptation to skelp him.

McQueen found himself once again making the boat journey back to Manoel Island, taking Sergeant Galea with him.

'I'll make sure Police Superintendent Ellis knows it was you that first uncovered the grain theft, Sergeant,' he said as they were propelled through the water. 'That was good detective work.'

Galea's face lit up. 'Oh, thank you, sir. I thought, now Inspector Azzopardi's been put in charge, he might forget that... not that it matters,' he added hastily. 'I mean, we work together, don't we, as part of the police force.'

'I'm not sure Azzopardi sees it like that.'

McQueen saw his chance to ask Galea about Azzopardi. The man intrigued him, he was such a closed book. 'I wanted to ask you, Sergeant, what do you know about him? Where is he from? Valletta?'

'I'm not sure. I think he's from Marsaxlokk – it's a fishing village down south. He can handle a boat well, that's why he was in the marine police. I've heard he's from a good family, well-educated.'

'I thought as much. Do the other officers think well of him?'

'Yes – but he's so serious. Religious, I believe. He rarely goes out, no one has seen him take a drink, or even laugh – not once. They call him Stoneface behind his back.'

McQueen laughed. 'Well, he's dedicated, anyone can see that. Good luck to him. We'll soon see what he's made of.'

He wondered what he himself might be called behind his back. It did not bother him. He did not have many admirers back in Edinburgh, not since he testified against two fellow officers accused of corruption. The men were guilty, and he had no compunction about appearing on the witness stand, but it was an unwritten rule of the force that you never betrayed a colleague. The hope was that by the time he returned to his old job, people would have forgotten. Somehow, he doubted it.

When they landed at the Lazzaretto, they went straight to the parlatorio where Sciberras had been told to expect them. Not the best of conditions, interviewing in separate parts of a room, through a wire mesh, but it would have to do. McQueen was relieved to find him there. Clearly, he had realised there was no way out for him, he would have to face the music.

Straight away, McQueen could see that Sciberras was not going to give them any trouble. All his bluster had gone. He sat deflated, sunk down in his chair, legs stretched out before him, arms crossed in front of him. The expression on his face was like that of a child caught pilfering sweets, guilty but looking to escape punishment.

'Right, Sergeant, I want you to take down everything this man says,' he said to Galea as he sat opposite Sciberras. Galea pulled up a chair nearby, pencil and notebook at the ready.

'Mr Sciberras. As Keeper of the Lazzaretto, you have made much of your highly important responsibilities. D'you not agree?'

Sciberras nodded. 'I've carried them out with—'

'Enough. I don't want to hear your stories. You've been revealed to be nothing more than a thief. The whole operation is being investigated. We know you've kept false records. We know you've been selling goods from the quarantine stores, as well as dealing in reduced price inferior products, while keeping the profits.'

'It wasn't much. It's not so serious.'

'It's extremely serious. The penalty is very high. Going back thirty, forty years, it would've been death by hanging. You'll be lucky if you get less than thirty years in prison. And how old are you? Forty-five or more? I think you'll be living the rest of your life behind bars.'

Sciberras looked at the floor, the folds in his face sagging.

'It wasn't my idea,' he pleaded. 'It was Borg. He came to me with the plan.'

McQueen drew his chair closer to the wire mesh.

'Look, the only way you can help yourself is to talk to us. Now. Tell us everything. If you're shown to be compliant, helpful even, it may help to reduce your sentence.'

Sciberras held his head in his hands for a while, breathing heavily. When he finally looked up, his eyes were blank. He appeared to be utterly defeated. 'What do you want to know?'

'Give us all the information we're looking for. When it started. How the operation worked. What you've done with all the profits you've made. Don't leave out any details.'

'All right.'

Sciberras talked for a good two hours, as Sergeant Galea took down the details, McQueen asking all the questions he could think of to get the full story. It was a case of opportunity and greed. The worst of it, of course, was that the goods could potentially be contaminated with disease, and sold on to unsuspecting customers. At the same time, people in quarantine were not being kept in clean, disinfected conditions. Corner-cutting leading to the spread of disease. McQueen grew more and more irritated with all the excuses, as Sciberras tried to present himself almost as a bystander, allowing the theft to happen, rather than facing the seriousness of his crime. Finally, when he felt they had as much evidence as they needed, McQueen switched to what he really wanted to know. Had Buchanan discovered what was going on? Was this in any way connected to the captain's death?

'You must conceal nothing. Tell me about Captain Buchanan. Can I remind you of the importance of telling the truth?'

Sciberras rolled his eyes wearily. 'Yes, of course. I will answer.'

'When Buchanan's body was discovered, you appeared to know nothing about his disappearance. Can you categorically confirm you didn't know anything about his murder?'

'Yes. That's right.'

'What about the dagger? Did you have any idea who could've taken it from the storeroom?'

'Grech told me. It was a few days after the dagger was found. He said Gilbert Browne removed it when he went to check on the diamonds in his luggage.'

'Why did you not say anything?'

Sciberras paused for a moment. 'I was going to ask Browne for some money, to keep quiet about that, and the diamonds.' He coughed, looking away. 'Only he died before I could do that.'

McQueen raised his eyebrows. 'Is that right? Well, well. Didn't I tell you that, Sergeant? Strangely enough, we guessed how you might behave, knowing your character. You and Grech are a fine pair, up to all kinds of mischief between you. Grech has been particularly busy, he seems to pop up everywhere. D'you know anything about a mysterious woman who Grech said sent Buchanan a message the day before his murder?'

'No, nothing.' His voice was slightly croaky.

'So, is there anything else you can tell us about Buchanan's murder? Are you sure you didn't witness anything the night that he was killed?'

Sciberras shook his head. 'I promise you, I've told you everything. I did find out what Mr Browne was up to, but I knew nothing about Captain Buchanan. All I knew was that he was supposed to be guarding the prince. When he died, I thought that no-good Indian had killed him with his precious knife.'

McQueen stood up. He had had enough.

'That's us done for now. As I understand it, Colonel Ellis will send some officers to arrest you later. For now, you're to stay confined to your office. Sergeant Galea, get one of the guards to take this gentleman back to his room and lock the door. Good luck, Mister Keeper of the Lazzaretto. See you in court.'

As the *dgħajsa* pulled away from the Lazzaretto, it was beginning to get dark. The wide edifice loomed over them as the boat dipped and rolled past. McQueen thought about all the events that had happened behind the walls, from the moment when the passengers from the *Poonah* arrived until the day Gilbert Browne had been buried. Sciberras had revealed nothing new, it was a case of whether he was to be believed or not. But McQueen had a thought rattling around in the back of his head. Somebody had said something significant, but he could not quite remember what it was. He had to get back and go through his notebook again. He felt sure that the answer lay there.

When they landed in Valletta, he sent Galea home for the

night. He went back to his office at the Auberge d'Auvergne, nodding at the police constable on duty. He lit a lamp, put his feet up on the desk and started to slowly read his notes, going through every page since the investigation started. He wrote down all the salient facts, with dates and details in a grid. It took him an hour and a half, after which he stood up, put on his jacket and picked up his hat. He headed to the nearest bar for a celebratory drink. He knew the truth now, he was sure.

CHAPTER THIRTY-ONE

Valletta, Malta. Saturday, 30 October 1880

McQueen had his team assembled. Maria had arrived at the police office early in the morning. She had come to find out the latest on the case and he had asked her to stay. It was a team he trusted: Carstairs from the governor's office, Sergeant Galea and Maria Tanti. The only person missing was Dr Bonnici, who was still in quarantine on Manoel Island. However, the doctor had already provided information that helped to unlock the case.

'Glad to see you all here,' McQueen began. 'We're at a crucial stage in the investigation. I think I now know the truth of what happened to Laurence Buchanan and Gilbert Browne. The problem is, I have no evidence. I need your help to work out what we do next to put the person responsible behind bars.'

'Who is it?' Carstairs asked eagerly. 'Is it that scoundrel Sciberras? I bet he did it to cover up his tracks.'

'No, it's not Sciberras. He's guilty of deception and theft, but he knows nothing about the murders. The person responsible is a most unlikely suspect.' McQueen drew breath before announcing, 'I believe the killer is a woman: Miss Eleanor Templeman.'

'I knew there was something strange about her!' Maria said loudly. 'But how could she have done it? And why?'

'I don't know why, but I found out she knew Buchanan much better than she claimed. I got to her through a process of elimination. Everyone on Manoel Island could account for where they were at the time when Gilbert Browne was murdered. Miss Templeman claimed to be by Miss Copeland's bedside, but Dr Bonnici was unable to corroborate that. The early morning was often the time she would slip away for breakfast. Also, there are very few people who know how to administer a hypodermic injection. She is one of them.'

'But that makes no sense,' Carstairs said. 'Why would she do that? What could he have possibly done to her?'

'I'll get on to that. When I returned from Manoel Island, I went back through my notes, right from the very beginning of the investigation.' He opened his notebook, found the right page and tapped it. 'When she was first asked about Buchanan, Miss Templeman said she hardly knew him, that she had only met him fleetingly in Bombay and then on the voyage to Malta. But she described him as arrogant, a typical Old Etonian. I noted her exact words. That was the thing that unlocked it for me. We found out where he went to school through Browne. But how would *she* know his school, unless she had known him a lot better than she let on?

'I think she must've been holding on to a secret about him, their relationship. She must've hated him, enough to arrange to meet him outside the Lazzaretto and stab him. The person who did this knew exactly where to plunge the knife, to instantly kill, which again fits with her nursing experience.'

'D'you think she had a liaison with him, in Bombay?' Carstairs asked, eyes wide with incredulity.

'It's possible. Miss Templeman was dismissed from her last position as a lady's companion, for unclear reasons. It could be linked.'

'Oh, my goodness,' Carstairs said. 'Is there anything else that backs this theory?'

'Grech said a mysterious woman gave him a note for Buchanan. It could've been Miss Templeman, getting him to come out and meet her.'

'She's tall, probably stronger than she looks,' Maria said.

'Aye, that's true enough. Also, the body was rolled down into the water. It wouldn't have taken a great deal of strength.'

'But what about Gilbert Browne?' Sergeant Galea asked. 'Why would she have killed him?'

'I think she got the dagger from Browne's apartment. He'd taken it from the storeroom. He would've thought of it as an item he could sell. It was an antique, valuable. She would've perhaps thought of it as a weapon that could throw suspicion on someone else.

'Then, when we found out about Browne smuggling diamonds, she may've thought it was too dangerous, that we'd get to the truth of where the dagger had come from. He might even have worked out who'd taken the *kirpan* from him, perhaps tried to blackmail her. For whatever reason, he had to be silenced. She slipped into his room in the night, while he was sleeping. She knew he took opium. She also knew how much morphine to inject to make sure he didn't wake up again.'

'I can't believe it,' Maria said. 'She's been so kind to her friend, looking after her all this time. How could she be a killer?'

'I don't know. But I'm convinced of it. Also, that she has to be stopped. But we've got nothing we can use as evidence, nothing that will stand up in court.'

'I've just met her and Miss Copeland. I went to see them two days ago. They're out of quarantine now, staying at the Grand Hotel. They're planning to sail to England as soon as Miss Copeland is strong enough,' Maria said.

McQueen raised his eyebrows. 'Is that right?' The first he had heard of it.

'Yes, I've been interviewing everyone who stayed in the Lazzaretto, for an article in the paper. It's in today's edition, here, see?' She held up a copy of the *Malta Post* she had brought with her. 'I really liked Miss Copeland, but I did find Miss Templeman perplexing. She didn't want to talk. I couldn't get much out of her.'

'Dr Bonnici also said he found her difficult to read. Despite spending so much time with her at Miss Copeland's bedside.'

'Listen, Inspector, I have an idea!' Maria jumped up and began to pace the room, her eyes shining. 'I left the two of them on very friendly terms. I'm seeing them this afternoon, at a lecture about the ancient temples at Ħaġar Qim. Why don't I arrange to go on a tour of the ruins with them, so that I can ask more questions? I could see if I can get Miss Templeman to reveal what reasons she might've had to kill Captain Buchanan.'

'Don't be ridiculous. It could place you in danger. An unacceptable risk.'

'Yes but, Inspector, what else can we do? You said yourself there's not enough evidence to proceed. I'm sure I can do it. I'm positive I can get you something you can use, even if it's just to question her further.'

'We've got nothing else at this stage, Inspector,' Carstairs said. 'And you know how keen the governor is on getting this case sorted.'

'Very well,' McQueen said reluctantly. 'I'll have a think about it. Perhaps we can work out a plan.'

Around midday, McQueen made his way to the *Malta Post*, at the foot of Strada San Giovanni. There he found Maria in the printing office, deep in conversation with a member of staff. She looked well, he thought. Taking on the responsibility of printing the newspaper had given her a serious and confident air that suited her. Her face lit up as he came in, and she quickly finished the meeting.

'If you could do that by tomorrow lunchtime, that would be perfect. Thank you, Pietro.'

'Yes, *Sinjorina*.'

Pietro left, clutching an armful of papers. Somewhere in his forties, he had deep-set eyes under a furrowed brow. He avoided glancing at McQueen as he left, which made him look slightly anxious.

'He'll do anything for my father. He's devoted to him,' Maria said as Pietro closed the door behind him. 'Been working here ever since the newspaper began.'

'How is your father?' McQueen asked.

'He's much better, thank you. The doctor says he can work full time again. He'll be back on Monday.' Maria sighed. 'I'll be happy to have him here, but I must admit I've enjoyed the challenge of getting these two editions out. It's been hard work, but I think they're good. What do you think?'

McQueen shrugged. 'Not much time for reading,' he said. 'If you're happy, I'm sure they're fine.'

'Well, I haven't had any complaints. People want to know what's been going on in Manoel Island, and I've given them a lot of detail. Now they just want to know if the cholera threat is over, and if the murderer has been caught, so they can sleep soundly in their beds. So, what about my idea then? Have you talked about it with Colonel Ellis?'

'I have not. His focus is all on Sciberras and Borg at the moment. He's got everything lined up for them to be arrested tomorrow. They'll be brought in for questioning and he wants me involved.'

'I'll need to know all about that for the paper.'

'You'll have to talk to Ellis. He'll let you know what you can print.'

'I'll go and see him later. And shall I make arrangements to go on a tour of the temples with Miss Copeland and Miss Templeman?'

'I think so,' McQueen said slowly. He sat down and picked up a copy of the newspaper, glancing at the column headings. 'See if they'd like to go on Monday or Tuesday. I want Sergeant Galea to go with you though. He's the only person I can trust. I'll ask him to keep an eye on you, incognito. He can be there if you need any help. And I'll be on hand, nearby.'

'Have they not met the sergeant? Will they not recognise him?'

'He was with me at the parlatorio when I questioned Miss Templeman. But he was in uniform, in the background. If he's in plain clothes, disguised, I don't think there's any chance she'll know him.'

He was uneasy at the thought of Maria being in the company of a woman who clearly could be dangerous. But if they were out in public, at a tourist destination, he felt they should be reasonably safe. It would be a good challenge for Galea, to try and blend in with a party of people and keep watch. He smiled slightly, imagining how seriously the young sergeant would take this role.

'Try and keep your questions light. We don't want to raise any suspicions. Just aim to find out a bit more about Miss Templeman's time in Bombay. She must've known Buchanan there, perhaps they were keeping company? It could be that if you talk to Miss Copeland on her own, *she* could give you more information. Send me a message if you manage to book a tour. I'll get Sergeant Galea booked on the same one, and I'll school him in the art of surveillance. He'll be your shadow, and a dogged one, I'm sure.'

'How exciting!' Maria said. 'I'll let you know what they say, after we've been to the talk.'

Again, McQueen felt a pang of unease. He got up, putting his hat on. 'It's not *exciting*,' he said. 'It could be dangerous. You need to take this seriously. Miss Templeman mustn't guess what you're doing.'

'Oh, I'll be careful, don't worry.'

The mischievous glint in Maria's eye was a concern. If he had any other way to proceed, he would not sanction a covert operation involving someone outside the police force. But he knew he had nothing that would persuade Superintendent Ellis to take seriously his suspicions about a young English gentlewoman. Much as he hated allowing other people to carry out the work, he had no choice. The trip would have to go ahead.

CHAPTER THIRTY-TWO

Valletta, Malta. Monday, 1 November 1880

Just as dawn was breaking, Maria met Miss Copeland and Miss Templeman outside the Grand Hotel. They were dressed sensibly in plain dresses, wearing hats and gloves, and carrying parasols. The weather forecast was for a fine day. Louisa greeted Maria warmly.

'This is exciting,' she said. 'I'm so thrilled you managed to book us on the tour.'

Professor Attard, who had delivered the archaeological lecture on Saturday was taking a group of tourists around the Ħaġar Qim temples. Maria had secured three places on the tour. She had been told that Sergeant Galea would be joining them, in the guise of an amateur archaeologist called Vincenzo Brincat. They had to make their own way to the site by carriage, where they would meet up with a party of around twenty people.

Eleanor Templeman seemed less enthusiastic. She nodded

briefly at Maria, while handing over a handkerchief to her friend.

'You need to be careful, Louisa. I fear this is too soon after your illness.'

'I'll be fine, I promise you. I can't wait to see those statues the professor talked about.'

'Ah, here's *Sur* Brincat,' Maria said brightly, trying to mask her amusement at the vision who approached. The young sergeant was wearing loose-fitting brown cotton trousers and a linen sack coat with a bowler hat, very different to his normal smart uniform. His moustache was gone. Without it he looked strangely vulnerable, like an awkward schoolboy dressed up as an adult.

'Good morning,' he muttered, hardly able to look at the women. Maria had been wondering how he would play the part of an archaeologist. It looked as though he had decided on acting hopelessly shy and withdrawn. Probably the best approach, Maria thought. She doubted he had much knowledge about ancient temples.

The journey in the carriage took over an hour and involved a hair-raising steep slope down into Qrendi. Louisa asked many questions about the landscape, which Maria was happy to answer. The fields were mostly empty of crops at this time of year, but there were still flowering shrubs and prickly pear cacti to be seen amongst the low rubble walls marking out the many small farms. Galea looked steadfastly in front of him, answering occasionally if Maria addressed him directly in Maltese, but not taking any other part in the conversation. Eleanor joined in from time to time but did not appear to be interested in her surroundings.

Maria asked about the women's experiences in Bombay, what they had seen and done while they were there.

'Oh, we couldn't do a great deal,' Louisa said. 'It was too hot.

Hot and humid. In the summer it got so bad we had to travel to the hill station at Shimla. At least there, it was bearable. In monsoon, when the rain came, it was unbelievably heavy. I've never seen anything like it.'

'The best thing about Bombay was leaving it,' Eleanor said. 'I couldn't stand the place.'

'What was Shimla like?' Maria asked. 'I hear that all the British go there in summer as it's so much cooler.'

The two women exchanged glances. Eleanor pursed her lips and subtly shook her head. Louisa coloured slightly.

'Very tiring,' she said. 'Too many parties.'

'It draws all the wrong people,' Eleanor said sharply. 'Appalling.' She looked out of the carriage window.

Louisa sighed. 'Oh, I can't wait to get back to England,' she said. 'It's been too long. I need to see my beloved Matthew again.'

Eleanor patted her friend's hand. 'Not long to go,' she said. 'Soon you'll be safely married.'

Maria wondered slightly about the use of 'safely', but as they were just arriving at Ħaġar Qim, she did not have time to pursue it. The carriage stopped alongside a group of people standing around in the sunshine and they clambered down to join them. Maria counted five other women, each holding a parasol, and around fifteen men, variously wearing top hats, bowlers, even a couple of straw hats. Professor Attard was standing in the middle of the group, with everyone turned toward him listening intently to what he was saying. A small, slight man in a black coat, his top hat was too big for him, sitting on top of his ears. His heavy moustache covered what seemed like half his face, but his dark, bird-like eyes conveyed his enthusiasm brilliantly. He clapped his hands as Maria's party approached the group.

'At last, we're all together now! Come, let me show you all

the parts of the temples. You'll see everything I talked about at the lecture.'

The professor led them up a rocky path to the top of a ridge where the massive Ħaġar Qim stones stood proud, marking out the prehistoric temples. He walked the group through the ruins, excavated nearly forty years earlier, pointing out pillars, chambers and an altar. He explained again the latest theory that they were built by the Phoenicians thousands of years ago, for worshipping gods thought to be protectors of sailors. Maria found her mind wandering. It was getting uncomfortably hot. She saw Eleanor watching Louisa closely, then leaning toward her to whisper in her ear. Louisa nodded, looking pale under her parasol.

'My friend needs shade and some water,' Eleanor said loudly. 'She's not strong.'

The announcement seemed to split the group. A few were solicitous, gathering around Louisa and offering advice. Others muttered and hung back. Maria could almost hear their thoughts of *well, why did she come along then?* Professor Attard stopped his lecture.

'I'm sorry to hear that,' he said. 'It does happen sometimes. It's exposed here, hot. Especially for the English, who are not used to it.'

Eleanor glared at him. He seemed to step back a little, his dark eyes blinking.

'We still have the temples at Mnajdra to visit,' he said. 'It will take some time. Can I suggest that you ladies walk back to the carriages? You can wait there. You'll have water and shelter from the sun.'

Eleanor caught Maria's eye, and they both nodded. Galea spoke up suddenly. 'I'll go with them,' he said. 'Make sure they have everything they need.'

'Very good, young man,' the professor said, clearly relieved the women would be looked after, so he could clear it from his conscience.

Maria was pleased the sergeant would be staying close. The rest of the party set off for Mnajdra, a third of a mile away toward the coast. Galea began to lead their small group back toward the carriages. Eleanor followed behind him, walking briskly in a fashion that suggested she was not in good spirits.

'I'm so sorry, Miss Tanti,' Louisa said, looking toward her friend. 'After all your efforts to get us on the expedition. I shouldn't have come.'

'Nonsense,' Maria said. 'We didn't know it would be so hot today. Besides, at least you've seen Ħaġar Qim. You'll feel fine again soon, I'm sure. Let's get you back to the shade.'

As they walked, the other two some distance ahead, Maria took her chance to ask more questions. It might be her only opportunity, so she decided to jump right in.

'You know, I got the feeling when you were talking about India that something disagreeable might have happened? When you were in Shimla?'

Louisa's face was flushed. Strands of hair were sticking to her cheeks.

'I can't talk about it,' she said. Her gaze was fixed firmly on the ground.

'Was it anything to do with Captain Buchanan?' Maria asked, knowing she was taking a big risk.

Louisa stopped in her tracks. Her eyes filled with tears. 'What do you know?' she asked.

'Nothing,' Maria said softly. 'It's just a guess. I thought perhaps you'd met him, either in Bombay or in Shimla?'

Louisa put her hand up to shield her eyes, staggering slightly. Maria felt bad. She knew she was taking advantage of Louisa's fatigue, her weakness. But she needed to push for answers.

'Did you meet him? Was he the cause of something unpleasant?'

Louisa sat down abruptly on a small boulder.

'Well, all right then, yes. I met him in Shimla,' she said bitterly. 'Eleanor already knew him. She warned me about what he was like. But I had no idea how awful he could be.'

Maria sat down next to her and put her arm across Louisa's shoulders.

'I'm so sorry,' she said. 'You don't have to tell me anything you don't want to.'

Louisa shuddered. 'He was a vile man. A seducer. Cared nothing for the consequences of his actions.'

Maria was taken aback by her venom. 'You mean he—'

'Took advantage of me, yes. Even though he knew I was betrothed.'

'And Miss Templeman had warned you?'

'Yes. He'd treated her in much the same way.'

'I'm so sorry. That's terrible.'

Louisa looked at her guiltily, as if suddenly aware of where she was and what she had just revealed. 'I shouldn't have said anything,' she said, clutching Maria's arm. 'It's a difficult subject for both of us. Please, don't say anything to Miss Templeman.'

Maria could see that Eleanor had stopped and was looking back at them. She seemed to sense that something was up. She started to stride back toward them.

'Come on, we're nearly there,' Eleanor said crossly as she approached. 'What are you two talking about anyway? You look very intense.'

Louisa said nothing. Her eyes were brimming with tears. She stood up, but all the energy seemed to have drained out of her.

Eleanor turned on Maria. 'What have you said to distress her? Can't you see how weak she is?'

'I just asked about Shimla,' Maria said. 'I'm so sorry, I had no idea it would upset her in this way.'

Eleanor quickly took Louisa by the arm, helping her along. She glared at Maria.

'Old history,' she said. 'Not something we want to talk about.'

When they got back to the carriages, Galea was waiting, chatting to the driver. He walked over to them with a flask of water.

Louisa sat down in the carriage drinking the water gratefully, while Eleanor dampened a handkerchief and held it against her friend's forehead.

Maria watched on, feeling uncomfortable. She could see the tension in Eleanor's fingers, though nothing showed on her face. Had she asked too many questions? Had she made it obvious she was fishing for information? She feared she had.

Eventually Eleanor spoke. 'Well, it's a shame to call it a day so soon, Louisa, don't you think?' She looked at Maria. 'We should go to those cliffs you told us about. Dingli, wasn't it? They're not too far from here, are they? The air will be fresher there. Louisa can rest on the way, then we can enjoy those fine views.'

'I... I'm not sure that's a good idea,' Maria said. 'It's still so warm. Perhaps it would be better to get Miss Copeland back to the hotel?'

'I don't mind,' Louisa said quickly. 'If Eleanor thinks we should go, then we should.'

'Yes, I *do* think we should. Get in the carriage, would you, Miss Tanti?'

Maria hesitated. What was Eleanor planning? Should she go along with her demands, or stay behind? If she refused to go, any pretence of a friendship would most likely be over.

Making up her mind to continue, she stepped into the carriage.

'I hope you'll join us, *Sur* Brincat,' she said over her shoulder, before sitting down.

'Yes, of course,' Galea said, moving forward.

But Eleanor had been talking to the carriage driver in an undertone. As Galea put his hand out to open the door, she called out sharply, 'Go, now!'

The carriage lurched forward.

'Aren't you waiting for *Sur* Brincat?' Maria asked, alarmed.

'Absolutely not!' Eleanor said. 'No reason to. He's interested in temples, not in us.' Then, to the driver, 'Quickly, cabbie, go as fast as you can.'

Maria put her head out of the window. She could see Sergeant Galea standing in disbelief as the carriage moved away. Short of running alongside and throwing himself into it, there was little he could do.

'Don't worry about me,' she called out in Maltese. 'I'll be fine.' She tried to sound more confident than she felt.

They left him behind, looking perplexed, his cap in his hand. She kept watching until he had been completely swallowed up by the cloud of dust from the carriage wheels. She was very much on her own.

CHAPTER THIRTY-THREE

Dingli Cliffs, Malta. Monday, 1 November 1880

Dingli Cliffs were over an hour's ride away. On the journey, Maria tried to talk to Eleanor, but she refused to engage. Her face was impassive as she looked out of the window at the rugged landscape. Louisa had closed her eyes, giving every appearance of being asleep. Maria's mind was whirling. Eleanor must have guessed she was digging for information because she suspected her of Buchanan's murder. What did she have in mind now? Why was she taking them to the cliffs? Maria prayed Sergeant Galea had gone straight to McQueen and that they were following close behind.

When they arrived at the viewpoint, Maria descended from the carriage with the two English women. She immediately regretted it when Eleanor spoke to the driver and sent him away.

'We're going for a walk,' Eleanor said. 'We'll be at least two hours. Don't return before then.'

Maria felt uneasy as she watched the carriage retreat into

the distance. There was nobody else around. No people, no other carriages. Silence, apart from the sound of the wind.

'Right,' Eleanor said, linking arms with Louisa. 'We're going to go and have a look at this famous view.'

The carriage had dropped them in front of St Mary Magdalene Chapel, perched on the cliff edge, looking out over a stunning view of the Mediterranean. Maria had been inside the tiny chapel before. She longed now for its safety, the solid reassurance of the stone walls and wooden pews.

'Shall we go inside the chapel?' she said, trying to keep her tone light. 'It's such an interesting little building.'

'No, we shall not,' Eleanor said. 'We're going to walk to that viewpoint. Looks like it commands an even better view of the sea.'

She pointed to a protruding spur of rock, some distance away to their left. It was bare, exposed, the ground dropping away beneath it. Maria felt sick at the danger she would be in, but she could not think how to get out of the situation. She would have to go along with it, for now at least.

'Come on, follow me.'

Holding Louisa by the hand, Eleanor led them along the rough, stony cliff edge. The ground tumbled away to the right, toward the sea. Maria could see shrubs, grasses, and prickly pear cacti hanging on to rocky ledges. The path was narrow, scarcely wide enough for two people. Maria picked up her skirts, navigating the stony ground, the wind whistling around her as she walked behind the two Englishwomen. Her boots were good, but every now and then she would slip on the sandy soil between the jagged rocks.

The sky was a strong light blue, with only a few wispy clouds breaking up the solid colour. The sea, eight hundred feet down, was flat. It stretched out to the horizon, where it met the sky in a hazy line, a vast expanse of blue with just a few white horses indicating any movement. On any other day, Maria would have admired its beauty, but now all she could focus on was how to deal with the plight she was in. She was terrified of what might happen when they got to the viewpoint.

'I'm not sure we should go much farther,' she called out. 'It's not good to go too close to the cliff edge. It's not safe.'

'But we must go right to the edge,' Eleanor said. 'It's by far the best place to get the view. It's such a lovely day. Come along.'

Louisa looked over her shoulder at Maria, her eyes expressing concern.

After about five minutes' walking, they reached the top of the stone outcrop. It was an area about the size of a small living room, tapering out to a narrow viewpoint. The limestone underneath their feet was rough and pitted. Scrappy clumps of grasses had given way to nothing but a few dried-out grey sticks on dusty bare rock. There was just about enough room for the three of them. Eleanor took Louisa to the end of the outcrop, then turned to face Maria.

'Right,' she said. Her voice was loud and harsh. All pretence at normality had gone. 'Now I've got you here – what are you up to? Why all the questions? All that pretending to be our friend, when all you were after was information. What is it you want?'

'Nothing. I *am* your friend. I promise you.' Maria had to speak up to be heard above the unceasing rush of the wind.

'Don't lie to me. I've brought you to this spot because now there is no one to hear us.' She was holding Louisa's arm tightly. 'Tell me what the police know. Did Inspector McQueen send you to get us to talk? Why was the sergeant with you?'

'It was my idea, I promise.' Maria put her hands up, stepping slightly forward. 'I've been following the investigation. I wanted to find out your side of the story. Sergeant Galea was sent by the inspector to keep an eye on me.'

Eleanor stepped back a similar distance, Louisa clamped to her side. They were terrifyingly close to the edge. Maria desperately wanted to get them to move away.

'Stay back,' Eleanor ordered. 'If you take another step forward, I can't answer for what I'll do. Clearly Inspector McQueen thinks I'm dangerous. Well, maybe I am.'

Louisa's eyes were wide with fear, as she clutched on to her friend. 'Please, don't, Eleanor. Why are you doing this?'

'You know why! This reporter here, this newspaper *hack*, she thinks she knows what happened on Manoel Island. Don't you?'

'No, I don't know,' Maria said, trying to keep her voice calm. 'I only wanted to find out how well you knew Captain Buchanan.'

'And I suppose Miss Copeland here told you what he did? What did you say, Louisa?'

'Nothing. I didn't say anything, I promise.'

Eleanor narrowed her eyes. 'I don't believe you. I can see from your face. You told her he took advantage of you, didn't you?'

'Not really.' Louisa wiped away a tear.

'I don't need to know any more,' Maria said loudly. 'I won't say anything. Your secrets are safe with me. Come away from the edge, please.'

'No. If you really want to know what happened, I'll tell you. Just don't come any closer.' Eleanor gripped Louisa's arm as she spoke. 'I want you to know the full story. So you'll understand that Laurence Buchanan *had* to die. He ruined our lives.' She locked her eyes on Maria's. 'If I tell you, will you help us? I want the police to know that Miss Copeland is not to blame for what took place.'

Maria nodded, swallowing down her fear.

'When we were in Bombay I fell into Buchanan's clutches,'

Eleanor said. 'I was a fool. He told me he would marry me, and I believed him. He soon discarded me, though, when he saw a prettier face. I'm not proud of it. I lost my position as a result. My employer heard of our liaison.

'But what was worse, much worse, was that he seduced Louisa, when we were in Shimla. Even though he knew she was betrothed. Treated her as though she was less than nothing.'

Louisa hung her head in shame. 'I don't know how he could be so cruel. It was awful. Then weeks later, when we were back in Bombay, I found out I was with child. It was the worst news. I had to find a doctor, go to him in secret, I had to lose the baby.'

Eleanor took up the story again. 'When we found out he was on the *Poonah*, we couldn't believe it. He didn't even acknowledge us. I talked to him one night, told him we would expose him for his behaviour when we got back to England. But he simply laughed. He threatened to tell Louisa's fiancé, knowing she couldn't afford for that to happen. I was so angry, I vowed to myself I would make him pay.

'When we got sent to the Lazzaretto, I took my chance. I saw the dagger, that Indian knife, in Gilbert Browne's room. I'd gone to see him with some headache powders. He'd been complaining of head pain. The dagger gave me the idea. I stole it, knowing it would throw suspicion on Prince Sundar. I sent Buchanan a message to meet me outside. I told him I had money for him, to keep him quiet. We walked down toward the water's edge, then I gave him an envelope. He opened it, found only pieces of paper inside. There was no money.' She laughed, a harsh sound, without any mirth. 'His face was a picture when he looked up. I was right next to him. I knew exactly where the knife needed to go and I pushed it in, hard. He fell to his knees. I watched him die, then I rolled him down and pushed him into the water. I waited until I saw him disappear.'

Louisa gave a loud sob, tears running freely down her face.

'What about Gilbert Browne?' Maria asked. 'Did you kill him too?'

'That idiot. He worked out I'd taken the knife from his room. He tried to blackmail me. When day and night I was by Louisa's bedside. Can you imagine that?' She laughed again. 'It was easy. He was locked in his room, but I knew where the key was. I took it, got inside, injected him while he was still asleep. Morphine stolen from the doctor's bag.'

Maria had all the answers she needed. She felt emboldened. She was sure she could persuade Eleanor to give herself up.

'The police don't know the whole story yet,' she said. 'Come back with me now. We can explain. I'll help you.'

She stepped forward confidently, holding out her arm. She managed to grab Eleanor firmly by the wrist and began to pull her away from the edge.

But Eleanor was tall, with a wiry strength. She would not budge. Maria was pulling hard, when she heard a shout from the path, a loud Scottish voice. McQueen! Momentarily distracted, she turned toward him. At the same time, Eleanor wrenched her arm out of her grip. Maria lost traction with her feet, slipping backward. With a lurch in her stomach, she felt herself falling out into nothingness. She screamed for help, but it was too late.

CHAPTER THIRTY-FOUR

Qrendi, Malta. Monday, 1 November 1880

McQueen was in the village of Qrendi, close to Ħaġar Qim, waiting impatiently for news from Galea. He had Battista and Genovese with him. The two constables were playing cards outside a café in the village square. He was sitting at a nearby table, unable to concentrate. Every two minutes he took out his pocket watch and checked it. When Galea arrived on horseback, it was immediately apparent something had gone wrong. The young sergeant was out of breath. He had lost his hat, his hair was in disarray, and his clothes were white with dust.

'Inspector, they've gone to Dingli Cliffs. I couldn't stop them. I'm so sorry.'

'Damn and blast it! I shouldn't have let Miss Tanti go on this trip. She's in danger now. We need to get to her, fast. How far is it?'

'About six miles. It's farther along the coast, not too far.'

He ordered Battista and Genovese to follow in a police carriage, while he and Galea took horses to get there more quickly. He was not much of a horseman, but a *karrozzin* would take too long. The road was dusty and uneven. It soon started to climb steeply. About halfway to the top of Dingli Cliffs, McQueen saw a two-horse carriage rolling past in the opposite direction, empty of passengers. There was no time to waste. He pushed his horse on, the poor creature lathered with sweat. Finally, they got to the viewpoint, where a small plain chapel sat looking out over the sea, at the top of the cliffs. They jumped down and tied the horses to posts in front of the building.

There was no one around. McQueen scoured the cliffs around them. Where had the women gone? Movement to the left caught his eye. He could make out the silhouettes of three women on the top of a spur of rock, around three hundred yards away. They appeared to be standing, talking. But two of them were very close to the edge.

He turned to Galea. 'It's this way. Quick!'

They raced along the path toward the stone outcrop. As they got close enough, McQueen could see that Maria had stepped alongside the other two women and had taken Eleanor by the wrist.

He shouted, 'Stop! Police!'

They were about thirty yards away. He was desperate to get to them, to prevent the drama he feared lay ahead. But his feet could not move fast enough. Before he could get there, he saw Maria slipping and falling backward. He heard her scream as she tumbled into emptiness. It cut through him like a knife. He stopped in his tracks, hardly able to believe what he had witnessed.

Eleanor stood frozen, her eyes wide in shock.

'She just fell!' she said. 'Oh my God! I didn't mean it. I was just... I don't know what happened.' She sounded panicked, her voice tight with fear. She was still holding on to Louisa by the wrist.

McQueen could not take in the horror of what he had just seen, the vision of Maria plummeting from the cliff edge. He had to push down his feelings, to try and control the situation. He started moving slowly toward the two women, his arm outstretched.

Eleanor pulled Louisa tightly toward her. 'Keep back,' she said. 'Don't come any closer.'

Louisa was crying quietly, deathly pale. She looked at McQueen pleadingly, unable to speak.

He could see Eleanor was beyond reasoning. She was desperate. He needed to keep her talking, to get her away from the edge.

'You don't want to do this,' he said, keeping his voice as level as he could. 'Face it, it's over. I'm arresting you for the murder of Captain Buchanan. You need to come with me now.'

'No. I'm not going.'

Louisa found her voice. 'Please, Eleanor, tell them. Tell them what happened.'

'No, I won't!'

'Please, tell him how it really was.'

McQueen knew then that his suspicions were correct.

'I believe I know already,' he said, speaking clearly to be heard over the wind. 'You worked together, didn't you? You plotted to take him out of the picture. Because Buchanan had seduced you, Miss Copeland, hadn't he? Was he threatening to tell your fiancé?'

Louisa nodded, tears running down her cheeks.

'You've no idea how cruel that man was,' Eleanor said bitterly. 'He left her with child, with no thought as to what might happen to her. She could tell no one, apart from me. We had to go to a terrible place to deal with it.' She held her friend's hand close to her heart. 'I'm so sorry, Louisa. Sorry for everything you've had to endure.'

She turned back to McQueen. 'When we ended up on the same boat with that devil, it was too much. He threatened to tell Mr Fenton, her betrothed, that she was of easy virtue, that he had enjoyed her company many times. It was wicked. Louisa nearly died, Inspector, because of him. She may never be able to have children. And I suffered too. I lost my position because of him. We decided the world would be a better place without him. When we all had to go to the Lazzaretto, we saw our chance to be rid of him forever. I'm glad we did it. I'd do it again.'

She was looking around wildly now. McQueen feared she would jump, taking Louisa with her.

'Let Miss Copeland go,' he said. 'She's suffered enough. You both have. Come back with me, now. I'll make sure you're treated fairly.'

'You don't expect me to believe that.'

'You can trust me.'

'Inspector!'

Galea's voice came from a few yards away. He had been edging around the group and was close to the point where Maria had fallen. 'It's Miss Tanti. She's alive. I heard her, and I can just about see her, I think.'

McQueen felt a surge of relief, but he could not afford to take his eyes off Eleanor. 'Are you sure?' he asked.

'Yes, she's caught on a ledge, a few yards down.'

'Tell her we'll get to her as soon as we can.'

He heard Galea calling down to Maria but remained focused on Eleanor. He felt a renewed energy, a determination to bring the situation to a close. He had to get Eleanor and

Louisa into custody as quickly as possible so he could rescue Maria.

'This has to stop,' he said. 'Before anyone else dies. Give yourself up.'

'Why should I? I'll hang. You know I will. I might as well die here.'

'It might not come to that. Give yourself a chance.'

She laughed, a brittle sound carried away by the wind. 'Are you thinking of a plea of insanity, Inspector? Defect of reason due to disease of the mind? Well, how about defect of reason due to a man's hold over a woman? How about defect of reason due to pressurising, cajoling, being forced into a position you don't want to be in, then holding it against *you* when there are consequences? Do you think that will stand up in court? Of course it won't. There is no way out for us now, whatever you say.'

'Listen to me. Miss Copeland wasn't the instigator. It's been you from the start, I know it has. Think about *her*. Give yourself up, so she has a chance.'

Eleanor appeared to deflate a little. Her shoulders sagged. She looked at Louisa and then back at McQueen.

'And what if I did?' she said. 'Would you let Miss Copeland go free? Nobody needs to know she was involved. She knew nothing about Gilbert Browne. Promise me you won't charge her, and I'll surrender.'

'I'll do what I can,' he said. 'I promise.'

'But that's not the truth!' Louisa cried out. 'I wanted Buchanan dead. I'm guilty too.'

'For God's sake, Louisa. Don't say that. I'm trying to help you.'

Sensing Eleanor's hesitation, McQueen readied himself to pull the two women to safety.

Before he could move, though, Louisa wrenched her hand

out of Eleanor's grip. 'I'm sorry, Eleanor,' she said steadily. 'There's no way out for us. It has to end here.'

With her eyes fixed on McQueen, she started to walk very slowly backward. 'It's all gone too far. Too many people have died. It stops now. I can't live with this. I've looked death in the face. I'm not afraid.'

'No! Louisa, please,' Eleanor begged, reaching out for her friend.

McQueen lunged forward, but Louisa was too close to the edge. He could not get to her. Quietly and calmly, she stepped backward and was gone. The last he saw was her white face, turned toward him, her eyes empty of emotion. She had been through too much. She was accepting her fate.

Eleanor gave a single cry and sank to her knees. Fearing she might attempt the same desperate act, McQueen took her firmly by the shoulders and drew her back. She did not resist. She remained motionless, as though she neither saw nor heard, her eyes fixed on the place where her friend had fallen.

The remainder of the day passed in a blur. McQueen felt empty, detached, going through the motions like an automaton. Genovese and Battista arrived soon after Louisa had fallen, bringing ropes and volunteers. McQueen insisted on rescuing Maria himself. Working together with locals from the village, he was lowered down to the ledge where Maria was lying. He tied the rope around her waist and strapped her to his chest, so they could then be pulled up, inch by inch. She was conscious when they reached the top, but clearly in a great deal of pain. She was given a few drops of laudanum by the village doctor, who then took her in a carriage back to Valletta.

McQueen's last task was to send a party to retrieve the body of Louisa Copeland. She had fallen hundreds of feet, hitting many jagged rocks on the way down. She was pronounced dead at the scene. It was many hours later, when darkness had descended that the wagon carrying her body finally trundled into Floriana, to the mortuary behind the hospital. Weighed down with guilt, McQueen walked to the police office and began writing out his report.

CHAPTER THIRTY-FIVE

Valletta, Malta. Tuesday, 2 November 1880

The next day, McQueen was standing in the hallway of the Tanti household, turning his hat around in his hands as he waited to find out how Maria was faring. At the same time as the maidservant appeared to take his hat, Michele Tanti walked down the stairs, talking to a doctor who was following him.

'We can do that, Doctor,' he said. Then when he saw McQueen. 'Ah, Inspector. So, you've decided to pay us a visit. Brave of you. This is our family doctor, *Dottore* Mifsud.'

McQueen could see the tension in Tanti's face. He could understand that Tanti would be furious with him for putting his daughter into such danger. It could so easily have ended differently.

'How is the patient?' he asked. He was anxious to hear the news. It had been a ten-foot drop onto a rocky ledge. The injuries could be life-changing.

'I think she'll survive,' Mifsud said cautiously. 'To some degree, she's been fortunate. She's sustained a broken ankle, broken ribs, extensive bruising, and a laceration to her face, but she doesn't appear to have a severe head injury.'

'My sister Paolina is with her now,' Tanti said. 'We're grateful to you, *Dottore*, for stopping by to give your opinion.'

'It's a clean break to the ankle. I think the bone will set well. I've applied a plaster-of-Paris cast, which she will need for three months at least. It'll just be a matter of time, and patience.'

'How's she feeling?' McQueen asked Tanti.

'She's sleepy, a bit confused. The doctor has prescribed laudanum. The pain comes and goes, but it can be intense.'

'Can I see her?'

'Go on up if you have to,' Tanti said testily. 'I'm aware that you saved her, Inspector. That it was you who risked your life to pull her up from the side of the cliff. Don't think I'm not grateful. But I also know she wouldn't have been there if you hadn't involved her in your work. She could have died. What were you thinking?'

'Aye, I know, it's bad,' McQueen said. 'I'd feel the same way myself. It won't happen again, that's a promise.'

'It had better not. Thank the good Lord she's out of danger. We must hope that the injuries will heal well and that she'll be able to walk again.'

McQueen stood in the doorway of Maria's bedroom, raising his hand in greeting at *Zija* Paolina. She gave a loud sniff and glared at him, no doubt thinking the same as Maria's father, that he was largely to blame for what had happened. The room was dimly lit, the shutters all closed. Maria lay propped up on pillows, covered with blankets. Her left leg was in plaster from the knee downward, elevated on a wooden box. He walked toward the bed slowly so as not to make any noise. Maria's face was lit by the orange glow of the oil lamp next to her bed. Vivid red weals covered the left side of her face from her cheekbone down to her jaw. The light accentuated the dark circles around her eyes. McQueen felt intensely guilty. He could hardly bear to think what this accident had done to her, and what the outcome could have been.

As he approached, her eyelids flickered and opened. For a moment, she did not seem to register who he was.

'It's Inspector McQueen, *ħanini*,' *Zija* Paolina said, 'come to see you.'

'Hey, soldier,' he said. 'How're you feeling?'

Maria's eyes focused. 'Inspector.' She attempted a smile, then said, '*Ajma!*' putting her hand up toward her face.

'Now, now, Maria, keep still, it's important!' *Zija* Paolina gently dabbed Maria's wounds with a damp flannel.

'Looks painful, sorry,' he said.

'Not too bad,' she said, her speech a little slurred. 'Doctor says I'll be fine. I'm a bit dizzy. Painkillers must be working.'

'You're in good hands anyway.'

Maria closed her eyes for a second, then opened them suddenly, as if remembering something. 'Is Miss Templeman all right?' she asked.

'She is. She's been taken into custody. She's quiet, compliant.'

'Good.' She sighed. 'She didn't mean for it all to go so badly wrong.'

McQueen thought of the two murders, the suicide and Maria's accident.

'That may well be, but it doesn't make for any defence in my eyes.'

Zija Paolina clapped her hands together, clearly wanting to draw the chat to a close.

'That's enough, Inspector. You must leave *Sinjorina* Tanti to rest.'

'That's fine, I just wanted to see the patient and wish her well.' He started to walk back to the door.

'I'll be up and about in no time,' Maria said weakly from her bed.

'Aye, I bet you will. Wreaking havoc no doubt,' he said, winking at *Zija* Paolina, who sniffed loudly again.

He left the room feeling sombre. He hated to see Maria like this. He never should have let her take on a mission by herself. He hoped to God she would make a good recovery.

McQueen started to head back toward his lodgings. It was nearly midday and still busy on the streets. As he zigzagged through the groups of people milling around St George's Square he caught sight of Trapani's associate, Luigi, handing out leaflets. Without thinking, he marched up to him and grabbed him by the collar. He had not seen Trapani since he had left him at the Manderaggio. He felt they had unfinished business.

'Where's your pal Trapani?' he asked. 'I need to see him.'

Luigi shrugged him off, glaring at him but saying nothing.

McQueen remembered that he did not speak English. 'Giuseppe Trapani? Where is he? *Fejn*?' One of the few Maltese words he had learnt from his landlady's boy, Antonio.

Luigi muttered some words in response, which McQueen could not understand.

'I need to see him, now,' he said more forcibly.

Luigi continued to hand out leaflets to passersby. He had a cobra tattoo coiling down the right side of his neck, which added an air of menace to his look. McQueen waited for a moment. Finally, when all his leaflets were gone, Luigi gestured for

McQueen to follow him. He walked across the square and along a couple of streets, stopping outside a battered pair of doors. The sign above the doors read 'Stamperia Bartolo, *Giornali, Gazzette, Manifesti e Volantini,* Strada San Cristoforo, 23'.

A printing shop. He knew that Trapani was a printer by trade. This must be where he worked. Luigi banged on the right-hand door with his large fist. A voice called out from within, and Luigi answered in a torrent of Maltese. McQueen caught the words *L-ispettur tal-pulizija.* The door opened almost immediately. He followed Luigi into a dark storeroom full of boxes of paper and printed material. Trapani emerged from the back of the room. He was wearing his usual shabby work clothes, his hair tied back, tucked under a black cap. His hands were ink-stained, and he was attempting to clean them with a greasy grey cloth.

'What do you want?' he asked.

McQueen thrust one of the leaflets toward him. 'What does this say? What is it about?' he asked. The words '*Malta per i Maltesi*' were written in bold letters at the top.

'It says, Inspector, that we expose the British for corruption. That the murderer of Captain Buchanan is caught and she's British – a woman. The British treat Prince Sundar Singh, an innocent man, badly. We ask Maltese people to join us to fight colonial rule.' He tapped his finger on the headline. '*Malta for the Maltese.* We want British gone.'

'You didn't waste any time, did you? We only arrested Miss Templeman yesterday.'

'I work all night, printing many leaflets,' Trapani said with some pride. 'Come, I show you.'

He opened a door in the right-hand wall and led McQueen into a busy workshop, smelling strongly of engine oil and ink. He stopped in front of a mechanical printing press with a large flywheel, operated by a treadle. He started up the machine, put a piece of paper in, which was pressed into the plate, then took out the printed leaflet.

'See, here is one. Five hundred I print.'

'And what do your employers think of you using the press for this?'

'They are happy. They believe in our cause.'

'Yet, while you're taking advantage of the situation, stirring things up, printing this rubbish, Miss Tanti lies at home with a broken leg, bruised and bleeding. *You* are the one who involved her in this. You tried to recruit her to your cause. You used her to get information about the police investigation so you could snatch the prince and use him for bargaining. Now look at what's happened. She could have died.'

Trapani laughed and raised his hands up in front of him. 'Oh, no, Inspector. You accuse the wrong person. You involve her first. You ask her for information. She want to help you, not us.'

'I'm sick of your antics. You've caused no end of problems. Do you realise how lucky you are not to have been arrested for kidnapping the prince? It's only because the Anti-Reformers spoke up for you that you've been let off the hook. Even though you jeopardised their position in the government council, Marsat persuaded the governor you were not a real threat.'

Trapani pulled over a box of ready-printed leaflets, opened it and started stacking leaflets into individual piles.

'Look, Inspector McQueen, you are outsider, yes? You see what happens here is not right for Maltese people. I tell you, we will not give up. We fight – whatever way we have to. Perhaps we are not "real threat" now, but you wait. The Anti-Reform Party is happy to go slowly, slowly. We are not.'

Trapani called Luigi over and handed him a few stacks of leaflets, sending him on his way with a slap on the back.

'For now, we recruit. More people. Not just in Valletta. We

go to villages, towns. We tell people how Malta is better as independent state, part of Italy, our neighbours, our family. We tell people the British want to stop teaching Italian at school, only English, that they want us to be like English slaves. We say no. No more.'

McQueen was tired of Trapani's rhetoric. The lad was deluded. Malta was far too strategically important to the United Kingdom of Great Britain and Ireland to ever be granted independence, let alone be ceded to Italy. Even he, who had been there for just a few months could see that. Trapani would never get anywhere with his half-baked ideas and his naïve attempts at political sabotage.

'Just stay out of my way,' he warned. 'And leave Miss Tanti alone.' He nodded toward the printing machine. 'If you cross the line and involve her in anything like this again, I'll put you through that press, bit by bit, until the only thing you resemble is one of your pal's tattoos.'

CHAPTER THIRTY-SIX

Manoel Island, Malta. Tuesday, 2 November 1880

All Souls' Day. The day of prayer and remembrance for the faithful departed which follows All Saints' Day. The light was fading fast as Bonnici made his way to the Cappella Funeraria di San Giorgio. It was a short walk from the hospital, but the path was uneven. He made his way carefully, cane in his right hand, making sure his left foot did not catch on any stones. Deep fatigue had set in but, God willing, this could be the last of the funeral requiems he had to attend for some time.

The chapel was tiny, just enough room for one coffin, a small altar and two plain wooden chairs on each side. As he entered, he removed his hat and made the sign of the cross. *Dun* Niccolò, in black vestments, was walking slowly around the coffin, swinging the incense burner to sanctify the space. Bonnici sat down on one of the chairs on the left, placing his hat and cane on the floor next to him. The coffin was raised on a low bier, covered with a black cloth. On both sides stood four tall iron candlesticks and four brown candles, flickering slightly in the air, dense with the woody, earthy smell of incense. *Dun* Niccolò carefully set the incense burner on a corner of the altar and began the service with the familiar words '*Requiem aeternam dona eis, Domine.*'

The body in the coffin was Patrick Cavendish, seventy-five years old. Bonnici had thought he was on the road to recovery but three days ago, pneumonia had set in, and the old man had been unable to pull through. He had breathed his last in the early hours of the morning. The fifth person to die from cholera, but Bonnici was hopeful this would be the last, as none of the remaining passengers had presented with any symptoms. Five was too many, but if they had managed to prevent the disease from spreading to the islands of Malta and Gozo, it would be a relief.

In the shadows of the chapel, however, Bonnici was not feeling thankful. In his coat pocket he was carrying a note from McQueen, informing him of the death of Louisa Copeland. This news had brought him very low. He had been so quietly pleased that he had saved Louisa from cholera. A gentle soul, a young woman about to set forth on the next stage of her life as a wife. He had seen her in his mind's eye, happily married, with a brood of young children. But now, suddenly, gone. A melancholy settled on him, not helped by his fatigue after sixteen days of round-the-clock care for his patients.

As he automatically responded to the *Kyrie eleison*, he thought about Eleanor Templeman, and the care, dedication and love she had shown toward her friend. How did that weigh against the wickedness of her deeds toward the man who wronged her? McQueen had explained that Eleanor had come up with the plan to murder Buchanan, for revenge. Louisa had been by her side on that fatal night and had helped move the body. But Bonnici knew she would have been unwilling, and that she likely suffered mental anguish as a result. The burden of her conscience, especially when she discovered Eleanor had also killed Gilbert Browne, must have been too much for her to bear. When she stepped off the cliff, he was convinced that she was not responsible for her own actions.

Bonnici's faith was strong. The Church's doctrines, sacraments and traditions were a solace for him. The Church taught that suicide was a sin, but he felt sure the circumstances, the mental distress Louisa had been in would mean her soul would be in Purgatory, awaiting purification. It somehow felt auspicious that he heard of her death on this day, All Souls', when the priest would lead prayers for all the departed. He prayed silently for Louisa, for God to have mercy on her soul. It felt like another heavy loss, one that would stay with him for the rest of his days.

The Mass drew to a close, Bonnici joining in with the words so familiar to him: '*Libera me, Domine, de morte æterna in die illa tremenda*' – 'Deliver me, O Lord, from death eternal on that fearful day.' He watched as *Dun* Niccolò stood by the coffin and sprinkled it with holy water. The priest then picked up the incense burner and swung it in three slow circles over the coffin, a final blessing before burial, the last words resonating around the small chapel: '*In paradisum deducant te angeli*' – 'May the angels lead you to paradise.' Two of the Lazzaretto guards arrived at the entrance to the chapel as silence fell after the blessing. The guards crossed themselves and without a word stepped forward, lifted the coffin, and carried it outside. It would be buried there in the quarantine cemetery, alongside the many cholera and plague victims who had died on Manoel Island.

Bonnici stayed in his seat, paralysed by the thoughts that crowded in on him. The grief he still carried for his wife, the shock of Louisa's death, his guilt for the patients he had recently lost, his sense of his own mortality. How much longer could he carry on, caring for the sick, his body letting him down with muscular aches, joint pain and stiffness? There was just one comfort, one seed of hope. He allowed himself to think for a moment of Carmela Caruso. She was ten years his junior, but she appeared to care for him. Could he think of a future with her? He was not in love, he knew, but he could help her. He would be offering her financial security, a respectable name, someone to support her in bringing up her son.

Dun Niccolò seemed to sense his sombre mood. He pulled a chair opposite Bonnici and waited until he looked up. The priest's eyes were dark and questioning under his white eyebrows and deeply-wrinkled forehead. 'What is troubling you, my son?' he asked.

Bonnici took a breath, shook his head. 'I don't know, Father,' he said. 'There's something on my mind. It shouldn't be so difficult. When you're young, marriage is an easy decision. You marry to be with the person you love. There's no question about it. You're desperate to join your lives together, to have children. It feels like you have your whole lives ahead of you. But, when that's gone, if you've lost the person who was everything to you, what do you do? Should you ever think about marrying again? What does the Church say about marriage later in life?'

'I think you know the answer to that, Doctor. If you care for someone, you absolutely should marry. Marriage is about commitment, sacrifice. It's for the good of both of you. It's one of the seven sacraments, a holy and binding covenant before God, whatever your age.' The priest smiled at him. 'Can I assume, then, you have a woman you're close to?'

Bonnici nodded. 'Yes, there is someone.'

'Then, what is it that's making you hesitate?'

'I don't know exactly. I've been on my own for so long. That brings some fear. There are also many things I don't know about her yet. I don't even know what I should ask, what I should find out first. I have feelings for her, strong feelings. I care for her and seek to look after her, but it's not the same. It doesn't feel the same.'

He was not sure he was finding the right words to express the deep-seated anxiety he was feeling. He felt trapped in his circular thoughts. How could a priest even begin to understand?

Dun Niccolò gave a gentle cough.

'Are you afraid that the basis for the marriage is more for convenience than for love?'

'Perhaps.'

'But you know that love's not just a feeling, it's a virtue. One that strengthens with duty, care and sacrifice. You can't expect the infatuation of youth. If you make the commitment, it should give you the grace to endure life's hardships together.'

That was exactly what he was thinking. It was that idea that was giving him hope. But was it enough?

'Thank you, Father, you've given me much to ponder.'

'You've had a difficult time, Doctor. You've been living on the edge of death for many days. Give yourself time to think, to pray. Trust in God's grace that you'll make the right decision.'

Bonnici stood up, putting his hat on his head and leaning on his cane. He had a job to do, to get the hospital back to full working order. The crisis was over. He would give it seven days. If there were no more cases, he would declare the cholera outbreak to have been successfully contained. He would be able to return home to Valletta. Carmela had written to him, saying how much she had been thinking of him and how fearful she had been while he was away. He felt sure of the decision he would make.

CHAPTER THIRTY-SEVEN

Valletta, Malta. Friday, 5 November 1880

'Telegram for you, Inspector. It's marked urgent.'

Sergeant Galea was standing in the doorway, holding a printed message as if it were a piece of touchpaper ready to ignite.

McQueen looked up from his desk. He was alone in his office, finishing off some overdue paperwork. It was the end of the working day. The sunlight was fast fading, and he was looking forward to drinking a beer before heading back to his lodgings.

'Let me have it then,' he said with a sigh, holding out his hand.

As he read it, he sat bolt upright. Marked Immediate/Priority, his eye was drawn to the name of the sender, bottom right of the form: *Miss Nellie Byrne, Southampton, 12.30pm.*

The last person he wanted to hear from. What on earth was this about?

He read it and reread it, trying to work out what she was saying.

> *SORRY INSPECTOR PRINCE SUNDAR ADAMANT MUST RETURN INDIA FULFIL DESTINY STOP ALSO SPOKE OF AVENGING BLOOD OF SIXTY-SIX BROTHERS STOP DO NOT FULLY UNDERSTAND BUT FELT MUST WARN YOU STOP FORGIVE ME NELLIE*

The steamship would have reached Southampton that morning. What did she mean? How was Prince Sundar returning to India?

'Have you any idea what this is about, Sergeant?' he asked.

'No, sir,' Galea said. 'The post-office boy just delivered it to the desk.'

They did not have long to find out. Loud footsteps came clattering down the corridor toward the office. Carstairs came crashing through the doorway, out of breath, brandishing another telegram.

'I say, McQueen, you'll never believe this! I had to come, straight away. What a fiasco!'

'Let me guess,' McQueen said heavily. 'It's about the prince.'

Carstairs looked at him suspiciously. 'How did you know?' He held up the telegram. 'This is from Scotland Yard. The *Arcadia* docked in Southampton this morning. Two detectives were waiting to pick up Prince Sundar Singh, but he wasn't there. He was never on board.'

McQueen sighed. 'How? How could that have happened?'

'No idea. There *was* an Indian manservant with Miss Byrne, but he wasn't the prince. Fooled everyone.'

What had Nellie Byrne done? Where the hell was the prince now?

'So the prince stayed in Malta?'

'Must've done. He's either in hiding, or he's escaped on another boat. I wager he's gone back to Bombay. Look, McQueen, the governor is away. He's gone to Egypt on a trip. And Police Superintendent Ellis is at some evening do at the Auberge de Castille. I can't contact him there. So I've come to you. What are we going to do?'

McQueen thought for a moment.

'Well, it's not an issue for Scotland Yard anymore, as the prince has now been cleared of any involvement in Buchanan's murder. You can send a response thanking them for the information but say that we'll handle it from here.'

'Will do.'

'Come back when you've done that. We do still have a problem. We must find the prince as soon as we can. Sergeant Galea, can you fetch Inspector Azzopardi? We need to work out what needs done.'

'Understood. Back in a jiffy.' Carstairs headed back out, clutching the telegram, his face a picture of self-importance, focused on his task.

McQueen sat back, feet up on his desk. Why would the prince not have got on the ship? Nellie Byrne had been clear she was taking him back to England, away from danger, on the orders of his father. Yet she had then covered for him, finding an imposter to travel in his stead. Singh must have persuaded her to let him go. He looked at the message from her. The prince was adamant he needed to go back to India, to fulfil his destiny.

McQueen could picture the young man's face, his assumed look of detachment. But, of course, the times he spoke with him, the prince was being held against his will. He had seemed intensely bored and frustrated. In truth, he was a young man who had set out with plans to prove he was a Sikh warrior, worthy of being the grandson of the Lion of the Punjab. Perhaps it was not so far-fetched that he would come up with this idea of deceiving the British authorities.

Nellie did not understand the prince speaking about 'avenging the blood of sixty-six brothers', but to McQueen it seemed clear. There was one person living in Valletta who had played a part in the execution of the Namdhari Sikhs. If Singh had found out that Colonel Ellis was involved, what reckless plan for revenge did he have in mind?

By the time Galea, Azzopardi and Carstairs had gathered in the office, McQueen had formulated a plan.

'Just as we thought it was all over,' he said, 'here we are again, on the hunt for a missing prince.'

'I've no idea how he has stayed hidden for all this time,' Carstairs said. 'Has no one heard or seen anything of him?'

'Not as far as we know.' He turned to Azzopardi. 'Have there been any ships setting off for Bombay?'

'None in the past ten days. Last ship to sail was on the twenty-third of October.'

'So, the next one is...'

'Tomorrow.'

'Right. Thank you.'

He turned to Galea. 'Sergeant, can you go and check the whereabouts of the *kirpan* – the dagger used to kill Buchanan? It was taken from the Lazzaretto and stored as evidence somewhere in this building.'

'Yes, sir.' Galea disappeared to the police strongroom.

'The thing is,' McQueen explained, 'I believe Prince Sundar Singh has decided the time has come to take up arms on behalf of his people. He's got it into his head that he needs to avenge the Sikhs who died at the hands of the British eight years ago. He must know that both Captain Buchanan and Colonel Ellis were involved with carrying out the execution. Buchanan has already paid the price, even though he was killed for a different motive, but Ellis has so far got away with it, without any repercussions.

'If the next ship to Bombay is leaving tomorrow, the prince has got to get Ellis tonight, before making his getaway.'

'Do you really think he's planning to kill Ellis?' Carstairs asked. 'I thought you said you didn't think he had it in him? When he was suspected of Buchanan's murder.'

'I may have underestimated him,' McQueen said. 'He's a young man. More hot-blooded than perhaps I gave him credit for. If you think about it, his whole adventure – setting off for Bombay, joining his cousin, becoming a Sikh – had fizzled out. He was returning with nothing to show from his time away. I think he wants to prove himself. He's after Ellis, I'm sure of it.'

At that point, Sergeant Galea came running back into the office, holding an empty box.

'This is where the *kirpan* was stored,' he said. 'It's gone. Someone has taken it.'

'That clinches it,' McQueen said. 'It's Singh. He needed to get his *kirpan* back. He's been clever, managing to steal it from under our noses. Thank God we got the information through in time. This is what we need to do. Azzopardi, get hold of Battista and Genovese. Go to the Auberge de Castille. Wait until Ellis leaves the dinner event and follow him back to his house. Don't let him know what's happening, just keep your eyes on him and be ready to tackle Singh if he appears.'

'Don't you think Ellis should be told?' Azzopardi asked. 'Warned that the prince might be after him?'

'No. Be it on my own head, I think it's better if Ellis behaves entirely naturally. I don't think anything will happen until he gets back to his home. It's too dangerous for Singh to attack him in the street.

'Sergeant Galea, Lieutenant Carstairs, we'll go and watch the house. Singh has had time to work out a plan for how he'll get in and ambush Ellis. We can stop him before he even gets close, I'm sure.'

'You'd better be right, McQueen,' Carstairs said. 'I don't like this. I don't like it at all. Seems to me we're taking one hell of a risk.'

One o'clock in the morning. Police Superintendent Ellis had returned home two hours earlier, but he had not yet taken himself to bed. It was just a short journey on foot from the Auberge de Castille to his place on Santa Barbara Bastion, a tall townhouse looking out over Grand Harbour. McQueen had sent Galea to watch the front of the house from the other side of the street. He had told Azzopardi and Carstairs to go home as they were not needed. He had stationed himself at the back of the house, in Strada Levante. He had a clear view of a small balcony, where Ellis had appeared an hour ago, leaning out over the iron railings, smoking a cigar. Then he had gone back inside. The room behind him was well lit. McQueen could only imagine that Ellis was now reading or catching up on paperwork.

From the back of the property there were several ways to get in, all of which he had in full view. On the road itself there was a padlocked wooden door and a shuttered window. These presumably led into the cellars. Then there was a pavement level, which could be reached from a set of steps to the left of the row of houses. Two doors belonged to the property, one wide set of double doors, one narrower wooden door. Both were locked. McQueen was sick of watching them. He had knocked on the door of the house opposite and persuaded the owner to allow him access to a tiny balcony overlooking the street. He was cramped, slightly chilled, hungry and thirsty. He had smoked about five cigarettes since he got there and his throat was dry and uncomfortable.

He kept thinking of giving up, going back to his lodgings. But he was convinced Singh was going to turn up. If he left his post and something happened to the police superintendent, it would never be forgotten or forgiven. He felt sure Singh had been plotting to make a name for himself by dispatching Ellis, to prove his status as a Sikh warrior. The young prince had to do something heroic to live up to his grandfather's reputation. McQueen shifted position again and started to roll yet another cigarette. He hoped Galea was still keeping watch, that he had not fallen asleep on the job.

Just as McQueen was pinching the tobacco out of the pouch, his eye was caught by a dark shape crossing the road, to the left of where he was standing. The shadowy figure was wearing a long cloak, with a hood. *Singh. He had been right.* He shoved the tobacco pouch back in his pocket, watching closely as the cloaked person silently crept up the stone stairs and along to the smaller of the wooden doors. Singh must have had a key cut, perhaps he had bribed a servant. It took him no time to quietly open the door and slip inside.

McQueen left his balcony and made his way down the back stairs, out onto the street. He followed the route the mysterious shadow had taken, finding the door had been left unlocked. Inside the house, it was dark. Knowing where Ellis had been sitting, he felt his way along the ground floor to the front hallway, and up the main staircase. It had been a couple of minutes. He hoped he was not too late. As he approached what he assumed was the study at the back of the house, he could hear raised voices. There was still a chance to stop Singh from doing something stupid.

He stopped behind the door. From here, he could see the figures in the room reflected in the mirror on the opposite wall. The young prince had discarded his cloak. He was wearing a turban, and a smart, long embroidered jacket. In his right hand he was holding the *kirpan*, the blade glinting in the lamplight as he brandished it in front of him. Ellis had stood up from his armchair. He had his hands up in front of him. McQueen could not see the expression on his face.

'There's no need for this,' Ellis was saying. 'It won't achieve anything. This doesn't help your cause in any way or form.'

'You have to die,' Singh said, his voice harsh and low. He was breathing shallowly, his arm shaking as he held up the dagger. 'I do this on behalf of my people. You murdered Sikh brothers in cold blood. You need to pay.'

He started to advance on Ellis. But he moved without conviction, as though unsure how to proceed. He still had the *kirpan* in front of him, but his feet moved falteringly, making little ground.

McQueen stepped into the room. 'Stop now!' he said. 'Give me that dagger.'

Singh wheeled to face him, his eyes darting from McQueen to Ellis and back again.

'No. I'm going to kill him.'

'McQueen, thank God,' Ellis said, backing away from the prince. 'He just appeared from nowhere. Disarm him immediately.'

McQueen pressed forward, holding out his hand. 'Give me your weapon.'

'No, I won't,' Singh said. 'Stay back!'

He turned toward McQueen, threatening him. But his arm

seemed to be losing strength, the *kirpan* held a little lower than it had been.

'I need to do this,' he said. 'This man murdered my people. He needs to face justice.'

'I understand. Believe me, I do. I agree that it's wrong. I agree that someone should pay for it. But it doesn't have to be now, and it doesn't need to be you.'

'It *should* be me. I am a Sikh, I've gone through the ceremony. I am a *prince*.'

The young man's voice wavered a little. McQueen could see the fight beginning to seep out of him. Then Singh gathered himself, holding the *kirpan* higher again, his arm locked in front of him.

'You are a prince, and now a Sikh,' McQueen said, standing firm. 'No one can take that away from you. But you need to give me that dagger, now. You have no chance of getting away, even if you carry out your threat. You'll achieve nothing that will help your people. You'll face the gallows. And if you're gone, who will take your place?'

'There'll be others to take my place. And I'll be a martyr, dying for my religion.'

'But you know you don't want that. You want to live. C'mon, hand it over.'

McQueen moved steadily toward Singh, who stood uncertainly for a moment, his fire and determination seeming to drain out of him. Then the prince tensed, readying himself for one last attempt, a steely look in his eyes.

'This is for the Sikh martyrs, you murderer,' he cried, lashing out at Ellis. McQueen stepped forward and kicked Singh hard in the gut, sending him off balance. The prince turned away, doubled over in pain. McQueen then grabbed Singh's right arm, pulled it up behind his back and twisted hard. The *kirpan* clattered to the floor. He pushed the prince down and cuffed his hands behind his back, before pulling him up on his feet again.

Ellis had been watching the scene from a discreet distance.

'What the hell's he doing here, Inspector?' he asked. 'Why's he not in England?'

'He's been in Malta, hiding, waiting for a chance to get to you. We just got word this evening.'

'I didn't get on the boat. I had to stay, to avenge my people,' Singh said bitterly.

'You don't get to speak,' Ellis said. 'Inspector, take this wretch away immediately and lock him in a cell.'

The superintendent was looking over Singh's head, as if he were no more than a nuisance beggar.

'I want a full report on this on my desk tomorrow morning, McQueen. I want to know how this happened. When did you find out what this heathen was planning? How did you let it get this far? You should have stopped him well before he could attack me, here in my own home.'

McQueen felt his anger rising.

'Lieutenant Carstairs can give you the details,' he said. 'We worked together. There was never any threat to your safety.'

'No threat? This savage went for me with a knife!'

'We were watching at all times. But never fear, you'll get my report in the morning,' he said tersely.

He made to leave, pushing Singh in front of him. He could hear loud footsteps clattering up the stairs, then Galea appeared in the doorway.

'Everything all right, sir?' the young sergeant asked.

'Aye, it is,' he said. 'Prince Sundar here got a wee bit carried away, but he'll be no bother now. Take him to the police office, will you? I'll meet you there.'

'What are you, some kind of sentimental apologist?' Ellis demanded. 'You need to arrest him for attempted murder. I'll see the magistrate and get him charged first thing tomorrow morning.'

'I suggest you speak to the governor first,' McQueen said. 'You might find he prefers to brush this under the carpet. Too much opportunity for the prince to have his say in court, too much being raked up for public scrutiny.'

He glanced back at Ellis as he left, allowing himself a small smile. The superintendent reached for the brandy, his hand trembling as he poured another glass.

CHAPTER THIRTY-EIGHT

Valletta, Malta. Tuesday, 9 November 1880

It was first light on Marsamuscetto. McQueen stood by the quay, where *dgħajjses* were waiting to take passengers to the SS *Poonah*. Prince Sundar Singh was getting ready to embark on his journey back to England. The governor had decided it was in nobody's interests for the prince to be charged, he was instead to be returned immediately on the next boat. McQueen had taken Singh to the landing place. Antonio, his landlady's son, had insisted on coming with him. Desperate to meet Indian royalty, he was brimming with excitement, bombarding the prince with questions.

'D'you have lots of jewels at your house? Lots of diamonds?'

'Some, not many.'

'D'you have elephants? Tigers in the garden?'

'No!' Singh laughed. 'I've never even lived in India!'

'I'm sorry about this wee rascal, he asks too many questions,' McQueen said.

'Oh, I have three little brothers at home. I'm used to it.'

McQueen looked at his pocket watch. 'Ship sails in half an hour,' he said. 'Time to get on board. I hope you're definitely going back to your old life in England this time?'

'Yes,' Singh replied. 'I'm looking forward to seeing my mother again. I've been thinking about it all. I'm not sure I'm cut out for being a hero or a martyr. I should look after my own family. Our father abandoned us. Living in exile, he's still harbouring dreams of revenge and rebellion. I went to India because I didn't want to disappoint him, but now I can see my mother and my siblings need me more. I'll find a paid position, perhaps in banking. That way I can make sure they're well looked after.'

McQueen was heartened by these words. Perhaps the young prince had scared himself to the point that he genuinely did want to get back to a more mundane existence in England.

'You'll need to be careful,' he said. 'Although Ellis has let you go, I've no doubt the powers-that-be will keep a good watch on you.'

The prince sighed. 'I know. But it's a fair price to pay, I suppose.'

'Let's hope you have a less eventful journey this time.'

'Indeed!'

They shook hands.

McQueen watched as Prince Sundar Singh, looking confident in an elegant silk-embroidered tunic and a rich, royal-blue turban, stepped into the *dgħajsa* and was taken to the ship. A great deal had happened since the *Poonah* had last arrived in Malta a month ago. He felt the young Sikh was leaving with a very different outlook on who he was and what he represented. *Good luck to him*, he thought. Proud of his heritage, yet reliant on the British who had deprived him of his status. It was a role fraught with complexity and contradiction.

When they got back to the lodging house, they found *Sinjura* Caruso had laid out a generous breakfast of bread, cheese and fruit. They tucked in, Antonio chattering about India and all the animals he would like to see.

They were interrupted by a loud knock at the front door.

Antonio scampered off to see who was there. McQueen poured himself a cup of tea and drank it.

Antonio came back slowly, holding a note out.

'There is funny man at the door. He give this to me. For you, Mister McQueen.'

McQueen took the note, skim-read it, then put it in his jacket pocket.

'What is it, who's it from?' Antonio asked eagerly.

'Never you mind, you wee rapscallion,' he said. 'Time for you to go to school, and for me to get to work.'

As he picked up his bowler and prepared to leave the house, McQueen wondered what he was heading into. The note was from Captain Borg. The former police superintendent was waiting at Il Cantuccio, a bar in Strada Stretta. He wanted to talk.

Despite their mutual dislike and distrust, McQueen was not concerned that Borg wanted to speak to him. Ellis and Azzopardi had charged Sciberras with theft and had sufficient evidence to charge Borg with receiving stolen goods and fraud. Whether he would be able to wriggle his way out was another question. Although Borg had been dismissed from his post, he had still not faced charges for perverting the course of justice, as uncovered by McQueen during his last case. There were constant delays and legal barriers. McQueen strongly suspected that Borg had at least one of the magistrates in his pocket.

Strada Stretta was a short walk away. Il Cantuccio was at the other end of the street from the bar McQueen frequented. A tiny place, on the corner of Strada Vescovo, it was known to be a low haunt, where dubious dealings were done. Sergeant Galea had told him that it was one of the establishments owned by Borg and his brother. Being early morning, there was no one there as he walked in, just the barman cleaning glasses with a grey cloth. The man nodded in the direction of the back of the bar. 'Downstairs,' he said with a strong accent. 'He is waiting.'

McQueen had to squeeze his way down a set of narrow stairs leading to the cellar bar. The room was bigger than he expected. As narrow as the bar above, but reaching farther back, with space for at least ten spindly tables, coupled with stools on thin, wrought-iron legs. The light was murky. Borg was sitting at a table opposite the foot of the stairs, his heavy features lit by a wall-mounted gas lamp to the right of him. He had a cup of coffee in front of him, and a plate of *pastizzi*. Camilleri and the two thugs from the warehouse were sitting at the next table, staring at McQueen with open hostility. Borg himself looked almost affable as he half stood up, gesturing for McQueen to sit opposite him.

'Well, well, Inspector McQueen. So, we meet again. Welcome to Il Cantuccio. How do you like my establishment?'

McQueen hesitated, not wanting to sit too close. Eventually he pulled across a stool from the next table, a good couple of feet from Borg.

Without his flashy police superintendent's uniform, Borg looked less imposing, but he still had a presence about him. Short and immensely broad, he was wearing a dark-grey suit with a matching waistcoat. With very little neck, his jowls appeared to rest on his collar.

'Not got the best reputation, I hear,' McQueen said. 'Why d'you want to see me?'

'Would you like a coffee, Inspector? I can recommend it.'

'No, thank you. Just tell me what you're after, so I can get out of here. I've a lot to do.'

'I'm sure you have, Inspector. I'm sure you have.'

Borg picked up a lump of sugar, dropped it into his cup and stirred his coffee, all the while staring at McQueen.

'The thing is,' he said, 'we have had some unfortunate – shall we say – "encounters" over the past few months. In fact, ever since you arrived in Malta.'

'Aye, we have. Especially with this pal here.' McQueen nodded his head toward Camilleri, who scowled at him.

Borg took a sip of his coffee.

'This is true. And this is what I wanted to talk to you about. Now, I don't know how long you're going to be in Malta, but while you're here, I am sure I'll have to keep sending someone to hurt you. To remind you I don't want you interfering in my business.' He reached out his right hand and clapped Camilleri on the shoulder.

'Now, Inspector, you've managed to show you don't approve of this. My friend here has many bruises as a result. But you can't stop me. I'll keep sending people to teach you a lesson. You might fight back, but the lesson will get harsher and harsher. It may well be – and this would be very unfortunate, but sadly all too possible – that one of my men here will go too far. It won't be my fault, but you know, sometimes they do get carried away.'

Looking at the bruisers next to Camilleri, McQueen could well believe it. They had the hard, expectant eyes of two crocodiles watching a piece of meat on a fishing line dangling in front of them.

'Go on,' he said.

Borg took a big bite from one of the *pastizzi*, flaky pastry dropping from his lips. He chewed and swallowed, then wiped his mouth with the back of his hand.

'Well, there is another way. This is how I see it. If you decide to work with me, rather than against me, this could be to your advantage.'

'In what way?'

'I can see, Inspector, that you're not a man of great means – even just looking at your clothes. It's possible I could make a lot of money come your way. All I would ask of you is to look in the opposite direction, ignore some business dealings you might find out about.'

He finished the pastry in two more bites, all the while keeping his eyes on McQueen.

'Think about it,' he said. 'I'm giving you a chance to make a sensible decision. One that works for both of us. You're perhaps not going to be in Valletta for long. You know that the city is mine. If you don't step on my toes anymore, I'll make it worth your while. But if you carry on as you have been, then it'll be the worse for you. What do you say?'

So, that was his game. Bribery and corruption. McQueen sensed an opportunity to push for information. He sat forward.

'I'll tell you what. I'll have that coffee, after all.'

Borg settled down in his chair, his jowls folding even further over his collar. 'Go get the Inspector a coffee,' he said to Camilleri.

Camilleri shot McQueen a dirty look as he went past.

'Tell me more,' McQueen said. 'What're we talking about here? You and your brother run a dodgy property company and an import/export business, dealing with stolen goods. You extort protection money from local businesses. What else is there? What exactly are you asking me to turn a blind eye to?'

'Look, Inspector, Valletta is a small place. It's good I don't hold public office anymore. Now my influence is everywhere.

Whatever people need, they have to pay me. Grog shops, bars, gambling dens – all are part of my business. For years I've been safe, no one can touch me. Now the police are looking too close, the governor even. This detective department – Malta doesn't need it. Things were working fine.'

Camilleri came back down the narrow stairs. The barman followed behind him, carrying a cup of coffee. It slopped a little as he placed it on the table. McQueen took some sugar and dropped it in. He took a sip and pulled a face. It never seemed to get any more pleasant, this bitter, spicy drink.

'There's one thing I wanted to ask you,' he said. 'Why did you help Nellie Byrne rescue the prince from Trapani?'

Borg shrugged. 'She offers good money. She is a clever woman. She arrives in Valletta and straight away she finds the right person to ask, to get a job done.'

'Why did you then go back and try to extort more money from her?'

'How d'you know about that?' Borg stared at him, then a light came on in his eyes. 'Ah – so it was you who was with her that evening. Interesting! You like this woman, yes?'

McQueen said nothing.

'Watch out for her. She has connections with dangerous people. She's not to be trusted.'

You can say that again, McQueen thought.

'She didn't even pay what she promised,' Borg said. 'She went back to England without the last payment.'

McQueen was impressed that Nellie had managed to outfox Borg, allowing himself a small smile.

'So, come on, Inspector. Back to my question. I can pay you as much as two times your salary every month while you're here in Malta, if you stay out of my business. What's your answer?'

McQueen took one more sip of the disgusting coffee, then stood up, putting his bowler hat back on.

'You can go and boil your head,' he said. 'If you think you can get away with *everything* through bribery and corruption, you can think again. It's obvious you have at least one person at the top of the justice system who's in your pay. While I'm in Malta, I'll make it my mission to find out who that person is and expose him.'

'You're making a big mistake,' Borg said. 'You'll regret it. The only person here who's happy now is Camilleri, isn't that right?'

Camilleri sneered at McQueen, exposing the gaps between his few remaining teeth.

'He'll be watching for a time when you're on your own, Inspector, and I'm sure he'll have some friends with him.'

'Him and these two? I've seen better heads on a pint of beer. I'll not be losing any sleep.'

CHAPTER THIRTY-NINE

Valletta, Malta. Monday, 22 November 1880

Maria leant her crutches against the side of her desk and lowered herself into her chair. The walk from home to the printing office had taken twenty minutes instead of the usual five. She had been helped by Rożi, but the age-worn limestone steps and paving stones were difficult to navigate, slippery with the autumn mist that hung in the air. She was tired, but triumphant, having proved to herself that it could be done. She had been quietly going mad sitting at home, itching to get back to work, even if only for a few hours.

Her father came bustling in, holding some papers and looking flustered, his spectacles pushed up on his forehead.

'Maria! What are you doing here? You shouldn't have made the journey!'

'I couldn't stay at home any longer, Papà. I needed to get back to work. Besides, *you* should be taking it easy, yourself.'

'You're right, *ħanini*. We're as bad as each other.' He peered at her face. 'You're pale. You must not overdo it.'

'I'm fine, I promise. I'll only stay a while. And we can get a *karrozzin* back home, instead of walking. Come on, Papà – what do we have for this week's paper so far?'

Her father leant back against his desk and smiled.

'Well, as you're here...' He pulled his spectacles down and held up the proof copy in his hands. 'We're leading with the story about Miss Templeman and last week's preliminary hearing before the Court of Magistrates. I've commented that both Laurence Buchanan and Gilbert Browne's families will be incensed that the defence lawyer has claimed the accused was suffering from a mental disorder at the time of the crimes. He's asked for extra time for Miss Templeman's mental state to be assessed by a specialist doctor, so the trial will be delayed. Who knows for how long? Given that she's confessed to two murders, it seems unnecessary to me.'

'I know, Papà, but don't forget I knew her a little. Honestly, she has suffered so much, and I do think she was not in her right mind. It would be so wrong for her to be hanged for murder.'

'Pah! I think you'll find most people will disagree.'

'Where is your compassion?'

'My compassion is with the victims. To me, there's something evil about what she did. A sharp dagger, in just the right place to kill Buchanan. A deliberate injection of morphine, enough to end Browne's life but make it look like an overdose. It's calculated. And it's terrifying. To think that a woman, who is meant to be caring, and who is even acting as a nurse could do this.' Her father shivered. 'It chills my soul.'

'We can't write about *why* she did it until the trial, whenever that happens. I somehow feel the public will condemn her before she gets there. I wish people could know about Buchanan's cruel treatment of Louisa. It's so wrong.' Maria sighed.

She took the proof from her father. 'What else have we got?'

'My editorial is about the first meeting of the government council. By all accounts it turned into a real battle between the Reform Party and the Anti-Reformers. They can't agree on anything. *Sur* Ricci accused the Reformers of rolling over for the British, going along with the proposed reforms to line their own pockets. He told them they're forgetting they are Maltese. I don't think he's capable of seeing another side.'

Maria read the column her father had written. '*Ajma*, Papà,' she said. 'Do you think you might have gone too far?'

'No, I think Ricci has gone beyond reason. He should face up to the reality of our situation and work out how best to work with those who govern and protect our island.'

'Plenty won't agree with you.'

'I know, but that's one of the good things about our newspaper. It's a place for informed debate.'

Maria would love to agree with her father, but she had a horrible feeling his comments in the paper would just encourage more of the bitter and acrimonious exchanges they had seen so much of in the run-up to the election.

'I think the governor and the chief secretary love to see all this in-fighting,' she said. 'It helps their cause to say the Maltese shouldn't be given more say in government affairs, if they can't even agree amongst themselves.'

'*Mela*, Maria, you're so wise! I think you're probably right. But it's still good that we're airing our views. It's progress, yes?'

Maria rolled her eyes. 'I hope so.'

She gave the galley proof back to her father. He put it down on the desk, saying carefully, 'Now, Maria, something you should know is that Inspector McQueen said he was going to call round to see me this morning. He should be here any minute.'

Instinctively, she put her hand up to the scar on her face. It was one inch long, red and raised. Dr Mifsud had taken care to minimise the scarring, using fine silk stitches to close the wound. The stitches had come out after a week and he said it was healing nicely, but she did not know how bad the final scar would be. She was not sure she was ready to be seen yet, but at the same time, she wanted to show McQueen how well she was doing.

The memory of her fall from the cliff edge was a complete blur. How she had managed to save herself and land on the ledge, she would never know. What she did remember was how long it seemed to take before she could be rescued. When McQueen had reached her on the ledge, having been lowered on a stout rope, she had felt an overwhelming sense of relief. He hardly spoke to her. Breathing heavily, he was intent on tying the rope around her waist as tightly as he could before shouting at the police officers to pull them up. She had to put her arms around his neck, her head pressed against his chest. It was terrifying, especially when she looked down, but she had trusted his strength, and she had felt safe.

Seeing him again would be strange. She did not know how she would react, or how he would be toward her. She smoothed down her hair, wishing she had a mirror to hand.

'Thank you for the warning,' she said. 'I hope I don't frighten him too much.'

'Don't worry, *ħanini*. You look fine, much better than the last time he saw you.'

At that moment, the bell rang at the front door of the office. Her father laughed.

'Right on cue. That'll be him now. I'll go and meet him.'

McQueen had asked to see Tanti with a delicate matter to discuss. He knew that the *Malta Post* was going to run a news report about Sundar Singh, based on Maria's interview when the prince was in hiding. He wanted to see if Nellie Byrne's name could be kept out of the account. Suspecting that Maria would not take kindly to what she would see as interference, he had wanted to talk to Michele Tanti man to man. So, he was a bit taken aback when he saw Maria sitting in the office. At the same time, he was pleased to see her up and about.

'A pleasure to see you, Miss Tanti,' he said, doffing his hat. As she turned to greet him, and he saw the scarring on her face, he felt a pang of compassion. It was going to be hard for her, he imagined. But she raised her hand, smiling, and seemed her usual self.

'See,' she said, gesturing toward her plaster cast. 'I can get about now, even with this thing on my foot. I have my trusty crutches.'

'That's the spirit. I knew there'd be no holding you back,' he said.

'I had to get to work. Any more time looking at those same four walls at home and I would have gone insane.'

'Take a seat, Inspector,' Tanti said. 'What can we do for you?'

McQueen sat down, putting his hat on the desk beside him.

'I came to find out when you're going to print the news report about Prince Sundar Singh, now he's back in England.' He cleared his throat. 'I have a favour to ask.'

'Oh, yes? I think you want to speak to Maria then, as the piece is all hers.'

'What is it, Inspector?'

He felt awkward. Not knowing exactly what she would be writing, he could be putting his foot in it. 'I just wanted to know – I'm aware you met Nellie Byrne, and she helped you get the interview. I don't know how much you're planning to include, but I need to ask you to keep her name out of the story.'

He watched Maria's reaction. True to form, her eyes flashed with irritation.

'Oho! So it's like that is it?' she said. 'You're trying to stop me from writing the truth, are you?'

'Not exactly. Just to leave some of the details out.'

'Why?'

'It's complicated. Look, this comes from the governor and Colonel Ellis as well. Miss Byrne is... let's just say of special interest. She has a unique role, and it has to be kept quiet.'

'You mean she's a spy!'

'Something like that.'

'I don't understand. Who exactly is she? Who is she working for? Why is she so important to *you*?'

McQueen felt colour rush to his face. 'She works undercover. Being independent and wealthy, she can mix with all kinds of people the government want to know about. We have to keep her out of the press, to keep her safe.'

'But she's twisted and turned so many times. I don't know how you think you can trust her. She's certainly got you at her beck and call.'

'Maria!' Tanti said sharply. 'No need to be rude to the inspector.'

'It matters not,' McQueen said. 'Miss Byrne is living in Paris again. She has no plans to return here.'

'I still don't like this. I don't like being told what we can and can't publish. Don't you think people have the right to know the truth?'

'Maria,' Tanti remonstrated gently. 'If the governor says we can't print this, I'm afraid we must comply. Clearly, it's important.'

'What about the freedom of the press?'

'We have to balance truth with recognising the importance of our role. We mustn't endanger someone through exposing him or her unnecessarily. I trust the governor on this. I know he supports free expression. This is a matter of security.'

Maria folded her arms, glaring at them.

'If you want to know, I wasn't going to put her in the report anyway. I'm not interested in her. She's not important to the prince's story.'

His mission had gone about as well as he had expected. Relieved, McQueen picked up his hat. 'Well, thank you anyway,' he said. 'I must be off.'

Tanti stood up and shook his hand.

'Inspector, I'd like to invite you to join us for a celebration. The eighth of December is the Feast of the Immaculate Conception. There's High Mass at St John's Co-Cathedral, then the procession in the afternoon. In the evening, we have a special meal. All the best food, I promise you.'

This idea seemed to cheer Maria up. 'Please come,' she said. 'We'll have honey rings. It'll be fun.'

McQueen thought for a moment. His father would recoil in horror at the idea of him standing in a gold-decorated cathedral, surrounded by incense, the congregation praying to the Virgin Mary. It represented everything rejected by the Church of Scotland doctrine. The thought amused him. There was also some appeal to watching the pageantry and a huge appeal to enjoying the evening feast.

'Well, you never know,' he said. 'I might do just that.'

CHAPTER FORTY

Valletta, Malta. Tuesday, 23 November 1880

McQueen had been summoned to the Governor's Palace for 5pm sharp. The note from Carstairs told him 'smart attire', saying he would find out why when he got there. Not having anything smarter, he had resorted to brushing and pressing his normal tweed suit and giving his boots a polish. That would have to do.

Arriving at the entrance, he was met by Carstairs, wearing full ceremonial uniform.

'What's all this then?' he asked. He felt a bit disconcerted, not knowing what he was being dragged into.

'Oh, you'll find out,' Carstairs said, flashing him a brief smile. 'Follow me. I'm to take you to the Tapestry Chamber.'

Their heels clacked on the marble floor as they trekked up the main staircase and along the corridor lined with suits of armour and paintings of the Grand Masters of Malta. The Tapestry Chamber – so called because of the ten-foot tapestries lining the walls – was where the Council of Government meetings were held. McQueen had been taken there by the governor once before, and had found it oppressive with its ornate ceiling, busy frescoes and colossal wall-hangings. He continued to feel mystified as to why he had been summoned there.

As Carstairs opened the door, McQueen saw Sir Thomas Grant, the governor, seated on a gold throne in front of a large mahogany desk, dressed in full military regalia. Grant stood up as they entered, motioning for them to approach. Colonel Ellis, also in dress uniform, stood at the front of the rows of desks and chairs normally reserved for the government council. McQueen's heart sank. If he could have turned around on the spot and walked out, he would have. Carstairs marched up to the desk and saluted first the governor and then Colonel Ellis. They both returned his salutes. McQueen felt like a claymore at a garden party, completely out of place.

'Detective Inspector McQueen,' Grant said in a rich, formal tone. 'So glad you could join us. I wanted to thank you for the role you played in protecting Police Superintendent Ellis from attack and murder in his own home by the Sikh prince, Sundar Singh.' He cleared his throat and picked up a sturdy piece of paper. 'I've taken the liberty of writing a report commending you for your bravery, which I've sent to the Superintendent of the Edinburgh Police and the Colonial Office. This is a copy of the report for you.'

The governor held out the piece of paper, which McQueen felt obliged to take. He glanced over it, then put it down on the desk.

'I wish you hadn't,' he said. 'It wasn't anything. Singh is young, easily dealt with. He wasn't much of a threat.'

'You don't know that,' Ellis said. 'He might be young, but Singh was set on bloody revenge. I saw it in his eyes. He was determined.'

McQueen sighed. He clearly was not going to get through to them. 'We'll have to agree to differ,' he said.

'Listen, McQueen, I do have to admit you were right about one thing. Obviously Singh was not guilty of killing Buchanan. I was convinced it was him, and that did make me blinkered. In my defence, I've good reason to distrust the Sikhs, having served in the Punjab.'

McQueen felt his anger flare up again. 'You never clarified what part you played, Colonel, in the execution of Sikhs at Malerkotla. *Did* you give the order to fire? Did you kill all those men, brutally, without a trial?'

A shadow crossed Ellis's face. His eyes narrowed as he looked at McQueen. 'I did what was necessary,' he said tersely. 'I had direct orders from the deputy commissioner. He wanted to make an example of the prisoners, to quash potential rebellion.'

'I have to say, it didn't go down well,' Grant said. 'Questions were asked in Parliament. The press didn't like it, nor the wider public. People saw the act as brutal, unwarranted. The deputy commissioner was removed from his post. It's not a great part of our recent history.'

'What part is?' McQueen retorted.

Carstairs, ever diplomatic, stepped in. 'That was some time ago,' he said, 'and in India. We're in Malta now. Can we not leave all that behind us?'

'Yes, Inspector,' Ellis said. 'We have a job to do. You agreed to stay in Malta for as much time as it takes to set up a detective department. Seems to me there's still a great deal to do before that's achieved.'

McQueen thought about his team, especially Sergeant Galea who had contributed so much to the investigation. He did not want to let them down. Could he continue to work with Ellis? Could he trust him to support his ideas?

'Give me additional men, and the means to see this task through, and I'll achieve it,' he said.

'You'll get everything you need, Inspector,' Sir Thomas Grant said. 'I thank you again for your contribution.'

McQueen turned and started to walk away.

Carstairs put his helmet back on and smartly saluted. Picking up the piece of paper from the governor's desk, he left with McQueen.

'Well done, Inspector,' he said under his breath. 'That's a major honour; like being mentioned in dispatches.'

'Just get me to a bar, Carstairs. Soon as you can. I need a drink.'

He took the paper from Carstairs's hand, scrunched it up, and drop-kicked it along the corridor, where it skittered to a halt on the fine marble floor.

McQueen was due to dine at his lodging house around seven. He was looking forward to seeing Dr Bonnici again. He had heard about the doctor's promotion and had bought a modestly priced bottle of champagne to celebrate.

Antonio came scampering up as he opened the front door.

'Mister McQueen – the doctor is here. We wait for you!'

McQueen ruffled the lad's hair. He was a bright wee thing. His English had improved so much in just a few months.

'Give that to your mother,' he said, handing over the bottle. 'But don't shake it up or it will explode.'

He laughed to see the serious expression on Antonio's face as he carried the champagne into the kitchen, treating it like a stick of dynamite.

Bonnici came out to greet him and they went into the dining room together. The doctor looked healthier than the last time he had seen him. He looked less exhausted, more at peace with himself.

'Congratulations,' McQueen said. 'I believe I'm now addressing the Chief Police Physician of Malta. Be careful the power doesn't go to your head.'

Bonnici smiled. 'It'll be good,' he said. 'I can make the changes I think we need to ensure our country is safer and healthier. Although it'll mean more meetings. Many, many more meetings. I'm not sure how I feel about that.'

Sinjura Caruso appeared with a tray of glasses and the champagne.

'You have to open this bottle,' she said. 'I've no idea how to do it.'

Bonnici opened it with a loud pop and quickly poured three full glasses and a tiny shot for Antonio. 'Here you are,' he said, handing it to the boy. 'Just a sip for you.'

'A toast,' McQueen said. 'To Dr Bonnici – may your patients be grateful, your staff be sane, and your whisky be never watered down! *Slàinte!*'

Bonnici smiled and took a sip. 'There's another thing,' he said. He looked over at *Sinjura* Caruso, his eyes asking a question. She smiled warmly and nodded.

He held up his glass. 'While I was on Manoel Island, I had much time to think and reflect. I came to realise that my life was lacking something very special. And as soon as I could leave the island, I came here to ask this lovely lady if she would consider becoming my wife.'

McQueen could hardly believe what he was hearing.

'And I'm happy to report that she said yes.'

'Well, now this really is a big celebration,' McQueen said. 'Let's all have some more champagne.'

The happy couple stood together and clinked glasses, engrossed in their own world. He was delighted for them, but he noticed Antonio was not so sure. The lad did not seem to enjoy the champagne. He put his glass down on the table, his face empty of expression. McQueen put his arm over the boy's shoulders. He could feel him wanting to pull away. Things were going to change. Perhaps the boy was not as happy about it as his friend might hope.

Later, his belly full of the Maltese baked pasta he had grown to love, McQueen went outside for a cigarette. Bonnici came out to join him – unusual – as he seldom smoked.

'Couldn't be happier for you,' McQueen said. 'It seems to me you share a good understanding.'

'I believe so,' Bonnici replied. 'I realised I wanted to be close to someone again. We're not so young, either of us. It feels like we'll suit each other well.'

'When d'you think you'll wed?'

'Oh, not for some time. There are many things we need to sort out.' Bonnici drew a tin of cigarillos from his jacket pocket and took one out. McQueen struck a match and held the flame steady. The doctor lit his cigarillo, exhaling the smoke with some elegance. 'Champagne and tobacco in one evening. How decadent,' he said. 'Tell me, did you hear from the American woman again? What was her name?'

'Nellie Byrne. Yes, I did.'

Nellie's letter was folded in his breast pocket. He knew it almost by heart.

> *Dear Inspector,*
>
> *Quite the adventure we've had. I hope you've forgiven me for the part I had to play.*

It was good to meet you. At another time, in another place we might have gotten along well, I believe.

I'm living in Paris again. Interesting times. Perhaps our paths will cross again one day. I sure hope so.

Nellie

'She left quite an impression on you, yes?'

He dropped his cigarette and ground it on the flagstone floor. 'About as trustworthy as a snake in a silk cravat, but yes, she did intrigue me.'

'So, what next, Inspector? Any plans?'

He thought about Jeannie, back in Edinburgh. There was nothing there for him. She did not want him anymore. Should he throw caution to the wind, follow Nellie Byrne to Paris? No, that was fraught with difficulty. The idea of staying in Malta had far more appeal. He needed to achieve what he had set out to do, before he could think about going back.

'I've some things to straighten out, some systems to set in place. I'll be around for a few more months, I think. If you hurry up with the arrangements, I might even be here to see you wed.'

'Take your time, Inspector. This is the Mediterranean. We're known for a more leisurely pace of life. Come, let's have another glass of wine.'

'You'll not need to twist my arm, Doctor. Lead the way.'

THE END

AUTHOR'S NOTE

Although this is a work of fiction, I have attempted to reflect some of the events and concerns of the day.

In 1880, Malta was an important strategic part of the British Empire. Six thousand troops were stationed in Malta, and it was a key naval station. Between seven and nine thousand ships of all types, carrying passengers and goods, would have stopped in the harbours each year, taking on coal and provisions.

Political Situation

Governors of Malta were generally military men without experience of civil administration. The Council of Government included elected members representing the Maltese people, but these were outnumbered eight to ten by members appointed by the governor.

A petition from the Maltese people for representative government and a civilian administrator, signed by nine thousand people, was sent to Parliament in 1879 and again in January 1880. The reply from Lord Kimberley, Secretary of State for the Colonies, published in August 1880, was very badly received, saying that as Malta was an 'Imperial Fortress and a Naval Station', it could not be treated as a normal colony.

A new nationalist movement emerged in 1880 in the form of the Partito Anti-Riformista, under the leadership of Dr Fortunato Mizzi. The party protested against a series of reforms announced in 1880, following reports commissioned by the British government. The proposals included the reform of taxes and public administration, and the Anglicisation of the educational and judicial systems, starting with English being taught at primary school instead of Italian.

Government Council elections were held between 13 and 16 October 1880, with the results announced Wednesday 20 October. Of the eight Maltese elected members, five were from the Partito Anti-Riformista.

Poverty was a real problem within the Maltese population at this time. The Bread Tax made it difficult for working classes to afford basic foods. Overcrowding and insanitary conditions in the Mandraġġ – an infamous area of Valletta – had been highlighted in petitions to the British government.

The breakaway group Gruppo Militante Pro Italiano is a fabrication. Italian irredentism in Malta advocated for the incorporation of the Maltese islands into Italy. Around this time, Governor of Malta Sir Arthur Borton expressed concern that irredentist ideas were gaining influence among young Maltese men, though there was little evidence to support this view.

The Lazzaretto

The Lazzaretto of Malta, located on Manoel Island in Marsamxett Harbour, was established in 1643 as a quarantine station to control diseases such as plague, yellow fever and cholera. Expanded over the years, it became a complex of stone buildings used to isolate travellers and disinfect cargo. During the first half of the 19th century, thousands of people were held in quarantine when ships arrived from ports reporting outbreaks of plague or cholera. Regulations were exceptionally strict, enforced by health guards known as 'guardians'. By 1880, however, quarantine measures were applied much more sparingly and the Lazzaretto saw much less use. Communication with those in quarantine had once been conducted through the parlatorio in Valletta, near Barriera Wharf, but this facility was no longer in use by then. I had to invent a parlatorio at the Lazzaretto to enable the characters to communicate with those from outside.

The last Maharaja of the Sikh Empire

I was inspired to create the character of Prince Sundar Singh by the story of Maharaja Duleep Singh, the last Maharaja of the Sikh Empire, which I read about in Anita Anand's wonderful book *Sophia: Princess, Suffragette, Revolutionary*. Sophia Duleep Singh was the daughter of Sir Duleep Singh, the youngest son of Ranjit Singh, the so-called 'Lion of the Punjab'. Duleep Singh inherited the title of Maharaja at five years old but in 1849 was deposed by the British, separated from his mother, and placed under the care of the British authorities.

He was sent to England and raised as a Christian by a British guardian. A great favourite of Queen Victoria's, Duleep Singh lived as an aristocrat, fully embracing British culture. However, from 1861, after being reunited with his mother, he began to question his upbringing and the loss of his kingdom.

In the years that followed, Duleep Singh tried to reconnect with his Sikh heritage and reclaim his status. He attempted to return to India and reconvert to Sikhism, but the British government arrested him at Aden and sent him back to Europe. He later tried to rally support for a rebellion against British rule, even seeking aid from Russia, but his efforts ultimately failed.

He left his wife and family, spending his later years in Paris, in financial and political exile.

The execution of Sikhs at the Malerkotla Parade Ground, in the Punjab, in 1872 is true. The event took place after a failed rebellion led by the Namdhari Sikhs, also known as Kukas, who were followers of Guru Ram Singh. The British authorities captured the rebels and Deputy Commissioner John Lambert Cowan had them executed – by being blown from cannons – without trial.

The Maltese language

At this time, Italian was an official language of Malta. It was the language of the wealthy, the law courts and the university. Maltese was the language of the common people, but written Maltese was still in the process of being established. The Maltese language is unique. It is the only Semitic language written in Latin characters, and is derived from a dialect of Arabic, heavily influenced by Italian. The modern Maltese alphabet and grammar systems were published in 1921 and 1924.

I have used Italian versions of first names of the main Maltese characters as this was standard for the time. For the servants/working classes it was more common to use Maltese names, so I have reflected this. I have used the Maltese spelling for *Sinjur*, *Sinjura* and *Sinjorina* although sources from 1880 mainly use Italian spelling. In Valletta in 1880, street names were written in Italian. Any errors are entirely my own.

Lynne Marie Taylor
Wiltshire, February 2026

ALSO BY LYNNE MARIE TAYLOR

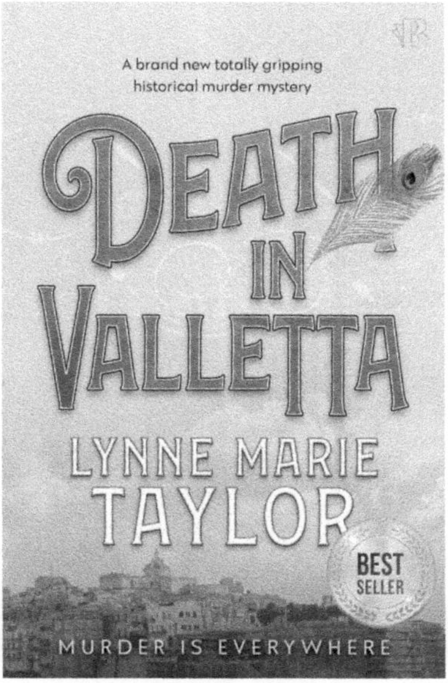

Death in Valletta

An Edinburgh police detective is summoned to the island of Malta, in this gripping and atmospheric murder mystery set in the Victorian era.

ACKNOWLEDGEMENTS

This book was made possible by a Developing Your Creative Practice grant from Arts Council England, which funded essential writing time. It also enabled me to benefit from the brilliant advice and support of my mentor Vaseem Khan. Thank you, Vas, for your time and patience!

Many thanks to my manuscript readers: Lucy Banks, Richard Tudor, Anya Taylor, Anhad Bhatia, Simon Tudge and Margot White. You all gave me such useful feedback, helping this book on its way. Additional thanks to Anya and to Sara Miles, for your much-appreciated help during research trips to Malta. And to all my family and friends who have supported this work.

In Malta, my thanks go to Denise Falzon, who took me to Dingli Cliffs (and other lovely destinations in Malta – you were so kind!), to Simon Wallace and the Gozo Book Club, and to Giancarlo Azzopardi, who helped with questions about the Lazzaretto. Also, my thanks to the helpful staff at the National Library of Malta and the National Archives of Malta. A special thank you to Ann Gingell Littlejohn for eagle-eyed reading of the manuscript and expert advice on the Maltese language content.

I am hugely grateful to the team at Bloodhound Books, especially Ian Skewis, Betsy Reavley, Hannah Baxter-Deuce, and Tara Lyons. Many thanks to Harvey Heap for the excellent map of Valletta.

Thank you, finally, to my first reader, Colin – you patiently listened to all the 'what if' questions and offered that endless support needed to get the project through to the finish line. I am ever grateful.

A NOTE FROM THE PUBLISHER

Thank you for reading this book. If you enjoyed it please do consider leaving a review on Amazon to help others find it too.

We hate typos. All of our books have been rigorously edited and proofread, but sometimes mistakes do slip through. If you have spotted a typo, please do let us know and we can get it amended within hours.

info@bloodhoundbooks.com

www.ingramcontent.com/pod-product-compliance
Ingram Content Group UK Ltd.
Pitfield, Milton Keynes, MK11 3LW, UK
UKHW040618080226
467794UK00002B/61

9 781917 705622